CYDONIA

Rise of the fallen

SEYI DAVID

ArrowGate

Published by Arrow Gate Publishing Ltd
London
15 14 13 12 11 10 9 8 7 6

Arrow Gate Publishing's titles may be purchased in bulk for educational, business, fund-raising, or sales promotional use. For information, please email arrowgatepublishing@ymail.com

Arrow Gate Publishing Ltd Reg. No. 8376606

A CIP catalogue record for this book is available from the British Library

ISBN 978-0-9575930-3-9

www.arrowgatepublishing.com

Arrow Gate Publishing Ltd's policy is to use papers that are natural, renewable and recyclable products and made from wood grown in sustainable forests. The logging and manufacturing processes are expected to conform to the environmental regulations of the country of origin

Printed in the United Kingdom

TO KAY

. 'And I saw an angel come down from heaven, having the key of the bottomless pit and a great chain in his hand.

And he laid hold on the dragon, that old serpent, which is the Devil, and Satan, and bound him a thousand years,

And cast him into the bottomless pit, and shut him, and set a seal upon him, that he should deceive the nations no more, till the thousand years should be fulfilled: and after that he must be loosed for a season...'

–REVELATION 20: 1-3

1

The Beginning

Stonehenge site, Salisbury, Wiltshire, July 31

Kate's eyes were on her man. She stared at him with longing and a quick sigh escaped her slightly parted lips. Her boyfriend tilted his head to one side as he studied the stones. She watched him intently as he moved closer to the nearest one, touching it lightly.

A brief smile breezed past her face. Her eyes lingered on his serious face, strong jaw, and broad shoulders.

He is handsome, she thought, but troubled. She felt giddy and light headed, like someone intoxicated. Reluctantly, she turned her attention to the bright blue sky and noticed a dark, tiny cloud forming, but she dismissed it with a shrug. A light wind gently caressed her face, and she wrapped her arms around her chest, as a contented smile lightened her face. *He loves me, what more could I wish for.* She thought with a satisfied sigh.

Her eyes strayed to the soft green grass, finally lingering on the enigmatic site before her. The ring of standing stones set within the Wiltshire countryside always amazed her. The site seemed to ooze an aura of secrecy; a secret apparently guarded for thousands of years. The strange stones had stood proudly and majestically for more than five-thousand years, but Kate's mind was neither on the beauty nor the mystery surrounding the origin of the stones. Her clear blue eyes fastened on the handsome man gushing with delight at the prehistoric monuments. He reminded her of Calum, her two-year-old cousin. The thought of Calum brought a chuckle to her lips.

Kate walked up to him, and his face broke out in a broad grin.

'I can't believe you brought me here Katie. I've postponed it for so long, this is an awe inspiring place...' and he paused briefly, 'my sister would have loved it here,' he added as a shadow crossed his face.

She slipped into his arms and they kissed passionately for a moment before he lifted his head. He swallowed hard and his eyes turned mysteriously dark. His face looked grim; his features seemed carved out of granite. Kate wanted to laugh but knew it would be awkward. She managed to control herself by resting her head on his wide chest, avoiding the gloom she saw in his eyes, and, at the same time, inhaling his manly scent.

'I love you so much,' he murmured into her hair, his voice breaking, 'you should always know that Katie, no matter where the wind of life blows, always have that at the back of your mind.'

She nodded, unable to speak.

Kate wanted to reassure him that life would be good to them, but his lips found hers again and she was lost in his arms. The pleasure of his lips shot waves of indescribable joy all over her being. She lifted her face and locked eyes with the love of her life,

'I love you too,' she said simply.

Hands entwined, they strolled through the surrounding grounds, which ditched slightly downwards. The weather was cool but not cold.

They walked down the sloping landscape and Kate stole a quick look at his face. *Nothing will spoil our fun today; not the ghost of your sad, extraordinary life or the tragedy that has engulfed your family and now threatens our happiness at every turn,* she thought, determined to make a success of their relationship.

They left Salisbury very late.

Kate had insisted on driving; she wanted him to explore the beautiful countryside as they drove away from Stonehenge, and that was exactly what he did.

He fastened his eyes on the site, lost for words, and in his own little world. Kate wondered what was going through his mind, but she did not care anymore. They were together now; even the odd expression that sometimes crossed his face had ceased to worry her.

The future held no fear for Kate. For now, the present was more than enough for her.

It happened in a fleeting second.

Kate took her eyes off the road briefly to have a final look at Stonehenge.

Then, there was a deafening sound as she slammed her Peugeot 206 car into an oncoming vehicle. She heard the sound of shattering windscreen and the wrangling of metal. She screamed as her car burst into flames.

That was the last thing she remembered before everything went blank.

THE BIG clock in Ilford town centre in East London resounded at seven in the evening. The town centre was still bustling with shoppers when a glittering black GMC 4x4 slid past the shoppers and came to a screeching halt at Cranbrook road, a few miles from the town centre. Three men got out of the jeep and dashed into the Golden Oaks pub, brandishing AK-47 assault rifles.

CYDONIA

The pub was packed full of people that cool Wednesday evening, and the men heralded a tense atmosphere as they barged in. There were muted gasps from everyone. Aaron Cohen was among the throng of people in the pub. Instantly, he knew they were looking for him.

A woman stifled a sob and her whimpering grated on Aaron's nerves. Slowly, he slipped his face cap down to hide his identity: it would do him good to stay hidden.

There was complete silence.

Aaron waited anxiously, praying fervently for the men to leave. People watched with apprehension as the men flaunted their rifles. One of them started shooting into the air and people ducked under their tables for cover.

Someone coughed among the terrified revellers in the crowded pub and the armed men turned in the direction of the sound. It was a young, brown-haired woman with tears streaming down her face. When the men faced her, she covered her face with trembling hands, whimpering quietly.

Then there was total silence.

The men frowned as they scrutinized people, their cold eyes picked through the faces in the crowd, but their man was not among the terrified faces. Frustrated, they prepared to abort the operation, but their leader, a tall, scraggy faced man with a permanent scowl shook his head. He was suspicious of a young man in a black shirt and beige trousers who had obviously made every effort to keep his face hidden with a cap pulled over his eyes.

He marched towards the young man with purposeful strides, his face a mask of rage. He yanked Aaron to his feet, dragging him along the floor. Aaron protested violently, his worst nightmare had finally happened. He tried wrestling himself free from the clutch of his captor but it was a death like grip; the man simply refused to let him go.

Everyone inside the pub was horrified. They were all helpless in the face of the dangerous weapons the men were brandishing, and the men knew that too. One of them fired a warning shot into the air, and again everyone ducked their heads, but one brave man stood up and spat out angrily, his chest heaving in and out,

'Who the hell are you guys? What on earth do you think you're doing?'

The men silenced him in a hail of bullets.

The intruders made a hasty retreat from the pub, shooting sporadically. Their reign of terror had lasted approximately two minutes.

They shoved Aaron roughly into the back seat. One of them sat with him in the back. The driver gunned the engine, and the tyres screeched loudly as they took off with the speed of lightning.

Aaron looked around wildly, a deranged look on his taut face. He then gave an ear-splitting scream. Duct tape materialised from nowhere, landing on his mouth with such viciousness that he almost passed out.

In the pub, people were speaking in hushed tones after the shots had faded away. A man rushed to help the young man bleeding on the floor: they had shot him in the stomach and his vital signs were faint. One of his friends had already called an ambulance.

After driving for about ten minutes, the powerful 4x4 came to an abrupt halt. The stern faced man beside the driver got out and opened the back door.

'What do you want from me?' Aaron mumbled through the duct tape. He tried to break free but a punch landed on his stomach and he passed out.

The man dumped Aaron inside the boot of the 4x4 and they sped off into the night. Aaron regained consciousness slowly and opened his eyes briefly, but it was pitch black.

Aaron knew his kidnappers well.

He had anticipated their every move and had managed to evade them for some time. He was not surprised that they had finally caught up with him; he was certain a death sentence was hanging over his head now. How he wished his brother, Simeon, was around to witness his abduction, at least, he would have believed him. But it was too late, his so-called paranoia seemed to have materialised.

Aaron had joined the priesthood after rebels murdered his brother in Africa. Simeon died in the hands of Somali rebels while working for the Red Cross, and the fractured Somali government failed to recover his body despite spirited efforts by the British government.

Before Simeon died, Aaron had repeatedly told him about his visions of a planet different from earth. The soil was as red as blood, and an unquenchable fire continually surrounded him, but the raging inferno did not harm him. Much like the biblical Hebrew boys who defied the king's order, his brother had refused to believe or even listen to him.

Simeon repeatedly told him off, disregarding it as the effects of the numerous books Aaron had been reading. After a while, he stopped talking about it altogether.

Aaron knew something sinister was going on when he realised that anytime he confided in anyone about his visions, they were killed within a month, or sooner.

He woke up one grey winter morning and decided to call it quits with the priesthood. The bishop of his diocese was patient and tried to reason with him, but Aaron was adamant, and he left. Nevertheless, his visions increased in intensity. It was terrifying, and that was when Aaron realised that he could not outrun fate. It was as if something, or someone, powerful and bigger than him was controlling his life.

He still believed in God, but after the gruesome fate met by his entire family, he wondered if God really cared for him. Aaron just wanted to live a normal life, to have a semblance of what a normal life entails, and if that was possible and achievable, he had absolutely no idea how to go about it.

The 4x4 stopped abruptly and Aaron gritted his teeth, fearing the worst. He heard the men coming out and speaking in hushed tones. He strained his ears and heard movements coming closer and closer, and one of the men lifted the boot of the 4x4. He shut his eyes again as rough hands dug into his flesh and one of the men pulled him out forcefully.

He stood unsteadily on his feet and opened his eyes, he had problems walking because he was sandwiched between the two men; the stench emanating from their bodies was dreadful.

After walking a few paces, Aaron looked round to take in his surroundings, but the only thing he could make out was the outline of what seemed to be a country house. His hopes of escape slowly disintegrated as they inched closer and the truth dawned on him: unless a miracle happened, he might not make it out.

They followed the scraggy faced man who kept muttering to himself. Aaron trudged on in silence, his thoughts in turmoil as different questions raced through his mind, and then his tummy began to rumble again.

They got to the imposing door of a palatial Victorian house and scraggy faced man knocked three times. A shrivelled old man whose dark, penetrating eyes sent shivers down Aaron's spine opened the door. The man stepped aside and they entered.

Aaron glanced around wildly; it was a perfect Victorian house but the décor was odd, from the window blinds to the chandelier, everything was black. They took him to a damp room and one of the men said gruffly,

'Sit down,'

Aaron obeyed meekly, the man yanked the duct tape off roughly, and he screamed out in pain, rubbing his bruised lips.

The man left the room abruptly, banging the door so loudly that he jumped.

The light in the room was dim, but he could just make out a single bed and a small reading table. He sat on the only chair in the room as his eyes travelled to the brown drape curtains, which hung ominously over the window, and he felt trapped. His heart sank when he weighed his options. I don't believe any force on earth could save me. He let out a frustrated sigh as his thoughts went back to his deceased family.

His Jewish grandparents had fled Poland at the outbreak of World War Two. They had settled in New York and within a few months, things rapidly changed for the young family of four. Daniel Cohen was a successful baker while his wife, Abigail, stayed home to raise their two young sons. The Cohen family had gradually integrated themselves into the Jewish society of Brooklyn.

The sons grew up and became successful in their respective fields; Joshua, the first son, became a famous lawyer while the younger brother, Benjamin, Aaron's dad, was a journalist. Things went on smoothly until Benjamin met and fell in love with a British girl. His father was furious, and, to make things worse, the girl was a devout Catholic.

That was the last straw: his father never forgave Pope Pius XII, and used to call him Hitler's Pope. Daniel Cohen believed the Pope was anti-Semitic and that he ignored the total annihilation of six million Jews all over Europe and for that, he regarded all Catholics as enemies of the Jews.

Benjamin had eloped with his pregnant fiancée, Anna, to England. They married and settled in London - life was hard, but they scraped by. Anna's father, who was the editor of the Guardian newspaper, came to their rescue by offering Benjamin a job with the pen name of Jonathan Potter. The deal worked brilliantly and the young family settled into a very comfortable life.

However, a sudden tragedy nearly destroyed the young couple. Their first child was stillborn. Aaron's mom told him that she was a golden haired girl whom they called Amber. Her birthday was quietly marked every year until his parents died. Amber's death was very painful, and his mother was depressed for several years but, gradually, she came out of it.

Ten years later, Simeon was born. The family grew as Aaron came five years later, followed by the last child, Rebecca.

Tears cascaded down Aaron's cheeks and he made no effort to clean his face when the thought of his vivacious little sister, Rebecca, assailed his mind. She was bold, funny, and very beautiful. Her laughter always filled the house - there was never a dull moment with her. How he loved her so. His soul filled with anguish and he wept bitterly.

After their deaths, Aaron had toyed with the idea of going to America to visit his uncle, but decided against it.

He was angry with his uncle. Aaron remembered the look of sadness on his dad's face whenever he talked about his extended family. He knew his dad had missed them terribly but no one tried to get in touch with him.

Aaron bowed his head as memories flooded his entire being, he remembered when his dad went back to Brooklyn once to see if he could see his parents, but he came back dejected. His dad had met new tenants in their family home and, with no forwarding address, there was no hope of reconciliation and that was the end. His dad died without making peace with his family.

The door opened abruptly, ending Aaron's painful reminiscences.

A huge, dark figure entered, his hair was jet black, and it flowed down his back. Aaron noticed his hands. His right hand was large, and stubby with claw like fingers with the index finger missing. He wore black flowing apparel and his eyes seemed lifeless and empty.

They were like two dark holes.

He seemed to fill the room with his presence and Aaron stared at him in disgust; he recognised him instantly. Aaron was finally meeting his tormentor - the shadowy, menacing figure who had repeatedly tortured him in his dreams for years.

He is a real man, not a nightmare anymore, Aaron wished Simeon had seen the 'figment of his imagination' as he had mockingly described his visions. Now his imagination had materialised. I know you would have believed me Simeon, if you had seen the gigantic man standing right in front of me, he thought sadly, wriggling his hands in desperation.

'I don't think I need an introduction,' the man bellowed, laughing with a wicked glint in his eyes that seemed to have gone through a quick transformation, 'you sure know me, but let me introduce myself properly. My name is Tyrus and...' before he could finish the sentence, Aaron slumped to the ground in a faint.

Tyrus's laughter increased in tempo and his voice echoed deep into the night. When Aaron regained consciousness a few minutes later, Tyrus was still towering over his crumpled frame, looking at him intently as if contemplating what to do with him.

'Young man, I need a favour from you,' Tyrus began in a conversational tone, but Aaron was afraid; it was as if his lips were glue together. He was still on the cold, hard floor when his eyelids fluttered to a close. He wanted to speak to his captor but it was as if his spirit had left his body, the welcoming embrace of darkness enveloped him.

2

Michael Crest Howard stared at the man in front of him in disgust. He was unsure on how to react. He wondered if he should punch him or simply walk away. Instead, he said crisply,

'Mr. Armstrong, do you know what you are talking about? You're deliberately threatening my family. I'm not afraid of your family's connection and I absolutely do not intend to satisfy the fantasies of your father. I'm now a writer, no longer a scientist.'

Michael took a sip of his beer wondering what had gotten into him. Normally, he would have stormed out of the pub. He rubbed his hands together fighting the urge to knock the smug look off the face of the man sitting directly opposite him.

'I'm not threatening you, I daren't do that. It's simply a proposal, and you can either take it or leave it.' Jude Armstrong said quietly, studying the good-looking man sipping his beer and he noticed Michael's shaky hands.

Jude took a generous sip of his beer, his eyes swept through the empty pub, and as if on cue, three men strolled in, giving Michael a cursory glance.

When Michael noticed the men, he sat up straight. Deep down he cursed his secretary for setting up the meeting. He had thought it had to do with his second book, which was due to come out in autumn.

'Look here Michael,' Jude's tone was now patronising, 'you have nothing to lose and don't forget that it's not for free: you'd be well paid. Just see it as a service to humanity. I want you to write another book and tell the story of your capture by terrorists with our own angle, or better still you could use a ghost writer,' he stared hard at him, his penetrating eyes made Michael flinch and for the umpteenth time, he wondered why he'd agreed to the meeting.

Keep calm, Michael thought, listening to the raspy voice of Jude Armstrong.

He continued, 'My parents are your biggest fans, they really want to meet up with you. They want to hear the story from the horse's mouth.'

'Tell me something,' Michael asked with a husky voice and people who knew him would steer clear: it was an indication that he was warming up to an explosive outburst, 'how did you come about the name Armstrong? I know who you really are; you can't really hide under that cloak of pretence.'

'Who am I?' Jude was getting pissed off too, he would have loved to pump some uranium bullets into Michael's stubborn head, but his dad was the one that had instigated the meeting. He had other means of coercion.

'You're related to a member of a powerful family in Russia; meanwhile, your great grandmother is related to one of the most hated families in Germany. You should be able to solve the equation by now.'

'I'm impressed,' Jude clapped his long, thin hands, impressed with Michael's background check on his family.

He gave a short laugh before gulping down the remaining contents of his glass, 'but that takes us back to the issue at hand: you will be doing the world a big favour by doing this.'

'Or trading with the devil, I'm not interested. I'm not writing any book for your devilish cause, I'm through with that part of my life.' Michael stood up and left the pub.

'Don't be late mate,' Jude hollered after his retreating back, an evil smile lighting up his smooth features, 'I'll be expecting you, you've already dined with the devil and you can't wash your hands clean buddy.'

Michael hurried home. Angry for even seeing Jude in the first place: his wife would be furious if she knew. They had been through hell and survived, he must never compromise his stand again, never again.

His thoughts went straight to Hammed, the man who kidnapped and locked him up in the barren lands of northern Nigeria. In a twist of fate, they later became close pals and he could only speculate where the poor guy was. Hammed had simply disappeared after he was freed and his discreet questioning and enquiries about Hammed were met with a brick wall, all his queries were unsuccessful.

No one knew anything, not even his best friend, Keith, and the more he tried to find answers to the numerous questions on his mind, the more his wife grew angry. He decided to let sleeping dogs lie, as the saying went.

He had written what he thought people wanted to read about his disappearance and what he went through in Nigeria. The problem was, there were some things people would simply not believe. The fact that he met with angels and fought the devil, no one wanted to read such tall tales.

Several hours later as he drove into his driveway, he saw Kate Summers, his neighbour's daughter, standing in front of her parent's home. The expression on her pretty face was grave. Michael hurriedly got out of his car and approached her warily, afraid that something terrible had happened.

'Hello Kate, are you all right?' he asked in a very concerned voice.

Kate shook her head and stifled a sob. Michael was perplexed, he took her by the elbow and they walked towards his front door, they entered his house and Kate went straight into the living room. She sat down on the sofa while Michael went to get his wife.

A few minutes later, he came out with Evelyn, and they both walked towards the young girl. Evelyn asked her husband to leave the living room while she sat down beside Kate. She glanced at the older woman and started speaking,

'I got a call from a friend yesterday asking if I could join him for a drink...' she hesitated for a moment and then continued, 'this friend of mine used to be a priest,' and as the words came out, her eyes filled with tears, and she began to cry.

Evelyn gave her a handkerchief, which she accepted graciously, dabbing it on her eyes that were already red and swollen with weeping.

'Shortly before I got to the pub where we were to meet, I saw three hefty men with assault rifles, dragging my screaming friend on the floor. The men looked mean and dangerous.'

'Have you called the police?' Evelyn asked gently.

She nodded and continued her voice was already hoarse.

'I jumped into my car and followed them. They got away in a black GMC 4x4 with tinted glass. I stopped before they got to the house where I suspect he'll be murdered.'

'No, don't jump to any conclusions yet, I'm sure he'll be fine,' Evelyn said reassuringly, embracing her, 'he will be all right.'

'He's gone through hell,' she sobbed on Evelyn's shoulder, 'I hope they don't kill him.'

THE LIGHT radiating from the mountain was very bright and a force seemingly drew him towards it. He approached it cautiously, as a child would approach fire, and when he got to the foot of the mountain, he sat down, resting his head on the cold hard surface.

He must have dozed off because he later felt someone tugging at his robe and when he opened his eyes slowly, he was surprised to see his brother, Simeon, standing in front of him with a stupid grin on his face. He looked well: handsome, healthy, and full of life.

Aaron jumped to his feet and gave him a bear hug.

Simeon did not speak though his bright, twinkling eyes suggested that he was happy to see Aaron. When Aaron released him, Simeon kept pointing backwards, he looked back in the direction but saw nothing, and when he turned to speak to Simeon again, he was gone. Instinctively, Aaron looked up and saw his brother flying upwards, his white apparel shimmered with brightness. In a matter of seconds, the clouds sucked him in, and he disappeared.

The encounter shook Aaron to the marrow, he had lost his brother again, 'but he looked all right,' a voice whispered kindly in his mind, 'he is safe.' That ought to have put his mind at rest but it did not stop his feeling of uneasiness.

Suddenly, weariness crept in and to worsen his situation, a rumbling sound emanated from the bowels of the mountain, rocking it to its very foundation. As the mountain seemed to expand in size, Aaron took a few steps back expecting the worse; *could it be a volcanic eruption?* He thought sadly and his heart sank.

His eyes went a shade darker and he gritted his teeth expecting the worse. His terrified gaze revealed his precarious situation; the clouds had gathered in dark plumes, spurting in anger like warriors ready for battle. Howling winds began to blow as guttural voices joined in the clamour of loud noise. Aaron clasped his hands over both ears to shut out the horrifying sounds. He felt a wispy touch on his feet and looked down in horror as the brown, grainy sand turned white.

At that instant, Aaron feared for his life.

He moved away from the mountain and took to his heels, and then he noticed that everywhere was suspiciously silent. He glanced up and saw the clouds clearing to reveal a bright sky devoid of any ominous signs.

'How in heaven's name did I get here?' He thought aloud and stopped running. Without thinking, he inched towards the mountain again and a gentle voice whispered his name.

'Aaron,' the voice was coming directly from the clouds.

'Move closer Aaron,' the still small voice commanded.

Aaron was no longer afraid because the voice gave him some sort of power. The cloud descended ever so gently and soon enough, it enveloped Aaron in its awesomeness. His brown eyes widened in curiosity.

'Who are you and how do you know my name?' He asked quietly, his legs shaking. He swallowed hard, waiting to see what would happen.

'I am He who lives forever more!'

'Show your face, don't hide in the clouds!' Aaron croaked out, he could hardly believe himself, *what a raw nerve!* He thought with pride, *it's better to stand my ground than run away.*

As if in slow motion, a man appeared in front of him and Aaron's mouth opened in surprise. The stranger strode towards him with easy strides and Aaron's mind went into overdrive as he considered all the options left for him, but none of them was attractive or realistic. Nervously, he wiped his face with the back of his left hand as sweat poured from every available pore on his body.

He was amazed when two girls materialised from nowhere, chasing each other, and as their rich laughter drifted to him, he felt at ease. Strolling behind them was a woman in a white dress, barefooted, and on her head was a golden crown, her thick brown hair falling luxuriously to her back.

The children lifted their hands and waved, Aaron merely nodded his head in acknowledgement; he was not sure his hands would move. He turned his attention back to the man and took in his appearance. He was tall with strong, powerful arms, his coffee brown hair was long, and almost reached his waist, his clean-shaven face looked kind. However, his eyes did the trick – they were blue and clear, Aaron had never seen such beautiful eyes in his life.

The man wore an ordinary plain white shirt with blue denim jeans. Aaron realised that the man's feet did not touch the ground.

He didn't need a soothsayer to spell it out - he was experiencing the supernatural.

The man now stood in front of him and when Aaron managed to hold his gaze, all his fears melted away.

But there was still a question nagging at him, *Am I dead?*

They stood close together, eyeball to eyeball. Aaron sensed a powerful force oozing out of the man's body and he tried to avert his gaze but could not; what he saw in the stranger's eyes transfixed him to the spot. 'Who in heaven's name is this guy?' He thought.

The man laid his hand on Aaron and repeated quietly,

'I am He who lives forever more. Walk with me and be perfect.'

'Where am I?' Aaron finally plucked up the courage to ask.

'Don't be afraid,' was the gentle reply, 'you're not dead, you're very much alive.'

At that revelation, Aaron heaved a huge sigh of relief. They walked together like two friends enjoying a stroll in the park.

The stranger chatted easily with him, his hands in his jeans' pockets, and threw him a sideways glance occasionally. Aaron listened with rapt attention but hardly understood a word. He had a quiet way of speaking, but underneath his gentleness, Aaron could also sense overwhelming power - he had felt the full force of that power earlier.

After walking for about a mile, they got to a river and in the middle of the river was a tree. It was a very peculiar tree with green leaves and a mere twelve fruits on it.

The man sat down and scooped some water in his palms, he drank from it, offering some to Aaron who stretched forth his hands, and drops of water touched his palms.

'Drink it,' the man commanded gently.

He obeyed and it tasted like honey mixed with lemon. Aaron wondered why it tasted like that and threw a cursory glance at the river. It was as clear as crystal, and when he saw his reflection he could not believe his eyes.

He was wearing a bluish type of robe, which reminded him so much of those worn by the high priests who worship in synagogues in Israel. Out of the corner of his eye, Aaron noticed that the man was watching him intently and he wondered what might be going through his mind.

Then it dawned on him: he actually was wearing the same garments the ancient high priests wore. He felt the hair at the nape of his neck stand on end and his pulse quickened as he tried to contain his excitement. Aaron stared closely at the clear flowing river, on his head was a turban; he touched it with a smile on his face. It was made of white linen and attached to the turban like-hat was a gold plate with the words *'Holiness to the Lord.'*

'Incredible.' He muttered under his breath.

The word 'Ephod' jumped to his mind; he was wearing the holy garments of the high priest.

He looked at the river again and noticed the square breastplates of judgement embedded with twelve precious stones, on his shoulders were extra ones, gleaming in the reflection of the water. Under his beautiful robe, he wore a white fine linen woven tunic.

Aaron could not breathe properly, he tore his eyes away, and that was when he noticed that the man was no longer with him. Aaron looked up and saw him floating in mid-air. He looked different. The man wore replica garments; his eyes gleamed, and radiated fire. When he spoke, his voice sounded like thunder.

'Aaron, you are the earth priest: the stones are yours, keep them close to your soul, because in it, is a great power the world has never seen or known; you can't begin to imagine how powerful it is. You are the keeper of the stones of fire. You will avert the total annihilation of your race. There's also a chain on your neck with the twelve stones of fire, wear it always.'

'Huh, okay,' Aaron said staring at the awe-inspiring transformation as the man's clothes changed into a bright red robe.

On his head was a crown of gold, and a golden band around his waist. He held a massive sword in his left hand and his eyes were like flames of fire.

The ground began to vibrate with such brutal force that Aaron almost slipped. Then the mountain slowly opened up, finally Aaron realised that he was in heaven. He saw armies of winged beings on white horses, flying in the clouds. They wore fine white linen and their faces were like the sun. Aaron wanted to run but knew it was futile. The atmosphere seemed charged with electricity.

Aaron was amazed when he saw a sword coming out of the man's mouth. The man floated back as his armies rallied round, he mounted a very big white horse, and the sword was now in his right hand. Aaron squint his eyes at the inscription on the man's garment, 'King of Kings and Lords of Lords.'

'Yeshua!' Aaron screamed on top of his voice, a tremor passed through his body and he almost fainted with disbelief. *Why didn't I notice? It's unbelievable that I've spoken to the son of God.*

Suddenly, everywhere was quiet.

'I'll be with you, always.' Yeshua's voice echoed through the air and Aaron swallowed hard, as Yeshua disappeared with the host of heaven into the clouds.

Aaron was rooted to the spot. His hands touched his neck briefly and he felt the tiny gold chain. He had seen the stones in his visions but not like this. He turned away from the river and headed for the mountain.

'Where am I going?' He asked stupidly, unsure of what to do.

Without warning, someone slapped him so hard that his neck almost snapped.

He opened his eyes and saw the scraggy faced man and his pimps. They towered above him and pulled him up.

'Get up,' they growled, their eyes turned to slits, 'you're free to go, Tyrus will seek your audience another day.'

Scraggy faced manhandled and dragged him through the corridor, opened the door and pushed him out, cursing him repeatedly at the top of his voice. He slammed the door shut with such force that Aaron almost jumped out of his skin.

The visions were over.

'Yeshua,' Aaron whispered the name softly and then checked his clothes, the holy garment was long gone but the gold chain was still around his neck; he felt different and light headed.

'What did you expect to see,' he said aloud and almost stumbled as he walked to the main road.

He saw police cars coming in his direction and wondered who had called them.

Aaron trudged towards the oncoming police cars, his mind on the weird experience he had just had. The son of God had entrusted the stones of fire to his care, but that was all he knew, he had no clue what would happen next.

He thrust his hands into his jeans' pockets, lost in thought, then a smile appeared on his face, at least there was a consolation, he thought happily, Simeon is safe and at peace, for that I am grateful. He turned to have a last glimpse of the house but there was nothing, just an expanse of land, full of tall grasses.

He stopped short, staring at the empty space and at that instant; he knew he had to go to Rome. He needed answers fast, sensible answers to the questions on his mind before he ended up in a psychiatric ward. No one would believe what he had just experienced.

3

The next day, Aaron opened his eyes slowly, his head was banging with such ferocity that he felt faint. He wanted to stay in bed all day but knew that was a pipe dream. He threw the duvet cover off his tired frame and glanced at the wall clock. A grunt escaped his throat; he felt like a warhorse.

To compound his problem, it was quarter past twelve in the afternoon, and that would mean a lot of explaining to Kate, his friend; at the thought of 'girl-friend', he went bright red. She would want to know the reason why he fled his apartment and was staying in a hotel.

But he felt safer in the cold, impersonal feeling of the small cosy hotel just a stone's throw from his apartment. He was a man prone to a lot of accidents and unwanted burly visitors. He wanted to minimise the dangers to the lowest level.

He yawned and was reluctant to get up. He had slept through the morning and had totally forgotten about his date with Kate. She would be worried if he did not show up.

Kate was hysterical on the phone when he called to tell her that he was okay, a slow smile crossed his smooth features at the memory. The blast of her fury almost destroyed his hearing. She was furious and remembering it still made him cringe from her shrieking on the phone.

She was adamant and wanted to know more about the people who had abducted him, and he promised to tell her everything, but that was just to shut her up - he certainly did not intend to do anything like that. He had learnt his lesson the hard way. Immediately he dropped his phone and crashed into bed fully clothed and slept like a log.

All the bones in his body screamed out in protest when he tried to stand up, he was extremely tired and drained of energy. His thoughts slowly turned back to the bizarre events of the night and the unexpected arrival of the police.

It was obvious that the police did not believe his story. They simply told him that a concerned motorist saw him wandering in the woods and called them. As much as he tried to explain his ordeal to the police, they politely advised him to visit his doctor for a thorough check-up, took down his details, and drove him home.

On the drive home, Aaron asked the officers about the man who confronted his attackers but his question drew a blank. The officers glanced at each other with a knowing look and asked if he was on any medication or drugs. When he persisted, they told him that there was no evidence of any shooting and that they had gone through the CCTV cameras inside the pub. There were no witnesses and the pub owner denied any knowledge of the supposed kidnap.

Aaron was lost for words at that.

The phone beside his bed rang shrilly, cutting his reverie short and he knew it must be Kate.

'Hello,' he said wearily, yawning again. It was Kate, she was already at the lobby, and he asked her to come up to his room. But something didn't seem right, her voice sounded hoarse. Aaron rubbed his face and stubbly jaw.

'I'm getting paranoid again,' he muttered and stood up, removed his shirt, sauntered to the bathroom, splashed some water on his face, and trod back to the room.

His swollen feet tingled when he walked and he knew it was because he had slept without taking his shoes off. He bent down, removed the shoes, and flopped back on the bed.

Then there was a knock on the door and he sighed at what was to come.

'Come in Kate.'

The door opened and his nightmare began all over again.

Lalibela Ethiopia, Aug 2

Twelve men assembled around a stone table at Medhane Alem Church Lalibela, Ethiopia. Stretching forth their hands, they murmured inaudibly, swaying back and forth like leaves dancing in the wind.

They were all clad in white linen robes, on their heads were turbans with golden lines at the base. Inscribed on their chests was the cross in red and every single one of them was barefooted.

In each man's hand was a staff with the cross on top, and the room was thick with the scent of frankincense.

They were chanting in an extraordinarily powerful language that priests had used in prayers for over two-thousand years in Ethiopia. They finished the mantra and rubbed their hands together, murmuring to themselves.

After a while, Caleb, their leader, cleared his throat to signal an end to their mantra, saying in flawless English, his eyes glassy as if he was still in a trance,

'I had a vision. There is a young man with incredible power at his disposal, he needs us and we must protect him, or he could be murdered within days.'

'He has the stones of fire, no man born of a woman can kill him... he is the destroyer.' One of the men interjected loudly, his voice shaking.

The eleven other men in the room fixed their gaze on Nathaniel, the man who had just spoken. Caleb frowned, his steely eyes spoke volumes, but before he could reply to the interruption, someone else did.

'Who are we talking about here?' asked the youngest of the men, whose name was Peter.

'The earth priest has been found in London, and he is in grave danger.' Caleb answered but his eyes never left Nathaniel's face for a second.

'I have also seen him Caleb,' Nathaniel said slowly, his parched lips barely moving, he looked determined, 'his name is Aaron... he is staying at a hotel in the eastern part of London. I saw him in a revelation early this morning.'

Caleb did not say another word he was simply astonished.

Nathaniel was divulging classified information known only to the Pope and a few cardinals. God speaks to them and through them. He stared at Nathaniel as if seeing him for the first time, he quickly made up his mind to keep this fresh information, he would not disclose it in Rome, at least, not all of it, he thought.

Peter's face glowed at the revelation and he gushed out in delight.

'This is what we have been waiting for, for three-thousand years: the earth priest!' His eyes brightened and almost sparkled.

'We have a mammoth task on our hands brothers, we must contact Rome immediately.'

Caleb said finally, turning his attention back to the men.

'Rome cannot be fully trusted,' Peter said quietly and the others nodded in agreement, 'Pope Clement V did nothing for the Knights Templar, King Phillip killed them and turned them...'

'That was centuries ago, this is different, it's beyond us now.' Caleb cut in gently, 'we must trust the Vatican, Peter,' he called his name softly, 'don't be naïve, there are things beyond us now, but there are also things we can control. We have centuries of riches in our land, we must protect our heritage and what God has entrusted to our care: that is why we exist. We must protect Ethiopia, we must protect the mandate God gave to King Lalibela. We must protect the Ark of the Covenant and that is our duty, our calling. We are a religious order ready to lay down our lives for the service of God and the protection of His saints - we must not forget that. We must not forget our lineage of honour.'

There was a brief silence as the men pondered on Caleb's words.

'What do we do now?' Asked Yohanes quietly, he was one of the priests in Beta Medhane Alem church in Lalibela where they were having the meeting.

'I'll go to Rome tomorrow morning, I already have an appointment to see the Pope on Friday, everything has been arranged by the elders in Rome and anything the Pope tells me to do, I'll let you know. All things being equal, I should be in London by Sunday morning and by God's grace, I should be back by Monday evening.'

'Are you going alone?' Yohanes asked in the same quiet voice.

'Yes.' Caleb answered looking at the men, trying to see their reactions.

'We have enough funds for three hundred people to go,' Peter quipped quietly.

'And I say no.' Caleb said coolly, and all the men glared at Peter disapprovingly.

Caleb had been, and was still, a very great leader: the men trusted him totally, though everyone was entitled to air his views, Peter was restless and reckless. Many of the men might agree with him sometimes, but they knew he was young with abundant energy and little wisdom about the Order of Lalibela and their programmes.

'We will pray for your success and the safety of the young man.' Theodore said in his husky voice, smiling broadly. He was the oldest member of the group and very jovial, he loved the Order and believed in their leader. That seemed to ease the tension caused by Peter's incessant questions.

They talked more on the upcoming trip while Peter gently tapped his bare feet on the cold, hard floor, angry with Caleb. His mind drifted to the past, at that first chance meeting, or was it? He thought indignantly.

Peter was a graduate of economics. He'd studied at the prestigious London School of Economics and was one of their most brilliant students, but he left Britain shortly after his graduation, refusing several lucrative job offers. He loved Ethiopia and was a devout Christian. He came back home, married his fiancée, Mariam, who was a scientist and didn't really care about religion. She had two loves in her life: her husband, and her job. Religion had no place in her heart; Mariam worked for the government.

Peter joined his father's construction company in Addis Ababa as the account manager and was doing pretty well. But his life changed on a seemingly uninteresting day.

Precisely two years earlier, he had gone to Lalibela to visit relatives and decided to worship at the Beta Medhane Alem church. They had just finished Mass, and as he knelt down and kissed the cold stone floor, he felt someone beside him. He stood up facing the east, ignoring the intruder whom he felt was trying to break his concentration. Looking straight at the scarlet curtain and the golden cross, his gaze fixed on the replica of the Ark of the Covenant and he felt a strange sensation. It was a languid feeling of elation, something he usually experienced anytime he worshipped in the ancient historic church.

He tore his gaze away briefly, staring at the apertures on the walls above, and when the service was over, he picked his way gently through the trench, as there were many worshippers. He got outside and felt someone tap him twice on the shoulder; he turned and saw a tall, good-looking man, who was somewhere in his sixties. Initially, he thought the man was white because his skin was extremely fair, but on closer inspection, Peter decided he must be a Tigray man, a native of the village.

The man held him by the elbow and Peter wondered at the familiarity of the stranger as they walked to the only main road in the historic village. The man began to speak softly, at first his voice grated on Peter's nerves, but the man had the strangest effect on him. The man and the village seemingly merged into an intricate image of perfection. Peter's attention turned to the beautiful sight of crested hills, and at the same time, the man's voice droned on. He admired the rugged foothills with jagged mountains soaring to the sky as a proud maiden paraded in front of her fiancé (male). The noise of the bleating goats permeated the atmosphere as they roamed around the luscious green landscape, it was early august and the rains had not stopped falling. For that, he was grateful; he did not want a repeat of the 1984 disaster where over one million Ethiopians perished.

'I love this remote and beautiful place, I am proud to be the son of the soil.' Peter said and the expression on his face was akin to someone who had seen heaven, and then he turned his attention back to the tall, handsome stranger who stood in front of him, looking at him closely, the man's face struck a chord. Then the man smiled, revealing snow-white teeth.

'My name is Caleb Negasi and I would like to invite you to a very important meeting, something to do with our great country.' The man said smoothly in a deep baritone voice, while at the same time stretching out his hands for a shake. Peter shook the man's hands and felt his clasped in an iron like grip.

'Sorry,' Caleb Negasi apologised with a shy smile, 'my hands are hard and tough like the skin of an elephant, I don't like shaking hands, but it is the courteous thing to do.'

'I know you,' Peter said, recognising him and he quickly tucked his hands safely in his trouser pockets; he didn't want any of his bones broken, 'you are the former Minister of Tourism. You resigned on personal grounds.'

'I wouldn't like to go into the sordid details young man,' Caleb said easily and there was surprise on Peter's lean features as they continued walking across the rugged landscape while worshipers thronged past them in droves.

The white clad crowds trotted up the hills towards their mud houses with thatched roofs. He was in deep discussion with Caleb that day as they went up the mountain to a strange, simple home, perched precariously on a jagged surface. There, he met some of the members of the Order and, two weeks later, he became a member in a simple ceremony in one of the monolithic churches in Lalibela.

That was how he became a part of an Order with over three thousand members: the Order of Lalibela, a religious organisation recognised and respected by the Vatican.

He had been a member for two years and had never travelled with any of the committee members and, as the treasurer; he knew how rich they were. They had members all over East Africa and Europe; as a result, money was not their problem.

Peter was jolted back to reality when he saw Caleb watching him with a funny look on his face. Caleb smiled and said jokingly,

'Our knight had been transferred to the third heaven.'

Everyone laughed and Peter could not help but join in.

They ended the meeting and all the members left, except Peter and Caleb.

They stared at each other shyly, and then Peter rushed into the older man's arms. He could afford to be a little boy with Caleb. It was like a bond between a father and his son. Caleb held him tightly and rocked him as he would a child.

'I am sorry son,' he said, his voice laden with emotion, 'I am going on a dangerous journey, I can't afford to have any one with me, I may not return.'

'Don't say that.'

Peter moved away from him, his eyes moist, 'Why are you hiding things from me? Why?'

'It is for the safety of the Order and for your safety,' he replied softly with emphasis, 'we have more enemies than you realise, not only the Somalis and Eritrean but also enemies you cannot see.'

'I know all about it.' Peter said meekly.

'No,' Caleb shook his head firmly, 'you don't, but you will in due course.'

'You're not coming back on Monday are you?' Peter asked with a sick feeling in the pit of his stomach.

'I can't be definite. I'll be back if the Lord wishes.' He replied evasively, looking at him closely as if engraving his image, his facial features, into the fabric of his soul so as not to forget him. He loved him as he would his own.

Caleb moved closer, holding him again, he closed his eyes and the picture of his son blown to pieces in a car bomb flashed through his mind. A shudder went through his body as he wiped tears from his eyes with the back of his hand. In Peter, he could hold his son again. The death of Girma killed his wife of thirty years - she died of a broken heart while he stood by helplessly, unable to save his family.

He would give his life to make the world a better place, and the first thing would be to find Aaron before anyone else did; the young man held the key to everything.

Caleb moved out of the embrace saying softly, his lips barely moving, his eyes was red and swollen, as if he had been crying for days,

'Goodbye son.' He walked out of the cavernous room, which was deeply entrenched in the ground. Peter watched him disappear into the shadows. He took the lantern from the stone table and, with a heavy heart, slowly followed. His footsteps padded softly on the stone ground as he trudged his way out of the shaded, damp room.

He met a monk who bowed his head in greeting. Peter acknowledged him with a nod and continued to the aisle. It was getting dark but he could not move, his feet were glued to the cold hard floor as he stood riveted, gazing at the finely carved columns.

With head bowed, he whispered a prayer,

'God of the ages, please bring Caleb back safely.'

Then he made a sign of the cross and stood still, expecting something to happen. But there was nothing, except for the rapid beating of his heart, which ardently filled the ancient chamber.

Through the centuries, thousands of feet have walked through the ancient vaults, chambers, and tunnels. There must be a reason why the incredible structures hewed out of rock are still standing. God is here, he affirmed in his heart, amidst the war over the centuries, the plundering, the famine, the poverty - the face of God was like an indelible mark in this glorious and ancient structure.

Nevertheless, Peter was afraid. He was scared of the enemy he did not know, a faceless enemy who could be lurking secretly in a corner, ready to pounce. He felt miserable as he walked through the trench to the main road towards his car. He had wanted to sleep in Lalibela but suddenly changed his mind. He wanted to hold his wife and daughter in his arms.

His heartbeat increased in tempo and he quickened his pace. Peter had a terrible premonition that his life was about to change drastically. He shivered uncontrollably when the chilly mountain air slammed into him.

He gritted his teeth and opened the door of his car.

4

Aaron jumped from the bed, raced to the window, and crashed out, landing on the hard ground with a heavy thud. He heard a whooshing and saw a hand grenade without its safety pin cruising towards him. He stood up to run but the sheer force of the explosion flung him to the ground again.

He picked himself up effortlessly, and ran out of the hotel premises.

He almost collided with Kate's car, she expertly brought the car to a halt, and he jumped in. Two men dressed in black slacks and leather jackets came out of the hotel, shooting in rapid succession.

Aaron's heart was beating fast and he took a quick glance back as bullets hit the windscreen and pieces of glasses went flying in different directions a stray bullet hit Aaron in the shoulder and he screamed out in agony.

Kate checked the side mirror and saw their assailants in hot pursuit in a black 4x4. Her foot hit the pedal as she flew past red lights.

'Hold on tight, I'll get you to the hospital in a sec.' she said through clenched teeth, her face flushed with perspiration.

'No!' Aaron screamed, 'we'll be dead meat in a hospital, just get us to Kent, out of London as far as you can,' he grimaced when he saw blood flowing from his shoulder and on to the brown leather seat, 'I'm going to ruin your beautiful car,' he added grimly, his brow furrowed in pain.

'Will you shut up and let me drive,' Kate snapped irritably, she was still in shock and her whole body was shaking.

'Yes ma'am.' Aaron managed to say and kept quiet.

After driving for about twenty minutes in silence, she asked, throwing him a sideways glance,

'Aaron, are you all right?'

'No I'm not, but I'll be fine,' he mumbled, his shoulder on fire. After a short pause, he added, 'I wonder how they knew you were coming to see me, I would bet my life on it that it was you I spoke to on the hotel phone.'

He kept looking back nervously.

'Those guys were desperate to kill you,' was all Kate said. She looked very worried.

Pain racked Aaron's body but he kept a brave face. He was glad that he was shirtless; the cool air-conditioning in Kate's car helped against the unbearable heat.

Kate slammed her feet on the accelerator, and the car shot forward. After driving silently for almost an hour, they arrived in Kent.

'Please drive to the Bromley Court hotel. I have some friends there.' Aaron leaned forward, holding his wounded shoulder in a bid to stem the blood flow.

Kate nodded and drove on, parking carefully in the hotel premises.

'You're in no state to go inside the hotel. People will simply call an ambulance, or the police.' Kate said quietly and touched his forehead. It was warm, and that was when she noticed the gold chain with the strange stone pendant. She wanted to ask him where he had got such a beautifully crafted stone but decided against it.

'Please give me your phone.'

He asked faintly, he had lost so much blood he was now dizzy.

He made a few calls and in less than ten minutes, two men rushed to the car, opened the door, and helped Aaron to his feet.

They gently led him away through the hotel's back entrance.

Kate followed them, mortified for allowing Aaron to have his own way; she should have taken him to the hospital.

The men took them to a very cosy little room - one of the men left and came back with a first aid box. They cleaned the wound and Kate was relieved to see that it was not very deep. The bullet had merely grazed his shoulder; in a matter of minutes, one of them had treated the wound and dressed it. Aaron lay on the bed and was soon snoring.

The men left the room and beckoned to Kate. Reluctantly she followed them, looking back at Aaron's sleeping form. She didn't want him out of her sight.

Kate followed the men down a long corridor. They entered a big suite and one of the men turned to her with an easy smile and said,

'My name is Kai, and this is Dave.'

Dave's bland expression did little to reassure her.

Kai walked briskly to the bed, picked up a small travelling bag, and gave it to her without a word. Kate managed a weak smile, looking at Kai for more explanations, but none was forthcoming. Kai and Dave left the room and she followed suit.

When she got back to their room, she was relieved to see Aaron still sleeping.

Kate strolled to the bed staring at him for a long time. She felt her throat constricting and swallowed hard. Aaron slept on his back with his right hand carelessly thrown on the pillow next to him.

He looked innocent, alone and sexy. She studied his strong, dimpled jaw; his dark, coarse hair; his well-shaped nose; and his full, inviting lips, and a slow smile crossed her face.

'More like the lips of a woman,' she murmured huskily and bent down, kissing him lightly on the lips as desire raced through her body.

She felt guilty for having such impure thoughts and knew her mother would be appalled if she knew what was going through the mind of her 'pure' daughter.

She removed the ribbon in her hair and allowed it to cascade down her shoulders. Her mother was Egyptian and she had inherited her dark looks from her. Her long dark hair tumbled down her back as she stared at herself in the mirror. She knew her compelling looks could get her any man she wanted, except Aaron. He seemed oblivious to her physical beauty, and was such a Gentleman. They had dated for a month and the thought of being in such close proximity to him was unsettling, even for her. She felt her body hardening at the thought of what could happen.

CYDONIA

They met at the birthday party of her goddaughter, Vivian. Aaron was still a priest then; as soon as she set eyes on him, she knew he would not stay a priest for long. Not if she could get her long fingers on his well-toned body. Her legs turned to jelly as her erratic mind played around. Kate had fancied him from the onset, but he had not been as enthusiastic - almost aloof.

Six months later, she had heard from her goddaughter that Aaron had quit the priesthood. Aaron was very close to Vivian's dad and Kate immediately got Aaron's phone number from him. Within a week, she had summoned enough courage to call him, and when she did, she was pleased that he still remembered her, and that was how their relationship began. She shook her head, was it really a relationship? She wondered with a rueful smile.

She was more or less the one making all the effort. Aaron was irritatingly distant, yet she knew he loved her. He seemed not to have any interest whatsoever in the opposite sex, saying very little whenever they managed to be together. She made excuses for him and put it down to his tragic past, but, deep down, she could discern that he was not secretive and cared for her in his own way. She would just give him time to adjust to being a layman, and no longer a priest.

Aaron groaned, muttering inaudible words, yet he was still fast asleep.

Instantly, she was by his side, a worried frown on her smooth forehead.

With a deep sigh, she moved away and turned her attention to the bag Kai had given her; rummaging through it, she found two shirts and pairs of trousers, a penknife, a map of Rome and a passport. She opened the passport and was surprised to see that Aaron would be travelling to Rome the next morning.

She zipped the bag up and lay down beside him, thinking of how complicated things were. She had fallen in love with an ex-priest. Her mother would simply kill her, and at the thought of her mother, an involuntary grunt escaped her throat.

'What a complicated life!' She muttered under her breath, and slipped into a deep and troubled sleep, her hands resting loosely on Aaron's thigh.

'I want you Aaron,' she murmured in her sleep and Aaron's eyes flipped open. He had heard what she said. He turned to his side, staring at her beautiful oval face, knowing that he may never see her again.

5

Pope Nathaniel III glanced through the paper in front of him with a short gasp. Written in red were the words, 'the Earth Priest'. He read the twenty-five pages quickly and rested back on his chair, the expression on his face was very grave.

He closed his eyes and shuddered; 'the Earth Priest', those three words kept echoing in his mind - they were like daggers to his soul.

Church and civilisation as a whole is in peril, the young man must be found and quickly too, thought the Pope.

Chilean Cardinal, Fernando Salvarado, and the Pope's private secretary, Monsignor Bacilio Alvarez, watched the Holy Father's reaction from afar.

An hour later, the Pope summoned the Cardinal Fernando Salvarado into his private chambers. The two men knew trouble was brewing.

Monsignor Bacilio Alvarez was pacing outside his office, visibly agitated: he looked tense and on edge. His shrewd brown eyes could not stay still.

Monsignor Bacilio was privy to the investigation on Aaron Cohen and the claims he had made to his bishop in London about his visions regarding the stones of fire. Could this Aaron be telling the truth? Could he be the Earth Priest? What would be the fate of the Holy See, would he take the position of Pope?

Surely, the Vatican would not allow such travesty.

Monsignor Bacilio's face was the epitome of uncertainty while different thoughts raced through his mind.

The church came into existence centuries ago with the Pope as head and the Supreme Pontiff of the universal church and no one can change that fact. The tomb of Peter, the Apostle of Christ, lies buried underneath St Peter's Basilica; the great Apostle was the rock of the church, no one can lay claim otherwise. Aaron Cohen cannot be a threat to the Papacy, there must be a reason for his appearance.

Monsignor Bacilio grunted aloud and ran his hands through his brown hair, pacing up and down in his black robe, his eyes cold, his arms clasped behind him. We must find the young man, I am certain the Holy Father will find a way, and if he asks for my opinion, I'll gladly give it.

His gut instincts may not count now, but he had a hunch the young man was harmless.

But who could really tell nowadays, so many prophecies about the end of days. He clenched and unclenched his fists until his knuckles turned bright red. When it became unbearable, he walked out of his office and knocked on the massive door of the Pope's chamber.

'Come in,' it was Cardinal Fernando Salvarado's voice and it sounded tough and crisp.

There was subtle rivalry between the two men, but the Pope pretended not to notice; they were both trustworthy and loyal and that was the end of it.

Monsignor Bacilio Alvarez opened the oak door and went inside.

The Pope sat behind his large table, the expression on his face was grave, but he said lightly,

'I think we might have a little problem.'

Alvarez stiffened at the revelation. The Pope had confirmed his worst fears.

'We must find Aaron Cohen before anybody else does: he holds the key to so many riddles,' the Pope smiled briefly and continued, 'he was God sent; he is not evil but he could be corrupted, and then we would all be in serious trouble.'

'What can I do your holiness?' Monsignor Bacilio asked quietly.

'Contact his uncle in Washington, and Cardinal Albert Freeman in Chicago. Invite them for an audience with me; Cardinal Salvarado will handle the rest.'

'Yes your Holiness.' Monsignor Bacilio said with a brief bow, and left the room.

The Pope turned to his trusted friend and asked quietly,

'Are we too late?'

'May God have mercy on us,' Cardinal Salvarado replied and stood up, bent down on one knee, kissing the signet on the Pope's hand.

'I don't think we're too late,' he emphasised before leaving the Holy Father.

At last, when he was alone, Pope Nathaniel III stood up and ambled across his large office. He stopped at the window and peered down at St Peter's Square. A verse in Revelation 5:10 popped into his mind,

'And have made us to our God kings and priests and we shall reign on the earth.'

This verse must have a correlation between the young man and the end of days, he thought sadly.

Cardinal Salvarado had to organise an urgent meeting with the two-hundred-and-two cardinals. Something sinister was brewing; he felt it in his frail bones. Surprisingly, he remembered the text he was reading recently about Jacques de Molay, the last grand master of the Knight Templars. Molay had asserted that the

Order was innocent of the charges against them, but King Philip IV of France ordered him to be burnt at the stake on October 13, 1314. Jacque de Molay also referred to the earth priest.

The text would never see the light of day, he affirmed as Molay's words echoed in his mind and he shuddered at the prospect of such prophesies coming to pass, 'The earth will melt into vapour, and the anger of the ancients will arise upon the sons of men...'

The Pope prayed silently that the ominous clouds hovering over him would disappear.

He folded his arms over his chest, gravely worried about his dreams. He always woke up covered in sweat, disturbed by the memories of those vague, meaningless dreams. How annoying was that? He cringed at the prospect of blaming it on old age, but now he was not so sure.

He would be seventy-four in December and had never felt better. It could not be old age, he reasoned; he believed there was a message from the Lord that was not yet clear. He sighed and turned away from the window.

Who is Aaron Cohen? Pope Nathaniel mouthed the name and trembled at the thought of such great power in the hands of a young man. The church must find Aaron before the hordes of hell realised his importance.

The Pope mopped his forehead with the handkerchief in his hands. He was sweating profusely and his hands were shaking.

The door opened and Cardinal Salvarado came in, he looked tense with his brow furrowed; the look on his face suggested that he had very bad news.

The Pope clasped his hands together and waited calmly.

'Aaron Cohen, as his name suggests, is Jewish. His parents and sister were killed in a plane crash some years back. Aaron was left with a brother who also died a couple of months later, in the hands of Somali militias,' he paused briefly and continued, 'I knew Anna very well and her death affected me greatly, she was Aaron's mother...'

'You never told me you knew Aaron?' The Pope interjected with a frown.

'I wasn't sure that he was... that he was Anna's son,' he stammered and turned his gaze away from the Pope's scrutiny, it was getting worse than he had thought.

'How well did you know Anna?' the Pope questioned quietly, not liking the idea that Salvarado might be harbouring a secret.

Cardinal Salvarado swallowed hard: if the Pope had any reason whatsoever to distrust him, what he had spent his whole life building would disappear instantly.

He had to tell the truth; he had always had trouble lying anyway, which was why he lost Anna.

'I was in love with her, but she preferred Benjamin, Aaron's father.'

'Would you have left your vocation if she had agreed to marry you?'

Cardinal Salvarado stared at his friend and mentor but could not answer the question. It was a long time ago, he forgave her, and before her death, they were close friends. Although thoughts of her pale white skin on his body kept him awake most nights, that was his cross, he dealt with it his own way.

He refused to answer the question and walked away from the Pope, but on second thoughts, came back and knelt before him, kissing the ring on his right hand. He clasped his hand tightly and the Pope winced in pain but said nothing, sharing his friend's pain and loss.

'I loved her so much,' he was sobbing now, 'I loved her totally, but I couldn't have her, as much as I tried.'

After a couple of minutes, he composed himself and stood to his feet. He brought out a white handkerchief and wiped his face with it and, at the same time, began his story,

'We met in Brooklyn a long time ago, she was like an angel; so lovely, gentle, and fragile, but Anna only had eyes for the rugged looking Benjamin Cohen. I heard from her neighbours that she'd eloped with him, the rumour was, they had fled to England to escape their parents' wrath,' he paused briefly as if to recollect his thoughts, 'two years later, she got in touch and I wrote to her regularly, but her letters were sporadic. Some years passed and the letters stopped abruptly. Then, out of the blue, she wrote to me again, saying she wanted to meet; she came with Aaron.'

Cardinal Salvarado paced up and down the large office, his eyes looked sad and the Pope's heart went out to him.

'Something died within me when I heard the news of her death. Aaron survived because he'd gone camping with his older brother, Simeon.'

'Then what happened after that,' the Pope asked softly, dreading the end of the story.

'I went to England to see the boys.'

The Pope's eyebrows shot up in surprise but Cardinal Salvarado merely smiled.

'It was on official duty your Holiness, but I used the opportunity to see Aaron and his brother. I knew there was something powerful about the boy but I couldn't figure it out until the day he called me about an incident.'

The story was getting more captivating and the Pope listened with rapt attention. Cardinal Salvarado fixed his gaze upon the Pope and said slowly, as if weighing the words,

'They were just fooling at a friend's place when one of his friends brought out his father's gun, not knowing that it was loaded - he pointed the gun at Aaron and shot him at close range, close to the heart. Aaron told me he fell down and fainted, but before the ambulance came, he was back on his feet and the bullet popped out of his body: he was miraculously healed.'

'Why didn't you tell me about this boy, Sal!' the Pope exclaimed in a sad voice.

'I thought it was irrelevant.' He could not look the Pope directly in the eyes now.

'So,' the Pope said quietly, 'tell me more about him.'

'Your Holiness, it was more than that,' and there was a pensive look on Salvarado's oblong face, his copper coloured hair looked strangely out of place with his bronze skin, 'Aaron Cohen has the twelve stones of fire.'

The Pope's mouth hung open. It was a huge bombshell, but he could not bear to show too much emotion, after all, he was still the revered spiritual head in the world. Nothing could come as a shock to him. Cardinal Salvarado saw through the Pope's façade; it was akin to a photographer and his rolls of negative pictures.

'The twelve stones of fire?' the Pope asked, staring into space as some of his dreams played out before his eyes. He was in the middle of a blazing inferno, but mysteriously the fire did not scorch him. He had woken up with a nasty headache; he was still a cardinal when he first had the dream. It was so eerie because anytime he saw himself dancing in a dream or around a fire, he would always have to make an important decision in his life or ministry, and it was always a tough decision.

The Pope let out a deep sigh and whispered,

'The stones of fire are real, but they are nothing to worry about.'

Cardinal Salvarado knew he could say no more, he kissed the Pope's ring and left.

'The stones of fire,' Pope Nicholas III whispered repeatedly as deep gloom settled on his soul.

6

Washington D.C, Aug 3

Joshua Cohen lay rigid on the bed, staring intently at the pictures with tears streaming down his wrinkled face, one in particular caught his attention, and he checked the back of the picture and saw the familiar handwriting of his father. The date was 17th of October, 1958 and a tidal wave of emotion hit him so hard it was as if someone had slammed a sledgehammer on his head.

He caressed the picture and his heart filled with unimaginable sorrow. Joshua stared at his brother, Benjamin, for such a long time that his vision blurred with tears. He put the picture down and his mind travelled to happier times in their small, but beautiful apartment in East Flatbush, Brooklyn, New York.

Benjamin was the darling of the family, his ruddy appearance and cheery, chubby face endeared him to people. Everyone who met Benjamin loved him to bits. He was funny, energetic, and very intelligent. Joshua admired and loved him too, but problems began during their teenage years. Benjamin was not too keen on religion, but their dad was a strict, orthodox Jew who made sure that they attended synagogue every Saturday. When Benjamin turned thirteen and had his 'bar mitzvah' it was a great occasion, but Joshua saw through him; the important Jewish tradition meant little to him. Their parents, on the other hand, exuded joy as they watched their beloved son absorbed into the fabric of their religion. He watched with apprehension as the day wore on. His parents threw a lavish party to celebrate the day, but Joshua noticed the bored expression on Benjamin's face and his heart lurched with fear at the impending doom that would surely come when his brother reached adulthood.

Joshua took a deep breath as memories flooded his entire being. His dad had been highly respected in the Jewish community in Brooklyn and a brief smile crossed his face when he remembered how his old man assumed the responsibility of modelling how a Jewish family ought to live and behave. They faithfully observed and celebrated all Jewish festivals, Yom Kippur, (Day of Atonement) and Rosh Hashanah. As they matured into young men, Joshua saw the fleeting look of uncertainty on Benjamin's face.

One day after school, he caught up with Benjamin in his room and asked to have a word.

'Ben, do you have something you'd like to share with me?' he had asked, looking at him directly.

'Nothing you'd be interested in Josh,' he had answered nonchalantly.

Joshua had left him alone, and now he wished he had not. Gradually, Benjamin's principles and way of life tore the family apart. Things came to a head one fateful night when Benjamin announced that he was getting married. He had just graduated from the University of Maryland, had not really secured a permanent job, and was still freelancing as a journalist. Nevertheless, Benjamin was adamant and when their mother encouraged him to bring the girl home, he did, and it was a shocker. The girl was a Catholic.

Joshua remembered his dad maintaining a stoic silence until the leggy, beautiful girl who had captured his brother's heart left, and when Benjamin returned home, all hell broke loose.

Joshua recoiled in horror as the memory of that late winter night assailed his mind. His dad's baritone voice filled the massive living room while he narrated the story of how they were some of the lucky few to have fled occupied Poland in 1941. His voice quavered while he spoke; Joshua saw the sadness creeping into his voice as he recounted the story. He told his rapt listeners how their relatives died in death camps like Auschwitz, Treblinka, and Belzec.

'As far as I'm concerned, Pope Pius X11 was not sympathetic to the annihilation of Jews, and I dislike Catholics with a passion,' at that instant his voice broke and tears spilled from his eyes, although he continued nonetheless, 'Benjamin, if you don't listen to me, and follow the laws of the lord our God, but follow the killers of your people, you and your descendants will never find peace, you will be forgotten and disappear like a fog in...'

'Stop this at once Daniel! Words are powerful; don't say what you'll later regret!'

Joshua heard his mom's voice cutting sharply through his dad's tirade of curses. Joshua closed his eyes as the acrimonious scene played out. He saw tears roll down the cheeks of his mother and knew things would never be the same again.

Benjamin did not say a single word at the outburst. He just stood up from the sofa and stalked to his room, slamming the door so hard the apartment shook, and from that day onwards, Joshua hated his brother with a passion.

Things got worse, and a permanent gulf was created. Shortly after the incident, Benjamin eloped with his fiancée to England, and that was the last time they set eyes on him.

One hot summer morning, his dad collapsed while walking to his car - he died at the hospital. It was sudden and so severe that his mother could not cope with the loneliness, and she followed suit three months later.

Before their deaths, his parents had refused to mention Benjamin's name, but he knew they longed to hear from him. Looking at the forlorn expressions on their faces, Joshua saw bleakness and sorrow brutally advertised for all to see. His parents were heartbroken, but there was nothing from Ben, just a terrible wall of silence, which was a tragedy.

There was no forwarding address, there was no way Joshua could have traced Benjamin to tell him the sad news about the loss of their parents. Joshua resented his brother because he believed Benjamin was ultimately responsible for their parent's demise by having chosen to marry a girl they strongly disapproved of, and he never forgave him for that.

Yet years later, he secretly longed for his companionship.

Then, one humid summer night, he heard of his death on the television; Benjamin had perished with his wife and daughter in a plane crash - they were on their way to Mexico when disaster struck. The devastating blow left him inconsolable.

Joshua immersed himself in work in order to escape his woes, and in the space of ten years, he became one of the most celebrated lawyers in America. He married his college sweetheart whom he had met during high school in New York - his parents had approved of his choice before they died.

Joshua picked another picture. His wife looked very pretty in a sleeveless dress, her auburn hair was piled on her head, and her eyes were clear and innocent. His lips parted slightly in a smile, I miss you darling,' he thought sadly. They had a beautiful but childless marriage, and she had passed away four weeks earlier, which rather informed his soul-searching exercise.

Joshua turned his attention back to his brother. Benjamin's tragic end haunted him daily and he held himself responsible. He believed his thoughts had a life of its own, which in turn destroyed Benjamin. Bitterness gnawed away at his soul like a cancer, its destructive effect resulted in the tragedy; superstitious? Yes, he believed in old wives' fables, and the fact that they never reconciled before his death was catastrophic. However, there was a glimmer of hope; Benjamin had a surviving son called Aaron, and he planned to find him if it was the last thing he did.

He would find Aaron and ask for his forgiveness.

Joshua put the picture down with a sigh and closed his eyes. He wondered how Aaron would turn out. Maybe he would be as stubborn and stupid as his father. Only time would tell, yet the thought of meeting him for the first time filled him with both expectation and apprehension at the same time.

Joseph, his assistant, had convinced him to hire a private detective, and now his only hope was pinned on a stranger, and the thought filled him with dread. Joshua loved being in control; relinquishing it was making his life miserable. Joseph had reassured him the detective was the best in New York. Well, I'll have to wait and see. For my sake, I hope the investigator strikes gold, or else I have lived in vain. He thought and turned sideways, staring at his hands.

He could not bear the thought of the shadows chasing him any longer, although his psychologist had dismissed his fears, saying he was imagining things. He yearned for a peaceful closure but was aware that it would not be an option. Joshua stared long and hard at his hands; spots of blood appeared unexpectedly, and, knowing it was another horrific illusion, he closed his eyes for a few seconds, and when he opened them again, the blood was gone.

He was hallucinating again, at least that was the diagnosis, but he knew better. His heart lurched painfully at the atrocities he had committed in the past. His face turned pale and he had trouble breathing; the memories kept rushing in like a tidal wave. His eyes turned bright red, no use crying over spilt milk, he thought sadly.

If he could turn back time, if only... he shrugged his frail shoulders at the futility of it all, and stood up from the bed heading for the toilet.

7

Aaron sat by the window as the plane taxied down the runway. Though it took him a while to board an aircraft after his family perished in a plane crash, he had simply refused to allow fear to dominate his life. He wanted to live a normal life, which was why he needed answers from the man his mother had trusted like a brother.

He relaxed back in his seat ready to take a nap. He had had a hectic week; he might as well catch up on it. When the plane took off, he covered his eyes and promptly drifted off. Seated beside him was a tall, fair-skinned man who was tapping his long fingers on an old, ragged looking book on his lap. It was the Bible written in Ge'ez, an ancient Ethiopian language.

Caleb cast a quick sideways glance at his co-traveller and trembled with excitement. He had followed Aaron from a hotel in Barking, having witnessed him flee with a girl in a car. He tailed them in a hired car to another hotel in Kent; somehow, Caleb knew Aaron would be going to the Vatican, consequently he had booked his own flight earlier, and as fate would have it, he was sitting right beside him.

Tension cruised through Caleb. He knew things could easily go awry, but so far, there seemed to be no problem, however until they had landed safely in Leonardo da Vinci-Fiumicino airport in Rome, he would not be able to relax. He could not stop scrutinizing the unsuspecting man snoring beside him. He finally tore his eyes away after what seemed like an age.

He felt a little uncomfortable knowing that he might be an object of scrutiny himself. He took a sweeping glance around the plane and was not surprised when he saw a passenger behind looking at him with interest. He focused his faltering attention on the Bible on his lap, trying to appear unconcerned.

Caleb flipped through two pages absentmindedly, and then remembered Cardinal Salvarado's promise to send helpers.

By now, he was restless and the Bible verses made no sense to his warped mind. Again, he scanned the entire row of passengers and noticed two men in dark sunglasses. They sat in the next row, one of the men bared his teeth in a supposed smile, but it was more like a snarl, and the hairs at the nape of his neck stood on end.

Caleb stood up hastily and went to the toilet. He had a funny feeling in the pit of his stomach. Who were those men? He thought frantically, they don't look friendly at all. Could they be the cardinal's men? He doubted that very much.

A sharp knock on the toilet's door almost made him jump out of his skin. He flushed the toilet and waited; he wanted to open the door but decided against it.

'I must be overreacting,' he mused but that did not stop beads of perspiration forming on his forehead like ants in a feeding frenzy.

He wiped it off defiantly with the back of his hand and opened the door.

One of the men he had spotted earlier stood outside the toilet; he was almost seven feet tall, and when he removed his sunglasses, his eyes were like steel. There was a nasty scar from the side of his face to his chin and it made him look more menacing, his nostrils flared like a goat in heat. Caleb hated the look on the man's face.

He pulled Caleb out of the toilet and slammed the door in his face.

'That was not gentlemanly mister!' Caleb hissed in protest and stalked back to his seat in rage.

He rarely lost his temper but the man's rudeness was beyond explanation. Caleb controlled himself with great difficulty, but the thought of jeopardising his mission finally did the trick.

'Calm down old man,' he whispered but felt like standing up and punching the sneer off the man's face. The man strolled out of the toilet and Caleb felt the man's eyes boring into the back of his head. He rolled his eyes sideways to check out his rude neighbours and, sure enough, they fixed their eyes on him. He finally decided to ignore them, and it worked.

They landed safely in Rome; Aaron slept through the entire journey, and when they disembarked, Caleb tagged along after him, hoping to introduce himself.

They passed through immigration and he tried striking up a conversation with Aaron, but he breezed past him, walking with long strides - he was almost running.

Not to be outdone, Caleb hurried after him and saw Aaron disappear inside a tobacco shop, probably to buy tickets.

He seemed to change his mind; Caleb saw him emerge from the shop hailing a cab, and he sprinted to catch up with him but it was too late: the car zoomed off. Only then did Aaron's frowning face rest on his briefly, their eyes interlocked for few seconds before the car screeched out of sight.

Caleb stood still for some time, he could feel his body vibrating with disappointment, there goes the powerhouse, he thought and waited for the cardinal's contacts. Barely a minute later, someone tapped him on the shoulder; he turned round sharply, expecting to see Antonio, his usual contact, but was shocked to see the two arrogant men he had travelled with on the plane.

'Yes, can I help you?' Caleb asked calmly, there was no need to panic as they were in public. Throngs of people milled around them, going about their various activities, he was sure they would not abduct him in broad daylight. Surely, they cannot attack me, he reassured himself.

'You are to come with us,' Scarface said brusquely; Caleb had nicknamed him Scarface for his own amusement.

The man took Caleb by the elbow, while his partner followed close behind. He decided to obey rather than cause a scene. 'The Cardinal must have sent them,' he reasoned with himself, apart from the Order of Lalibela, no one else knew about his trip.

He was marched into a black Mercedes Benz and as Caleb sank into the plush leather seat, he masked his emotions well. Scarface opened the driver's door while his partner got in the back with Aaron.

Expertly, the man eased the car onto the road while Caleb struggled to make sense of it all.

AARON GOT out of the car, paid the driver, and walked briskly towards St Peter's Square. It was a lovely sunny day with tourists strolling leisurely with cameras slouched around their necks. Some were taking pictures while others posed for the cameras, their faces the epitome of joy.

Aaron felt relaxed and safe.

He inhaled the fresh crisp air and allowed himself the luxury of a smile that rapidly turned into full-throated laughter.

He had been fascinated with the Vatican ever since he visited the historic city with his mother as a kid, he had been enamoured with the smallest nation in the world ever since.

It was around eleven in the morning as he patiently manoeuvred his way through the teeming crowd, there was a festive feeling in the air, and it was infectious. Aaron walked with quick strides towards a yellow Vatican postal box on the side of St Peter's Basilica and saw a Swiss Papal guard with his brightly coloured uniform, he grinned with delight; the guards' uniforms never ceased to amuse him.

As he passed the guard, the cardinals and bishops in their scarlet and purple vestments distracted him. He stopped briefly to admire them, a smile clearly etched on his face, *'I've come to the right place,'* he thought happily.

The cardinals disappeared from view and Aaron strolled through the square, taking in the structure and basking in the knowledge that he was part of a mystery. He wondered why the primordial city and everyone associated with it seemed steeped in hallowed history; even the shadows seemed to whisper.

He quickened his pace as an impulsive urgency gripped him, Aaron realised it would be impossible to see his mentor, Cardinal Salvarado, immediately, so he decided to check into the only hotel in St Peter's Square. He sauntered into the monastery-turned-hotel, went straight to reception, and paid for a room for the night. He got the keys and went to the lift. When he came, he opened the door of his room, and felt miraculously alive. The cherry wood furniture, the tiled floor, and the big white bed cheered and lifted his spirits for a few minutes.

Then his mood changed again, foreboding swiftly replaced his optimism, an ominous heaviness enveloped his soul. He crashed on the bed totally drained of energy, his shoulder throbbed with a slight pain, but it was nothing compared to the heat, which gradually built up inside him.

He tried crawling out of the pit of darkness creeping in on him by focusing the remnants of his energy on the reason behind his trip. A persistent, silent voice urged him to take his bag and leave the hotel, while his rational mind dismissed the idea. Although he felt physically weak, his thinking faculties were still on high alert and his mind was sharp.

Aaron had noticed that the man beside him on the plane had been too close for comfort. Aaron had also sensed that someone was following, but none of it bothered him - as long as he could have audience with the cardinal. He was in the Vatican to get answers, and he was sure he had made the right decision, yet the lingering feeling of uneasiness stubbornly persisted. Aaron was sure Cardinal Salvarado would not be pleased he had left the priesthood, but it was nothing compared to the burden on himself; it was like a heavy cloak on his body.

His stomach rumbled, he had nothing to eat on the plane. He picked the phone beside the bed and ordered a large meal. He could eat a horse, he was that hungry. Aaron dragged himself from bed and went into the bathroom, took a quick shower and hurriedly changed into a casual shirt and beige trousers.

Deep down he wished he had a gun because he suddenly felt defenceless and exposed. He lay on the bed for a couple of minutes and was almost dozing off when someone knocked on the door.

'I'm coming.'

He called out and stood up from the bed, opening the door. A pasty-faced man stood by the door with a trolley laden with food. Aaron gave him a ten-pound tip and he left. Aaron shut the door with his right foot and sat down to eat.

He attacked the food voraciously; it was as if he had not eaten for a month. After his meal, he made a cup of tea and relaxed on the bed, waiting for the cardinal's phone call.

He did not have to wait long. Twenty minutes later, his mobile phone beeped twice and, palms clammy with sweat, he answered the call. He listened as beads of sweat gathered on his brow; Cardinal Salvarado promised to be with him by nightfall, and Aaron protested feebly. He had no intention of spending days in the city.

'Why not pay a visit to the Castel Sant'angelo Museum,' suggested the cardinal smoothly, 'you'll be surprised how time flies, I will soon be with you.'

'Okay,' Aaron agreed lamely, 'I hope you won't be too long because I am meant to be in France by tomorrow noon.'

They chatted briefly, and ended the conversation.

Aaron angrily threw his phone on the bed, deflated by the abrupt change in plans and his mood plummeted further: to compound his problems he was becoming suspicious. He had noticed the cardinal's voice had seemed detached, warning bells began ringing again but he ignored it.

I'm tending towards paranoia if I kept suspecting everyone. I need to have faith in someone, and I choose to trust the cardinal. Though it dawned on him that if the cardinal should betray him, he could be dead in minutes.

Patience was the least of his virtues and it was obvious that he had no choice other than to wait. He dropped his head on the pillow with his thoughts in disarray. The cardinal was his only option for now and that was not good. Out of boredom, he began twitching his fingers and noticed that his hands were cold. He stood up, went to the window, slowly parted the curtains, and peered outside.

The sun was shining brightly but the temperature in his hotel room was steadily dropping, the hair at the nape of his neck stood on end. He turned away from the window, indecisive: if he stayed indoors, he might be able to reduce his exposure to danger, but staying indoors now seemed ill advised.

Restless, he began pacing up and down, grinding his teeth in frustration. He knew there was something in the room, but his sharp eyes didn't see anything extraordinary. Then he noticed a brilliant glow from the centre of the room, magically, the brightness increased in intensity.

Aaron was astounded as he watched with fascination and dread. He was mesmerised by the radiant light that had steadily grown into a blaze accompanied by a mist, which steadily clawed its way from the centre of the room and was now engulfing him. By now, his fascination was turning to outright panic, and he felt the overpowering presence of the supernatural. He pinched himself to confirm that it was real, but this time he was not dreaming, it was not like his abduction by Tyrus's gang.

Surges of electricity coursed through his body and he began to tremble as his heartbeat increased in intensity, and, at that particular moment, he wished his dad were still alive. He had a unique way of making light his fears.

Without thinking, Aaron grabbed his bag from the bed with the intention of running out of the room when someone grabbed him by the elbow and turned him round: he saw a very strange sight.

'Where do you think you are going?' Asked a very good-looking man in a light blue robe, he had a red band around his waist with a gleaming golden sword securely attached to it. His eyes were bright, his bronze-like skin glistened and his dark hair was thick and long, falling down to his waist. Aaron heard a distinct sound behind the man, and his eyes flicked to the stranger's hand; he held a big golden scroll.

'My name is Uriel... I've come to take you away from here.'

Aaron was not amused.

'Next thing, you'll tell me you're an angel,' he said sarcastically.

'You are perfectly right, how could I have made such an entrance without even knocking,' Uriel answered laughing, but his eyes were serious, 'I'll lead the way,' he said and turned away from Aaron. Walking towards the door, his wings opened up in a slow motion.

'How else could I have gained access to your room?' He repeated again when he reached the door.

Aaron moved closer and inspected the wings, and when he touched them, a powerful tremor went through his body. He stepped back quickly.

'You are real!' He exclaimed.

'Yes of course I am, don't be dumb!' Uriel's eyes gleamed when he spoke, 'I made a great entrance; you could at least give me that credit,' and he grinned, 'now, we have to leave this room in the next ten minutes: your life is in danger here.'

'How do you mean?' Aaron asked, dreading the answer.

'From you know who: your cardinal.'

Aaron detected a note of sarcasm in his voice, 'If you don't leave this hotel now, you will be dead and the Almighty wouldn't like that, so He sent me to save you.'

A cold rage steadily built within Aaron as he stared at the man standing in front of him, suddenly he cried out angrily,

'Where was the Almighty when my whole family were wiped out? Where was He?'

8

Uriel averted his gaze.

He knew there was nothing he could say that would ease Aaron's pain. He listened as Aaron ranted on and was visibly upset.

'Why did the Almighty fail to protect my only brother? I couldn't even see his body!' He shrieked uncontrollably and his voice quavered with sadness.

Uriel closed the short distance between them and held him by the shoulder with his free hand. Aaron saw kindness in his eyes but was past caring.

'He is always with you Aaron. He never let you out of His sight for a second.'

He moved out of Uriel's grip and said in a crisp, impassionate voice,

'I am going sightseeing because I don't understand what your God wants from me. I am very upset and in pain if you hadn't noticed that by now,' with that Aaron left the room. But outside the door, he waited briefly and took one last look at Uriel, whispering hoarsely, 'by the time I come back I want you gone, and take your theatrics with you.'

'Wait...!'

Uriel tried to stop him but Aaron hightailed it to the lift and, when the lift's door pinged to a close, he half expected Uriel to be inside, floating and begging him to leave the hotel, but there was nothing. He got to the lobby and dropped his keys at reception, the short bald receptionist glared at him without a blink; something in his gaze caught Aaron's attention, and he lingered briefly, watching him. He almost turned round to go when he noticed the receptionist's protruding jacket. Then he remembered Uriel's warning and froze in his tracks.

At that same instant, the man brought out an AR-15 automatic rifle and Aaron did not wait to find out what would happen before diving to the floor, desperately searching for a hideout, but finding none.

Bullets rained in torrents around him and Aaron put his hands to his ears to blot out the rasping sounds of the gun. He closed his eyes tightly mumbling the last rites: he believed he was going to die.

Ten seconds seemed like a thousand years and when the shooting stopped abruptly, Aaron waited for the worst to happen as his breathing came in shorts gasps.

When nothing happened, his eyes flipped open. He had expected to see the barrel of a gun pointed at him by a deranged killer but instead, a tall, intelligent looking man approached him slowly. When the man came closer, Aaron recognised him as the man who had sat next to him on the plane. The man was speaking but Aaron could not make out the words; he was temporarily deaf.

The man stretched out his hands and Aaron took them gratefully. He looked round the lobby in disbelief. The level of carnage unleashed within such a short period appalled Aaron, but for the timely intervention of his newfound friend, he would have been killed. The man at the reception desk had disappeared too. His gaze swept the lobby, people sprawled in different postures of death, glass strewed on the floor, and a steady stream of tourists had already gathered at the entrance. Ten men had lost their lives, and it was a shocking discovery that the men wore the brightly-coloured uniform of the Swiss Papal guards. The church was on his trail.

'What happened here?' He finally found his voice.

'My name is Caleb,' said the tall stranger who extended his hand again for a shake.

Aaron shook Caleb's hand and winced.

'I believe you must have been forewarned, but you stubbornly refused to leave. I think we should make haste while the sun shines. We're not out of the woods yet. Besides, a trigger-happy guard could be hanging around. Let's go catch a plane.'

'I don't understand,' Aaron began with a non-plussed look on his face, 'who are you? And why am I being followed, how do you know me...?'

'I'll explain everything to you,' Caleb said patiently and steered Aaron through a back passage toward a waiting car.

Aaron kind of liked the tall smiling man, but was disappointed that he would not be able to get the answers he needed from his mother's friend. It was as if the whole world was fighting against him, and the cardinal's betrayal further confirmed his predicament.

When they entered the car, Aaron asked in a diminutive voice,

'Where are we going, if I may ask?'

'We are going to a safe house in Rome where the Pope will see you, and then we will be on our way to Ethiopia.' Caleb answered softly, his eyes fixed on the road.

'I hardly think that is a wise decision. The Pope wants me dead!' he exclaimed, 'and what the hell are we going to do in Ethiopia?'

'No!' Caleb snapped angrily and his reaction took Aaron by surprise, 'the holy father knows nothing about this,' and then he lowered his voice to a whisper, 'it must be one of his trusted aides, the Pope wanted to meet with you right now, but I think Ethiopia is the safest place for you to be.'

'What if I refused?'

'You can't,' Caleb replied kindly, 'you wouldn't last a second.'

'Why can't I be left alone? Why can't I simply be a normal guy?'

Caleb had no answer to Aaron's questions; he merely shook his head and turned away. The silence in the car was somehow eerie and Aaron wanted to it break but later decided against it. He glanced briefly at his new friend - at least he could call him that, after all, Caleb's timely intervention saved his life even though he knew little or nothing about him.

There was no use making small talk while he had mountains of problems to mull over. Their driver, a sullen Italian with a permanent scowl on his face, who only grunted when spoken to, was the worst driver he had ever had the misfortune of seeing behind the wheel. He hoped the Italian police would ignore the driver's erratic driving through the streets of Rome. If police flagged them down, things could get worse. He stole a quick glance back and could see that they were rapidly leaving the Vatican behind.

His mind kept wavering all over, in the midst of his anguish, Kate's image suddenly loomed large before him, his heartbeat increased in tempo, and it was precisely at that moment that he knew he had truly fallen in love with her. His entire countenance changed radically at the thought of her kind, beautiful face. She was a gentle, selfless human being who always put others before herself, and she was a hopeless romantic. Kate loved flowers, candlelit dinners, going on endless strolls in the park, and his heart lurched painfully at the awful realisation that he would not be able to provide such simple pleasures of life to her. He wished he could give her more but was so limited, and not the kind of person who could love her in the right way. He had a whole lot of issues to deal with.

'She deserves better,' he whispered softly to himself.

He sighed and felt guilty that he had not been able to call her, but he was reluctant to drag her into an adventure that would be dangerous and could endanger her life. He had no idea what would happen the next day, where he would end up, and was relying on people he hardly knew to make decisions on how to keep him safe.

As much as he tried to wrestle control from fate, his life seemed to be spiralling out of control.

He swallowed hard as thoughts of his future lingered on his mind, 'can I be allowed to nurture a beautiful relationship of that sort in the madness that is my life? I don't think so,' reluctantly, he pushed thoughts of her to the furthest part of his heart, but his wayward mind kept turning back to her.

A shy grin spread to his face and he rubbed his hands together. The thought of her brown skin on his would be heavenly, but dwelling on that intimate aspect of their relationship was pure torture. He had never been with a woman and, at the ripe age of twenty-five, he was somewhat ashamed, but could not discuss that with anyone.

As though Caleb knew what was going through the younger man's mind, he turned to Aaron and patted him on the hand reassuringly. Aaron nodded, grateful for Caleb's kindness as he watched the Italian's furious driving through the crowded streets.

Aaron's vacant expression was a ploy to hide his turmoil but he was determined to appear strong, even if he felt a crippling weakness consuming him. He stared ahead, intent on an inner resolve to conquer his fears.

He remembered his dad had told him about a relative in America; Aaron was determined to explore that part of his family though he knew it may not make any difference to his plight, but it was good to know he had a family elsewhere.

He removed his hand from Caleb's and clasped them together, his future didn't look promising, rather, it appeared bleak and capricious, but one thing was certain - he would fight to stay alive. Silently, he prayed for God to have mercy on his soul and save him from the clutches of darkness.

9

Brooklyn, New York, Aug 5

The sniper placed the twenty-four pound .408 CheyTac LRSS intervention M200 rifle with scope on a table. He moved it very close to the window and bent down slightly, scanning the tactical ballistic computer, which already contained relevant information in the database intended to make his task a smooth one. He paid attention to every minute detail to avert any mistake. He had painstakingly planned every aspect of the operation: he wanted to avoid a botched job at all costs.

He gazed through the telescopic sight of the CheyTac rifle and gritted his teeth as his stiff head seemed to move to the rhythm of a song in his mind; sweat gathered on his forehead while his trained eyes were glued to the apartment on the next street.

His target was about two-hundred yards away and he was confident that the mission would be an easy one. He knew it would be a clean shot but something else kept troubling him, it was like a slab of concrete on his mind: no matter what he did, it lay there like a heavy weight, or a conviction of some kind, but he shrugged it off defiantly. He couldn't be bothered anymore; he didn't have any hope of redemption and he planned to take as many people down as possible. Besides, he had a grudge against his subject and it was more or less a personal vendetta for him.

He focused his attention on the building and a little girl emerged from nowhere, bouncing on her feet excitedly. She radiated an aura of innocence and, to make matters worse, she was not alone.

She entered the building with two adults, probably her parents, he thought with gritted teeth. The sight of the girl caught him off guard, 'would you kill an innocent girl who knew no sin?' His tortured mind cried out. He ran his hands through his hair and thought for a microsecond of abandoning the job, no sooner had the possibility encroached on his mind than he fiercely chucked it out.

His bloodshot eyes trailed after the girl until she disappeared inside the building with her companions. His breathing became ragged, forcefully torn out of his throat. He visualised her long dark hair, which tumbled down her tiny waist, with her brown, glossy skin. She could be no less than six years old, and the thought of killing such a young girl was doing his head in. He wiped sweat off his face with the back of his gloved hand.

'The girl is very pretty,' he mused and knew he was going into uncharted territory if he went ahead with his plan. Rather than think of the disastrous fate that awaited the little girl if he made good his threat of bombing the building, another saddening thought assaulted his mind like a ferocious storm.

The sniper almost lost focus as unpleasant memories flooded his mind and a single teardrop rolled down his lean cheek. His daughter's murderers had been acquitted, and the man he was going to kill in a couple of minutes had convinced the jury that the two Latin American men who raped and killed her were innocent. They had been set free, free! His eyes turned icy cold at the judgement.

He screamed in his mind as he imagined his daughter's helplessness in the hands of her murderers, and he was glad he had avenged her death. The only man left in the equation of injustice was the subject he had come to silence. It was a job, and he desperately wanted to relish every moment of it. He had wanted to give up on the killing aspect, but when the phone rang and he heard the name, he jumped at the chance. The subject was a cocky, arrogant lawyer who had denied him justice; so he would get it by himself.

He was an army sniper at the U.S Army Sniper school at Fort Benning, Georgia, and was an outstanding student, one of the best in the school. He had served in Iraq during the Gulf War, and later became a shadow leader in the 2nd squadron and the 33rd regiment at the onset of renewed hostility in Iraq. But he had to be sent home after sustaining an injury to his shoulder and, as a sniper, the severity of his injury meant the end of his tour and he came home disillusioned.

He licked his dry lips while his angst-ridden mind played it out, his glassy eyes stared straight ahead. His hands began to shake as the painful memories rushed through his conscious being: it was as if it had just happened.

It was a cloudless day in May, and I had gone to the court seeking justice for my daughter. But my dreams came tumbling down with such force that I almost fainted. After the trial, I watched with anger as the families of my daughter's killers rejoiced at the 'not guilty' verdict.

I felt some tightness in my chest but continued watching nonetheless; hatred filled my heart with such intensity that I could hardly breathe. After a lot of struggle and restraint, I finally tore my gaze away from them and led my grief-stricken wife out. Our lawyers followed closely behind, our defeat showed on their slumped shoulders.

We walked out of the courtroom with deliberate steps while my wife clutched my arm tightly. She was devastated but I guess she knew we would not be able to elude the packs of reporters waiting impatiently to descend on us. Sure enough, the road that led to the courthouse was awash with news vans, and journalists of all shapes and sizes filled everywhere.

Reporters swarmed around us like a company of bees shoving microphones and cameras into our ashen faces.

'How do you feel about the verdict?' I locked eyes with the pretty ABC reporter who had asked me the question and I answered tersely,

'I leave judgement to God,' and our attorneys whisked us away while my wife stifled a sob. We got into our car and drove away from the scene.

Throughout the journey home, my mind was working out what I had to do, and then, slowly, the perfect plan came to me.

The sniper stopped his sad reminiscences and turned his attention back to the building. All thoughts of the young girl had vanished from his deranged mind while he had been trying to justify his actions. Though he had been waiting patiently for more than two hours in the same position, his physical strength had not faltered.

His hands itched in the sweaty gloves but he ignored the discomfort. He felt the rapid beating of his heart; setting aside his own revenge, his subject was a prey to be killed at all costs, or else he would become the hunted. Once the man was dead, he would finally be able to close a painful chapter in his life, and possibly move on - but at the thought of his wife, a shiver ran down his spine.

Their marriage was plainly over.

He became a shadow of himself after the death of Diana, who was their only child; he withdrew into his shell and became almost comatose. Naturally, his wife was distraught, but she tried to move on. He could not.

The sniper let out a long breath.

They just grew apart after their daughter's death. It was hard to believe that the power of his grief could actually turn him into a monster.

He ditched his erratic thoughts when his sharp, well-trained eyes noticed movement in the building he was shadowing.

He saw a man approach the window of the apartment directly opposite and part the curtains. He picked up his binoculars and studied the person in the room; then he put his binoculars down and stared at the man through the telescopic sights of the rifle. A wide, evil grin spread over his taut features, without hesitation, he muttered under his breath,

'Good night old man.'

Shots rang out with supersonic velocity; the window of the apartment crashed into thousands of pieces as fragments flew about in different directions and, in a matter of seconds, it was all over.

'Mission accomplished and accurately done,' he said gladly with a satisfied grin on his face.

He could imagine his victim, or victims, depending on who had been in the room, falling down and groaning with agony as their life slowly ebbed away - but he was not done yet. He took the rifle from the window and quickly disassembled it. He removed the barrel, the optics, and suppressor.

He worked quickly, packed the receiver group into a military rucksack, and gently put the barrel into a black weapons case. He left the rifle in the room, staring at it for a while; he hated parting with such a reliable weapon but he had to, that was the agreement in the contract. He questioned why such an expensive weapon should go to waste, but he was not the one calling the shots.

He shrugged his wide shoulders and walked out of the room. Strolling through a long corridor, he leisurely took a Cuban cigar out of his pocket, lit it, puffed it out, and threw the cigar into the living room.

He left the apartment and heard the loud wailing of a siren, which was coming closer. He entered the lift, pressed the button for the ground floor, and waited patiently. When he got to the ground floor, he checked his wristwatch and waited anxiously as the seconds ticked by.

He was motionless for a while as the image of the little girl and her companions crept into his mind; he felt sick and was sorry she had to die, but he regarded her as a victim of war.

Suddenly, there was a loud bang as a series of explosions rocked through the apartment block. He had seen enough, it was time for him to stop for the day.

'I should not have waited this long to kill that wicked lawyer,' he muttered under his breath as he walked briskly to where he had parked his car. He got in, put the key into the ignition, and the car spurted to life. He drove away while looking into the rear view mirror with a wicked grin firmly pasted on his face. Finally, he had the closure he had desperately longed for but, deep down, something kept gnawing at him. He had expected elation and relief but was surprised that he felt sad. It was a strange, uneasy feeling that slowly ate through him like a cancer, it must be my conscience, he thought gloomily.

When he got to his church, he drove straight to the underground parking lot. He had been ordained the previous weekend as a reverend and he laughed at the irony of it all. His unsuspecting congregation had no inkling of the kind of man he was, and he had pulled off the charade for too long.

'Something will have to give soon,' he thought as his mind drifted to his wife, 'she will leave me if she finds out I am a hired assassin.' His congregation would be devastated if the secret came out that their beloved pastor was not who he had made out to be.

He stroked his chin and grunted, got out of his car, took out his phone and dialled a couple of numbers. He waited for about a minute, and then a call came through, but he ignored it. Instead, he switched off the phone and slammed it to the ground, crushing it under his military boot.

He picked up the remnants of the phone and entered the church, stopping briefly at the altar with his eyes riveted to the stained-glass window on the second floor of the church. He walked away, but his conscience pulled him back - he swallowed hard, went back to the altar, and sank to his knees.

He bent his head for a brief prayer but his mind was blank; his susceptible mind had retained the picture of the little bouncing girl and he found it hard to expunge the memory.

'Help me lord,' he cried out in anguish, frustrated by his own weakness. Angry, he stood up, walked past the empty pews, and was about to open his office door when his second mobile phone began to ring: he knew who it was and felt guilt ridden.

It was the church overseer, Right Rev John Lake - the older man loved and believed in him. He ignored the call and took long strides towards his office. He knew it was time for him and his wife to leave the beautiful congregation of 'Time of God Ministries' and start their lives elsewhere. Personally, he would prefer Alaska, but knew that his wife and her family would furiously contest his decision. She had lived in New York all her life and the decision would jolt her for sure.

He pushed the thoughts of his wife aside, switched off his second mobile phone, and went straight to his office.

In a matter of minutes he had removed his leather jacket, black jeans and boots - he folded them neatly and dropped them into a black bag, tied it securely, and put it on his desk, making a mental note to discard it on his way out of the church.

He changed into his pastoral robes and sat on the chair behind his big oak table littered with papers. Heaving a deep sigh of relief for a flawless operation, he waited patiently for the call. Precisely ten minutes later, the landline phone on his table rang shrilly and he snatched it up in a flash.

'Good job, I loved your preaching on Sunday, it was directly from heaven,' said a crisp sharp voice at the other end, 'how is the bazaar committee? Hope things have cooled down considerably Reverend Peters.'

'Yes,' the sniper, otherwise known as Reverend Mathew Peters, chuckled into the mouthpiece, 'I hope to see you soon on the proposed hunting trip...' there was a short pause followed by a cough, 'I badly need a break your eminence.'

'You deserve it Reverend, but we need to pay a short visit to the Vatican tomorrow for the meeting of the cardinals. My letter was faxed to me this morning.'

Revered Peters kept quiet for a long time.

He had thought the lawyer was his last assignment and the prospect of going to the Vatican filled him with dread, but he had to.

Or maybe not... and a plan slowly formed in his mind.

'Yes your eminence, when do we move?' He asked quietly, his mind working like an overcharged battery.

'Tonight,'

'Okay, I'll be at your residence in an hour.'

'Good,' said the voice at the other end - there was a clicking sound, and the line went dead.

Reverend Peters dropped the phone, and, immediately, it began to ring again. He picked it up and held it in mid air as realisation finally dawned on him, but his reflexes were too slow and too late.

The explosion ripped through the building and seemed to tear it into shreds. Reverend Peters was pinned against the wall while huge balls of fire raged all around him. I knew I should have call off that operation, he reasoned candidly, as the flames engulfed him. He knew the little girl he had murdered in cold blood was a curse on him. He had been killing for money while parading as a man of God, but the cardinal was wrong, thought reverend Peter in agony, the cardinal will burn with me whether in this life or the next. His blackened face contorted into a grim mask and his breathing came in short gasps. Coughs racked through his huge frame as he frantically searched for a way of escape but everything was a blur. He screamed out in agony, thrashing wildly about the room.

His entire life flashed before him in an instant, and he asked God for forgiveness for profaning His name. His flesh began to burn slowly but he stubbornly clung to life, death was not a very good option for him, but neither were his chances of survival; his situation was very grim indeed.

As the Reverend in charge of the largest church in the district and a wartime hero, his descent into criminality was very slow, but after his first kill, he realised that it was easy and found he could no longer stop. He had received the Distinguished Service Cross for fending off Iraqi insurgents and killing several of them in a raid, which could have inflicted horrendous losses on his regiment.

He collapsed in a heap and waited for death.

10

Forty-eight hours later, a parcel arrived at the New York Police Department addressed to the police commissioner. The contents of the parcel sent shock waves through the country. Cardinal Albert Freeman of Chicago was the head of a cartel of drug dealers, while Reverend Mathew Peters was the cartel's hit man. And in another twist of fate, Reverend Peters was the first cousin of the police commissioner. It was a terrible scandal, from which the Vatican reeled for days.

The Catholic Church was under a lot of pressure to get its house in order. The humiliation inflicted by the newest scandal grieved the pope, whose sagging frame could hardly take in the fresh allegations. He collapsed while addressing the College of Cardinals in a meeting hastily organised to salvage the image of the church. Temporarily, Aaron Cohen appeared forgotten, his case no longer considered a priority. The pope withdrew from official duties for a while he recuperated in an undisclosed Rome hospital.

Barely twenty-four hours later, the police commissioner committed suicide – as well as being a relation of Reverend Peters, he was also a very good friend of Cardinal Albert Freeman. It was only a matter of time before someone fingered him as a collaborator in the murky details, so he took the easy way out.

The Vatican simply refused to issue any comment.

Back in London, Kate leafed through the newspaper in her hand, her sleeping and waking thoughts were on Aaron, and she hoped the sordid stories going round had nothing to do with him.

She had woken up at the hotel in Kent the next day to find the other side of the bed empty.

Aaron had gone but had left a short note on the bedside table. It gave little away - just the word 'sorry' scrawled on a plain sheet of paper, and that was all. It had been two days since then and she had not heard anything from him. The silence was slowly driving her insane.

Kate had left the hotel in a hurry, terribly annoyed and beside herself with rage. When she arrived home, she got into a huge row with her mum, venting her pent up frustration at her. Her mother had demanded to know why she did not call to tell her she would not be coming home, but Kate had ignored her and gone up to her room.

When she entered her room, she flung her bag angrily on the bed, and immediately convulsed with tears.

Two days later, still nothing, no call or even an email; anger quickly turned to anxiety, and anxiety to worry as fear over his whereabouts gripped her heart. She could not bear to imagine what might have happened to him.

She stayed glued to her laptop for hours but there was nothing, which was utterly infuriating. She felt he should have informed her when he landed in Rome, at least that would have definitely put her mind at ease.

She felt lost and withdrawn; her mother noticed her despondency and pestered her for an explanation, but she refused to budge, and stayed holed up in her room all day. She hardly ate or bathed. It was as though she were in mourning. Exasperated and at her wits end, her mother told their next-door neighbour Evelyn about her concerns, whom she had noticed was quiet fond of Kate.

Shortly after that, there was a knock on her bedroom door. Kate stood up grudgingly from her rumpled bed wondering what her annoying mother wanted.

She staggered to the door in a daze as though she had been drinking. To give her room a semblance of sanity she carelessly pushed the empty cans of Carlsberg under her bed. She had not slept for two days and, even in her state of stupor, she was aware of a terrible odour oozing out of her body - not that it mattered to her.

She opened the door and saw the fresh face of Evelyn. Kate's face turned bright red when she thought of the state of her room, her mother glared at her in disgust and walked away.

'Come in,' Kate said demurely and moved aside while Evelyn entered the room and closed the door. She went straight to her bed and continued reading the newspaper.

Evelyn gave the room a sweeping glance and began tidying up. Kate was miffed but said nothing. She continued reading while Evelyn rearranged opened the windows to let sunlight in, gathered the cans of beer from under her bed into a heap and opened her built in wardrobe, groping through her clothes. She found a clean pair of black jeans and a white shirt, and placed it on the bed.

'It's time for a hot bath.' Evelyn declared softly but firmly.

Kate nodded meekly, stood up from the bed, and went obediently to her bathroom where she stayed for over half an hour. When she came out, Evelyn had changed her bed sheets and the room smelt of her favourite air freshener. Beside her bed was her breakfast on a tray: eggs, bacon, baked beans and toast with a cup of strong, black coffee, but her friend was nowhere to be seen.

Kate was grateful for Evelyn's kindness - she dressed and ate the food. When she had finished, she took the tray downstairs to the kitchen and met her mother in a deep discussion with Evelyn.

Kate smiled politely at their astonished faces and dropped the plates in the dishwasher, then went back to her room.

Half an hour later, Evelyn popped back to Kate's room and sat down on the newly made bed, her sad blue eyes not leaving her face for a second; Kate felt uncomfortable under the scrutiny but did not make any comment nor utter a word.

'I'm going to tell you a short story and, please, I don't want you to interrupt me.' Evelyn began quietly while her eyes glistened with unshed tears. Kate was shocked at the obvious display of emotion but managed a weak smile and said softly,

'I won't.'

Evelyn nodded and the compelling story flowed effortlessly.

'Precisely seven years ago, before you moved to this neighbourhood with your parents, my husband disappeared, and straight away I knew something wasn't right. He left a note for me and a cheque for one million pounds. But I knew that we couldn't afford that kind of money, except if we had won the lottery.'

She smiled at that and continued, 'My immediate suspicion was that something sinister was going on, so I called his best friend Keith Morgan, who took the next flight from the States to see me and my little girl Caroline.' She paused for a brief moment and her face betrayed no emotion as Kate listened with rapt attention.

Evelyn continued speaking quietly again, her voice hardly above a whisper, her eyes were sad as if the words coming from her mouth were being forced out.

'I never believed that there would come a day like this, when I would be telling someone an unabridged version of the story of my life. My husband's surname used to be Crest, but we changed it when his family publicly disowned him for helping a country in West Africa acquire nuclear power.'

Evelyn stopped speaking, it was as if she was waiting for a reaction, but when there was none forthcoming from her audience, she continued,

'When my husband disappeared, I felt so isolated - all my friends deserted me when they were privy to the fact that he might have left for Nigeria with little or no coercion whatsoever. His best mate, Keith, stood by us though. He was with us for a couple of weeks, which was also short-lived - his son was brutally murdered.

To cut a long story short, I followed him to New York and stayed with his family for a year and a half, but, somewhere along the line, I lost the plot to a very sad story, and slit my wrists. I died before I got to the hospital. Unbeknown to me, the day I decided to kill myself was the day my husband landed at Heathrow Airport; he was miraculously released and had wanted to make a surprise entry.'

'You died?' Kate asked quietly, disbelief evident in her voice.

'Yes I died.'

Evelyn repeated firmly, her eyes gloomy and mystifying, her heart shaped face contorted as though in a spasm.

She stood up and turned her back on Kate, her pale skin glistened with sweat. She ground her teeth and continued speaking, facing Kate again,

'I bargained for my life, I didn't stay dead for long; what I want you to learn from my story is this... life is not as simple as it looks. There are spiritual forces that control things, whether good or bad, it all depends on which side you are on my dear girl. There is life after death, believe it or not,' her voice was solemn and her eyes wide, 'we are not here in this world by mistake, and just forget the stupid Big Bang theory propounded by scientists. There's a life apart from this world, there are demons and there are angels, and worlds beyond what any human could describe - there is heaven and hell!'

'How on earth did you bargain for your life?'

Kate asked in a trembling voice, the story was surreal yet she believed the regal, strong woman standing in front of her.

The hair at the nape of her neck stood on end and she felt a kind of numbness in her body; the way Evelyn was speaking, it was obvious she had experienced something profoundly extraordinary which could not be explained or rationalised in the natural sense of human reasoning.

'I slept with a demon.' Evelyn declared quietly but there was a harsh tone to her voice.

'But you said it yourself,' Kate said shaking her head with a confused look on her now flushed face, 'you were dead... how could you possibly be dead and still... live?'

'That's the mystery I want you to solve,' Evelyn declared with a smile on her pretty face, 'this should definitely take your mind off your man for a couple of weeks, or days at least.'

Kate saw the challenge, though if she pressed further, she knew Evelyn would have succumbed and spilled the truth anyway. As absurd, as it sounded, Kate knew without a doubt that Evelyn was trying to help her solve, or accept the possibility of, the mystery surrounding the disappearance of Aaron by leading her to solve an incredible story.

And Kate believed every single word, knowing Evelyn to be a very intelligent woman who would not cook up a tale just to jolt her back to life. The story fascinated her, though it was somewhat spooky and bizarre, the kinds of story, which make you wonder how something like that could have happened. This is one mystery she would love to solve, she loved adventures, and this promised to be one.

'I'm going to New York,' Kate announced and they stared at each other, 'I'm going to find out how you died and still lived, at least from the medical perspective.'

'A word of caution,' said Evelyn quietly, 'things are not as they seem, you may be loaded with explanations about me going into a coma and still being able to survive. I want you to explore the other aspects; the realms of the spirit.'

'I'll remember that,' Kate said and locked eyes with her friend, 'but what about your daughter, where is she?'

Evelyn turned away at that and Kate wondered if she had overstepped the boundary. She really wanted to know, because Caroline's picture adorned Evelyn's living room and she often wondered where the blonde haired girl could be.

'She's in a hospital in New York, she has a mental illness,' the lifeless words stumbled out painfully and it heralded a floodgate of tears. Kate stood up from the bed and embraced her tightly as she cried. When the tears subsided, Evelyn muttered,

'Maybe I should tag along with you to New York; I haven't seen my daughter for almost a year, which has obviously been too long.'

'Then let's get packed.' Kate said gleefully, staring at her friend fondly and her heart filled with compassion for her. She intended to unravel the remaining mystery surrounding the stoic but beautiful Evelyn.

11

Ethiopia, Addis Ababa, Aug 6

Aaron inspected his hotel room with a tired and almost frightened expression etched on his face, unlike his riotous thoughts, the opulence of the hotel was almost staggering, it was a most peculiar contrast.

'Oh well,' he mumbled under his breath, 'life is the survival of the richest, not of the fittest.'

He was staying at the Sheraton Addis in the central area of Addis Ababa.

The hotel was luxury epitomised: located on a hilltop overlooking the National Museum, it oozed beauty and wealth.

He marvelled at how Caleb was able to lodge him in such a luxurious hotel, there is more to the man than meets the eye, he thought fondly, his respect for Caleb was growing in leaps and bounds as the day went on.

His eyes took in the massive, neatly made king size bed and slowly, he walked towards it. There was a 42 inch flat screen television on top of a table and he cringed at the thought of what could be happening back home in England.

Aaron dropped his luggage at the foot of the bed and sat down, suddenly tired and drained of energy. He saw no end in sight; the endless flights, fleeing from enemies and, to make things worse, there was a constant throbbing pain beneath his rib cage. It was like a burning sensation and at times, he felt like crying aloud, but he clamped down on it as best as he could.

Caleb on the other hand had noticed that something was wrong and assumed Aaron must be coming down with a fever. He had phoned his family doctor who came to examine him, but Aaron was declared as fit as a horse and was probably suffering from jetlag.

Aaron stood up and sauntered to the window, parted the curtains and peered outside - he liked what he saw; the Ethiopians flirtatiously displayed their grandeur, a landscape of vibrant greens and colourful wildflowers seemed to kiss the African sky, but Aaron's eagle eye also noticed the surrounding slums, their opaque presence still gleamed in the bright morning sun. On a good day, he would have loved to tour the ancient city to his heart's content but sadly, it was out of the question.

The burning sensation in his chest had intensified in spite of the doctor's diagnosis. He sighed and tried to take his mind off his ailing health by studying his environment.

There was something truly magical about Ethiopia and he felt it deep within his bones. Ethiopia may finally answer his questions or, miraculously, even find a cure for his malady and the numerous nightmares, and maybe bring closure to the beast called Tyrus.

He had always dreamt of going to Africa but after the brutal murder of his brother, he was wary of embarking on such a trip. He was not afraid of the continent, quite the contrary, but his feelings of hesitation boiled down to the unknown and, in a way, he felt pretty much alone, that the details of his life seemed to be in the hands of strangers, and that his future was shrouded in secrecy, even from himself.

He grunted in frustration and ran his hands through his hair. He had finally decided to take each day as it came, that way nothing could come as a surprise to him. He turned away from the window, opened his bag, and took out the Bible he had brought with him.

Caleb had advised him to read it and there had been a twinkle in his eyes as had he said it, Aaron had laughed and reminded him that he was an ex-priest who knew the Bible thoroughly.

'You never know the fresh insights you may find when you read it again.'

Caleb had persisted in his gentle way and Aaron could not refuse him: Caleb was his knight in shining armour in Rome and he would not forget that in a hurry.

'I will,' He had promised.

Aaron sat down and the pages turned to the middle, lifted by a breeze that seemed to caress his face. His eyes scanned everything in the room in a flash; he felt a presence but could not see anything or anyone.

He turned his attention back to the page and began reading from the book of Ezekiel, chapter twenty-eight. His hands began to shake when the name Tyrus leapt out at him from the page, and when he got to verse thirteen he read it out aloud,

'Thou hast been in Eden the garden of God;
every precious stone was thy covering, the
sardius, topaz, and the diamond, the beryl,
the onyx and the jasper, the carbuncle, and
the gold: the workmanship of thy tabrets and
and of thy pipes was prepared in thee in the day
thou was created.'

He stopped reading to catch his breath as realisation finally dawned on him: Tyrus was real, he must have lived thousands of years ago, why had he chosen him now? Aaron had no interest in antiques or ancient relics, neither was he a collector, but now he must uncover the truth. He continued and at verse fourteen, the hairs at the nape of his head stood on end.

'Thou art the anointed cherub that covereth;
and I have set thee so: thou was upon the
holy mountain of God; thou has walked up
in the midst of the stones of fire.'

At that precise moment, everything clicked into place, and he was petrified of the magnitude of the task before him. Tyrus was the bad man and he the good man - the good man always wins, he reassured himself.

'Are you sure?' He heard a hoarse voice mocking him in his mind.

Aaron slumped back on the bed with the Bible over his face, and realised the reason why he seemed to court trouble everywhere he went, and why anyone in on his visions ended up on a cold slab. His eyes turned back to the pages as he lifted it up while still lying on the bed, he mouthed the words slowly,

'Thou wast perfect in thy ways from the
day thou wast created until iniquity was
found in thee.
By the multitude of thy merchandise they
Have filled the midst of thee with violence,
And thou hast sinned: therefore I will cast

thee as profane out of the mountain of God:
And I will destroy thee, O covering cherub,
from the midst of the stones of fire.'

Aaron let out a big sigh and closed the Bible, pondering on the words. Different questions raged through his mind like tidal waves: why did God chase Tyrus away from the midst of the stones of fire? Why did God choose him out of the billions of people in the world?

He remembered when the nightmares began - it was the night of his seventh birthday. He had partied with his friends all day, although he felt a strange heaviness in his heart, he had shrugged it off defiantly, determined to enjoy himself and when the party ended, he was reluctant to go to sleep.

Aware that he was stalling going to bed, his mother finally ordered him to his bedroom - when he refused to budge, she had more or less dragged him upstairs to his room. An hour or so later, he was snoring deeply, and then he'd had the weirdest dream. He was in an unfamiliar environment, a different, reddened planet, bizarrely depressing and so very hot that his feet was almost on fire, but it was nothing compared to what he saw next.

A huge man dressed in golden robes was fighting a tall, dark angel who seemed to growl with every muscle in his body; the angel was equally massive but angrier.

Aaron strained his eyes because he could not see clearly; he inched closer, watching the unfolding scene with apprehension.

He looked on in amazement, by then oblivious of the pain in his feet. When the man's robes came off, Aaron saw sparkles that were like little dots of light emanating from the robes. They were twelve precious stones. Suddenly, the dark angel gave an unearthly, guttural shout and Aaron almost fainted with fright; it was the cry of a victor and then Aaron saw hailstones and fire landing on the massive man who was now naked and shaking, but the huge, dark angel showed no mercy as two flaming swords of fire ripped through the man's weakened body.

Aaron cried out at the display of such brutal violence, he wondered why the man was being punished so severely. Nevertheless, he could not draw his eyes away.

He saw a sea of men dressed exactly like the man in the golden robes, now naked, helpless, and shaking like a leaf in the wind. A lone fire engulfed their bodies and sucked them in, yet Aaron watched still, his long skinny arms began to shake as the planet began to implode.

The scene was unbelievably cruel as the bodies of the men disintegrated. Hailstones fell in torrents until there was nothing left, and then an uneasy silence reigned.

Aaron tore his eyes away and began to cry. Unexpectedly, he found himself in the arms of the dark angel. Aaron's eyes were puffy and red with tears and his breathing was fast and hard.

'Who are you?' Aaron asked with tears still streaming down his face.

'I'm your friend.' The angel answered in a surprisingly gentle voice.

'Why are you destroying this planet?' He asked, although he was afraid.

'These men are bad people and had to be punished.' was the simple reply.

'What did they do?'

'They betrayed their father.' The angel answered, his eyes glowing with kindness.

Aaron liked him, and he was quiet as he thought about his next question.

'What is your name?'

The angel smiled, revealing sparkling white teeth.

'My name is Barachiel, and you are in the Cydonia region of mars, now you have to run along. Don't tell anyone what you have just witnessed.'

Barachiel put him down and gave him a gentle push, but Aaron turned back and tugged at the red robe the angel was wearing. Barachiel stared at Aaron for a long time and then did something unexpected. He tore a piece of his robe and gave it to Aaron. He then instructed him to go and never turn back. Even if he had wanted to, the sound behind him would not let him; it was akin to the roaring of a very angry lion, and then he heard the unmistakable sound of clanging swords, the battle raged on and that surprised him: he thought the battle was over.

He woke up with a start, screaming at the top of his lungs. His parents had come rushing into his room and he had recounted everything he had witnessed, even the part where the man asked him not to say anything about what he had seen.

His parents exchanged knowing glances as Aaron's confused gaze rested on his right hand and he showed them the red silky cloth. When they saw it, his mother screamed. From that day onward, things rapidly went downhill.

That was the beginning of a series of visions, dreams, and nightmares. His parents took Aaron to see priests who performed exorcisms, but the dreams continued to grow in intensity. In the end, he gradually became a recluse, burying himself in comic books, and as he grew older, he became shy, but his family showered him with love and affection; he lacked nothing.

That was until a succession of tragedies turned him into an orphan, but he kept the piece of red silk as evidence that he was not paranoid or hallucinating: it was a solid reminder that he was not just imagining things.

As his mind clung to the fears of the past and present, palpable sorrow descended on him. His life had been one steady stream of pain and, in a way, he was quite used to it.

Finally, he succumbed to a troubled sleep. A few hours later, he felt a heavy hand on his shoulder: his eyes flew open, and he saw them.

12

A Pungent odour filled the room as the men glared at Aaron. They looked the same: ugly, mean, and dirty. The same men who had kidnapped him in London had traced him to Ethiopia. Enraged, he charged at them, fighting like a bull, his eyes literally red, his nose flared in fury.

The men fought back angrily but were surprised at Aaron's strength. Bloodied and shaken, two of them escaped through the window while the last man cowered and moved away from Aaron, his chest heaving up and down like a man running a marathon.

'I am a demon, you dare not kill me!' He growled, baring his teeth.

'I eat demons for breakfast now!' Aaron roared and grabbed his throat, the man managed a feeble punch to Aaron's stomach, but it had no effect - within seconds, he went limp and slid to the floor.

Aaron bent down and as soon as his hands touched the man's body, he evaporated. Stunned, Aaron staggered back, watching from a safe distance. Excitement coursed through him like a tidal wave and he stared at his hands in disbelief, but there was no difference, he was still the same person.

His mind went straight to his college days when he was doing his A-levels. One of his classmates had described him as dull and uninteresting and the words stuck to him through his adult years. Although he failed to acknowledge it then, now he knew better. He was not a dull, bland, or uninteresting bloke, but an empowered man ready to conquer all forces of evil. He could feel his sense of identity somehow coming back.

Now, Aaron was confident that he could fend off any aggression directed towards him. Then he remembered Kate and his expression turned grave as his hands fell limply to his side. How he missed her!

There was a knock on the door. He went to open it and saw a young Ethiopian boy of about fourteen with a broad smile on his face, and Aaron returned his smile. The boy gave him a bulky parcel and a frown crossed his smooth features as he took it, thanking him in English for his kindness. The boy hesitated with an expectant look on his face, and then he understood. He dipped his right hand into his pocket and gave him a five-pound note, a big grin spread to the boy's black face as he thanked Aaron profusely and bowed slightly - Aaron closed the door with his foot.

He wondered who could have written to him, and how they had known his whereabouts. He tore the parcel open and pictures fell to the floor. His blood turned cold. He bent down to study the pictures; it was his uncle, and he looked frail, almost lifeless.

Aaron read the note that accompanied the pictures and his heart sank. He would have to leave for New York at once: his uncle was dying.

Aaron was torn about informing Caleb about his uncle's condition. He desperately wanted to meet his only living relative - if he died, Aaron would not forgive himself. With his mind made up, he went down to the hotel lobby and spoke to the receptionist, asking if he could get the number of an airline to book a ticket to New York. Her face tightened up in what Aaron interpreted as a smile, but it was actually a grimace. She told him to hold on while she spoke rapidly on the phone.

As he waited, two soldiers entered the hotel lobby and at once, he knew they were looking for him.

Aaron turned away from the receptionist and faced the entrance of the hotel so the men got a proper look. Sure enough, when they spotted him, they approached with deliberate steps and their stony expressions spelt trouble. Aaron saw the guns and stood rooted to the spot, then he heard a soft moan and a thud behind him and knew the receptionist must have fainted. The men opened fire, but the bullets bounced off his body and fell to the ground. There was pandemonium as people screamed and ran out of the lobby. Realising the futility of their mission, Aaron's attackers fled but he chased them to the street, but the men merged with the crowds and disappeared. Aaron stopped the chase, panting furiously.

'Cowards!' He shouted and went back to the hotel, furious with himself and the never-ending cycle of violence. When he entered the lobby, it was like a ghost town: completely deserted, not a single soul in sight.

He strode back to his room to wait for Caleb, 'my uncle will have to fight on without me' he thought aloud. Besides, the tightness in his chest had returned with full force. Twenty minutes later, the door to his hotel room opened and Caleb came in with two men.

Aaron was pleased to see him but the pain in his chest was so severe he could hardly speak. The men carried him out while Caleb took his luggage. By the time they got outside, a small crowd had gathered; news had travelled fast about the death defying white man.

Inside the car, Caleb touched Aaron's forehead and was dismayed by his temperature. They sped through the noisy streets of Addis Ababa.

'What's wrong with him?' Peter asked quietly, looking at the pale white young man.

'It's the stones on his chest. We have to make some offerings tonight.' Caleb answered with his brows furrowed together.

'Is he going to die?' Peter asked again, he sounded scared.

'No he is not!' Caleb snapped and the tone of his voice suggested he would appreciate a quiet journey, but Peter was apprehensive as he cast furtive glances at Aaron who was too weak to talk.

'I shouldn't have left him alone,' Caleb mumbled to no one in particular.

Their car cruised through Laitu Street towards Bole road, to the residential area of the city. They stopped at an imposing white house and the driver hit the horn twice. The gigantic gate of the house opened and they drove in.

Aaron resisted any offer of help and wobbled on, taking in the imposing house and well laid lawn.

Caleb walked with him while Peter carried his luggage.

They entered the expansive, sparsely decorated living room and Caleb led him down a long corridor, before opening the door to a room. Aaron collapsed onto the bed, his breathing came in short hissing gasps, his body racked with pain. Within minutes, he was fast asleep. Caleb stuck to his side, watching him like a hawk.

Peter lingered outside, his gaze rested on an old man approaching with a limp from the garden. They shook hands briefly.

'Where is the young man?'

'He's in the bedroom,' Peter answered and lowered his voice, 'in very bad shape.'

The old man nodded and moved away from Peter. Men dressed in fine white linens with turbans on their heads began to arrive in a convoy of cars. Peter welcomed the men and reverently ushered them into the living room. They took their seats in the vast living room, conversing in the ancient Ethiopian language, Ge'ez.

They talked in hushed tones, casting surreptitious glances at Peter who beckoned to Caleb. They moved to the balcony where he spotted stern faced soldiers with AK-47 assault rifles. Peter dismissed the men with a single wave of his hand and they disappeared from view.

'Do we need to have armed guards?' Peter asked with an edge to his voice.

'We do,' Caleb answered, 'we need more than armed guards Peter. People will kill to have a pound of Aaron's flesh - he is the mystery of the present age.'

'How do you mean?'

'His blood contains the stones of fire, his flesh cannot rot, and he can't die - at least not our kind of death. He is the only man alive that can stop the plans of the devil and his cohorts,' and then he added with emphasis, 'he is our only hope.'

'But who were the military men who shot him?'

Caleb glared at him and stalked back inside.

Peter was frustrated.

He hated Caleb's obsession with Aaron, yet he left him in a hotel by himself, he thought with a frown. Luckily, the receptionist was kind enough to alert them of Aaron's plans to go to New York, or else they would have missed him, and Caleb would have embarked on another ill-timed trip.

Peter was becoming increasingly apprehensive about the older man. Caleb was not getting younger, and deep down Peter didn't believe the world was facing any real threat from anywhere, let alone from a faceless foe.

He shrugged his shoulders and went back to the living room to wait for the arrival of the priest and caretaker of the Church of St Mary's Zion in Axum.

Caleb watched Aaron anxiously and blamed himself for leaving him alone in the hotel. But he'd had to, he reasoned. As soon as their plane had landed in Addis Ababa he had told Aaron that he must inform the elders of the Order of Lalibela of his arrival, and the next day he was supposed to go to Axum with the caretaker of the Ark of the Covenant.

Caleb walked away from the bed, deep in thought; the betrayal of Cardinal Salvarado had come as a surprise - I could have been killed and it was a miracle we were not harmed in the attack, I will be eternally grateful to the Pope's private secretary, Monsignor Bacilio Alvarez: he was able to thwart the cardinal's devilish plans.

He turned his thoughts away from the treacherous cardinal back to the Order, how will I convince them of what I am about to do? Aaron can only achieve the purpose of his calling in the relative safety of St Mary's. He let out a deep sigh. Convincing the elders would be a massive task, the incessant questions from Peter were already driving him nuts, and he knew their lives could be in danger because the extent of Aaron's power was still unknown.

They could die protecting him. His eyes turned a shade darker as he scratched the stubble on his face. He had not shaved for days and knew he must look a wreck, but his appearance was the last thing on his mind.

Caleb brushed the negative thoughts plaguing him aside; his only consolation was the caretaker of the Ark. He was one of holiest men he had ever had the privilege of knowing. Instinctively, the caretaker of the

Ark of the Covenant must be aware of the stones of fire or he would not have agreed to come to the impromptu gathering. As the caretaker, he was not supposed to leave the church premises for any reason whatsoever.

A thunderous explosion outside the gate destroyed the fragile peace and Caleb almost collided with Peter as he rushed into the room shouting,

'Fire, fire, we must evacuate the building at once!'

'Calm down,' Caleb said quietly, 'we cannot be harmed while he's like this.'

Peter was confused, and then he followed the direction of Caleb's gaze.

Aaron looked different, almost transformed as an ancient Israeli Priest, yet he was still fast asleep. They moved near the bed, staring at him in amazement; he was wearing an ephod - it was an apron like garment, but what captivated them was the breastplate of judgement and the gleaming precious stones. A bright yellow light glowed from his chest sending its brilliant rays into the room, there was a mist and a cloud appeared above the sleeping Aaron.

It was an amazing sight.

At that same instant, the caretaker of the Ark came in with the rest of the Order. There were gasps of admiration and shock at the strange sight before them.

The caretaker was a smallish man with dark, intelligent eyes. On his head was a black cap and he wore a brown robe, his feet were dusty, more like the colour of the brown sandals he wore, and he carried an Ethiopian Coptic cross, in the other hand was the key to the treasures. A young man stood silently behind the caretaker, with a brightly coloured umbrella in his hands.

'My assistant Obed,' said the caretaker, introducing the young man in a booming voice, which resonated round the room, and Obed bowed briefly in greeting.

The caretaker scratched his white beard, his eyes on the sleeping form of Aaron whose face seemed to glow.

One by one, the members of the Order averted their gaze.

'He is in a trance,' and his eyebrows twitched slightly, 'he is the descendant of Aaron the high priest, the high priest we've all read about in the scriptures. We have to take him to the Ark immediately or else we will not see the light of tomorrow. The son of darkness seeks him.'

The ground began to shake. Simultaneously, they began to pray as successive explosions rippled through the building, and the sound of rushing feet was clearly audible.

'Disregard it,' said the caretaker in a more solemn voice, 'it is the work of demons: they don't want him to be taken to the Ark, but there will be sacrifices...', and he left the statement hanging.

'I think we should stay here,' said Peter in a very small voice.

There were murmurs of approval from the others. The light radiating from Aaron's chest was getting brighter, and they had to close their eyes. There were continuous sounds of rushing feet as another explosion outside rattled the building and at the same time the room was completely engulfed in a bright light.

Peter opened one eye and found Aaron's eyes staring at him. He closed his eyes again praying fervently for the noise to stop but it didn't, rather, it intensified.

13

Kate had been totally against the idea of staying with Evelyn's family friends but she knew she was fighting a losing battle; Evelyn insisted until she buckled under the pressure and, finally, she succumbed, albeit grudgingly. It would save her the cost of a hotel room and she would be able to explore New York to her heart's content.

She began to unpack her bag but could not shake off the lingering questions: what happened in Evelyn's room that fateful night? How could someone die and still live?

Kate shrugged it off, and a rueful smile played around the corners of her mouth as she remembered her mother's reaction to her impending trip.

'New York? What in heaven's name are you going to do there?' her mother had asked in a high-pitched voice.

'Adventures mum; I'm going to have fun,' Kate had replied light-heartedly, hoping her mother would get the drift. She was going on the trip, and no one would stop her, not even her father.

'What am I supposed to tell your dad when he comes back from his expedition in Africa?' she'd asked coolly, too cool for Kate, and her defences shot up in earnest.

'Tell dad that I'm twenty one years old; an adult, who will soon be moving to her own apartment. I have to go because I'm going insane in this house!' she had replied hotly, her eyes shooting daggers at her inconsiderate mother.

Kate wanted to escape but her mother's cold hands held her wrists so tightly that she screamed.

'Mum you're hurting me!'

There was no reply, just a crazy glint in her mother's eye and a fleeting thought passed swiftly in her mind, was I adopted?

Without thinking, she blurted out, 'are you my real mother?'

That statement had the desired effect on her mother. She dropped her daughter's hand as if stung by a bee. The expression on her face had been one of horror.

'Why would you say that?' her mother's voice was hoarse and achingly sad.

Kate said nothing, but rather planted a kiss on her cheeks and left her mother with a nonplussed look on her face.

She had always had an explosive and highly charged relationship with her mother, at least that was how Aaron had described it, but her father was a different kettle of fish. She simply adored the ground he walked on, but he was never around. He was either on the rugged African plains filming lions, or on his way to the Himalayas doing one documentary or another. Although money was never in short supply, she was no fool - she saw obvious cracks in her parent's marriage and was brutally aware that in a couple of years, the pretence would simply crumble.

Although her dad was rarely home, he was a good father in his own way. They chatted daily on the phone and when she'd told him about her relationship with Aaron, she had sensed his hesitation, but he gave his blessing all the same.

She finished unpacking her bag and heard movement behind her. Kate stood still as the hair at the nape of her head stood on end. Slowly, she turned round and saw a dark shadow on the bed; a tremor passed through her body and she watched the shadow move in a circular motion, and then it was gone.

Kate closed her eyes briefly, when she opened them, she scanned the room, satisfied that she was alone, she moved away from the bed. Trying to control herself, she took quick steps out of the room and closed the door.

'That room's haunted.'

She heard a distinctive male voice behind her, and she turned round to see who it was. There was no one.

'Calm down, Kate,' she whispered softly and walked slowly down the steps as her skin began to crawl with fear. When she saw Evelyn's smiling face and her hosts at the dining table, her fears took a back seat and she sat down to a sumptuous meal.

The next morning, Kate and Evelyn left the house very early for Central Park. The weather was gloriously warm, people looked happy and there was a festive feel in the air. Kate decided to jog while Evelyn preferred a stroll.

The park was brimming with people. Children screamed with delight while parents sat on the grass, their eyes following every movement of their children. Kate and Evelyn parted ways with a promise to meet up at the Wollman Memorial Skating Rink, but after jogging for a mere fifteen minutes, exhaustion finally set in. She collapsed on the soft grass, staring at the clear blue sky.

After a while, she stood up and moved closer to the tall trees within the park, once under the shade, she lay back down on her back and closed her eyes.

What an idyllic environment, she thought happily, content with the weather.

A couple of minutes later, a howling wind disturbed her peace and an eerie silence seemed to descend on the park. She swallowed hard and opened her eyes, staring into space.

Everywhere was deathly silent.

Kate stood up and almost fainted at the scene before her.

A few minutes earlier, the park had been bustling with activity; teenage boys playing football and children chasing each other, their laughter echoing in her ears. But they had all vanished. There was not a single soul in the vast park. Then, she saw him.

He was a huge man, roughly seven feet, and was dressed in black overalls with a hood shielding his face. Kate watched as leaves danced around him in circles, the sound of the wind was akin to that of a wolf, and her heartbeat was annoyingly loud. That was when she noticed the brute.

It was a snarling black bloodhound, its tongue hung out dripping blood. He was a very large dog, its wrinkled face contorted in rage.

Kate watched keenly; strangely, it didn't occur to her to run, besides, she noticed that there was no leash on the dog. A few misguided steps and she could end up as a bloodhound's lunch.

The stranger's appearance was bad enough but coupled with the dog, it was a double nightmare. She did not want to have a chat with the man or his dog. He came across as ancient and a character from out of this world.

The stranger and his dog approached quietly, mesmerising her with their presence. Her eyes darted everywhere, but it was as if a force had her suspended in a time warp. Something clicked inside her and she wanted to make a run for but she could not move: her legs were like rocks, glued to the spot, but her mind was working, trying to see if she could bluff her way out of it.

God! Where the hell is Evelyn? Kate remembered she had mumbled something about going to Cleopatra's Needle and, afterwards, visit the Wollman Memorial Skating Rink. Who would skate in such lovely weather?

They were inches away from her and the stench from their bodies was akin to rotten corpses. Suddenly, the dog's massive tongue lashed out, hitting her right leg and electricity seemed to surge through her body. Kate screamed in agony.

The stranger's gaze held hers and Kate stared into the abyss as dead hollow eyes stared back at her. Her whole body began to tremble uncontrollably. She tried to turn her face away from the monster. She succeeded, but he lifted his claw like fingers and jerked her head back so she was facing him.

'I need to see Aaron,' the stranger said as billows of smoke engulfed her and she began to choke.

'Where is he?' he asked roughly and opened his mouth wide. A snake emerged from his mouth, and Kate could not stop yelling.

'Leave her be,' said a firm voice and her tormentor disappeared in a puff of smoke.

Evelyn rushed to her aid and held her close, wiping tears from her eyes as she gently pulled her away. Kate was crying and talking at the same time.

'Where were you?' Kate shouted, 'I couldn't move, everybody had disappeared and...'

'Shhhhh...' Evelyn held a finger to Kate's lips and she calmed down.

But she looked worried when she asked, still holding her tightly,

'How well do you know Aaron?'

'Well enough to want to marry him,' she shot back.

'I think you should find out more about him before making any form of commitment.'

'I can't make any commitment to a man who's disappeared, don't you think?' a sad look crossed Kate's face when she said that, 'who am I kidding, I don't even know where he is!'

Evelyn led her away with her brows knitted in a frown. She looked troubled.

'Coming to New York was a bad idea. You can't possibly find anything other than what I've already told you.'

'It wasn't your call, I wanted to come remember?' Kate disagreed with a vigorous shake of her head, her full black hair dancing in the sun, 'I was the one who saw the shadow on the bed, and I was the one who got a visit from Mr Ancient and the dog from hell, not you.'

They lapsed into companionable silence as they walked to where they had parked their car.

'Tell me about the dog,' Evelyn said suddenly, breaking the silence.

'It was a black bloodhound...' and Kate's voice trailed off, she seemed to be reliving the horror, 'the dog had a long tongue dripping with blood, and an ugly drooping face with a nasty expression; not a very friendly dog. I don't hate dogs, but neither am I a great fan: the beast licked my right leg.'

'It did what?' Evelyn stopped in her tracks, her eyes almost popping out.

Kate's eyes travelled straight to her leg; it was red and blotchy, and she when touched it, blood started coming out.

'Oh my God, what's happening to me?' Kate asked as tears welled up in her eyes.

Evelyn was silent while she studied Kate's leg - it was beyond anything she had seen in her life. The poison was spreading fast.

She clenched her teeth in despair, desperately looking for ways to avert the looming tragedy. Evelyn kept a straight face betraying no emotion. Within two days, the leg would begin to rot; they would have to take the next available flight back home.

Evelyn was in a dilemma: if she took Kate to hospital, she would not last the night.

Her wound was unleashed from hell, and no hospital would dare treat that. Explaining the extent of the wound to Kate or her mother would be useless. Kate had been afflicted with an ancient curse from the pit of hell itself, a curse that would run its course within seven days and would culminate in death. Everyone Kate met would also die, except for her. From that moment onwards, they were practically homeless. How am I going to tell her?

'What's the matter Evelyn? Don't you dare hide anything from me!' Kate was on edge, something was wrong, she saw the uncertainty on Evelyn's face.

'We can't go back to the house...'

Evelyn struggled for the words, 'you're infected with the corrupted life of the bloodhound; it wasn't an ordinary dog, and by licking your leg, the dog's blood entered your skin and your blood stream.'

'Am I going to die?' Kate asked quietly, dreading the answer. She felt like a condemned criminal waiting for the verdict from the jury.

The day had begun innocently enough. Evelyn had wanted to stay home and just relax before visiting her daughter the following day but Kate would have none of it, so out they went.

On their way to the park, Kate had confided in Evelyn about the shadows on her bed and the voices ringing inside her head. Evelyn had laughed it off as a silly illusion, but Kate caught a wild expression on her friend's face; it was fleeting but it was there. And as if to confirm her suspicions, before they left, Keith, Evelyn's friend, had announced that he would be selling his family home.

Evelyn had shrugged it off but Kate was not buying it, she was certain that things were not as they seemed. Her eyes bored into Evelyn until she looked away and let out the bombshell.

'You've got seven days left, Kate. We must get to London as soon as possible.'

'I'm really going to die.'

Evelyn nodded, her eyes looked sad.

Kate was not religious in any way but, as an archaeologist, she had seen enough evidence during her numerous digs to know that history hides many secrets; especially about the Ark. Aaron had told her that he believed the Ark still existed and that it harboured ancient secrets. If that were true, then it would be spectacular, especially for Christians and Jews, but it made no sense to her. The Ark was just a relic: powerless and useless.

Evelyn's head dropped to hide her teary eyes. They were beginning to attract the attention of passers-by. People streamed past them but Evelyn was not bothered by the curious glances thrown their way. She feared for Kate's life. Her fear had taken on a life of its own and she shuddered as sorrow overwhelmed her.

Kate felt numb, it was surreal, but she felt it; it was like a ticking time bomb. She was really going to die. How she wished she had stayed home with her mother. If Aaron had not breezed into her life, she would not have been bothered, but even the mere thought of his name sent sensations down her body. She was still hopelessly in love with him. Kate closed her eyes and tried to pull herself together.

She still had seven days, and besides, Evelyn could be wrong.

Really?

A tiny voice kept ringing in her heart,

Your time is short...

The stranger was asking about Aaron, I wonder why that is.

Her eyes sought Evelyn's tear stained face.

'He asked about Aaron, he could help me...'

A short pause and Kate glanced at her swollen leg: it smelt like rotten flesh, exactly like the stranger's odour. Her heart sank when she realised that Evelyn had meant every word.

Seven days... Kate thought as a shudder passed through her body.

'Let's go,' Evelyn said hoarsely.

They raced to their car, parked on the bucolic loop road.

Kate disregarded the needling pain in her leg and gritted her teeth as she pushed her weight forward, but when she trotted past a crowd Kate noticed two or three people covering their noses.

They reached the car and got in, then zoomed out into Eighth Avenue. Kate felt terrible about the stench oozing out of her leg: it could flatten an army.

'Evelyn, I think you should take me to a hospital.'

'That's a bad idea,' Evelyn said firmly, 'this isn't something of this world, don't you see? It can't be treated with modern medicine.'

'Then what am I going to do?'

'I'll call my husband, he'll fly in tomorrow. Michael will know what to do.' Evelyn said and gripped the steering wheel so hard that her knuckles turned bright red.

'Where are we going to sleep?'

'We'll look for a church,' Evelyn replied, checking her rear view mirror, 'I'm sure he won't bother following us inside a church.'

'Do you think the stranger is following us?'

'Yes, I'm afraid so; why else would his bloodhound put a scent of death on you?' Evelyn answered and hated herself for saying it, but she had to, 'that beast from hell wanted Aaron, and since you're his woman...' her voice trailed off.

They lapsed into an uneasy silence, then Evelyn broke it, 'We're going to the nearest church to the park, I think there's one on West Ninety-Sixth street; it's a towering building, I'm sure it's a church and we'll be welcomed there. Then I'll go home and get some fresh clothes for you.'

'I'm sorry for causing so much trouble,' Kate glanced sideways at her friend who expertly manoeuvred the car towards the west side of Central Park and the Christ Movement Church.

'I'm sorry too kid,' Evelyn said quietly, 'I thought the trip would help you get your mind off your boyfriend for a while. I promise to get you home.'

Kate nodded, too tired to speak.

Evelyn slammed her foot on the gas pedal and desperately prayed for a miracle.

14

Cornell Medical Centre, New York, Aug 7

At Weill Cornell Burns Unit, on bed twenty-seven lay Reverend Matthew Peters with third degree burns. He had surprised nurses and doctors by clinging onto life dearly. His doctor had slated him for surgery in a couple of hours, and many such operations and skin grafts would follow. As far as the director of the burns unit Dr Rodney Heist was concerned, Reverend Peter's full recovery would be a medical miracle due to the severity of his burns.

In reception, his wife of thirteen years huddled in a corner, weeping quietly while a friend tried to console her.

In another wing of the hospital, Joshua Cohen was under heavy sedation following successful surgery. Doctors had removed a bullet lodged in his skull; he had sustained the wound to the back of his head, and though the surgery was successful, his prognosis was not good.

Joseph Shalev, Joshua's personal assistant of twenty-five years, trotted down the hospital's reception, a grave expression on his gaunt face. His tall thin frame looked ready to break, but despite his fragile appearance, he was a strong and competent man. A few minutes earlier, the lead surgeon had spoken to him.

'He has a fifty per cent chance of survival; we have to watch him closely. I suggest you go home and rest.'

The words bounced through his mind in frenzy. Fifty per cent chance of survival? Fiercely, as if contending with an enemy, he brushed the thoughts aside.

Joseph had ample faith that the old lawyer would pull through. *Joshua had suffered too much tragedy in his life to succumb to a sniper's bullet,* he thought.

A booming sound was all it had taken to destroy his day.

He had stepped out of the living room briefly to receive a phone call, when he'd heard the sound of shattering glasses. By the time he rushed back, it was too late.

Joshua was sprawled on the floor with blood trickling from the back of his head and right shoulder. Joseph's quick thinking had saved the day: within seconds, he had dialled 911. Afraid that the sniper may still be lurking around, Joseph had carried his boss into the lift, and he was glad that he had. By the time they had reached the ground floor, successive explosions had torn the building apart.

When Joshua was stabilised, Joseph took his picture and sent it via DHL to Aaron in Ethiopia; Joseph had information from the private eye they had hired about Aaron's precise location.

Months before the attack, Joshua had told him about his intention to meet Aaron, and Joseph had swung into action by hiring a private detective who had latched onto Aaron like a virus, though the poor guy had no idea someone was on his tail.

Joseph let out a worried sigh and trudged to one of the hospital chairs, sitting down heavily. Dense cloud seemed to hover over him; for no obvious reason, fear clung to him like a second skin.

He settled back on the blue plastic chair ready for a long day ahead. Glancing round casually, he noticed a red haired woman crying, and wondered where he had seen her before: her face looked vaguely familiar.

Try as he might, the woman's face remained obscure in his mind. Joseph took out his mobile phone to call the office, but decided against it. He had been running Joshua's law firm while his boss was fighting to stay alive and things were relatively calm: he prayed they remained so. There were no serious cases, which required the urgent attention of Joshua Cohen, the junior partners at the firm could handle most of the minor cases in court.

Joseph's calm exterior was a mere pretence to hide his inner conflicts, but his clammy palms gave him away. Restless, his roving eyes took in everything and everyone in the waiting room. The red haired woman locked eyes with him briefly and a chill went through his spine as he tore his eyes away. The woman stood up and walked out of the hospital. There was something arresting about the woman; he tried recalling where he must have met her, but could not. He racked his brain to no avail.

Frustrated, he lifted his head to watch the news bulletin on the television and a name flashed across the television screen: Reverend Matthew Peters, former soldier turned Pastor. The rest of the news was a blur.

Then his brain came alive.

The news had jogged his memory and it all came back in a flash, it was inconceivable that they had been in the hospital reception for the past hour.

The red haired woman was the wife of the former army captain whose daughter ... Joseph almost blanked out at his discovery.

He needed to get to the office fast.

Joseph stood up and stopped for a while debating whether his decision was the right one. The thought of leaving his boss alone in the hospital was heart wrenching, but he had to. He was not a detective but the coincidence was too damn strong.

When the news had broken a few days earlier about the reverend, he'd heard it in a passing statement from his wife and hadn't thought much of it, but his wife had been angry that a reverend could be a trigger boy for drug barons.

He had thought nothing of it until now.

Joseph walked out of the hospital and took quick strides towards his car.

'The police must know about this,' he muttered and opened his car door. He sat down, tracing his hands absentmindedly on the steering wheel. The whole scenario sucked but his problem was whether the police would believe his tale, or whether they would just dismiss it as the ramblings of a devoted employee?

Joshua Cohen had many enemies, including the police. He had saved the necks of countless criminals and had recently come into disrepute. He would not be surprised if they dismissed his story.

Glaring at the side mirror, he wondered what his son would be doing. Suddenly, an alien feeling crawled up his spine and into his soul; he couldn't lay his hands on it but he was afraid. He toyed with the idea of getting out of the car and going back to check on Joshua, but decided it was best if the police knew of his suspicions. But what was the probability that Reverend Peters was the man who had fired the fatal shots?

Joseph gritted his teeth and held the steering wheel tightly, still undecided on his next course of action.

A woman walked casually to his car, Joseph looked sideways and saw her face, and he froze as three gunshots rang out shrilly in succession, shattering the car's window and slamming with full force into his forehead. He died instantly. The woman put a hood over her head, and calmly walked away from the car.

His phone began to ring as blood trickled down his face onto his crisp white shirt.

15

Pope Nathaniel III rested on the bed, his sad eyes burrowed into his private secretary until Bacilio turned away; his face seemed impenetrable, but the Pope could discern that he was angry and was just trying to control his temper.

He spoke rapidly and the only word the Pope picked out from it was 'murder'.

'How long have you known this, my son?' he asked quietly and Bacilio saw traces of tears at the corners of his eyes.

'I have known about this for seven years, Your Holiness,' Bacilio answered, his eyes scanning everything in the room except the Pope's face.

'How many cardinals are corrupted?'

'I have been able to compile a list of several reverend fathers but to my knowledge, only two cardinals are entirely corrupted with little or no redemption.'

'Thank you,' the Pope mumbled and Bacilio kissed the signet on his right hand and left the room, closing the door gently.

The Pope was a very troubled man.

The wickedness and hatred in the heart of a man he had loved and trusted since he was a teenager growing up in the south of France alarmed him. Even the intensity of his dreams had increased.

He closed his eyes and a teardrop fell down his wrinkled face. The walls and ceiling seemed to be closing in around him and an image loomed in front of him - it was a man with a snake for a tongue and when the snake bit him, he almost died with fear. The Pope recoiled in horror as the image assailed his mind again and again: it was as if he was still dreaming.

He was aware that the dreams kept occurring for a reason. It was unthinkable that cardinal Salvarado had almost killed the young man who would not only save the world but his own soul as well.

The Pope prayed silently while tears poured from his eyes in torrents, he made spirited efforts to control them but could not. Like all things in life, a moment of calm came and he lay still. A few minutes later, he drifted into a dreamless slumber.

Outside the door, Monsignor Bacilio stood guard and listened, his heart crumpled at the severity of the deceit in the Church. If only he had a way of consoling the Holy Father, but in this regard, he was helpless. He knew the Pope was clearly courageous and had proved himself fearless by giving him an unspoken order. He was to weed out the corrupted seeds in the Vatican.

'What an honour,' he thought aloud.

He had to carefully plan his moves, and quickly too, or else the deceit of the cardinals would soon be public knowledge and the Church was trying to steer away from scandals as much as possible.

Bacilio nodded at the Swiss guards stationed outside the door and marched away.

He went straight into the Pope's private office. But when he entered, an uncomfortable feeling settled on his soul.

It was a choking, frightening kind of feeling. It seemed to suffocate him; it was akin to an evil spirit, the kind that exorcists find hard to expel.

Cardinal Bacilio picked up a paper from the table. He studied it but his mind strayed towards that fateful night when Cardinal Salvarado ordered assassins dressed as Swiss Papal Guards to attack Aaron. He was happy to have successfully thwarted Salvarado's wicked plots, but his concern was not the deceptive cardinal who was now under the watchful eyes of the real Swiss Guard twenty-four hours a day, nor was it the hired assassins, who had almost destroyed the peace at the Vatican.

Bacilio was worried about the recurrent visions that had become a daily routine in his life. He was now afraid to sleep and, somehow, he suspected that the Pope must have seen something similar. How he wished he had persuaded Aaron to stay for a while, but the young man had been understandably afraid. After the failed but brutal attempt on his life, Aaron had been in a hurry to leave Rome and its devilish men of God behind.

The amazing thing was the connection he felt between them; it was like a bond. It was strange that he had not even seen Aaron, yet, it was as if he had known him all his life. He would love to visit him in Ethiopia, but Bacilio knew he had to stay and resolve the crisis threatening the Papacy.

He turned his attention back to the paper in his hand and out of the corner of his eye; he caught the snarling face of a bloodhound staring at him. Dumbfounded, Bacilio's hands fell to his sides and the paper floated away from him, landing in front of the massive animal.

'It's a dog!' he said and took two steps backward.

There was a deep growling sound and the dog barked twice. Bacilio was in a state of disbelief; nobody had warned him that there would be a dog in the office.

He held his crucifix in his hands unsteadily watching the dog nervously. The dog's long black tongue hung out, dripping blood on the marble floor. Then a tall man in a balaclava emerged from the shadows. Bacilio was stunned, and he staggered back again, clutching his crucifix tightly. He watched the stranger's menacing approach and, miraculously, his fears evaporated in an instant. He had to conquer his fears now or die trying.

It was Tyrus: the horrible spirit that had tormented him in his dreams since he was a little boy, before Father Francis started visiting him late at night.

'What do you want?' Bacilio blurted out; he was almost angry.

'Where is Aaron? I've been trying to find him but I can't,' Tyrus drawled, he almost sounded bored.

He lifted the balaclava to reveal a hideous face that had begun to rot, 'I need to find that stupid Aaron: he has something that belongs to me.'

He stopped abruptly in the middle of the room and his yellow eyes almost twinkled, 'and by the way; why are you not afraid of me?'

'Why should I be?'

'You should be, you poor soul. Do you remember Father Francis? His stubby little fingers did things to you. I hope you remember the night you prayed for the avenger?'

Bacilio blushed.

'I have no idea what you're talking about!'

'You don't want me to start with you,' he warned.

'You foul demon from hell...' Bacilio began, but Tyrus hurled him to the wall with a flick of his long hand. He screamed in agony, watching the towering figure in disgust. Tyrus was now livid with rage; sensing his master's mood, the dog moved towards Bacilio's legs.

'Sit!' Tyrus snapped and the dog bared his fangs, emitted an eerie sound before sitting down on the marble floor, scratching it with his long dark claws.

Bacilio wondered why everywhere was silent. Tyrus and his dog were making enough noise to attract a crowd, besides; Castel Gandolfo was crawling with guards. It was almost impossible for the commotion to go unnoticed.

Tyrus's tongue metamorphosed into a black snake and Bacilio tried to stand up, but fell back weakly. I must show no fear, faith is what I need he thought, but all scriptures flew from his head as the snake hissed. It almost touched Bacilio's face but Tyrus pulled it back.

The room smelt like a sewer and Bacilio was beginning to choke: it was a pungent, stale smell of putrid, decaying flesh.

'Bacilio...' Tyrus hissed as the snake coiled in his mouth and disappeared down his throat, 'you called for me Bacilio and I slaughtered Father Frances. He committed suicide the following morning; is this how you are going to repay me? I did you a big favour and destroyed the man who made your life a living hell. Believe me old friend; you cannot escape your destiny.'

'My destiny is to serve God.'

A shudder went through Tyrus's back, he staggered, his knees buckled, and Bacilio was pleased but knew that the battle was far from over: he needed help.

'You wanted to sleep with Aaron,' Tyrus said and roared with laughter while the bloodhound groaned and growled.

Bacilio's face registered surprise.

'I have no such feelings... Aaron is like my own brother.'

Tyrus moved towards him with deliberate steps, his sunken eyes turned red as he said through gritted, arrow like teeth,

'I need to know where that stubborn stiff necked Jew is, he has the stones. We need to use them for our appeal. I'm here alone, and I think you should thank your stars I didn't come with my dad.'

Bacilio was unperturbed, 'What are you talking about? Besides, you didn't introduce yourself properly; who are you, and how did you get in here?' he asked as calmly as he could manage, struggling to his feet.

'I'm a wolf and my mission is to devour the lamb and eat its flesh and drink its blood,' Tyrus answered, his patience wearing thin.

Bacilio sniggered and said contemptuously, 'you amuse me pal, you're not making any sense.'

'I'm the king of the world and I'm my father's son. For the time being, I'm just keeping a low profile. Our case will soon be decided and I need those stones...' He allowed a slow smile on his face and almost looked human, but Bacilio knew he was a demon.

'I don't know where Aaron is,' Bacilio said stiffly expecting a volatile reaction. He was right.

'No!'

Tyrus opened his mouth and an ear-splitting, inhuman scream came out. The building shook to its very foundations, Bacilio heard stomping feet as people rushed about and he prayed for someone to come through the big oak door, but nobody did.

Tyrus flung furniture about, his eyes eternal pools of hatred. He hurled the Pope's massive table towards Bacilio who quickly dodged it as it crashed against the wall. Tyrus beat his chest with his fists and spewed fire from his mouth.

Terrified that the end was near, Bacilio began reciting psalm twenty-three, but Tyrus cut him short by flinging him to the wall. Crumpling to the floor in a heap, Bacilio groaned as pain racked through his entire body. Slowly, he limped back to his feet, pressing back against the wall, but there was nowhere for him to hide.

'For your information, I hate that particular scripture so, no more tricks.' Tyrus's eyes blazed with such intensity that Bacilio avoided his gaze. Surprisingly, Tyrus changed tactics by saying quietly,

'I'm not going to hurt you if you cooperate, I really need to know where Aaron is and believe me; I don't have much time left. I have never begged for anything in the world but now Bacilio,' and he rolled his name under what resembled a tongue, 'I really need to know where that young man is.'

In that instant, Bacilio knew he was living on borrowed time. His mind flew to his younger years and tears gathered in his eyes as he saw himself as a young child, running round in the garden laughing loudly without a care in the world. He could still picture his family home in Oslo, Norway.

He was an only child and his Spanish father had died in a boat accident off the west coast when he was only ten - his body was never found. His mother had remarried but his stepfather had disliked him from the start because he was the spitting image of his father and, to save her marriage, his mother had sent him off to Spain to live with his dad's relatives.

He enjoyed life in Madrid and soon decided to go to the seminary. He was a mild mannered boy and a devout churchgoer. He had decided to be a priest because of his constant dreams about a fiery planet. Tired of the intensity of his visions, he had confided in his uncle. His uncle believed God was trying to give him a message and they went to see the reverend father of their parish. The father had been impressed and advised him to be closer to God.

That was how he came to give his life to God's service, but Reverend Father Francis was a paedophile who abused him for nearly two years before he died. One cold winter morning, he had heard the delightful news that Father Frances had killed himself. Secretly, he was happy, but his visions of the smouldering planet intensified, and then came the nightmares and beatings from the disgusting being towering above him.

Bacilio made up his mind and said loudly, looking his foe in the eye,

'I don't know where Aaron is!'

'Then you have condemned yourself,' Tyrus said without remorse. Bacilio glared at him, and waited for death.

'The only thing I need is your heart, and I'm going to take it out right now; that way I will have the answers I seek.'

Bacilio was furious and yelled, 'Get away from me you stinking demon!'

Tyrus merely laughed.

'I'm not a demon. I'm the king of them all.'

Then the bloodhound attacked.

The Pope heard faint noises as Bacilio's scream echoed through the hallway and guards came rushing to the room, but it was too late. Monsignor Bacilio Alvarez died of injuries to the leg, face, neck, and torso. Blood was gushing from a deep open wound on his chest. It was a sordid scene.

Pope Nathaniel III knelt beside his bed, he tried to pray, but his mind was blank. Bacilio had been like a son to him and his grief threatened to overwhelm him. Later, when guards led him to the room, he finally realised the enormity of the attack. Walking slowly to the middle of the room, he noticed scratches on the marble floor, his favourite table was broken, and papers and files littered the floor. He almost fainted. The words of his mother rang shrilly in his mind,

"The spirit of the whore would eat the heart of the clean. The children of men would run for cover as fire falls like rain." He had insisted that he wanted to see things for himself, although paramedics had taken the body of Bacilio to the morgue, the scent of death still hung heavily in the air.

He went back to his room, heartbroken but determined to fight for the Church. The demons responsible for the death of his beloved Bacilio would rot in hell. He promised himself.

We have to arrange a quick burial, he thought with a frown. The thought of telling Bacilio's mother was like a stab wound to his chest. He was not looking forward to the next couple of days. The brutal killing seemed to have awakened him from a very long slumber.

The Pope ordered Cardinal Salvarado arrested and handed over to the Italian police in Rome; the police finally charged him with the attempted murder of Aaron Cohen. Ashamed and humiliated, Cardinal Salvarado killed himself with a poison he had hidden on his person when police him picked up from his residence.

Pope Nathaniel III mourned Salvarado and Bacilio but held meetings until late at night with the College of Cardinals.

When the Pope retired to his private chambers, his heart was heavy, and his soul weary; he lay on his giant bed but sleep deserted him.

Restless, he stood up and amused by the dozing cardinal who sat on a sofa opposite his bed. Cardinal Alfonso had insisted he would spend the night watching him sleep, but Pope Nathaniel had refused. The cardinal stuck to his guns and, at last, he had agreed to the bizarre arrangement.

'No one can share this sorrow with me, my son,' Pope Nathaniel murmured weakly, his eyes resting on the unstable head of the Cardinal; it was moving back and forth like a leaf in the wind. The Pope wandered to the window, his favourite spot in the room, and parted the curtains. The sky was dark and ominous.

'Even heaven knows,' he whispered and tears fell on his withered cheeks, his eyes had sunken and he looked and felt ten years older than his age: he would be seventy-four in December. He hated the tears but they kept flowing unhindered.

Let your mercy prevail oh Lord... he prayed silently as he remembered all the shocking details of the past terrifying hours. A brutal enemy seemed hell bent on destroying him and the faith he had nurtured since his teenage years. To make things worse, heaven was silent to his pleas for succour. It reminded him of the silent years in the Bible when God did not speak to the sons of men for more than four hundred years. It was as if he was groping in a dark pit and there was no way out. How he wished he had seen Aaron. It was a cruel thing to lose the two men he loved and trusted on the same day.

Pope Nathaniel suddenly felt cold, and heard a creaking sound.

He turned around sharply.

Two black eyes glared at him from the shadows. A black bloodhound moved stealthily, inching closer to the window, his deep breathing was like the voice of a multitude. His long black tongue was hanging out and it dripped blood.

They stood facing each other, the bloodhound growled, ready to attack and the Pope directed his fury to the beast from hell,

'And the angels who kept not their first estate, but left their own habitation, he hath reserved in everlasting chains under darkness unto the judgement of the great day.'

The dog disappeared with a howl. Cardinal Alfonso stood unsteadily to his feet. He approached Pope Nathaniel, knelt down and kissed his hand, then gently led him back to bed.

For the first time that day, the Pope allowed a grin on his scrawny face. He had won, and for now, he could sleep without fear.

16

Mogadishu, Somalia, Aug 8

Fatima Ali walked through the desolate street, shaken by the utter destruction; her beautiful country had turned into a ruthless and lawless society where human corpses decayed at street corners.

She held her bag loosely in her hand, her face ashen with the scale of destruction and chaos that had been unleashed around her. Her eyes caught two young boys appraising her with open admiration and she smiled in their direction. They turned away shyly but she was sure their sharp eyes followed her every move.

Her brother was against her visit to the city centre but she wanted to, after all, she was, and always would be, a Somali.

Fatima moved around cautiously and took out her camera, warning bells started ringing in her head, but she disregarded them. She took pictures of everything:

the bullet-ridden buildings, the deserted street. Her trained eyes caught everything as her camera clicked away, the sound was like a bomb in her head.

The boys inched closer; she saw them through the camera's lens and took their pictures. She was preparing to take another clean shot when sporadic gunfire erupted without warning. Fatima hastily dived for cover, taking refuge under a ruined office complex. Her heart was beating with such intensity that she felt faint, her breathing was quick and hard. She waited anxiously for about twenty minutes.

Eventually she ventured out of hiding scanning everywhere, but it was ominously silent. Fatima ambled out, tentatively watching the ground as if afraid to step on land mines. She looked around wildly, and then she saw them. An involuntary gasp of pain escaped her, and she clutched her heart tightly; right in the middle of the street were two bodies. The two boys lay on the dusty ground, their young bodies riddled with bullets. It was inconceivable that she had taken their pictures barely an hour earlier. Bending down with great difficulty, she touched their innocent faces and bitter, heart-wrenching sobs racked through her body; she wept bitterly for such wanton waste of human lives.

Fatima took their pictures and stood wearily to her feet, her legs almost buckled under her, she felt such an overwhelming pang of sorrow. She was about to leave the scene when the sound of raucous laughter disrupted the uneasy silence. Fatima turned round and saw two men emerging from the ruined office complex where she had hidden a moment earlier. They cradled AK-47 assault rifles in their arms like day old babies.

They were not Somalis; that was obvious by their strong muscular arms, and condescending looks. Oblivious to any attack, she faced the men and spat out angrily, 'Why did you kill these innocent children? They were still babies...'

The soldiers merely laughed, assessing her clean cut appearance; they knew she was not from the neighbourhood. One of them said flippantly,

'Your country men fired the fatal shots, unfortunately, they were casualties of war. I'd advise you to go home in your pretty dress, before you end up like those poor boys.'

They left her without a backward glance walking towards the Ministry of Defence headquarters. She stared at their retreating backs and hatred welled up inside her. It was so potent, she would have committed murder if she'd had a gun: killing those conceited Ethiopian soldiers would have made her day. Alarmed by her train of thought, she turned her attention back to the boys.

She lingered for a couple more minutes, unable to move. Her hands found her camera again, and she took more pictures. Then common sense prevailed, and she hurried home.

Her district, Hamar Jadid, was a complete war zone. The fact that she would be going back to Washington the next day saddened her, and her heart went out to her people. She would do everything within her power to shed light on the plight of the ordinary Somali child. Fatima rushed back to her car and jumped in, zooming off in a cloud of dust.

A few yards away, Mukta Mohammed gawked at the Volkswagen as it sped away, desire clawing at his groin

'Who is she?' Mukta asked his companion, a lanky youth whose bored expression indicated that he was not interested in what his boss was saying, but he answered nonetheless, 'she's the younger sister of Farouk.'

That took Mukta by surprise.

'Farouk Ali? He works for the American government?'

Rahal nodded, staring at his dusty feet. He was tired and hungry; they had been in the same spot for six hours. He was starving but Mukta was oblivious to his discomfort. He was like a mad man and his hatred of Ethiopians was legendary, but Rahal was tired of the constant fighting.

He wanted to go to school and have a semblance of something close to normal life. His three brothers had already gone to Britain, all thanks to him, and he was itching to join them. Once he was able to save enough money, he would gladly leave Somalia, never to return. His brothers were keen to see him safely in London but he had been putting it off. The pointless killing of those boys had been uncalled for; Mukta had said they were spies, but as far Rahal was concerned, he had had enough.

Rahal watched Mukta from the corner of his eye; he was still drooling after Farouk's sister. Then without warning, they came under heavy fire. Rahal trained his rifle in the direction of the attack but seconds later, his rifle was stuck. Mukta took one look at him and screamed, 'Let's get out of here.'

They ran across the street and jumped into their truck, speeding away as bullets trailed after their car. The two Ethiopian soldiers looked at the retreating truck and laughed.

'Bloody menace, they're like vermin,' one of the soldiers sneered and they walked away.

'That girl was beautiful you know,' the younger soldier commented with a sly expression on his face.

'Huh,' his partner grunted, he had a wife back home in Ethiopia with three children; he was not attracted to Somali women.

They trudged through the dusty, empty street, their boots making a single pattern on the road and the soldier who'd spoken earlier said again, 'I wish I could see her again.'

'And then what's going to happen?' his partner asked with a sneer, 'look here pal, I didn't come to this country for pleasure; I just want to be done here and get back home. I have three daughters and a beautiful wife.'

He took a long look at him and said shrewdly, 'you'd better face what you came here to do man, or you might go home in a body bag,' and he strode off angrily.

The soldier felt mollified. Keeping a short distance between them, he followed his partner but his mind was still on the tall Somali girl.

Safely at her family home, Fatima sat on the sofa and recounted her experience to her brother who was increasingly worried, there was a flushed look on his face and Fatima said calmly, 'don't worry Farouk, I didn't do anything stupid; when I saw that things were getting too hot, I came home.'

'That was why I was a little worried about coming home. Mum wasn't too pleased to see us anyway. She's obviously upset about our visit. Forget the surprise and all that, we aren't exactly the best tourist nation on earth right now,' Farouk said, his brown eyes widened in agitation.

Fatima understood his concerns.

They had left Somalia in the early nineties and, at that point, things had not deteriorated to the current level. The whole country was virtually in rubble; it was a heart-breaking story. Fatima had always wanted to come home and see things for herself and now she had, painful as it may seem, she had no future in Somalia, but her heart still went out to her war torn country.

There was a short knock on the door and Farouk looked at her sharply.

'Did anyone follow you home?' he asked with an edge to his voice.

'No!' Fatima looked scared. Their mother hurried out of the room, her huge brown eyes said it all. She hardly ever had visitors, and it could only mean one thing: trouble! With a frantic wave of her hands, she pointed towards the back door, they obeyed, and she went to open the front door.

They heard male voices and Farouk turned back, he had to intervene, he would not leave his mother alone with strangers - they could be rebels for all he knew. He told Fatima to get their bags and get out of the house.

She obeyed, went back to their rooms, picked their bags up from the bed, and ran outside into the blazing sun.

Fatima stopped short when she heard two gunshots. She ran back to the house and froze when she saw Farouk in a pool of blood. Standing beside him was a tall lanky youth with a deranged glint in his eyes.

She crumpled to the floor and screamed. Farouk opened his eyes briefly, his lips quivered as he struggled to speak.

'Shhhhh...' Fatima whispered hoarsely, her eyes searched frantically for her mother but she was not in the living room. She wiped blood from Farouk's lips, weeping softly. She clutched his white shirt, which had turned crimson with blood.

'I'm sorry Farouk, I'm so sorry...' She kept saying, her tears were like a river on his clean-shaven face. Then somebody came into the room. Fatima looked up and saw her mother; there was a gag in her mouth and her eyes were red with tears. A man followed closely behind and she recoiled in horror. She recognised him instantly; he was the second in command of one the most feared Islamic extremists groups in Somalia. Mukta Mohammed was an imposing, eccentric man, Fatima had read a lot about him and none of it were flattering.

'I'll bury your brother,' he said slowly.

Fatima couldn't take it anymore; everything became a blur and she fainted.

Half an hour later, she came round and found herself on a big bed in a small room, which reminded her of a maximum-security prison.

'Oh my God!' she exclaimed with a grunt, putting her hand on her head and closing her eyes tightly, trying to blot out the memories of the day. Breathing deeply to gain control of herself, she opened her eyes and listened to the rapid beating of her heart, then she sat up and her eyes swept the room. It was a clean but sparsely furnished room with a small reading table beside the bed. Someone had obviously gone to a lot of trouble to make the room presentable; she had clean sheets on the bed and neatly folded towels on the lone chair. A small radio and old copies of Glamour magazine were on the table.

Fatima stood to her feet and saw her bag on the bed; snatching it up, she unzipped it and rummaged through the contents. Her passport, camera, and jotter were missing but everything else was intact. She went to the door and tried opening it, but it wouldn't budge. She tried the small square window and a mirthless grin crossed her flushed face; she couldn't even squeeze her leg through it.

Fatima went back to the bed, thinking of Farouk and her mother and her eyes reddened with tears, but she wiped them defiantly. She would have to postpone her mourning until she and her mother were safely out of Somalia.

Although she realised that she would have to be careful.

A bitter smile played around the corners of her mouth when reality finally dawned on her; she was a hostage in her own country. It was ironic that she had written several articles on the subject.

She should have travelled to Nigeria on a fact-finding mission to unravel the mystery of the notorious Ijaw youths of the Niger Delta, who had driven expatriates working in the oil rich region aground through vicious attacks. Most of them were angry at the way foreign companies were siphoning their oil while the youths live in squalor. She knew it would have been a rewarding assignment.

'What an irony of fate, Fatima,' she whispered sadly.

The thought of Farouk's pregnant wife, the whereabouts of her mother and her own ordeal finally sent her over the edge and she screamed, taking the radio from the table and hurling it at the door.

Her breathing came in short gasps as she fought to control herself. She ran her hands through her thick, short hair. If only I had listened to Farouk, none of this would have happened, she thought in regret.

Farouk had wanted them to travel back to New York that same day, but she had nagged him until he agreed to postpone their trip and they had rescheduled their flight for the next morning. What a heavy price she had to pay stubbornness.

Her father had died in the early days of the war. A few months later, they migrated to the United States, living with relatives until her mother got a job as a journalist, and they moved into a small but beautiful house. She and Farouk went to school and performed well; Farouk studied business law while she studied international relations and communications.

After graduation, Farouk married and moved to New York; she got a job as a political correspondent with the Washington Post. Then a year ago, her mother decided to move back to Somalia. Fatima missed her terribly, and a few months later, she told Farouk of her intention to visit her mother in Somalia. Initially, he was against the trip, but eventually he changed his mind and went with her.

Her fiancé, Andre Negasi, was not too keen on the trip either, but Andre would do anything to keep her happy and she knew it.

Andre had taken them to the airport while Farouk jokingly told him to marry his sister before a Somali warlord did. They had laughed it off. Shortly before they went through Departures, Andre had held her tight and said,

'You know baby, I don't want you to go; my gut feelings...' and she had stopped him with a kiss.

'Don't 'gut feeling' me on this,' she had whispered, touching his lips with her index finger.

'I should have followed you, baby,' he had said softly and Fatima pushed him away gently.

'I have to do this, Andre,' she had said quietly.

Andre had felt like taking her home to their apartment. She had blown him a kiss and hurried after her brother. She turned back to wave but he was gone; Fatima was a little bit disappointed but knew how hard it was for him.

Fatima gritted her teeth in despair; she had to think of a way out soon. Then she heard the key in the door turning and Mukta stood in the doorway looking at her like a long lost friend. He closed the door and strolled into the room. Fatima licked her lips nervously.

'Who are you?' she asked in a surprisingly calm voice.

Mukta looked at her and felt desire rushing through him like a tidal wave. She was different from his two wives and all the other women he had slept with. He smiled and replied casually, 'My name is Mukta Mohammed and I'm a fighter for the liberation of the Somali people.'

'Why did you kill my brother?'

Mukta's eyes narrowed in thought and he kept quiet for a long time. This one will be a little tigress, he thought with a smile. No one had ever talked to him like that before.

His dark eyes softened and as Fatima watched him, she realised that he liked her; that was some sort of comfort, she reasoned, but Farouk's body flashed through her mind and she came to a very difficult decision.

Fatima lay on the bed as her long hands gently pulled her dress up to reveal a smooth brown thigh.

Mukta swallowed hard, and could hardly breathe. The sight of her naked legs drove him crazy. His eyes tried to lock onto Fatima's, but he couldn't think straight.

Then he remembered the dead man and he sobered up and said slowly,

'It was an accident. My boy Rahal wanted to cock the rifle to scare your brother and the bullets just hit him... it happened so fast.'

'Okay.'

Mukta was surprised. He had expected her to throw a tantrum and try to claw her way out of the room.

Fatima's eyes flicked briefly to his trousers and she was dismayed at the sight, but she would have to play her game very well.

'Where is my mother?' she asked softly, her big brown eyes never leaving his flushed dark face.

'She is in a secure location,' he answered huskily, his eyes tearing her clothes to shreds and claiming her as his own.

'I want her released please; she has hypertension,' she lied in a small voice; she would gladly give herself to him for that.

Mukta's eyes lingered on her thighs. Her full breasts seemed to taunt him in the flowery dress, and he made up his mind. He took out a phone from his jeans pocket and dialled a number, he spoke rapidly into the phone, listened for a few seconds, barked orders like a general, and then he looked at her.

'Where do you want her to go?'

'I want your men to escort her to the airport. We were supposed to fly to New York tomorrow, but I want her on the next available plane.'

Mukta hesitated briefly but when Fatima exposed her lacy pants, he quickly did as she asked.

'All done,' he said and swallowed hard, his Adam apple bobbing up and down like a Ping-Pong ball as his eyes feasted on her thighs.

'Can I speak to her later when you have finished making love to me, please?' she asked seductively, painfully banishing the handsome face of Andre from her mind.

'Yes my dear, you can do anything you want, my love,' Mukta said and held her face tenderly, planting a wet kiss on her lips. Surprisingly, he was gentle and she kissed him back. He groaned with desire but Fatima grimaced and dug her nails in his back.

He pulled back, staring at her and she smiled. He continued as Fatima vowed to kill him in her own time.

17

'When the ground shook and I heard screams from outside,' Abraham, the caretaker of the Ark began, 'I knew Aaron was the real thing.'

Caleb smiled and nodded, looking at Aaron with pride. They all stood under the shade of the old ruins of the Church of St Mary Zion in Axum.

The weather was pleasantly cool. Aaron smiled in contentment, he had gone through an unimaginable experience, and his new friends had nothing to say except that. He watched Caleb and Abraham exchanging banter; he felt at ease with himself, and with his new friends.

The caretaker seemed taken with Aaron, Caleb was pleased but he often wondered if the old man would not distract him, and, at the same time, he was afraid. The guardian of the sacred Ark should never step outside the church premises; it could be dangerous, and if the Archbishop of Axum were to find out, things could get complicated. But it was a risk Caleb had already taken and it had worked.

Finally, Aaron's real identity had been revealed, Caleb was glad that the guardian of the Ark was there to witness the transformation. The next step was the Ark, although Caleb knew he couldn't get close to the Ark - no one could except for the guardian – he was at least content in the knowledge that Aaron could.

Aaron watched the old men in amusement: everyone still appeared dazed. He had little recollection of what had happened, just the weightless feeling of floating without a care in the world.

The only snag was the press; the day's papers screamed his name, some people were calling him the 'Messiah', others, 'Death Defying Maverick', titles he vehemently rejected, but he had learnt one lesson, and that was the ability to take everything in his stride.

'It was a wonderful sight,' Caleb remarked, staring at the ancient church, but he was referring to the events of the previous night.

'It was,' Aaron agreed, watching a bird fly into the sky, its strong wings moving in consonance with the wind.

Caleb smiled as he remembered how they had held hands praying, but the commotion outside the house had increased in intensity. After praying for half an hour, they felt the presence of other people in the room with them. One after the other; they had opened their eyes and saw three men in the room. The men glowed from head to toe, dressed in plain linen. They had oozed power, and without any introduction, the men in the room knew that they were angels.

They had all burst into songs of praise and the three strange men joined in the singing. Fifteen minutes later, they stopped singing and waited. There had been complete silence as one of the men began to speak in a rich, clear voice, 'We have come to your presence today sent by the Almighty God to give you this message of hope. "Be careful, there are wolves amongst you, but I'll pluck them out if they do not repent. In a short while, you will all fight the fight of faith. You will fight with a powerful demon, be united together in faith."'

'What is your name?'

There had been gasps of disbelief from everyone.

The angel's blue eyes bored into Peter's, 'My name is Barachiel, and my friends are Selaphiel and Uriel.'

Peter nodded and the angels disappeared.

The men had filed out of the room silently, shaken by the experience. Aaron had opened his eyes briefly, turned on his side and promptly dozed off. Caleb and Peter stayed behind, watching him sleep. At last, when they were alone, Peter had turned to Caleb with an apology.

'I'm very sorry, I just wanted to be sure they were real.'

'Of course they were,' Caleb had retorted angrily, 'curiosity killed the cat and I sincerely hope you don't bite off more than you can chew one day.'

Peter had looked remorseful and Caleb's heart went out to him, moved with compassion he said quietly, 'I have never seen an angel before,' and he had grinned, 'you were incredibly bold to ask for their names, but next time just be patient; they probably had more things to say. Didn't you see that their departure was sudden?'

Peter nodded still staring at the floor. Caleb looked at him and changed the topic, 'Let's check what the furore outside was all about.'

They had left the room and taken the back door. They walked through the entire property but there was no sign of fighting or explosions. They saw soldiers still patrolling the compound, and everything looked normal. They had gone back inside.

Peter couldn't help asking, 'What happened? It was a full blown war while we were in the room praying.'

'Yeah,' Caleb had agreed, 'but don't you forget what the caretaker said: those demons were probably messing with our heads.'

‘Really?' Peter had difficulty believing it, 'are you pulling my leg or something?’

‘No, I'm not. C’mon, let's get back inside. We still have a lot of decisions to make.’

‘No,’ Peter had refused, moving away, ‘I’ve made a fool of myself today and those men in there are not going to forget in a hurry.’

Caleb had watched him until he disappeared from sight, and he knew he was right.

Aaron laughed suddenly. Such simplicity, Caleb thought, his mind coming back to the present. Aaron and the caretaker chatted away like old friends. The caretaker looked up and said in his booming voice, ‘I was just telling Aaron about the rich history of Axum.’

‘I see,’ Caleb said politely but his mind was busy thinking of what to do next. Everything they had discussed earlier was inconclusive; they have to find a way to control the power within Aaron.

‘Axum was the first Christian kingdom in the world and, I can say with all authority, the largest outside of the Roman Empire.’ Abraham paused for emphasis, then added as an afterthought, ‘My son, the time for telling tales has not come; I'd rather do that later. Let me take you round the church and inside the treasury, and, if you want, we can visit the most sacred part of the church.’

Aaron and Caleb exchanged glances.

'Now?'

Aaron thought it was a bad idea. He couldn't waltz in and out as he liked. He knew Ethiopians would gladly kill anyone who desecrated or stepped inside the treasury.

The Ark had been the object of furious debate and legend, and he wasn't too keen on inspecting the powerful and ancient relic. He had thought he would breeze in, admire the scenery, and bask in the glory and ancient history of Axum, not stay in the church or the treasury. He had intended to go back to the Sheraton Hotel in Addis Ababa.

'Don't you think we might actually need some sort of permission before we enter the church... or the treasury?' A short pause followed, then he added quietly, 'I mean apart from you.'

'No,' the old monk shook his head, 'I determine who enters this holy place,' and he waved his arms about, 'my ancestors would have done anything to be in my shoes today,' his wrinkled face exploded into an infectious grin.

Then his mood changed abruptly and he asked, 'Do you know much about your lineage?'

Aaron shook his head.

On several occasions, Aaron had overheard his mom teasing his dad endlessly about the duties of the high priest, and the fact that his dad's middle name was Eleazer, but he had thought nothing of it until now.

'You're a real descendant of Aaron, the high priest in the Bible...' Lightning flashed across the sky followed by thunder and the clear blue skies suddenly turned grey and gloomy. A tree caught fire as the earth began to shake.

'Let's get inside!' the caretaker yelled and they ran towards the Chapel of the Tablet. Aaron threw a look over his shoulder and saw a tall solitary figure, and then a big black dog appeared. The dog growled, and waited beside the tall figure.

'Run!' Aaron shouted and they sprinted to the rusty gate, then to the entrance of the treasury. The caretaker's hands shook slightly as he tried to open the door to the ancient church.

Finally, the church door budged, but Aaron hesitated.

'I'll join you guys later,' Aaron said and his eyes turned a shade darker.

'I don't think you should...' Caleb began but the look in Aaron's eyes stopped him. They stood at the church's doorway and watched.

The dog yelped and moved back when he saw Aaron sprinting towards it. The tall figure disappeared in a puff of smoke. Aaron panted, turned back, and walked to the church.

Caleb was grinning from ear to ear; the relief on his face was obvious.

'They're gone,' Caleb said in a matter of fact tone.

'Who was that?' the caretaker asked.

'You should know,' was the simple reply from Aaron and he wiped sweat off his face. His face brightened when he saw the dog running away, but his elation was short lived. The uneasy feeling had returned.

'Tyrus is obstinate, he'll be back.' Caleb said quietly.

'I know,' Aaron said and walked into the church. Caleb took a quick glance and saw that the tall figure was back. This time there were three of them.

He closed the door quickly.

18

New York, Aug 9

Three days after attack, Kate sat on the cold, hard floor writhing in pain. Her brow was knitted like a woman in labour and her sweat was like blood. Her parched lips trembled and she groaned, moaning with despair. Her eyes were a shade darker and she was running a fever.

She studied her environment with glazed eyes; the empty pews reminded her of the despair in her soul. Evelyn had bluffed her way into the church, despite the repeated but feeble explanations of the church's administrator that the pastor was away on a preaching engagement to India.

They had stood their ground, and the church administrator hadn't hung around. But Kate understood why the man had hurried away: the stench oozing out of her leg was horrible.

Kate felt like a leper and, for the first time in her life, she wished she had listened to her mom, but it was too late for regret. She had finally accepted the fact that she had days left. She would be happy of no one became infected through her, but Evelyn gave no assurance.

According to Evelyn, she had four days left to live, and now, she couldn't wait to die: death would mercifully bring an end to her suffering. Her mobile phone rang and she picked it up, it was the breathless voice of Evelyn, her husband was with her outside but police were guarding the church's entrance. Apparently, a church member had called the police.

'I'll see what I can do,' Evelyn promised before hanging up.

Kate was too weak to talk, the phone slipped from her hand and her reluctant eyes took a quick peek at her swollen leg.

The skin had begun to peel off. Somehow, she'd got used to the pungent smell.

She heard a knock on the church's massive door and two men entered; they were in white overalls with gas masks on their faces.

Kate began to count, 'One... two... three... four...,' by the time she got to nine, the men were roughly ten feet away from her. Suddenly, they made an abrupt U-turn and ran out of the church.

Outside, Michael glared at the teeming crowds. He turned to his wife with a frown, and asked quietly, 'What's really going on?'

Evelyn stared at her husband with that annoyed look which always spelt trouble, but something else caught her attention. Michael was wearing a white shirt, his hair neatly combed and his cheeks flushed and freckled. He was still a very handsome man. Evelyn knew she must look beat-up, rough, and unkempt. She had barely slept in three days and it was showing on her.

'It's just like I told you on the phone: Kate was licked by Tyrus's bloodhound,' she retorted as she ran her hands through her blonde hair, she was getting more frustrated as the minutes ticked by.

'Tyrus and the bloodhound cannot walk this earth any more without authorization,' Michael said as the muscles in his mouth twitched.

Evelyn realised that he was infuriated, but that would not solve her problem; she needed a solution fast.

Evelyn softened the tone of her voice; fighting or arguing with him would not solve any problem. She hadn't dragged him away from his writing to fight with him. She needed help.

'Who could have called the press?' she asked helplessly.

'Have you called Kate's mother?' Michael asked, ignoring her earlier question.

'I don't have the guts to.'

'Tyrus was a formidable foe and I'm amazed that he could walk the earth so quickly after the battle in the dungeon,' Michael said with a troubled expression on his face.

'I thought of calling your friend, in fact I did, but it seems like she's changed her mobile number.'

'Who are you talking about?' Michael looked at her strangely, his mind several miles away.

'Sharon,' Evelyn replied, her eyes drawn to the flurry of activity outside the church.

Three police cars breezed in as New York police officers trooped out of their cars. An ambulance also came to a screeching halt behind the police cars. Some officers began to cordon off the road, while others were redirecting traffic.

Evelyn was thankful that she had parked her car at Central park.

'Michael, I've just had an idea,' she said with an uncertain look on her face, 'do you think garlic and holy water could work some magic?'

Michael was relieved; why hadn't he thought of that before? Raw garlic could heal any wound and within two days the young woman may well be on the road to recovery.

'Yes darling, it could work wonders... how did...?' he didn't finish asking the question because he already knew where she had got the idea from.

Their next major problem was getting close to Kate, so they waited. Just as they thought, no one could go within ten feet of her; the stink coming from her leg permeated the atmosphere in such a way that anyone who moved close to her would choke to death, except for people like them who had dined with the devil and survived.

They waited for almost four hours before they saw their chance. The odour was already seeping out from the church, and in a couple of hours, the police would have sealed the area off altogether. Evelyn quickly went to where they had parked their car to collect the garlic and holy water. Since her experience with death, she didn't leave the house without garlic, holy water and a bottle of anointing oil.

She wondered why it had escaped her mind. Kate would not have suffered as much if she had remembered. Evelyn saw two men shadowing her car and she waited, watching. Judging by their appearance, Evelyn assumed they were car thieves, and they looked armed.

She did the sensible thing and went back, but Michael was not there. Maybe he's found a way into the church, Evelyn thought. She made her way back to her car and saw the men scurrying away. On closer inspection, the men had only smashed her windscreen and had left everything intact.

She opened the car door, fumbling through the clutter on the back seat. She saw the garlic and bottle of holy water, heaving a deep sigh of relief she picked them up, closed the door, and walked briskly back to the church.

She saw her husband peeping out from the corner of the church and quickly went to meet him.

'What took you so long?'

'You're so fond of asking questions,' she retorted brusquely, 'anyway, I saw two suspicious looking blokes by the car. I came back to tell you but you'd disappeared into thin air, so I went back, braved the odds and here I am.'

'Good,' he said and took her by the hand, 'let's hurry. She doesn't look human anymore.'

They entered through the church's entrance while the police officer on guard was talking to three women asking for directions. The potent smell assailed their nostrils when they entered; no wonder nobody could enter the century-old granite clad church.

They walked straight to the reading rooms that also doubled as an office. Opening the door quietly the sight that met their eyes traumatized them. There were three hyenas on the floor. Someone must have strangled the animals to death: their necks were twisted, and they were just inches away from the sleeping form of Kate.

'I didn't see any animals before I left,' Michael stammered, his eyes wide with fright. He looked perplexed. Who could have done this in a window of just ten minutes? Michael thought with a grunt.

'Forget the hyenas' darling; they would have mauled her to death anyway. C'mon, help me with her leg,' Evelyn said as she moved warily towards her.

The skin of Kate's leg was dark blue. Michael took a good look at her and prayed for a miracle; she seemed to be deteriorating fast. He crouched down beside her sleeping form and continued praying that the garlic would work. At the same time, he looked intently at his wife.

Evelyn peeled the garlic's skin and threw three cloves into her mouth. She chewed briefly, and spat it on the wound. She did it three more times before standing up and drinking some water. She sprinkled holy water all over the room, praying at the same time, and then she sprinkled holy water on the rotten leg and waited.

The first thing they noticed was the smell, it slowly dispersed and the air in the room smelt fresher, but there was a look of shock on Michael's face - Evelyn followed his eyes and saw Kate's face. Her face had metamorphosed into the face of the bloodhound, complete with the sagging skin and a drooping mouth dripping with blood.

They watched, unable to move. After a while, her face slowly changed back to normal. While they were busy staring at her face, her leg was healing up.

'Are you thinking what I'm thinking?' Michael asked with a smile.

'I'm thinking what you're thinking Michael Crest-Howard: let's get out of here.'

'Not so fast, guys,' someone said from the corner of the room.

Tyrus sat calmly beside the carcasses of the hyenas, he looked tired and defeated, but Michael knew he was the master of illusion.

'I need to know how to get close to her boyfriend,' he said softly, his dark lifeless eyes pleading.

Michael said nothing he was still watching Kate. But Evelyn was furious, when she spoke her voice was shaking with anger, 'You almost killed her, and now that she's out of your hands you think you can twist us around your slimy, wicked claws?'

'Fingers, my dear Evelyn,' he corrected her sharply standing to his feet.

His head was almost touching the ceiling and his nostrils flared in pain, 'I have fingers, not claws, and I'm in serious pain at the moment. I hate coming to His house.'

'You mean the house of God,' Evelyn taunted him mercilessly, 'I would like to warn you Tyrus...'

'You know my name,' he was clearly impressed.

'Yes I do, demon,' Evelyn said flatly, moving close to Kate. She looked at Michael and he moved towards Kate, bending down, he picked her up gently in his strong arms and shook his head sadly. Kate felt so light in his arms and she had aged considerably. He beckoned to his wife as he backed out of the room.

Tyrus roared in anger, his thick black nose flaring with rage, his dark robe slipped from his body as spikes protruded from his hairy body. His feet left the ground and Evelyn threw the garlic and holy water at him, she grabbed her handbag from the floor and fled. She heard him screaming obscenities after her, 'I'm not a mere demon you dickhead, I'm a king decked in glory, you shit face. I'm the king of the world... I'm the...' Evelyn couldn't bear to hear any more of it. Clamping her hands over her ears, she closed her eyes and ran past Michael, but she had forgotten about the steps, which led to the ground floor.

Evelyn lost her balance, and fell face-first down the stairs. Michael raced down the steps and laid Kate on the floor. He checked Evelyn's pulse, calling her name softly, but she didn't answer.

Michael was afraid, and it was alien to him. He had not felt like that for seven years. It slowly crawled up his spine and settled coldly on his soul. His daughter had been in a psychiatric hospital for a long time, Evelyn had been, and still was, his soul mate, friend, lover, everything, and they had gone through so much together. He would be lost without her.

He knelt beside her and took out his mobile phone but before he dialled the emergency services, two police officers rushed in with paramedics. He was shocked and confused, who could have called them? Michael thought. Something drew his attention to the auditorium arches. He saw Tyrus suspended in the air, his face twisted in agony and on fire. He flapped his powerful wings and flew out of the church, crashing through the extremely large blocks of white concord granite, shattering the roundels of concealed lighting. Everyone looked up sharply.

There were gasps from the paramedics but the officers reacted swiftly. They took aim and fired several shots, but he was gone. He left a massive gaping hole in the roof and some of the church's stained glass was cracked.

Michael was stupefied. He still wanted to find out who called the paramedics but the paramedics and officers looked distracted - they were staring at the ceiling and the gallery that wrapped around three sides of the auditorium, and the extensive damage done to the church by the powerful intruder.

'What in heaven's name was that?' one of the officers asked sadly, there were cracks in the rich French plaster on the ceiling, and the concealed light fittings were scattered on the marble floor.

'I don't know, maybe a burglar or... a big bird.' Michael answered and swallowed hard, his eyes downcast. How could he explain to the seemingly trigger happy officers that the being that just left the church could not be destroyed by their ordinary guns?

'You didn't see who, or what, it was?' the same officer asked again, sounding suspicious.

'No,' Michael said coldly fixing his gaze on the officer without wavering.

The officer said nothing as he walked through the Circassia walnut pews towards the auditorium.

'Mrs Evelyn Crest called us about ten minutes ago,' the ambulance woman broke in sharply.

She was not worried about the cost of repairs in the church, she was more concerned about the women on the marble floor, 'at least that was the name I was given.'

'That was my wife,' Michael said quietly, staring at the woman as if seeing a ghost. He was fast losing concentration but he was grateful for her attention, 'and ten minutes ago we were still in one of the reading rooms with this young lady,' and he pointed to Kate who was still undisturbed by the commotion.

'That's strange,' an officer said sarcastically. He was short with a strong, wide chest, his body was packed full of muscles and his thinning chestnut hair was brushed back. His face was very flat and expressionless, 'And how did you gain access to this church, Sir? Didn't you see the officer guarding the doors? You need permission to enter these premises.'

One of the paramedics bent down and examined Kate while the woman checked Evelyn for a pulse and signs of life.

'I'm sorry, Officer,' Michael said his eyes on his wife.

'Sorry my ass!'

Michael was shocked at his language but decided to disregard it. If it had been a normal day, he would have taken it up, but the day was anything from normal.

The officer took out a pen and a jotter, scribbled some letters, and asked for Michael's name. Michael told him and the officer looked at him sharply, a surprised expression on his otherwise blank face.

'Are you in any way related to the scientist-turned-writer Michael Crest-Howard? The one who wrote the terribly interesting thriller about some bunch of fools fighting the devil in Africa?'

Michael nodded and stood to his feet looking down at the officer, but before the officer could make any more comments, the paramedic cut in,

'Mrs Crest will be all right, the suddenness of the fall was responsible for her passing out, but she should be fine after a full day's rest. But I'm afraid we'll have to take the young lady to hospital immediately.'

'And you, Mr Crest-Howard, will be coming with us. We need to know what you were doing here and how you entered the premises.'

'I would love to do so, Officer,' Michael said smoothly, 'provided you allow me to take my wife home first. Then I'd be happy to go to the station with you.'

'That's all right,' the officer agreed and beckoned his colleague who sauntered towards them.

The paramedics placed Kate on a stretcher and wheeled her out while Michael gently carried his wife outside to the waiting police car.

19

Joshua Cohen's recovery was rapid despite still being very weak, and he kept asking for his personal assistant. The hospital was crawling with detectives; they were still investigating the gruesome killing of Joseph Shalev in the hospital's car park.

Rebecca Kolinsky, the chief medical director of the hospital, was shocked and speechless following the murder and she cooperated fully with the police by releasing the CCTV footage of everyone who had entered to the medical centre that day.

The police had already informed the deceased's family but the onus fell on Rebecca to make sure barrister Joshua Cohen's staff were aware of his desire to see his trusted PA.

She rang his office but no one picked it up, 'Strange,' she said, and rested back in her chair, deep in thought. Police were guarding the renowned criminal lawyer but Rebecca was suspicious. She assumed that the murder must have something to do with cases Joshua Cohen had handled in the past. *Any fool could put two and two together and get four,* she thought.

There was a short knock on her office door and an intern popped her head in,

'There's a young man here to see you about J.C.'

'Send him in,' she said, wondering who it could possibly be.

A tall, well-shaven, slim black man entered.

'How may I help, Sir?'

'I'm here to see Joshua Cohen. I have an important message for him.'

She took in his appearance. He was well dressed, wearing a well-tailored black suit with white shirt and a very nice blue tie. She caught a whiff of his cologne too Hugo Boss, not bad, Rebecca thought. He didn't look like a killer but she would not allow him to see Joshua Cohen. He looked like one of Joshua's junior lawyers.

'Are you from his office?' Rebecca asked, tapping the tip of her pen on the table.

He shook his head slowly before answering, 'No, I...' he paused briefly while he adjusted his tie, 'I'm a private investigator. I was hired to track down his nephew,' and he pressed his lips together as if he had said too much and would not say more.

'How did you know about his attack?'

He looked at her as if she was stupid, 'He's one of the best criminal lawyers in this country. Do you read the papers?'

Her face creased up in a smile,' 'I do Mr...?'

He got the drift, cleared his throat, and said huskily, looking her straight in the eye, 'I'm sorry, that was very rude of me. My name is Logan Stone.' And he stretched out his hand for a shake. She shook his hand and held it briefly, then Rebecca realised she was sending the wrong message. She snatched her hand away and brushed a lock of hair back from her face.

'Nice to meet you, Mr. Stone,' she managed to say, avoiding eye contact. In her mind, she was grinning from ear to ear; why was she behaving like a teenager? The boy was young enough to be her son. Aloud, she said briskly,

'Well...erm... he was brought in about four days ago with gunshot wounds and erm...' she couldn't find the right words. Looking at him squarely, she said slowly, 'his assistant, Mr. Joseph Shalev was also shot dead that same day.'

'No way, how can that be?' Logan exclaimed, 'that's really tragic.'

'Yeah,' she agreed and stood up, 'I'm afraid I'm very busy, and I'm sorry but there is absolutely no way you can see the patient. For his age, he's recovering really well, just give us a week then you can come back and see him.'

'Yeah, thanks anyway,' Logan also stood up and walked to the door. His hand was already on the doorknob, and then he turned back and asked, 'Does he know yet?'

Rebecca shook her head and mouthed 'No,' he stood there for a while as if considering what he was about to say.

'He shouldn't know about Joseph, the shock could kill him.'

'Why?' Rebecca asked although she knew the answer to the question: the few hours she had seen Joseph around the hospital, she had sensed his devotion to his boss.

'They were very close.' Logan said simply, came back into the office, and took out his card.

'Please call me when he comes round,' he whispered softly, his eyes lingering on the front of her silk blouse.

Then he was gone.

Rebecca sat on her chair, relieved; the young man had the strangest effect on her. She was forty-nine, recently divorced and the mother of two teenage boys. Her job deprived her of the thing she loved most in the word: her husband, James. He'd started an affair with her best friend's daughter. It was sordid, devastating, and cruel but she was a very strong woman; she had picked up the pieces of her life and moved on.

After that, she vowed never to touch a man with a ten-foot pole. She chuckled, searching through her purse, and found what she was looking for: her compact mirror. She admired herself in the mirror; her well-shaped nose, bright eyes and golden locks, combined with a very curvy figure made her one of the sexiest women in New York. However, work had killed her relationship, and she had vowed to devote her life to saving the lives of others.

Maybe fate would smile on her and she would meet a man who could replace James. Are there any man like that? Rebecca thought and gave a short laugh, then stood up. She was going to check on her favourite patient and afterwards attend a board meeting which Joan, her secretary, had rescheduled several times.

The door closed silently behind her. Had she seen the tall, dark apparition in her office, she would have fainted.

Tyrus saw the white business card and a crooked smile lit up his ghastly face: Logan Stone, not a bad name. He needed a human vessel and Logan seemed to fit the description very well.

Tyrus heaved himself off with effortless ease and flew out of the office. He had little time left, a mere twenty-one days before the appeal and he had not come close to getting what he came for. I will not be defeated, he swore silently.

However, the thought of his father sent a shiver down his spine. Tyrus had vowed never to return to the abyss, it was the worst place anyone could imagine, although his father had since got used to it, he could not.

Tyrus wanted redemption, something many other demons also desired, but it was so elusive. If only he had blood flowing through his veins. He would do anything to be flesh and blood, not flesh, and bone, which angels and demons are. However, he knew there was still a slim chance for him - a chance to live.

NATALIE PETERS swung her legs into the bathtub. She rested her long, tired legs and allowed the warm water to do its magic. She slid deeper in the bathtub and raised her head above the water. She mustn't cry. What good would it do anyway? Her husband was one of the most hated men in the country and her family had long since deserted her.

All her friends had started giving her one excuse after another and the more she tried to clear her name concerning the death of Joshua Cohen's PA, the more the police were pointing accusatory fingers in her direction. Then she remembered Logan, 'Oh sweet Logan,' she murmured huskily as she thought of his long, strong body packed with muscles how she desired him. But he was a man she dared not dream about.

Her sad thoughts turned back to her predicament.

The FBI had arrested her and they had grilled her endlessly but she'd refused to budge. *I'm innocent, I will not take the rap for something I know absolutely nothing about,* Natalie thought.

Simply because she fitted the perfect description and had, the motive did not make a criminal.

Anyone could have shot Joseph Shalev.

She clearly wanted both Joshua and Joseph dead because they had denied her justice, but all the same, her husband had crudely served justice. He had confessed to her just a day before he shot Joshua that he had killed the two Latino men who raped their daughter. He had shot them both in the head, execution style and, foolishly, she had confided in her mother who in turn told the police.

He had evaded arrest until he tried to kill Joshua Cohen.

Yet, he would climb the pulpit on Sunday mornings, preaching about heaven and goodness.

Natalie pulled herself from the bath, wrapping a big white towel around her pale, naked body, banishing every sorrowful thought from her mind. Tonight, she was determined to enjoy herself.

She padded to the bedroom and dried herself thoroughly. Sitting down at her dressing mirror, she saw something pass by swiftly. Afraid, she stood up and checked the entire room, but she was alone. Natalie went back to the mirror, moisturised her body thoroughly, and then brushed her red hair until it was silky. Satisfied, she went to her wardrobe and chose a simple black gown, she didn't want to appear too glamorous, but a dinner with Logan was something she wanted to make good use of. Who knew, he may console her in his bed that night. She would soon be a widow anyway.

She slipped the gown over her head and checked her reflection in the mirror. She had decided against wearing any jewellery. Natalie picked her perfume and sprayed it on herself, then carefully applied light make up. She was patting her hair when she heard a hissing sound. It was a distinctive sound and she turned in the direction that it had come from.

Natalie froze. A black cobra reared up, displaying a flattened head that formed a hood. The snake sprayed its venom, and she ran out of the room. Her earsplitting scream echoed through her spacious apartment but the snake was too fast, she tripped over the centre table and the snake struck.

Downstairs, two FBI agents were taking the lift to Natalie's apartment to ask a question or two about Joseph Shalev's murder. They were walking briskly through the long hallway when they heard the high-pitched scream and ran to her apartment. The door was ajar and they saw the snake still biting her, they took out their guns, firing repeatedly but the snake flew out of the window mysteriously.

Agent Stockwell called for an ambulance – but she was already dead. Logan was climbing out of a taxi when he saw the stretcher and ambulance, he rushed through the crowd and pushed people out of his way, but he couldn't see who was on the stretcher.

He hurried up the stairs and came out on the hallway; he saw federal agents and police officers in Natalie's doorway. He quickly retraced his steps and went back, taking the stairs two steps at a time.

When he got outside, the ambulance was just pulling away from the luxurious apartment block. He walked blindly along the street dazed by what he had witnessed. He stuffed his hands in his trouser pockets still in shock at what must have happened, could it have been a burglary turned sour? Logan thought sadly. He liked Natalie as a friend and things might have gone further, what with her husband being sick and all that: he could have been a source of comfort to her.

He'd first met the Peters when Matthew hired him to investigate the two men who allegedly raped and killed his daughter. Logan investigated and found them in Mexico. He finished the job and Peter had paid him a handsome amount of money. Two months later, he heard about their deaths on the news, he wondered if Matthew Peters knew something about it, but he shrugged it off: it was not his headache.

Two weeks later, he met Natalie in a shopping mall and they had exchanged phone numbers. Since then, they had kept in touch. Logan wished he had known her better.

He felt a tap on his shoulder and, when he turned to look, someone punched him so hard in the face that he tasted blood on his tongue, and darkness closed in on him.

20

Ethiopian-Somali Border, Aug 10

Hussein Mahdi groaned as excruciating pain rattled through his tall, thin frame. His driver drove furiously through the dusty roads as their comrades continued the onslaught on Ethiopian troops in the border town of Luuq in Gedo region, southwestern Somalia, but it was obvious that they were gradually losing ground.

Hussein closed his eyes and regretted the ill-timed attack; Mukta had warned him not to carry out the offensive; they didn't have enough weapons to fight the Ethiopians who could carry out air raids anytime they wanted. The Ethiopians' armoured tanks and sophisticated weapons were no match for their rickety trucks but Hussein would not listen. Initially, he had wanted to kill Mukta when he returned from his 'invasion' of

Luuq town, but it seemed he was now the victim and the leadership contest between him and Mukta was finally over.

Fear gripped him at the thought of what Mukta would do if the reins of power were to fall into his hands.

A handful of Ethiopian soldiers in military trucks noticed their camouflaged truck and turned their attention to it. There was a rapid exchange of mortar shells between the two enemies. In a matter of minutes, it was over.

The severely wounded leader of the notorious Liberation of Somali People conceded defeat. There was rapturous clapping from the exhausted soldiers as they rounded up and arrested the rest of the insurgents.

Back in Mogadishu, Mukta listened with rapt attention for news of the fighting and when the droning voice of the broadcaster announced Hussein's defeat, he was not surprised. He knew that Hussein was a weakling. Mukta clenched and unclenched his fists in frustration and, when he couldn't bear it anymore, he kicked a boy who was sitting down calmly watching the men in the crowded room.

The boy shrieked out in pain, tears rolling down his cheeks. There were jeers from the men in the room and the boy hurriedly scampered out before the irate militants mauled him.

Mukta growled and roared - the men knew why he was angry. The Ethiopians had captured Hussein, and Mukta was probably sad that they captured him alive, he would have been better off dead, he thought.

'I told him not to go but he wouldn't listen to me. He's too damn stubborn for his own good,' and he swore and cursed looking around wildly. One by one, the men left the room.

They knew that anytime he was in an irate mood, it was better to leave him alone. Surprisingly, two fresh faced youths stayed behind. Glaring at them, he ordered the boys out of the room but they stood their ground looking at him fearlessly. There was something daring and penetrating about their unflinching gaze, and that puzzled him.

'Who are you, morons?'

'We are the Taofik twins. We would like to have a word with you,' they chorused in unison.

Mukta's mood changed dramatically, the twins' father was a respected man in Mogadishu and he wouldn't dare hurt his boys, although he marvelled at their bravery, why would they risks their long, skinny necks to have a word with him? He had no idea.

'What would you like to talk about?' he asked impatiently. Sheik Taofik was a religious man and there had been rumours that he could predict the future, but Mukta was not into superstitions or any of that mundane stuff, at least that was what he considered fortune telling to be. Who cared about the future when one could enjoy the present?

The boys approached him, their brown eyes boring into his. Mukta' hands swiftly moved to his holster, 'Stay back, boys,' he barked out sternly, 'I don't want to hurt you, don't make me.'

'You'll be glad we came to you with this news,' they said looking at each other with a smile.

Mukta's patience was running thin but he controlled his volcanic temper and said as calmly as he could manage, 'Spill it out boys, I don't have all day.'

'All right, let me speak,' the shorter of the two said to his twin and turning his attention to Mukta he said with a boyish grin on his face, 'There is a white man in Ethiopia, his name is Aaron. If you can capture him, you will defeat the Ethiopians and anyone who opposes you.'

There was a trace of a smile lurking at the corners of Mukta's mouth; he had been right, the boys were as dim-witted as he had thought.

'Okay thanks for your information, can you both excuse me now?'

The twins looked at each other in surprise, 'You don't believe us do you?'

'No,' Mukta replied and gently pushed them to the door.

'We won't be around to help you when you need us Sir, but we're sure you will.' And they stalked out of the room angrily, but who cared, he hated fortune tellers; he dealt with cold, hard facts not mysteries or old wives' tales.

Rahal walked into the room and Mukta looked at him suspiciously.

'Did you allow those boys into this room?'

'Yes,' and he turned away from him.

'You dare turn your back on me?'

Rahal lowered his eyes, 'I'm sorry, Mukta.'

There was a look of emptiness in Rahal's eyes and Mukta was surprised. He had never seen Rahal like that. He had been loyal to him for the two years he had known him.

'What's eating you buddy?' he asked, softening his voice and playfully punched him in the stomach.

'I want to go and see my family,' he said quietly, afraid of what Mukta's reactions would be.

Mukta said nothing, he needed Rahal now more than ever, even if God had carved his heart out of stone, he dare not refuse Rahal. He had wanted to join his family for a long time, but Mukta had delayed him up until now.

'You've really been a good brother to me and I appreciate it,' Mukta held both his shoulders with a tender look on his face, 'but I need you to give me a few weeks to organise this rowdy group and see what we can get for you, you don't want to go to England empty handed do you?'

Rahal stared at him and shook his head, but Mukta could still see the sadness there.

'Anything else you'd like to share with me?' he prodded gently looking deep into his eyes.

Rahal hesitated briefly then blurted out, 'I'm afraid of Fatima, I don't like the way she looks at me.'

Mukta laughed, 'you killed her brother, what do you expect?'

'It was an accident,' Rahal defended himself feebly.

'She is completely harmless, forget her,' Mukta dismissed Fatima with a wave of his hands, 'besides, she is too westernised, she can't do anything.'

'Aren't you westernised Mukta?' Rahal challenged him fiercely, 'you were a medical doctor in Leicester, remember? It seems like centuries ago.'

Mukta fixed his gaze on him and said simply, 'I have to fight for my country.'

'You fought after your entire family was murdered by Ethiopians Mukta, revenge drove you to this.'

Rahal said with a glint in his eyes and walked out of the room.

His words stung Mukta because they were true. Sober, he sat limply on the only chair in the bare room, his eyes vacant as he stared into space.

He was born and raised in London, his father was a respected surgeon at the Royal London Hospital, and he had quickly followed in his steps. They were a close-knit family but he was an only child and was so lonely. His mother later gave birth to his little sister just before he completed his degree and he tried to see her as much as he could. He graduated with first class honours and married a Somali girl he'd met on campus. They started a family, having two kids in quick succession and his sister, Nisha, came to stay with them.

His father made it a tradition to go Somalia every year, mostly over Christmas, but that year was marred by violence. They left London anyway. That was the last time he saw them alive: his mother, father, and sister all died the same day.

His world practically ended. He went to Somalia, buried them, and went back to Leicester, where he was a general practitioner.

He harboured a strong hatred towards Ethiopians, and one day it came to a head. While he was waiting for a bus home, a tall, rude teenager slapped him hard across the face for stepping on his toes. Mukta apologised but the teenager landed another rough blow on his head while his mates cheered him on.

Mukta only meant to defend himself, but he just flipped. He always carried a penknife with him and he grabbed the boy and plunged the knife into his neck. It was a fatal wound and Mukta had known there was no way the teenager could have survived it.

He had pushed the fatally wounded boy away and had taken to his heels. There were bystanders at the scene, but no one moved to apprehend him. He later found out that the boy he killed in self-defence was Ethiopian. Shockingly, he didn't regret his actions.

That day, when he arrived home, he told his wife they had to leave Leicester and move back to Somalia. The next morning, he had cleared his accounts and they took the first available flight back home.

When they got to Somalia, his wife tried to talk him out of staying permanently in Mogadishu. She had a hard time adjusting to life in Somalia; different groups were fighting for the control of the country and she was scared, but Mukta ignored her pleas.

Their finances were depleting rapidly, his wife was afraid of the monster he was turning into and, most of the time, he was high on Qat, the narcotic leaf he had been against as a GP in Leicester.

One hot afternoon, his wife ended their relationship and left and was about to cross the border into Ethiopia when a group of boys caught up with her. She was gang raped and stabbed repeatedly in the chest.

She died on the spot. A neighbour who happened to witness the crime hurried home and told Mukta the gory details. He went with some of his cousins to the border town to take her body back home. They saw six youths meandering around the spot where his wife had been murdered. Suddenly, something snapped in him - he singlehandedly fought the youths and killed them, raving like a lunatic.

In the years following the gory incident, Mukta married two women, but the incessant violence had left a scar on his soul. There seemed to be no hope of redemption for him.

He joined different groups of men fighting for survival. While some were patriotic enough, most were religious fanatics and Al-Qaida supporters who were hell bent on causing chaos and anarchy.

Mukta was none of those. He was just a man living a borrowed life, he knew he could die at any moment and couldn't care less. At a later stage, he lost faith in God. What kind of God would allow such wanton destruction of lives and property?

But could he truly blame God for what had become of his country? The Horn of Africa? No, it was an emphatic 'No'.

He wiped tears from his eyes, human beings had free will, the power to choose; there was always a choice, and he had chosen to fight until the end. He even believed he no longer had a heart.

Rahal came back into the room expecting a tirade of abuse and anger, but he met a calmer Mukta. He had bad news for him and was at a loss as to how to break it.

'Rihanat, Halimat, and the kids are gone.'

'What are you saying?' Mukta asked in a deadly whisper, his eyes bloodshot.

'The Islamic Revolutionary Front took them, Mukta, we have many eye witnesses.'

'How is Fatima, is she awake yet?'

Rahal nodded, angry with Mukta for his misplacement of priorities. He knew Mukta loved his family, though he kept a tight rein on his emotions, but Rahal had hoped Mukta would have sent the poor girl back to America where she belonged.

Fatima's brother had been buried the same day he died; they even had an Imam pray for his soul.

Their mother was safely back in New York, but Mukta was still blinded by lust and refused to acknowledge the fact that he who played with fire would definitely get scorched. Rahal was determined to save his own skin.

Mukta stood up and said with a sneer, his mood changing swiftly like London weather, 'Mogadishu belongs to us. Let's go and kill some dogs, Rahal get some Qat for me.'

'I will boss.' Rahal left the room to rally other militias. He ran into the street and whistled. The summoned group gathered in front of Mukta's house yelling with manic, drug-fuelled expressions on their faces.

They lifted their rifles, shooting into the air.

Mukta left the room and ducked into a corner - he opened a door, and slipped inside. Fatima was huddled on the bed with a bored look on her face. She sat up straight when Mukta came near the bed, straightening her short dress with long, delicate fingers.

She looked at him expectedly, but her hopes were dashed by his next words.

'My family has been kidnapped, I need to go and bring them back,' he said gently, like a pupil talking to his favourite teacher, a teacher he had a crush on.

'I wish you God speed,' she whispered, her brown eyes red and puffy with continuous weeping. She had misjudged him.

Fatima had expected him to set her free, however it seemed Mukta would never release her. She needed to act quickly.

He sat beside her on the bed and started speaking in a solemn voice,

'You remind me of my first wife. She was raped and murdered here,' he seemed to chuckle and continued in a lifeless tone, 'I'm not a freak or a senseless killer. I was once a doctor in England.'

That got her attention, and she looked at him sharply.

'Yeah it's true, I know its weird; people have written different kinds of stories about me, but I'm also human.'

His mood did not fool Fatima, as far she was concerned, Mukta was a wild animal.

'Then let me go home,' she blurted out. She wanted to flee the dingy hole, but there was no way out. Revenge might be sweet but she would love to be free before planning her next move.

'You'll go home, my dove,' Mukta said huskily, his breath on her face as he pulled her towards him, kissing her passionately for a long time. When he released her, they were both lost for breath.

Mukta swallowed hard and controlled himself: he must save his family first so as not to lose the respect of the group.

'You're like a virus in my blood, Fatima. I have never felt this way with any woman, not even my Vivian. I'll be back soon and I promise to take you to a better apartment. I also give you my word that you will go home soon.' Mukta stood up abruptly and walked out of the room, locking the door securely behind him.

The colour drained from Fatima's face as she flopped back on the bed dazed. What is happening to me? Am I falling for a Somali warlord? *No*, Fatima thought and grimaced, *that would be so disgusting*. But there was no denying her unusual emotion. Mukta had been incredibly gentle with her, but he has forced himself on you, and was responsible for the death of your only brother, a voice whispered in her head.

I would never forget that, she thought.

Her intention was to seduce and kill him, then get out of the hellhole called her country, but she was slowly forgetting the way Andre used to touch her. Feeling like that was scary.

They were to be married in December and were already living together, even though Farouk had disapproved of what he called 'sinful cohabitation'. After his conversion to Christianity, Farouk had frowned on sex before marriage and believed absolutely in the sanctity of marriage.

'No,' Fatima said aloud, she would not betray her brother.

Mukta had not pulled the trigger, but he was responsible for what happened.

They buried Farouk nearby, and Mukta had allowed her to attend the funeral. For that, she was thankful.

She knew her mother would try to contact her but the lanky youth who killed Farouk had taken her phone.

Fatima blamed herself for Farouk's death. His young wife would be devastated by the news, and if she were released, how would she face Andre after she had willingly given herself to Mukta?

Her train of thought shocked her. She couldn't possibly be falling for her captor, her brother's killer, a militia who killed for the fun of it!

Fatima swung her legs from the bed and stood to her feet. Her restlessness grew as the harrowing minutes ticked by. She had racked her brain endlessly looking for an escape route but found none. The only window in the room had iron bars and it was very small. She sat on the bed and unexpectedly, rapid burst of gunfire tore the silence in the room into shreds.

Fatima stifled a scream and dived under the bed and something caught her attention. It was the covering of an opening, disguised with some dirty clothes. She pushed the clothes aside and pulled on the lid with all the strength she could muster, and it gave way. It smelt of damp earth and her heart leapt for joy: she had never smelt anything so wonderful.

She dragged the lid aside and slid into a hole, it was just big enough for her to crawl through; it was dark but strangely cool. It wasn't a big hole, but she kept crawling. She hurried along and then saw a flicker of light. The light became brighter as she inched closer with all the energy she had left.

'Freedom!' she shrieked, keep it quiet woman, she admonished herself but couldn't help the huge grin on her face. She had dreamt of the day she would be free and it was finally happening. She crawled on painfully, her knees were bruised and bleeding, but she pressed on until she came to the end of the makeshift tunnel.

Fatima's sharp eyes caught sight of a big iron bar - hope rose in her heart as she realised that it wasn't locked. She tried pulling it back but it stayed put. After closer inspection, she discovered it was a bit rusted. A sinking feeling of despair rose from the pit of her stomach.

Despair had been her constant companion and it reared its ugly head again. She was afraid and the cold claws of fear slowly crawled up her spine.

'Don't panic,' she whispered bleakly, how would she get out? She gritted her teeth and pulled with all her strength but the iron bar was unyielding.

You'd better get back, a voice whispered in her head as perspiration and an incoming flow of tears threatened her newfound joy. She was fast losing control of the situation, then she heard a sweet rich voice, it was a woman calling her kids.

Fatima listened warily, her breathing unsteady. There was the sound of tiny scurrying feet and then she heard steps that were more definite. She held her breath as the sound got closer, and louder. The iron bar guarding the small tunnel swung open. A woman with a cheerful face and a smile that could melt the heart of a lion loomed into view, and Fatima was speechless. The woman was speaking Arabic, but Fatima did not fully understand. She finally pulled Fatima to safety, and led her into a dark, modest kitchen.

Cooking utensils were scattered across the floor, but for Fatima, that kitchen was like heaven. The woman gave her a cup of water and Fatima took it with a grateful smile, drinking with relish while her rescuer dashed into an adjacent building like a flash of lightning. When the woman came back, there was a small carrier bag in her hand. She gave it to Fatima and said to her in halting English, 'Border, go now,' Fatima nodded and grabbed the hand of the woman, covering it with kisses. The woman led her through a narrow path behind the large compound and pointed into the forest, her dark face creasing in a broad smile. Fatima thanked her profusely and took to her heels. She stopped to catch her breath and turned back, the woman was still watching her. Fatima waved, and the woman waved back.

'God bless you,' Fatima whispered with tears of gratitude streaming down her face. She was free at last! She had endured two days of hell. Mukta had forcefully had his way with her more than ten times within a period of thirty-eight hours, but now she was free. Tripping over a large stone, she fell face down, but picked herself up effortlessly and ran for dear life.

21

The rain fell endlessly in the vast mountainous countryside, accompanied by gusts of wind. Aaron slept on a brown mattress on the carpeted floor of the Church of Tablet. The Ark of the Covenant was still hidden from view, buried somewhere underground beneath the church, and he did not attempt to go near it. The sound of rain hitting the roof was like a nursery rhyme and it was enough to send anyone into a blissful slumber.

Abraham, the caretaker of the Ark, stared at Aaron long and hard; if only the poor boy knew the amount of power he was carrying inside his body.

He would be jumping for joy, but he knew Aaron was a simple man.

Aaron murmured inaudible words as he slept while the caretaker cast furtive glances in his direction at regular intervals. Abraham adjusted his legs under the weight of the Amharic Bible but try as he might, he couldn't concentrate.

He reached for his walking stick and struggled to his feet. He was seventy years old and had started feeling the strain of his age. He knew the cold weather and incessant rain was not helping matters.

Walking had become a terrible chore but he masked his pain well; people mustn't see how fragile he was fast becoming. He certainly wished the young Jewish boy would rectify the situation; that's if he knows what to do, Abraham thought warmly.

He admired the young, pale faced man and, as much as he resented western influence on Ethiopia, he had finally realised that most of his reservations were unfounded.

He wandered to the centre of the room and fixed his gaze on the red carpet. Bending with difficulty, he lifted it to reveal an ancient map; the words on the map were in Hebrew. He took the map, put the carpet back and walked out of the room.

Abraham closed the door quietly; he didn't want to rouse his sleeping guest. He strolled along a long, dim corridor, towards the tail end of the long, gloomy passage; he stopped at a big oak door, and paused briefly before opening it.

The door creaked open and he walked through, leaving it ajar. He moved slowly towards the Ark, his eyes glowing with anticipation. The Ark always filled him with wonder and any time he approached the Holies of holy, his face always lit up in joy. He sank slowly to his knees and worshipped God.

His gaze rested on the Ark briefly and then he bowed his head and began praying quietly. But he was no longer the only person in the room. Aaron stood in the doorway, staring at the sacred relic in the centre of the room. The room was thick with the holy odour of frankincense.

It is true, Aaron thought as his heart raced with apprehension, the old monk had been right; the Tabot was real, and he couldn't bear to tear his gaze away.

The Ark was exactly as he had read in the scriptures. A wooden chest measuring three feet, nine inches long, by two feet, three inches wide and was lined inside and out with pure gold. How could they have protected the Ark all through the centuries? But Aaron couldn't ask Abraham, who seemed to have gone into a trance like state. He kept murmuring, rocking back and forth on his knees, his hands clasped together in a prayer position.

Aaron turned his attention back to the Ark and, as if drawn by a magnet, he tiptoed into the room, his heart beating wildly. He stared in fascination at the mercy seat made of pure gold; goose pimples appeared on his body. He couldn't take his eyes away from the two cherubim that were also made of pure gold that were on the two ends of the mercy seat. And the most exciting thing of all: inside the Ark was the testimony of the Lord. Or, at least, he hoped so.

Finally, Aaron tore his eyes away from the sacred relic. Suddenly, a brilliant white light began to shine in the room and he backed away towards the door and hurried back along the lengthy passageway.

He was not ready to come too close to the Ark; he had satisfied his curiosity and that was enough for the moment. As he walked along the corridor, a sharp, excruciating pain pierced through his body and he almost fainted. He leaned against the wall to rest for a while. When he felt stronger, he continued walking slowly. After taking five steps, another knife-like pain slammed into his chest and he began to gasp for breath.

His body felt like an enormous stone, he dragged himself forcibly back to the room and collapsed on the mattress as fatigue crippled him. I shouldn't have crept up on the old monk like that, Aaron thought in dismay. He hadn't officially been invited to enter the holy room, but curiosity had got the better of him.

His breathing was ragged but he controlled himself with difficulty, having a panic attack was out of the question, but the ache increased in intensity. His breathing was becoming irregular; he clutched his chest and closed his eyes - he really should see a doctor about the twinge. He tried another approach by holding his breath, but it was futile: the hammering pain persisted.

'I shouldn't have gone into the room,' he murmured, wondering what he was doing in Ethiopia. What had he come to do? But he had no answer to the question. At that moment, he wished he could see his dad, but knew such a wish was pointless. The thought of his dad exacerbated his discomfort and he stopped wishing for the impossible.

There was a knock on the door and he opened his eyes with great difficulty, the thought of walking to the door filled him with dread so he remained on the mattress, immobile.

Then he heard quick footsteps along the holy corridor, as he had tagged it.

Hurriedly, he shut his eyes again; the nice old monk must not find him awake.

Abraham went to the door and opened it slightly - it was Caleb, and he let him in. Caleb's flushed face looked ready to pop, he went to a corner of the room and sat down.

'What's the matter, my son?' Abraham asked gently and sat on a mat in front of Caleb.

'Our secret is out,' he gushed out hurriedly, 'we have been betrayed by...'

'What are we going to do?' Aaron interjected his eyes bright, the soreness in his chest temporarily forgotten.

They both turned to look at him. He was embarrassed and he stammered brokenly, 'I... over...heard what you were saying.'

'We're safe here,' Abraham said confidently, 'no one has any right to come in here without my invitation, not even the Ethiopian President.'

Caleb and Aaron were not convinced but the old monk was defiant and adamant, he stressed it forcefully, 'Anyone who ventures in here uninvited will be struck with an incurable disease and will die within seventy eight hours.'

'Really?' Caleb and Aaron exclaimed.

'Yes, and a great light will emit from the Ark chambers and consume trespassers; they will be totally annihilated,' Abraham added gravely his eyes shining.

There was a tense silence in the room. Suddenly, Aaron cried out in pain, clutching his chest. Sweat broke out on his forehead. Abraham and Caleb rushed to his side.

'I have seen the Ark,' he confessed.

'What!' Caleb screamed, 'you were not supposed to do that yet, I mean...'

'Are you all right, son? You look terrible,' Abraham asked, a note of worry creeping on his voice.

'It was nothing,' Aaron answered lightly, and he could feel the pain easing, 'it was just a slight tightening in my chest.'

Abraham chuckled, relieved that Aaron was fine, and then a twinkle appeared in his eyes as he said laughing, 'I knew you were there, in fact I lured you in since you had developed cold feet.'

Aaron was tremendously relieved to hear that Abraham wanted him to see the Ark.

'We have to do something about the archbishop: how did he find out that Aaron was here?' Caleb asked a worried expression on his face.

'But he reads the papers doesn't he? He must have known about the incident at the hotel,' Aaron answered slowly.

'Don't bother son,' Abraham said, his eyes glistening, 'God is here, and He will protect His own.'

Caleb was not convinced; he knew the monk was trying to allay their fears. His thoughts were on Aaron, he would protect him with his life if need be, but he wanted a clear signal before he shared his next line of action with his brothers. It appeared they had a mole amongst them, and he needed to find out who the person was. I may have to travel to Rome again, sooner than expected, Caleb thought with a worried frown.

He had refused to believe the findings of the surveillance group that was set up, and the information he'd received about the mole was disheartening to say the least. In the meantime, he would keep his fingers crossed and wait for the next move of the traitor. The archbishop must be furious knowing that they had allowed a stranger into the most sacred place in Ethiopia.

Caleb let out a deep sigh.

He shook his head sadly. He mustn't allow his mind to dwell on the fact that one of the brothers in the order could betray them. He stared forlornly at the ceiling, his thoughts riotous.

22

Manhattan, New York, Aug 10

Keith Morgan sat still for several minutes, lost in thought. He rubbed his right hand across his face and yawned. He had been having weird dreams of late and was worried. He kept seeing his dead son and was too embarrassed to confide in his best friend. He knew Michael would simply laugh it off and change the topic. He had not slept a wink for two days in a row and it was gradually showing on him. He was irritable, jumpy, and angry; his colleagues had been looking at him strangely, and he knew he had to do something about his mood swings.

He had just come back from a long holiday in the Caribbean so he couldn't complain of fatigue or blame his restlessness on stress. He'd had a brilliant time on the island. He felt refreshed, invigorated, and alive and was ready to tackle anything headlong but as soon as he set foot inside his house, his mood changed and an unexplainable wave of sorrow hit him like a Tsunami.

His wife was confused and tried to help but it was futile. To add to his woes, the presence of Evelyn, Michael's wife, and a young British girl who tagged along with her infuriated him for no apparent reason. It was a tense atmosphere while the young girl was in his home and he had been relieved when he heard that a dog at Central Park had attacked her. Understandably, he had upset his wife with his attitude, but he couldn't explain it.

Keith stood to his feet, hands in his pockets and head down. He paced his massive office, lost in thought, then without warning, an unexpected rumbling shook his office.

He took the remote control for the TV and flipped to check the weather forecast. The forecaster's voice droned on confidently about a clear, bright day. *So what was the tremor that shook my office?* Michael thought, his brow furrowed, definitely not thunder.

There was a lazy, almost bored expression on his tanned face - the day had been hot and humid, and he yearned for rain.

He returned to his chair and laid his head on the table.

After a few minutes, he lifted his head and questioned the reason behind his despondency.

CYDONIA

Keith was living the American dream and he was well aware of it. He had his own law firm and his reputation was soaring. His wife was finally able to conceive after losing their son seven years back, he was over the moon with the news, and at last, his twin daughters would leave him alone about having a little brother. His career couldn't have been better; his wife was loving, beautiful, and terrific in bed, while his daughters were doing fine in school. What more could a man want?

Things were working so well for him, he was surprised and wondered why he was tilting towards depression, but the heavy cloak of gloominess consumed him totally and he was so weak and powerless in fighting it.

He'd attempted suicide twice and, somehow, his wife had been able to read his deepest thoughts. She had advised him to seek professional help but he'd refused.

When he sank deeper into the quagmire of depression, she had pleaded with him to have a word with her pastor, but again, he had politely declined.

He chuckled at that, he used to go to church as often as his career would allow, but after the death of his son, he put the blame on God and slowly withdrew from participating in church activities. Lola had nagged him endlessly, after a while she decided to let him be.

'I'll be praying for you, Champ,' she would say every Sunday morning as she and the girls piled into the car and zoomed off while he stayed glued to the TV.

Now seeking any kind of help would make him look like a weakling. He believed in his innate ability to proffer solution to any problem, and seeing a psychiatrist or a pastor would not help, either way, he was not going to rehab.

The overwhelming feeling of sadness engulfed him full force as he swivelled his chair round and round, after a while he stood up again and walked to the toilet. While his hand was still on the doorknob, he felt a movement behind him, sharply, he turned round and swallowed hard. Everything was as it should be. He breathed in/out heavily and opened the toilet's door.

It was a small and compacted toilet. There was nowhere an intruder could hide. If there were anyone in the toilet, he would have noticed anyway. He turned on the tap and washed his hands. He stared at his brown fingers and the hairs at the nape of his neck stood on end, he felt slightly dizzy but with an effort, he calmed down. He allowed the water to flow in full force. Suddenly the tap stopped running; it had turned off by itself.

Keith believed in ghosts and demons, but was sure there was no reason why the spirits should target or haunt him. Calmly, he sauntered towards the hand-dryer and put his hands under it, but nothing happened. He mumbled to himself, trying to keep a tight rein on his emotions.

He glanced at his reflection in the mirror: his eyes were red, and he looked scared. He couldn't see whoever was there with him, but the feeling was very strong; there was definitely something in the room with him.

He dried his hands with a towel and left the toilet in a hurry.

Sitting back on his chair, he tried to get some work done by reading the files on his table. He would not be chased away by shadows and feelings.

His phone rang shrilly and the sound was so loud that it grated on his already frayed nerves, startled, he picked it up and barked into the phone angrily, 'Who the hell is this?' He listened for a few seconds and dropped the phone.

'Oh God, what is wrong with me?' he whispered brokenly, it was as though he was not the same person who'd left home that morning. He snatched his car keys from the table and walked briskly to the door, but he couldn't open it.

He grunted and kicked his door, then was about to walk back to his chair when he saw him, and he froze.

A naked baby stared at him with big blue eyes, and reminded him so much of his son. How did a naked baby get into the office? He wondered and bent down to touch him, but the baby moved out of his reach and crawled under his table.

'C'mon darling, come to me, let me take you to mummy,' he cooed in a silly little voice. Discouraged, he stood up and walked to his desk, but when he bent down to check the baby, he had disappeared.

Keith realised he was in serious trouble, and ran out of his office. He walked with long strides to the lift, but on second thoughts went to his partner's office, but it was empty.

That's strange, Michael thought.

He checked all the offices on the top floor but there was not a single soul - not even his chatty secretary. Where had everyone gone? Then he remembered the baby. Should he go back and pick him up? *Not a chance, I'm not going back into that office,* he thought and ground his teeth.

He went down the stairs, taking two steps at a time, screaming, but there was no response from any quarter - the offices were all empty, as though everyone had left in a hurry.

He walked into one of the offices, parted the curtains, and looked down. The sight he saw turned his blood cold. There was not a single soul on the street; everywhere was deserted. There were cars on the road with horns blaring but there were no people in the drivers' seats.

Everywhere was chaotic. He quickly turned away from the window, his heart beating so fast that he believed he might slump down and die of shock unless he pulled himself together. Fear clawed at his soul; it was alien and potent, and as much as he tried to control it, he failed woefully. Fear was not a pleasant feeling.

The only person on his mind at that moment was his wife. They were supposed to meet for lunch. With shaky hands, he wiped sweat off his face with the back of his hands, scratching his head in frustration as he ran his shaky hands through his sandy brown hair. He expelled air from his mouth and closed his eyes for some seconds before opening them again. How could everyone just disappear in a split second? But there was no answer, Keith knew something abnormal was going on and he didn't know how to unravel the mystery.

He had just spoken to his secretary, who reminded him of his appointment with a Mr. Logan Stone, but he couldn't even remember anyone by that name. He'd banged the phone down on her and during the brief time they'd been speaking and had heard voices on the background, so how could they all disappear in a puff of smoke? It wasn't Hollywood; this was his law firm, his life.

Keith had to go back to his office, his mobile phone was on the table, but the thought of it filled him with dread: the strange naked baby could still be crawling around. He fidgeted with his car keys, pacing back and forth and checking the window every now and then. Surprisingly, there was the welcoming sound of a ringing phone. Keith moved with the speed of lightning towards it. He found the phone on the desk of one the best lawyers the firm had, Jonathan Swift. Keith snatched it up and was relieved to hear the voice of his wife.

'Hello, darling,' and he couldn't control himself as he almost choked in tears and narrated everything to her. He was happy to learn that the strange phenomenon was limited to his side of the city and he promised to come home as soon as he could.

'Take care, Champ, I'll leave Kate and Evelyn as soon as I can,' Lola said breathlessly and then there was a clicking sound as she hung up.

He put the phone down and saw Jonathan looking at him strangely. He sat behind his desk, a pile of files in front of him. Keith glared at him, dazed, and he rushed out of Jonathan's office.

Keith strode through the corridor and some of the junior lawyers walked past him with smiles on their faces.

Everyone was all right - where had they all gone at the same time? But he was not in a position to answer that question and he didn't even want to try. *Surely, I'm losing my sanity,* he thought gloomily.

'Hello, Mr. Morgan,' a bright faced woman greeted him and he nodded with a fixed smile on his ashen face. He walked straight to the lift and pressed the button for the sixth floor. Then the same ominous presence he had felt in his office earlier overwhelmed him.

The lift door slid open and he strolled boldly into his office but he was far from being confident; he knew something was terribly wrong but the only thought on his mind was how to get home to his family. The hallucination he was having could not be rationalised - maybe he should take his wife's advice and see a psychiatrist.

He closed his office's door and turned the key, he wanted to be alone for a while. He combed the entire length and breadth of his office but everything was as he had left it. There was no sign of the naked baby, but as he walked with brisk steps to the centre of his office, he noticed a red silk cloth beside the windowpane and he frowned, studied it for a while, and decided to leave it there.

He picked his mobile phone up from his desk and a brutal force hit him hard on the back of the neck. He crumpled to the floor and the force lifted him up and slammed his head against the wall with cruel efficiency. He heard rushing feet as his secretary repeatedly knocked on his door, but he had already locked it. Her frantic cry for help was a brief relief but it was hopeless. The banging on the door grew louder and if she could, she would have yanked the door off its hinges to rescue him.

Keith tried to wriggle his way free but he was powerless against the rage of the unseen assailant. He fought hard, hitting empty air. After a couple of minutes, the attack stopped as abruptly as it had begun. Keith struggled to his feet and dragged himself to his desk, his Armani suit was torn, and he was bleeding.

He struggled to the door but fell midway, he crawled back to his desk, stood up, picked up his phone, and dialled his friend's number but he couldn't hold still as his knees buckled again and he crumpled to the floor.

Then Keith saw him.

It was the naked baby. His eyes were red, and when he opened his mouth, a black snake came out, slithering and hissing. Keith tried to use the last remaining strength in him but an invisible force dragged him and pinned him against the wall. The force yanked his jaw open and the snake glided in. Then whatever was in his office left him alone.

Keith eyes turned yellow and he rolled on the floor, choking as the snake tore his insides to pieces. Keith wanted to scream but could not because his voice was gone. Blood poured from his nose and splashed on the floor - in that instant, he knew his life was ebbing away fast.

Keith lifted his eyes and saw a hazy image of his dead son, Destiny. The boy was weeping and Keith tried reaching out to him but he failed, there was a wide gulf between them. Keith tore his eyes away and closed them; he knew what had possessed him was evil and the only way he could save his soul was for someone to kill him.

He made a last attempt and tried standing up, but an explosion in his brain thwarted his plans and he hit the floor with a thud. Keith welcomed the darkness that enveloped him as a friend, and his heart stopped beating.

23

When he regained consciousness, the enormity of the pain in his body stunned him. Logan rubbed the back of his head vigorously and staggered to his feet. His hands went to his face and he realised it was swollen. He tried to piece together what must have happened to him, but he could not. He felt so strange; it was as if someone had placed a ton of concrete on his head.

He glanced around him trying to take in his surroundings, and then it all came back to him. He had been on his way to see Natalie when he saw an ambulance and paramedics bringing out a stretcher from her apartment.

Then he recalled going up to her apartment and the place was crawling with cops and FBI.

He had dashed back to the street, wandering about aimlessly when someone punched him in the face on

Fifth Avenue at least that was the last bit he remembered.

He shook his head in a bid to clear it and tried to think but it was useless. He saw a man sleeping on a sofa and that was when he finally scanned his surroundings.

The room was big and tastefully furnished. It was kind of an open plan apartment. He took everything in: the plasma television, the blue couch, and thick red rug on the floor. In a corner of the room was a bar with a small refrigerator and beside it was a kitchen sink. His stomach churned wildly. The last time he'd had anything to eat was the sandwich he had after leaving the hospital. A cold beer would be heavenly, if only he could lay his hands on one, but he had to find out who had brought him to such a cosy environment.

He turned to his right and saw a gym complete with a treadmill and all the works. The room had a modern, contemporary feel to it. The décor was superb, and the thought of sitting comfortably on one of the sofas watching football with a chilled bottle of wine was so tempting that he started licking his dry lips.

He sat down wearily and turned his attention back to the man on the couch who was snoring softly. *That's one deep sleep,* Logan thought with a smile, and winced in pain. After staring at him for a while, the man stirred in his sleep and turned over. Logan had no choice other than to wake him and ask how he got into the plush basement apartment. The room had the unmistakable smell of an underground cellar, despite attempts to mask it.

He was about to stand up when he heard approaching footsteps and bouts of laughter, so he sank back into the chair. The door opened and three men walked in, one of them was a black man.

'Hey son, you've woken up - you were a wreck last night when we found you.' The man who spoke was short and bald but he had a very kind face. His mates dissolved into laughter and Logan joined in; they seemed like good-natured men.

'My name is Logan Stone,' he said and tried to stand but felt so dizzy that he settled back on the chair.

'You could've been killed by those Satanists, good job we were around the neighbourhood,' the man who spoke earlier said watching him shrewdly. This time, no one laughed, just silence. They were all watching him now.

But Logan was confused; how could he have fallen into the hands of Satanists? And who were Satanists anyway?

'I don't understand,' he murmured, almost to himself, 'I was on my way to see a lady friend when I was attacked and the next thing I knew I found myself here.'

'You're in the safest place in the world,' one of the men said kindly. He was tall and scrawny, his eyes sunken into his face, 'I was once a Satanist, and I worshiped the devil. Look at me now,' and he opened his arms and turned round, 'if not for the blood of Christ I would have died. You would've sold your soul to the devil yesterday if you'd slept with the dead woman; she was marked by the devil, and they won't find her killers.'

Their uncanny revelations shocked Logan. They spoke with such authority that he believed them without a doubt. Who were these people? Moreover, how did they know about Natalie? He looked at each man and said, 'Please, just tell me where I am, I can't recollect much of what happened.'

The three men glanced at each other and were quiet for a while. Then the tall, bony man walked to the big sofa in the room and sat down, while his two friends sat on the wooden floor, six pairs of eyes stared at him. The man sleeping at the end of the room was snoring loudly and the gaunt man chuckled before he began speaking, 'My name is Darren, and this is Zach, but I call him John Bull, but I'm the only one permitted to call him that.' Zach smiled revealing mission tooth, he was the short bald man, 'And my good friend here is Jonas the prophet; he can actually see into the future.' Jonas nodded his head but didn't speak.

Darren continued speaking, 'Our life histories could make Hollywood millions of dollars if turned into a film, but we don't dare venture into that now. Anyway, we were greatly concerned about you.'

There was a protracted silence as everyone took in the words of Darren and then he said standing up, 'We're living under the basement of the Fifth Avenue Presbyterian Church. You're in Midtown Manhattan. There are ten of us in this beautiful apartment, and by joining us since last night; we are now eleven. We are all homeless men, except you of course.' And he went back to the sofa and stretched his long legs.

'But how did you find me?' Logan asked.

Darren nodded towards Jonas whose voice would have drawn laugher from Logan had he not been sober. He could barely open his mouth due to the pain in his head and their act of kindness touched Logan deeply. He listened to Jonas, fascinated by his simplicity and love for him, something that was missing in his life. As he watched Jonas, his mind travelled out of the confines of the basement.

Logan hated going to church and couldn't really trace how he'd lost his faith. His mom made sure he went to church every single Sunday where the pastor preached about the end of days, hell fire and hailstones falling on children of disobedience. His rebellious heart was afraid of hell fire and every night he would tell his mom to pray for him so that if he died before he woke up, he would go to heaven.

Growing up in Jackson, Mississippi, was tough. They were poverty stricken but very proud. His mom made sure he never missed a day of school but his dad was rarely home; he was an unrepentant drunkard and a gambler, so the upkeep of the family fell on his mom's enormous shoulders.

One hot summer day, the sheriff came to their derelict apartment with a scowl on his face to announce that his dad had been involved in a brawl at the local pub and was seriously injured. They took him to the hospital, but his mom came back three hours later crying. He had died of his wounds.

Five days later, two men drove up to their house in a Jaguar with Cuban cigars dangling from their lips. Logan's mom was suspicious as they came into their sparsely furnished lounge. One of the men kept pulling faces as if he were in a dungeon . Logan was mad with rage and when his mom turned and saw him lingering in the doorway, she ordered him out of the room; he obeyed and went to sit with his three sisters.

His eldest sister, Natasha, was twenty-one, already mature. She kept peeping through the window, all her focus on the big, shiny car outside their home.

Unexpectedly they heard a scream and they rushed outside to see what was wrong. They met their mother crying, tears of joy flowing freely down her round, pretty face.

The men calmly left the house. As their mother later explained, their dad had apparently struck it rich on the tables before his premature death, and the manager of the casino had decided to play fair and send over his winnings. Seven hundred thousand dollars was a lot of money, and the shock had nearly given her a heart attack.

Within a month, they'd bought a bigger house and life in general improved, but once he finished high school, he told his mom he would be leaving for New York to make something of his life. He couldn't continue living off of her, even if she was rich.

He wanted to become an actor but it didn't work out, so he joined the Police Academy. But that too only lasted seven days. Shame of failure wouldn't let him go back to his family, so he decided to try his hand at becoming a PI - private investigator - and in a way had struck it rich. At least he had a roof over his head and a very fat bank balance.

Along the line, church lost its flavour and whenever his mom called, he had a ready lie.

He told her that he attended church frequently and was even in the choir, but when he visited her during Thanksgiving and Christmas, she had a way of finding out the truth.

And to compound his problems, she wanted him to get married. 'Don't be fooled by your young looks, son; you need to settle down and give your late father a son to carry on the family name,' she would nag him endlessly and he would murmur in agreement and say, 'Yes mom.'

At thirty-five, Logan looked twenty. He was simply a confirmed bachelor, and he wasn't sure that he wanted his freedom taken from him. He became aware of the movement of Jonas's mouth and focused his attention back on reality.

'I have been having visions about you for the past six months,' Jonas was saying, gesticulating with his hands and Logan noticed the well-manicured hands, *this man must be rich*, Logan thought. Meeting them could be profitable for him after all, and Logan's face broke into a wide grin.

'But it became clearer that your life was in danger when I saw a big python swallowing you up. That was when I decided that we should look for you. I had an idea from my visions of how to get to you, but we had to be fast and pray all through yesterday because we knew it would not be an ordinary task. We were going to war with demons and we had to be prepared. We decided to go to the east side of Fifth Avenue, through Ninth and Tenth Street.'

He paused for a while before continuing,

'We hung around there until it became dark. We didn't have to wait long when we heard the sudden piercing sound of a siren. We watched from our vantage point across the street as an ambulance screeched to a stop. We saw a woman on a stretcher and we waited patiently until I saw you, just as I had in my visions.' Jonas stopped speaking, watching Logan's reaction, and that was when he realised that his mouth was slightly open.

It was surreal and puzzling, to think that someone had been dreaming about him.

'Continue, please,' he managed to say.

And Jonas did, his small voice was raised a little for emphasis,

'We saw when you entered the apartment, and then we saw them,' he paused to flick imaginary dust from his shirt, 'they were three heavily built men, thankfully, I had my anointing oil with me and...'

'What was that...?' Logan interrupted him.

Darren answered him, 'It's always used for protection when you want to fight demons.'

'Oh,' Logan murmured, completely perplexed.

'As I was saying,' Jonas said, 'we saw you coming and moved towards you, but one of the men punched you in the face and we rushed forward, throwing the oil into their face.'

'And then what happened?'

'We brought you home, we had already hired a car. You might like to know that those demons dissolved into sulphur.'

'Demons?' Logan asked, and his heart skipping a beat.

'Yeah son, Tyrus wanted to take your body. He knows you could take him straight to the earth priest, and he needs a human vessel to be able to subdue Aaron Cohen.'

Logan was surprised.

Aaron?

They knew exactly what they were talking about, and they had heard about Aaron.

What had he walked into? He frowned and thought of everything that had happened to him; he could have ended up in a cold drawer in a mortuary... in a body bag, and very dead indeed. It was a very distressing thought.

His eyes rested on Jonas and he felt chastised for thinking they were beneath him. All humans are equal; at least that was how God wanted it. His pride was gone and he lowered his eyes.

They saved you, dog, Logan thought soberly, staring at them again, totally lost for words.

'We know Aaron is in Ethiopia,' Darren said with an air of mystery about him.

That came as a surprise to Logan.

'Who are you guys? Can you please tell me?' he croaked out in a voice he hardly recognised as his own. In that instant he felt so naked; the three men looking at him knew so much about him, but why were things about him being shown to them? Although he had no answer to that, he hoped they would enlighten him some more.

'We're ordinary men used by an extraordinary God,' Jonas said simply and stood up. At the same time, there was a knock at the door and Jonas went to open it.

Logan swallowed hard and wondered if these men were who they said they were.

Three more men ambled into the spacious room; they gave him a quick glance and nodded in his direction. Jonas disappeared with the men into what looked like a cupboard. Actually, he had thought it was a cupboard, but there was a concealed door, which opened when Jonas touched it. With Jonas gone with the three well-dressed guests, Logan glanced at his wristwatch. He ought to make a move.

'You have to lay low for a while. Tyrus will be on the lookout for you, don't forget you sent his demons spiralling into hell fire.' Darren said laughing while Zach grinned.

'I have to pick up some stuff. I can't just stay here; I have to call some of my clients.'

'One of your clients is housing Lucifer, Tyrus's father in his body right now,' Jonas said emerging from the other room, 'and if you don't believe me you should receive a phone call at twelve fifteen tonight. Don't answer it: the man calling you is the commander of the vicious demon we saved you from yesterday.'

The story sounded preposterous and he had the urge to laugh, but his instincts agreed.

'What should I do?'

'You have to stay here today and tomorrow; we may have to go to Ethiopia. Aaron is the one with the answers.'

'But I don't understand,' Logan said standing up, he still felt wobbly at the knees but he felt much better.

'I was hired by Aaron's uncle to find out anything I could about him. When I came back from Ethiopia, I heard that my client had been attacked. How can I expose myself to Aaron without blowing my cover as a private investigator tailing him?

'We'll cross that bridge when we get to it,' Jonas said with a shrug.

'I'm hungry,' Darren said, a relaxed expression on his face, 'anyone care for a Chinese?'

'I want mine hot and spicy,' Logan said and sat down again. He might as well make himself more comfortable.

24

Pope Nathaniel III flipped through the pages on his desk and adjusted his reading glasses. It had taken him the best part of an hour to sort through the deluge of mail and important documents. He beckoned to the prefect of the papal household, a tall, dark haired man with a crooked nose and a smiley face, whom he fondly called House.

'I can't get all the facts from this file, I need more. Could you also arrange for Monsignor Bacilio's mother to have an audience with me later this evening? I understand she's in Rome.'

'Yes, Your Holiness,' House bowed briefly and left the Pope's office.

The Pope had been inundated with problems from all sides; even though he was a very strong man, the scales of the crises were daunting. He would not bow to pressure from hell yet - even though he missed Bacilio and Salvarado deeply, he had to accept their demise as the will of God.

He had been in deep talks with the palatine cardinals, the bishop's assistant to the papal throne, the prince's assistant to the papal throne and a host of others. They had agreed on one thing: to wage war against the forces of darkness threatening Christendom in Rome, or anywhere else in the world for that matter.

He thought of Aaron and it was obvious that he must meet with him. Although, they would have to reassure him that no one would molest or threaten him in any way. His emissaries had already gone to Ethiopia. Aaron would be able to stop the menacing crisis that was looming over the Church.

He rested back in his chair with a yawn. He felt sleepy but he fought it off, his weary eyes turned upward, glancing at the big grandmother clock against the wall - it was twelve noon on the dot.

There was a short rap on the door, and the Pope's new secretary sprinted to the door and opened it, ushering in the preacher to the papal household. Father Giovanni Rossini was a tall, heavily built man with a husky, commanding voice and sharp, piercing eyes. The Pope relished his words of wisdom and always felt refreshed any time they had a chat or Bible study.

Father Giovanni breezed into the office and his enormous voice resonated soundly throughout the room. He strolled purposefully towards the Pope and knelt on one knee, the Pope stretched out his right hand and Father Giovanni kissed him. As his lips touched the Pope's hand, his head seemed to explode into a million fragments. The vision he saw was very frightening and his brow knitted as if he was in agony.

Flashes of lightning ripped through the dark night and Father Giovanni's hands trembled as he saw a man tied to a stake. Along with the condemned man on the stake were three others in filthy garments, their gaunt faces had despair written all over them. They were crying and an angry mob surrounded them; the crowd were waving their hands violently, their voices like the howling of the host of hell.

The visions came in the form of flashes and then there was a sharp intake of breath.

The Pope looked at his preacher and knew something was not right.

Everyone at the Curia knew about Father Giovanni's visions, and that they were always accurate and very detailed - that was why the Pope had stuck to/with? him for the past ten years of his Papacy.

Father Giovanni stood up and sat in front of Pope Nathaniel III, his expression was cool and calm. He was also famous for his ability to mask his emotions well, but the Holy Father knew without an iota of doubt that Father Giovanni had seen something scary. He could see his eyelids flicker briefly and for the kind of man he was, that was very revealing indeed.

Father Giovanni fixed his eyes on the Pope, it was as if what he was about to say was painful but he said it anyway, 'I saw Your Holiness on the stake,' there was a minute's silence, and then he turned away, his face the epitome of sorrow. 'It was you Holy Father. It was you!' he repeated in a hoarse whisper.

The Pope merely smiled and brushed it aside, 'that means that I might die soon: everyone has to die someday, Giovanni.'

He nodded and seemed to be considering what he was about to say,

'You can't see Aaron Cohen, Your Holiness; if you set eyes on him today you will die, and your bones will be begin to rot. He is carrying the curse of Jacques De Molay. You are spiritually connected to Pope Clement V, but I don't know how that is.'

'But it can't be,' the Pope exclaimed and was actually hit by the revelation, 'I'm Irish, I know my mother is French and I have cousins, relatives...' and he was gesticulating 'in France but how can they possibly link me to Pope Clement V? That is not possible, absolutely impossible.'

Father Giovanni kept quiet, this was one vision he wished he had concealed well and not revealed, but he had to say it all, 'Aaron must never set foot here again,

Your Holiness. He is like the angel of death that killed the first born of the Egyptians - heads will roll if he comes back here, many people will die...' he paused to let that sink in, then he added miserably, 'people like me, Your Holiness.'

Pope Nathaniel III stared into space.

Had his mother lied about his real father? How could he find out the truth? Whom could he send to unearth the secret of his parentage?

He bowed his head in deep thought, sickened by the enormity of the problems facing him. His papacy had been relatively peaceful. He spent the first two years travelling all over the world, and he heard from his staff that he had been nicknamed 'The Smiling Pope'. That name simply stuck like glue. He remembered fondly an orphanage he went to in Pennsylvania in the United States; a beautiful young black girl asked him why people called him Pope Smiley III. He'd laughed out loud, wiping tears from his eyes and patted the girl gently on the back, telling her kindly, 'Because I love to smile,' the girl had turned away from him obviously satisfied with the answer.

Pope Nathaniel sighed deeply; most of the time he was either frowning or desperately sad.

He turned his attention back to the only man allowed to preach to him. 'What do you think I should do?'

'Nothing, Your Eminence. What good could any revelation do? It would only exacerbate resentment from the descendants of the Knights Templar and those who are sympathetic to them.'

'I should do nothing,' the Pope repeated quietly, turning his face away to look at the decade old grandmother clock on the wall. His painting in full regalia as the head of the Church adorned the wall, and in the painting he was smiling - it was a very sincere and open smile.

It was the smile of a man ready to change the course of history by fighting to end wars in all nations on earth. A man of peace, and yet at the same time, the devil had made his home his domain. But if I don't find out now, what if someone else did? Then the whole world would be calling the head of the World Church a mere liar - the Lying Smiling Pope?' Pope Nathaniel thought miserably.

'I want you to commission someone we can trust, someone outside the Church who could find out who my real father is. It is easy, isn't it?'

Father Giovanni Rossini nodded and moved towards the Pope, bending on one knee to kiss his ring. He left the room a very troubled man.

25

Bellevue Hospital, New York, Aug 12

Kate slept on her side while Evelyn watched her keenly, worry lines appearing on her otherwise smooth face. She leaned back in the chair and glanced impatiently at her wristwatch; it was quarter past two, and her husband was late, which was very unlike him. Michael was never late. She rested her head on the chair and dozed off. A little while later, someone tapped her lightly on the shoulder. She jumped up, startled, and smiled when she realised that it was Keith.

'Hello Keith, this is a pleasant surprise!' Evelyn exclaimed looking up at him.

He seemed edgy; there was something tense and different about him. In fact, Lucifer currently inhabited Keith Morgan's body. He had come to take charge of the mission. He couldn't leave Tyrus alone to his devises for long. If he left things to his son, failure would be a common feature in his kimgdom.

'Lola asked me to pick you up,' he drawled, his eyes on the sleeping form of Kate; 'I heard she was being discharged today. Do you want me to hang around and wait for her too?'

'That would be nice of you, but don't you have a meeting or two to attend today?' she struggled for the words wringing her hands. She was uneasy and didn't quite know why.

'Nope, I've cancelled all my meetings. Besides, I don't do meetings on Sundays any more, Lola's seen to that. On the Sabbath day, I rest,' he said smoothly with a boyish grin exposing snow-white teeth. Evelyn's heart lurched painfully: something was definitely wrong.

Keith had been her husband's best friend since high school and that made her and his wife, Lola, great friends.

When Michael disappeared for fifteen months, seven years earlier, he was her rock, and they saw her through the most difficult time in her life. All the same, she wasn't comfortable.

'Evelyn,' he called her name softly and she turned to look at him.'

I have a surprise for you at home.'

She chuckled and asked, 'What might that be?'

'Caroline had been discharged and Michael is with her as we speak.' Lucifer held her gaze for a few seconds, and those seconds were excruciating for her as she tore her eyes away panting. There was something odd and evil behind the steely blue eyes but it seemed to soften when he smiled.

'And she looks absolutely gorgeous,' he added easily, tapping his left foot on the hospital floor.

Evelyn couldn't believe her ears, she had been with her daughter the previous day, and the doctors treating her were a little concerned about her progress. The new consultant assigned to her case hinted that her progress was slow and that she was not responding well to the latest medication.

'How could that be?' she whispered, searching the eyes of her husband's friend and what she saw chilled her to the bone. She shuddered and almost froze with fright. Evelyn was hundred percent sure that Keith was dead, or a walking dead man. Something else had taken possession of his body; a dark, sinister spirit. She couldn't wait to get out of the hospital with Kate.

At that exact moment, Kate mumbled some incoherent words and opened her eyes. Evelyn turned to her and shielded her from seeing Lucifer.

He wanted to say something but a beautiful nurse moved towards Kate's bed and drew the curtain, cutting out Lucifer.

Initially, the hospital had placed Kate in quarantine but when her leg stopped producing puss, they transferred her to the general ward and now they were ready to go home.

Evelyn had made up her mind there and then; they would not set foot in Keith's apartment. It would not be safe.

She threw a quick glance in his direction.

'Nurse, we're in trouble,' Evelyn whispered desperately to the nurse who made a show of checking Kate's legs.

'I know,' the nurse answered looking over her shoulder, 'your husband is right outside the hospital; we knew about the impostor. What we're going to do is simple; I'll distract that gentleman for a while, and that should give you a window of about five minutes to leave the hospital. I wish you good luck, Ma'am.'

Then she left them, and there was silence.

'Kate, we have to go now.'

'Was Tyrus here? I dreamt of him,' Kate asked weakly.

She was a little disoriented, but otherwise she had regained most of her energy and appetite.

'No, he's not here, but we have to hurry,'

Evelyn lied.

There was no way she could explain it to her, all she knew was that the man who came in as Keith was a demon. She now realised that the earlier they leave New York, the better for everyone.

Kate sat on the bed while Evelyn hurriedly slid her feet into the flat shoes she'd brought for her.

They left the ward through the front entrance. Kate would have preferred a wheelchair. She had come to have a sort of telepathic relationship with Evelyn, she knew what went on in her head, and she seemed tensed than ever.

They went through reception on level one, the trauma centre, and a young doctor who had tended to Kate while she was in intensive care saw her and came over.

'Hey, Miss Summers, have you been discharged?'

Kate nodded with a huge grin on her face. She liked the doctor. He had been so nice to her when she was in intensive care.

'Yeah, and she has a plane to catch.' There was a slight edge to Evelyn's voice. The doctor was delaying them.

'Okay, see you around,' he chuckled and added, 'I hope not, I guess.'

And he extended his hand for a shake. Kate shook it and felt a chill go through her spine. She snatched her hand away.

He stared at her retreating back with a contemptuous look on his face.

'I don't like that doctor. He could be one of Tyrus's boys,' Evelyn murmured under her breath as they entered the lift. They got to the ground floor and walked towards the entrance of the hospital but they didn't get far. Someone grabbed Evelyn's arm and she screamed out in pain, lashing out viciously.

Two men materialised from nowhere sandwiching Kate and Evelyn between them, they poked guns to their ribs, and they kept quiet, following meekly like lambs to the slaughter.

Meanwhile, Michael waited for over two hours in the hospital car park, checking his wristwatch constantly. He dialled Evelyn's number several times but, surprisingly, she had switched it off. Annoyed, he banged his fist on the steering wheel.

He was sure the nurse he'd hired should have been able to contact them, and if things had gone according to plan, they should have been with him. He stared at his watch again and gritted his teeth. We ought to have been on our way to the airport by now, Michael thought angrily.

He would love nothing better than to take Kate back to England, her mother had been on his back and he didn't know what to say to convince her that her daughter was fine. She had threatened to have MI5 on him if she didn't show up in the next twenty-four hours. He'd laughed it off as ludicrous; MI5 had better things to do than chase a girl who had gone on vacation.

'Dad, everything will be all right, you'll see,' Caroline said gently, breaking into his thoughts. Her golden locks fell on her pale face and her blue eyes were shining.

Michael looked at her and composed himself.

His daughter shouldn't see him falling apart, not when she had just been miraculously healed. The doctors were amazed at her rapid progress. They told him to take her back in a week's time to access her stability, but he was more worried about his friend Keith than his daughter; his friend looked and acted like a stranger.

Keith hadn't been himself lately and he seemed to be interested in Kate's welfare, which was rather unexpected because Michael thought Keith hadn't been too keen on the girl staying in his house. Now his wife had failed to respond to his calls.

'What can I do?' He didn't know that he'd spoken aloud.

'Let's go back to London, Dad.'

He threw a sideways glance at his daughter and pondered on her words: England. He would not leave his wife and Kate, but how could he explain that to Caroline? She would not understand. Gently, he pulled a lock of hair away from her eyes as waves of emotion rushed through him. He tried to explain as best as he could.

'Honey, we need to see your mom before we go; we're going home together.'

'What about Lola, is she coming home with us?' she asked.

He rubbed his eyes vigorously with his left hand before replying.

'She lives here with her family: she can't come with us.'

'She told me she would never leave me.'

'She can't come with us,' he tried to find the right words, 'but I'm sure we could arrange a visit soon.'

She seemed to consider that and then flashed him her brightest smile.

Michael started the engine and drove out of the hospital's car park. He had no choice other than to wait for Evelyn and Kate at the Sheraton Hotel, where they had spent two nights. At least he was relieved that he had taken Kate's bags from Keith's apartment, so there was no need for him to go back to the house. Michael's brow furrowed as he thought of Keith. He made up his mind to call him once he got to his hotel room.

He headed for midtown Manhattan, his mind contemplating his decision to leave the hospital, maybe I should have waited longer, but the thought of contacting the lady he'd hired to impersonate a nurse filled him with dread. He knew what he'd done was a criminal offence, but he was desperate to take Kate home to her mother.

He sighed as he changed the gear of the car. After driving for about ten minutes, he noticed an Audi on his tail and remembered seeing the car at the hospital. What struck him was the driver of car; he looked so much like Keith, but he wasn't. Michael kept checking his rear view mirror; the car was still behind them, although there were now two cars between them. When the other cars cruised past, the Audi car loomed into view and Michael knew he had to act fast.

He gunned the Mercedes-Benz through Madison Avenue and, to his surprise; the traffic was light at that time of the day.

As Michael raced on with the Audi in hot pursuit, his eyes strayed away from the road for a brief moment to stare at the shops. He had promised to take Evelyn shopping, and he wondered if they could still make it before they left for London.

He was furious with rage when he saw the Audi gaining ground behind him. In a split second, he made the decision to shake the Audi off his tail finally. He gritted his teeth as his foot slammed on the brake. The next thing Michael heard was a deafening noise as his car somersaulted three times and landed back on its wheels. He cast a quick glance at Caroline; she was staring straight ahead with a calm expression on her face.

As expected, a line of cars rammed into each other, but he hadn't thought it would be as bad as that. Cars were strewn all over the road; they had rammed into each other with such ferocity that three of the cars had exploded on impact, some had their horns blaring. But the Audi was nowhere to be found, which was a startling revelation to Michael.

He looked on in incredulity as he walked away from the mangled cars. His daughter was still sitting calmly, a serene expression on her face. He moved to the other side of the car and tried opening the door but he couldn't. His hand passed through the door handle and came out at the other side.

Michael was beside himself with worry. He watched with trepidation as police cars started pulling up. An officer dashed out of a patrol car and surveyed the scene with a grim expression on his face.

The officer walked with brisk strides towards Caroline, yanked the car door open with such brute force that Michael jumped with fright. Michael watched with fascination as the officer gently carried Caroline away from the wreckage and she began to whimper. Michael didn't understand what was happening to him; he wanted to hold his daughter but couldn't. He was baffled as he looked around, but nobody noticed he was even standing there. He went after the officer carrying Caroline, and then he heard a whooshing sound. He was surprised to see a woman standing closely beside him. She had a funny accent and flaming red hair.

'You fool, you caused the accident,' she accused him with blazing eyes.

He stared at her and saw paper white face, her feet did not touch the ground: she was floating. She must be a ghost, Michael thought moving back in horror.

'Who are you? And why do you think I caused the accident?' he asked furiously, his pent up frustration and anger directed at her.

'You shouldn't have stopped the car when you were doing a hundred and twenty miles per hour in such a busy street!' she snarled, her dead eyes mocking him, 'your braking the car abruptly was suicidal. Now you'll never walk her up the aisle to meet her husband,' and she was gone, leaving a trail of white light in her wake.

Fear swept through Michael as he turned his attention back to the car, his body was still pinned under the steering wheel with both legs broken. He watched with a sinking feeling at the pit of his stomach as paramedics and fire fighters battled to remove him from the car.

Michael stared at his body; there was no way he could have survived the accident. He gritted his teeth and accepted his fate: he was already dead.

'No!' he screamed as he felt a pulling force sucking him into a bright white light. He felt his body move with incredible speed, suspended in space, but the ashen face of his wife blotted out any feeling of peace and tranquillity he might have felt. His frantic thoughts ended his flight and he landed back on the ground with a loud thud.

'What was that all about, huh?' he shouted to one in particular, he didn't expect anyone to answer him, and there was no reply. He beat the air in fury and waited for the worst.

Maybe he was really going to hell... but he had been a very nice guy, he reasoned; he'd only cheated on his wife once and had asked for her forgiveness, which she grudgingly gave.

He went to church every now and then; he was what his mates would call a 'nice enough bloke with a good head on his shoulder.'

He died a foolish death. He shouldn't have stepped on the break at top speed. He waited patiently, staring at the activity going on around him and an overwhelming feeling of sorrow washed over him. He would never be able to hold his wife ever again, and the thought of what was coming filled him with dread.

He thought of his family; how would they survive without him? This was not the right time for him to die - he still had so many things to do.

Finally, the fire fighters removed his body from the wreckage of the Mercedes. He watched them working swiftly as they put his corpse in a body bag. Behind him, he heard an eerie sound and the hairs at the nape of his neck stood on end. A powerful force slammed into him and he staggered back, his stomach turning to knots at the horrible sound.

Michael turned in the direction of the sound expecting to see the devil in all his regalia, but the sight that met him turned the remaining blood in his body to ice. There were more than a thousand smelly black gigantic creatures. They closely resembled bats with their massive, monstrous wings. Transfixed to the spot, he watched them swooping down and descending on the piles of cars strewn all over the street.

The creatures screeched as they sniffed around, moving with such incredible speed that in a blink of an eye they had snatched five men and three women from some of the wrecked cars. The powerful creatures pounced on Michael, and he flung them off and took three steps back, but they kept approaching. One of them pushed its long razor sharp teeth into towards his face. Michael swallowed hard and stood perfectly still as they sniffed him. When their feet touched the ground, they metamorphosed into ogres with little semblance to human beings. They had big heads, long arms, and wide, hairy chests. They reminded him of

Neanderthals only they were more grotesque in stature.

Michael fixed his gaze on their yellow eyes and dripping noses. Incredibly, every ounce of fear he'd felt had fled. He faced them, his hatred protecting him like a Roman shield. They howled, pounding their hairy chests. He braced himself for the onslaught of the agents of the abyss. It came as a disappointment to discover what would become of his eternal soul; he had thought he was a nice guy.

Maybe he'd been wrong.

26

Evelyn's head ached incessantly but she endured the pain. Her thoughts were on her husband and daughter, Keith had hinted that the hospital discharged Caroline, but before they'd left their hotel room that morning, Michael had said nothing of the sort, maybe he wanted it to be a surprise. She consoled herself with the thought.

She squeezed her eyes shut as images of happier times invaded her mind. They had sort of grown apart after the crazy and terrible period in their marriage when he had disappeared of his own volition and gone to Nigeria to assist the military dictator in building nuclear weapons. Those were dark days and she wanted those memories blotted out of her mind forever, but her stubborn mind strayed on and she remembered when he was released. Their daughter suffered a nervous breakdown and had been in a New York psychiatric hospital ever since. What a blatant waste of childhood. Six years of her young life spent with strangers. A single tear rolled down her cheek.

The car stopped abruptly and Evelyn lifted her head, it was already dark and the outline of a very tall building loomed large, probably a hotel, she thought with a sinking heart. She heard cars whizzing past and the urge to scream was strong, but she knew it would not be wise.

The men who'd kidnapped them were extremely courteous and she began to wonder what they really wanted from them, they did not look like criminals.

'Sorry Ma'am, but we have to blindfold you, please cooperate,' one of the men said.

He was a tall, good-looking black man; he looked too clean and sleek to be a kidnapper. Evelyn threw a quick glance at Kate with a smirk on her face and she grinned back.

Evelyn was pleased at her recovery; her face had a new glow and she was more radiant, although her sunken eyes still revealed the trauma she had gone through. Their high spirits were surprising considering that they'd left the hospital with guns poked into their sides by stern faced men.

The men blindfolded them each man took them by the hand. After walking for about ten minutes Evelyn heard the sound of an organ playing, were they in a church? She thought and waited anxiously as their captors guided them down some stairs.

'Careful please, we'll be going down some steps: please do be careful.' They heard the silky voice of the good-looking black man; he spoke easily, as if he were talking to a customer.

'Thank you,' Kate said, and Evelyn detected some excitement in her voice; this was like an exciting adventure, but all the same, she was beginning to worry. Evelyn wished she could speak to her husband, she missed him terribly, 'After all this is over darling, I'm going to be the best wife to you, I promise,' she murmured under her breath.

They kept going down the steps and Evelyn was glad for the word of caution they'd heard earlier because she almost tripped.

The man holding her hand held her firmly to his side, a wave of sexual awareness sluiced through her body and she felt ashamed of herself. Strange men were leading her inside a building and her body was craving intimacy.

She clamped down on her desire and almost stumbled again, this time the man's hand mistakenly brushed her breast, and she gasped.

'I'm sorry,' he apologised.

'That's okay,' she whispered, her mind filled with visions of her husband's strong arms. She wished he would just appear and save them, but that kind of rescue only happened in films.

They came to a landing, one of the men pressed a doorbell, and, within seconds, someone opened the door and ushered them into the basement.

When they were safely inside, they took their blindfolds off and the first person Evelyn saw was Lola, Keith's wife.

She was shocked to say the least, and they embraced each other.

Evelyn moved back, surprised when she saw tears in Lola's eyes.

'What's happening? Who are these guys?'

'They're my friends,' Lola answered and beckoned to the men who'd kidnapped them, 'this is Logan and Jonas.'

'Can someone explain what's going on?' Kate asked in a loud voice and every one turned to her, she had made herself comfortable by sitting on the rich blue sofa.

Logan turned to her and said, 'We have reason to believe that Mrs Morgan's husband is possessed by the devil. There could be terrible consequences if nothing is done.'

There was a brief silence before Kate exclaimed, 'That's ludicrous. How do you guys know about him in the first place?'

'I did some business with him a couple of times... it's hard to explain, but in time you'll understand,' Logan said. He was beside her in a second.

Jonas handed back Evelyn's phone. She switched it on straight away, and immediately a call came through.

'Hello,' she said but there was no response for a couple of seconds. Then she heard her daughter's voice.

'Love, are you all right? Where are you, where is your dad?' her voice shook as she spoke; it was as if she'd had a premonition.

'I'm in the hospital with dad, please come and get me,' Caroline said slowly, her voice was faint. Before she had a chance to explain someone else came on the line and the colour drained from Evelyn's face as she listened, after a while she mumbled in a horror-filled voice, 'Thank you Officer, I'll be there.' Lola moved closer and held her by the shoulder. Evelyn turned to her and collapsed into her arms and a guttural, unearthly sound escaped from her mouth.

'Michael's dead,' she struggled to breath, 'there was an accident and he died, he died just like that. Can you imagine that?'

There was total silence in the room.

Kate cupped her face in her hands and wept quietly, 'I'm so sorry,' she said in a broken voice. She felt responsible for Michael's death; if she had not gone to

Central Park that fateful morning, none of this would have happened.

Evelyn was still reeling from the news but she managed to say, 'I guess I just have to get back to the hospital.' Kate also stood up, but Evelyn disagreed with a vehement shake of her head.

'No Kate, you stay here with Logan, I'll go with Lola and Jonas.'

Kate looked scared but Logan reassured her by holding her hand protectively. Lola and Jonas left the basement with Evelyn in tow, her head bowed. Incredibly, she seemed calm. After they had gone, Logan stood up and walked into the mini kitchen. Zach and Darren could not look Kate in the eye; they were guilt ridden.

Logan came back carrying a tray, he pulled up a table beside the sofa she was sitting on and set the tray on it.

She shook her head and said in a whisper, 'I'm not hungry.'

'Please eat something, you look tired and worn out.' Logan persisted, surprised at his concern for the girl.

She looked at him and Logan hated the look in her cold, hard eyes, 'You know nothing about me, why should you care?' she sneered, but regretted it almost at once; they were all just trying to be nice but she was not in the mood to be civil, she felt terrible.

'We know an awful lot about you, Kate,' Darren said speaking for the first time, 'they had to forcefully take you away from there at that point because of Tyrus or, as the case may be, Keith Morgan.'

'How, and what, do you know about him?' she asked curtly.

Darren laughed and said with a sad glint in his eye, 'Tyrus has taken over the body of Keith Morgan. He would've killed Evelyn by now if he had been successful. Lola's twin girls are presumably dead, so is Michael, but he needed you because of Aaron.'

A look of terror appeared on her face; it was more than she had bargained for. A knot of fear and dread tightened her heart, squeezing it until she felt she could no longer breathe, what is happening to me? She thought sadly.

'What are we going to do now?' Kate asked, scanning the faces of the men in the room. She felt compelled to assume they were together.

'We have to wait for Evelyn to come back. But at the end of the day, we might have to go to Ethiopia. That's where the story ends, I think.' Logan said.

'Is Aaron still in Ethiopia?'

Darren nodded.

This is getting more bizarre as the minutes go by, Kate thought. Loudly she asked, 'But how did you guys know about him?'

There was a deep sigh from Logan before he replied, 'Aaron's uncle hired me to tail him - report anything he might be doing. Joshua Cohen is one of the best criminal lawyers we have in this country and I know he has many enemies...' he paused for a minute as if trying to control the flow of his thoughts, his eyes on his well-manicured nails, 'so I've been following Aaron ever since. I got back from Ethiopia a few days ago thinking I would be able to give Joshua Cohen an account of my progress, but unfortunately he almost died before I got here, so I haven't had the chance to have a chat with him.'

She did not comment on what Logan said, but there was a look of relief on her face. She was really going to see Aaron. How would he react when he saw her? After all she had gone through in New York? It would be a welcome relief to be in Aaron's arms, but a feeling of utter sadness engulfed her when she remembered Evelyn.

Michael had been a good friend to her and news of his death would come as a shock to her parents. She stared into space as fear ravaged her body and soul.

27

Michael found himself in front of a mighty gate, when he turned to look back; there were millions of souls already queuing behind him. He scrutinised everything around him, expecting to catch a glimpse of the bat monsters but they had been an illusion. He tried to recall how he got to where he was, but failed.

He clenched and unclenched his fists wondering if this was truly the end. There is life after death after all. He was trying to rationalise the futility of life when a deafening sound disoriented him; it was as if billions of trumpets were playing. The great pearl gate swung open with such brute force that every soul gasped out in fear.

Michael's eyes were riveted to the celestial beauty and the innumerable precious stones used to decorate the gate. To Michael's untrained eye, the gate was made of pure diamond, and it gleamed in the bright morning sun. He gazed upwards and realised that it wasn't the sun that was shining, and the spectacle literally astounded him. Millions of angels filled the air in their white robes, snow-white hair, glowing swords, and trumpets in their hands. It was a fascinating sight.

Michael heard murmuring behind him, but he dared not look back. He was about to discover his fate, but he did something foolish; he pulled his sleeve up and went to look at his Rolex watch, but it was gone. A smirk graced his face, what would I need a wristwatch for in his present predicament? He saw a little girl that reminded him of Caroline; she flew down and touched his shoulder. A miracle occurred; he found himself flying with her.

'Bring him back,' shouted a man, his voice was guttural and harsh. The girl laughed and dived in the direction of the voice. The man left Michael to his own devices; he began to study his surroundings.

The sight that appeared before him was indescribable. It was different from anything he had ever seen in his entire life; there were skyscrapers built with solid gold and the city sprawled as far as the eye could see. He stared at what looked like roads, also paved with gold, while different kinds of precious stones adorned the twelve gates of the city and he could hear laughter and joyous voices. It was surreal, nothing he had ever imagined could have compared to it. He would have loved to capture the beauty of the eternal city and take it home to his family. It was simply awesome.

Michael swallowed hard, lost for words at the display of such breath-taking splendour at every angle he turned. He noticed a hill that seemed to descend from the clouds, it was like an extension of the city, and, at the same time, it was like a dome suspended in space. When he looked closer, it was a snow caped mountain with majestic buildings round it.

He shook his head in confusion, baffled by the city, the mountains, and the angels. He heard a sonorous voice singing and, strangely, he knew the words of the song; it was the Hallelujah chorus. Joy filled his heart as he flew, flapping the wings that had grown on his back.

The little winged creature came back and pulled him by the hand laughing,

'You have to go back, or you will be late for the roll call. But I promise to see you soon, and I'll find your mansion.' She flew away, giggling and amused by the look on his face.

Michael stood back in line, waiting for his judgement. He tried to think of something else besides the rapid beating of his heart. Suddenly, there were eruptions of clapping and the blasting of trumpets. Instead of the sound to be annoying he didn't like trumpets anyway, it was rather melodious, joyous, and at the same time hilarious.

He burst into laughter with tears streaming down his face. His happiness seemed to be infectious and millions of the souls queuing behind him joined in. Their merriment built in momentum and turned into thunderous laughter. However, amidst it all he heard his name clearly,

'Michael Crest-Howard.'

'Present!' he said with his hands lifted high, and he flew into a big cubicle beside the massive gate.

There was a very handsome man in the cubicle like structure sitting on a golden throne. In front of him were a gigantic scroll and a big screen, bigger than the ones he had seen in picture theatres. The big screen adorned the gold plated wall behind the man, the floor where the man sat was made of chalcedony, - it was transparent and greyish blue in colour.

Michael inched closer to the man and his heart almost popped out of his chest. When he stepped inside and saw the reflection of his feet on the floor, his eyes widened in surprise. He faced the man and waited.

'Hello, Michael,' the man on the golden throne greeted him in flawless English, and Michael couldn't take his eyes off his well-carved face. It was as if it was made of light; the glow radiating from the man's face was so strong that Michael had to look away. After a while, Michael summoned enough courage to fix his gaze back at the man.

'My name is Emmanuel,' the man was saying and at the same time flipping through the scrolls on his enormous diamond table.

Michael stood like a teenager with his hands behind him, his face flushed and expectant. There was a booming sound as his eyes travelled to the screen, and he saw the image of his mother. She was crying, and then he saw his wife with two black men, they were talking in hushed tones and, at that instant, she lifted her head and seemed to look right through him. Her eyes were red and swollen with tears; they were at the Bellevue hospital's morgue to identify him. The pictures changed to when he was born, as he grew up, all the accidents he had had, his first sexual encounter.

Everything was detailed; his first kiss, the first time he stole from the corner shop. He shuddered with fear; would he be thrown into hell or heaven? What kind of fate awaited his eternal soul? He stood there watching his life history play out. The screen showed when he became a Christian, his struggles with pornography, gambling and lying, and then he grew and became a better man, husband, and father.

'Now, what have you got to say for yourself, Mr. Michael Crest-Howard?'

Michael stared at the man Emmanuel and replied, 'I have nothing to say, Your Honour.' He didn't know what else to say.

'Then based on all the facts I have here, I can now pass my judgment.'

Michael's knees began to wobble as he waited.

The seconds turned to minutes and in Michael's befuddled mind, he was heading to hell.

The man Emmanuel smiled, and rapturous ovation erupted in the vast space.

'Welcome to the joy of your Lord!' He said

Michael's heart surged with joy, as eternity appeared before him. He felt movement behind him as his clothes changed and he transformed into his glorious body.

Ever so gently, he more or less floated away from the man Emmanuel, whose kind expression welcomed him into eternity. Michael flew towards the city of gold and he remembered his new friend. She spotted her amidst a group of angels, and she smiled when she saw him.

'Come,' she said sweetly, her voice rich with laughter, 'I'll take you to your house.'

'Thanks,' Michael said and they flew towards the sun, flapping their wings joyously.

28

Buhudle, Somalia, Aug 13

Fatima trudged along, weary and thirsty, but she persevered and kept on moving. She had barely slept a wink in three days and the incessant, rapid bursts of gunfire between warring factions and Islamic militias had kept her awake. She was afraid to close her eyes and the lack of sleep was beginning to tell on her body. Hunger was now a familiar companion, but she would gladly go without food for weeks just to seal her freedom.

She sensed without an iota of doubt that she was getting closer to the semi autonomous border town of Buhudle.

Fatima opened the bag in her hand, took out the big bottle of water, and drank the last drop. She had passed several houses, or at least what had resembled houses, riddled with bullet holes, she'd heard voices but she dared not show her face for fear of being captured again.

She knew that Mukta would be livid with rage when he found out that she had escaped, and very soon his thugs would be combing the surrounding forest, but she had mastered the art of survival skillfully. She was positive that no one would be able to capture her again; she would rather choose death.

A feeling of total despair engulfed her entire being; she still had a lot to do before she got to America and she had wisely decided to live one day at a time, but at times, the overwhelming ill luck that had been dogging her steps since she'd left home a few days earlier weighed her down. It would be very easy to give up and wait, but if she did then she might as well go back to Mukta.

At the thought of his name, she began to shiver uncontrollably.

Fatima pulled herself together and focused her attention on her escape.

The morning sun shone brightly and she decided to rest under the shade of a tree for a while.

Sitting down on the ground, she scrutinized her surroundings. Satisfied that she was alone, she relaxed, staring into space, her vision blurred as exhaustion crippled her tired frame. In a matter of minutes, she slipped into a troubled sleep.

Half an hour later, she felt a hand on her shoulder and woke with a start, jumping to her feet in fright.

But it was a harmless boy, he was around ten and he was looking at her with a smile on his brown face. The boy laughed and said to someone in the thick bush, 'Papa, she is awake.'

Fatima dusted her skimpy skirt and ran her hands through her hair, trying to appear decent and clean. She saw a family of three staring at her and she flinched under their piercing gaze.

She forced a smile on her sleepy face, but felt very uncomfortable.

They took in her dirty appearance and the tall, thin man looked at her and asked in a high-pitched voice, 'Where are you going to, my daughter?'

She did not answer; what if they were some of the numerous militants scattered all over Somalia? The man noticed her hesitation and said in a more reassuring voice, 'We are crossing the border into Ethiopia and my son wanted to urinate; when he saw you he called us. Sorry for intruding on your privacy.'

'Not at all,' she replied hastily, 'I came from America to see my mom...' she paused wondering if she'd said too much, but there was something about the man and she continued, 'I was caught up in the fighting, I'm trying to get across the border and see if I can get to Ethiopia.'

'Aren't you Mukta's woman?' the man's wife asked shrewdly as she coldly appraised her short skirt.

'Keep quiet, woman!' the man snapped angrily.

Fatima knew trouble when she saw it, and she had got too far to involve herself in a fighting match with a jealous wife.

She picked up her carrier bag and faced the forest, but the man called her back, 'Let us help you: we all know how bad Mukta is. I'm sure you were kept against your will. By the way, my name is Mustapha.'

Fatima was scared; they had discovered her real identity, and her cover had been blown, if she walked the remaining miles to Ethiopia, one of Mukta's men could spot her.

Looking at it critically, in a way she had nothing to lose; she would take the man's offer, and just keep quiet, that way she would be able to save herself a whole lot of trouble.

'Thank you Sir, I'm so grateful for your help,' and she lowered her eyes.

The woman disappeared and came back with a long black dress, she tossed it at Fatima, and she caught it.

'Cover your nakedness with it,' she hissed and walked away, her hips swaying in the tight wrapper around her waist.

'Thank you,' Fatima said, but the woman didn't bother to answer.

The dress was bigger than her size ten figure, but she was pleased with it: no one would be able to recognise her now.

She tagged along and the boy kept looking back smiling, Fatima loved his bright, wide eyes. They walked along the footpath in silence and came to a dusty road, and then she saw their truck. She climbed into the back of the truck with the boy. Then she saw him, and froze.

It was Rahal, Mukta's right hand boy. Fatima sat back stiffly and waited as Rahal's van pulled up beside their truck.

She overheard their conversation faintly. Rahal was cursing Mustapha but the old man stuck to his guns - it seemed Rahal wanted to seize their truck forcibly. She heaved a deep sigh of relief when she heard the sound of Rahal's van revving loudly, and later become a faint echo.

She rubbed her dirty hands over her face, but something made her turn and she looked out again. Rahal was still there, standing beside his van by the road some distance away, glaring at their truck. Their eyes locked for a brief second and he opened the van's door and jumped into the driver seat. Fatima bent down holding her head in her shaky hands.

'Are you all right, America?' the boy asked, his huge, innocent eyes blind to the atrocities committed around him, and she wondered when he would be drafted to join in the killing spree, the raping and murder.

She gritted her teeth and felt so helpless. The boy had called her America and it stunned her. It was a defining moment for her as she turned to him and managed a smile.

'Why did you call me America?' she asked pushing her sad thoughts aside for a while.

'You speak like them, in the films,' he replied and wanted to say something, but Fatima saw him hesitate.

'Tell me what's on your mind,' she urged him gently.

Shyly, he turned his face away. The truck hit a pothole on the dusty road, and suddenly he was in her arms. Her heart went out to him as he asked, his parched lips barely moving, 'Will you take me to America, please?'

Fatima had never bonded with a stranger the way she had with the boy, but she knew it was an impossible task. She was still trying to frame her response when a mortar shell hit their truck. The only thought in her mind was the boy she was holding in her arms, before everything went blank.

29

Aaron stared at the breath-taking landscape and was lost for words. He lifted his face towards the sun, basking in its beauty as the wind blew with a buzzing sound. He closed his eyes, his face shining with delight, and he felt ten feet taller.

Ten minutes later, he strolled round the treasury and the church, studying the fortress-like walls. A slow grin spread to his face as he let his imagination run wild; he imagined the wall's fortitude in standing against the oppressors that had raided the country countless times, but over the centuries, the walls stood firm, and so had the Ark.

With his arms akimbo, he glanced in the direction of the lone heavily armed guard in his bright red jacket, tie and black slacks with black shoes.

The guard flashed him a bright smile and Aaron returned it with a wave.

'What a great country,' he muttered quietly.

He strolled near the ruins of the fourth century St Mary's Church totally lost in thought, the sun bathed the church in its orange glow and he had the most serene feeling. There was a kind of joy bubbling inside him that he couldn't explain - he simply put it down to the spirit of the ancient town.

He had refused to go back to the holy room again. He chuckled at the general belief that the real Ark was underground somewhere in Jerusalem, but he had seen the real Ark. He was not a scientist, nor would he contest contrary beliefs about the whereabouts of the most holy relic in Christian history, but he was humbled and privileged to be part of something so wonderful, yet powerful at the same time.

He thrust his hands inside his jeans pockets, enjoying his early morning walk, a gentle breeze caressed his upturned face, and he inhaled deeply. He strolled on, heading for the field, marvelling at the granite obelisks, which stood roughly between ten and seventy-nine feet. The intricately carved obelisks fascinated him; he wondered about the history behind it all. He touched one of the obelisks, called the 'Obelisk of Axum,' and Abraham had told him it was over 1,700 years old, and at 24 metre-tall (79 foot) and weighing over 160 tonnes, it was a remarkable sight. The obelisk was ornamented with two false doors at the base and featured decorations resembling windows on all sides, the obelisk ends in a semi-circular top part, which used to be enclosed by metal frames.

Aaron moved away from the obelisks, a worried frown crossed his face briefly. Abraham, the caretaker of the Ark, had been feeling rather weak, although he tried so hard to put up a front Aaron knew there was something seriously wrong with him.

Aaron's eyes filled with tears when he remembered Abraham's heartfelt conversation with him. Abraham had spoken to him for a long time concerning his faith in God. It was interesting because, finally, he felt a release, a kind of peace that had eluded him since the death of his brother. He was able to let go, and the faith that began its slow ascent in his heart was rich and beautiful.

He felt sane, light headed and free due to the inspirational words from the mouth of the old, ragged looking monk from a proud town of derelict appearance. But imbedded within was great beauty, a town and a country which stubbornly refused to surrender to invaders and colonialists.

Abraham had finally shown him what he must do, how he must affect the lives of the ordinary citizens of the proud African country, even though he still had Tyrus to contend with, he knew that Tyrus would come looking for him, and he would be ready.

Aaron sank to his knees and kissed the ground, inhaling the fresh scent of earth. He took some sand in his hands and allowed it to trickle through his fingers.

Someone called the name 'Kate' softly. He looked around sharply; there was no one, but he was sure that he heard it.

He stood up and rubbed his hands together, 'Katie,' he whispered her name fondly, it was a name he would love to hear more often, but experience had taught him well. There was no one around but the voice was very near, maybe another trick up Tyrus's sleeves, Aaron thought, then said aloud, 'I've got to hand it to you man, after thousands of years you're still a sneaky little bastard.'

There was total silence as he walked in the direction of the obelisks, he had never felt at peace the way he was feeling now, not even when his parents had been alive. However, his peace was broken again by rapid footsteps behind him. He turned in the direction of the sound and saw Peter running towards him waving his hands.

Aaron swore softly under his breath but regretted it instantly. He looked around to see if anyone had heard him. His mother would have been very cross if she'd been alive to hear him swearing: she hated it with a passion. Peter got close to him, he was panting and beads of perspiration appeared on his forehead.

'Good morning Peter. What's up?' Aaron asked, hating him briefly for invading his privacy.

Peter's eyes were filled with tears, but he wasn't crying. He began to laugh, and Aaron wondered what was so funny.

'Good morning Aaron. My wife gave birth to a bouncing baby boy yesterday night, and I was wondering if you knew where Caleb was? I've called his mobile phone countless times but it's been switched off,' he said still laughing.

'Congratulations,' Aaron said shaking his hand, it was good news, and he couldn't be happier, 'I haven't seen him for two days now - I thought you might have an idea where he is,' Aaron replied a little bit confused.

'Negative,' Peter said quickly averting his gaze, but Aaron caught the look of uncertainty in his eyes.

'Do you think something's wrong?' Aaron asked.

'Not exactly,' Peter answered evasively. 'Would you mind coming to Addis Ababa with me, I would love you to meet my wife,' Peter asked.

'I would love to, but I can't - I'm sorry.'

Peter was hurt and it showed on his face, 'I've already told her about you and she's really keen on meeting you,' and he narrowed his eyes, 'she thought I had a mistress because I'm always up here...' he paused to let that sink in, 'so it's really affecting our relationship, I told her you were a tourist...' He looked embarrassed for saying the words, 'If you don't come with me she might leave me, and I can't raise our kids on my own.'

Aaron grinned and hit him playfully on the shoulder, 'You're a proud man you know. All right, but I'll just go back to the treasury and have a word with Abraham. I'd better tell him where I'm going.'

Peter grunted in protest. They walked to the church and he stood outside the gate while Aaron hurried inside.

He knocked but there was no answer. He pushed the door open and saw Abraham lying on the floor in a pool of blood. Aaron's blood turned cold as he rushed to him, cradling his head in his hands. Abraham's eyelids fluttered and opened, he managed to whisper, 'Don't let them take the Ark; guard it with your life.'

Aaron gritted his teeth as murderous rage built up in him, 'Who did this to you?' he asked, his eyes filling with tears.

Abraham began to cough out blood and he mumbled, 'Peter...the archbishop sent some thugs, but Peter was here looking for you.'

'I'm going to kill that son of a...'Aaron said forcefully, but Abraham shook his head and a single tear fell onto his wrinkled cheeks.

'Don't say foul words in here, my son. Take this,' and Aaron looked at Abraham's upturned hands: it was an ancient map.

'There are some important treasures on this map that you will find in Jerusalem. Although you do not need them now, you might need them later on. Please keep it with you always.'

Aaron took it and Abraham breathed his last. Aaron lay him down gently on the floor and folded the map, his hands shaking as he put it in his breast pocket. He let out a sigh; to think that he had been enjoying himself a few minutes earlier. Now everything had changed.

He stared at Abraham's lifeless face and a shudder went through him.

Now would have been a good time for Caleb to show his brown face, but he's vanished into thin air, Aaron thought, and realised that Peter would still be waiting for him. Like a bolt of lightning, he knew exactly what to do.

He carried Abraham down the long corridor and into the holy room. Whoever killed Abraham would die in a few hours, but he would do whatever he could to save the old man. He couldn't call an ambulance anyway, and if he showed his pale face outside the treasury, it could be the last thing he did; they would definitely pin Abraham's death on him.

As he walked along the corridor he heard loud banging on the door, but he ignored it. He wanted to find out the truth about the Ark now that he knew the practical power of the Ark. He entered the room and closed the door with his leg. He almost dropped Abraham when he saw three old men beside the Ark.

They appeared to be waiting for him.

'Come,' they said in unison, and he moved towards them with the body of Abraham held protectively in his arms.

30

The sky turned black with billows of smoke as explosions rocked through the Pope's seventeenth century summer residence and the adjoining Barberini villa. Guards and cardinals were running about bewildered.

Smoke filled everywhere, Father Giovanni's only thought was to get to the Holy Father in time, but as he raced from the Barberini villa into the inner courtyard of the papal palace, he saw the Roman bust depicting Polyphemus face down. Goose pimples appeared on his body as flashbacks of the dream he'd had the previous night assaulted him.

The Polyphemus must never touch the ground, and now that it had, heaven help them.

He hurried past the fallen bust and saw a guard writhing in pain on the ground. He was burning and his heart wrenching screams were unbearable. Another guard appeared and quickly poured water on him.

Father Giovanni began to cough from the smoke, but he was resolute in his pursuit. Until he set eyes on the Pope, he would not be at peace. He heard the distant echo of the fire engine getting closer and he prayed they got to Castel Gandolfo on time.

He entered the papal palace and could not see a thing. He held a wet handkerchief to his nose to prevent the inhalation of smoke and sank to his knees.

He crawled, but soon came to a sad realisation; he could not go on, and if he didn't go back he would die. He crawled out of the smoke filled entrance. On his way out, he collided with four firefighters coming through in their full protective gear.

He heaved a sigh of relief, salvation at last.

'The Pope is still up in his room,' he said, panting and coughing while pointing upward.

One of the men held him by the hand and pulled him towards the fire engine. Soon the whole place was a beehive of activity.

Three of the four firefighters moved cautiously into the entrance of the building, one of them had an axe in his left hand and his colleagues stayed close to him. They proceeded into the smoke filled room on their knees and, when they entered, a series of explosions rocked the building and they came out briefly.

A few minutes later, they went back in. One of them came out with the body of a Swiss papal guard.

The fire raged on in the private office of the Pope; his secretary lay sprawled on the floor almost dead, holding a piece of paper in his hand. He clutched it desperately as if his life depended on it. He heard faint footsteps, but was too weak to call out.

He was dead before the firefighters could reach him, but they took the piece of paper in his hand and gave to Father Giovanni who awaited news of the Pope anxiously.

Police officers and some of the surviving staff stood in the courtyard, their faces ashen with sorrow. Castel Gandolfo had never seen a fire so brutal - it devoured everything in its path.

After a protracted battle with the fire, there was a brief spell of success. The battle weary fire fighters and paramedics brought more bodies out. The Pope was not among them, but Cardinal Alfonso, the Pope's secretary, was.

Cardinal House, the prefect of the papal household, sat huddled in a corner, staring into space. A firefighter urged him to go in the ambulance to be treated, but he was adamant, he had to see the Pope before he could think of himself.

Father Giovanni folded the paper given to him and kept it under his black robe. He moved towards the

Prefect and neither of them said anything. The silence was later broken by a shrill cry from the Barberini villa, the incident officer of the fire brigade looked at the cardinal and ordered them to evacuate the area, but Father Giovanni refused.

'You can't tell us what to do! We need to see the Holy Father.'

'But you must be alive to see him!' came the reply, and there was a sting of sarcasm in his voice.

The prefect fixed his eyes on the incident officer. After a battle of wits, he relented and pulled Father Giovanni by the hand, 'Let's walk to the road, and watch what they are doing from afar.'

'Excellent idea,' remarked the incident officer as he scuttled off, angry at their obstinacy.

'He's lost about three men. I think that explains his behaviour,' the prefect said slowly.

'But that doesn't give him liberty to be rude.'

The prefect said nothing to that.

His mind was on the people who had lost their lives, and the fact that the fate of the Holy Father was still unknown. He glared at the scene before him and prayed for the deaths to stop. They were still mourning the sudden passing of Cardinal Bacilio and Salvarado. As if that had not been enough, a mysterious fire engulfed the Castel Gandolfo and the adjoining villas. It was a very disturbing scenario.

'Father, what's happening?' the prefect asked sadly, 'What, or who, do you think is responsible for the spate of tragedies in the papacy?'

Father Giovanni glowered at him ready to answer curtly, but thought better of it. Instead, he gawked at the carnage, which had wreaked havoc on the beautiful summer residence of the Pope. He realised that either his visions had been wrong, or he had mistakenly interpreted the visions verbatim.

Maybe there was something he'd missed, but he knew he had ignored nothing. The young Jewish priest had not set foot in Rome yet and they a catalogue of woes had assailed them from all sides. What if Aaron Cohen had seen the Pope? What would have happened? What would have been their fate?

His eyes turned red as the visions played through his mind; what had he overlooked? He knew if he didn't find out soon enemies he had yet to identify would raze the Vatican to the ground.

'Unfortunately I can't answer that question right now. I have to go to the Vatican archives. There is a document I must see,' he said in reply to the prefect's earlier question, and he hurried away.

The prefect was perplexed as he watched Father Giovanni scamper away. He had lots on his mind, but there was no one with a ready answer. His head fell to his chest in anguish.

31

Aaron's eyes never left the three ancient men. They had long facial hair as white as snow, and their eyes were as bright as the sun. Gently, Aaron lowered Abraham to the ground swallowing hard. His legs were becoming too weak and he tensed up for whatever was coming.

The hair at the nape of his neck stood on end and he tried very hard to convince himself that he was not afraid of the extraordinary men in the room.

One thing was clear to him since his peculiar but incredible adventure began; it was important to talk less, and to watch and listen more.

'Remove your garments,' one of the men ordered crisply.

The man's eyes seemed to twinkle, and Aaron nodded his head and obeyed. He removed his shirts and jeans, leaving only his boxer shorts and shoes.

Aaron's gaze rested briefly on Ark; the light radiating from it almost blinded his eyes, so he turned his attention. One of the men handed him a white linen robe and a blue tunic. They ordered him to wear it and he obeyed.

'Could you also remove your shoes, please? This is a holy ground.'

Aaron removed the white trainers, which had been a gift from Kate.

The man gave him a pair of brown sandals and he slipped his feet into them. He liked the way it made his feet feel; they were fluffy and very comfortable.

'For the next three days, wherever you are in the world, by five o'clock in the morning you must take a bath and change your raiment; new ones will be given to you before you finish bathing. This is crucial,' the man who had spoken to Aaron when he entered the room said in a quiet voice.

Aaron nodded and found his eyes on the lifeless body of Abraham. The man held out a long brown stick and at the tip of the stick was a white flower. Aaron looked at the stick and asked in a hoarse voice, 'What should I do with this stick?'

'You must have it with you always.'

Aaron was puzzled: how could he be seen carrying a stick with a flower at the tip? People would think he was a nut case. When the man saw his hesitation, he laughed and his eyes twinkled again, 'Don't worry, it's invisible to the naked eye.'

Aaron nodded, grinning foolishly, 'That's a good thing to hear.'

He collected the stick and it disappeared into his hands.

'Listen to me, the time for playing is over: you have work to do now,' the second man said and there was a stern look on his face, 'you have to take the Ark to the Fourth Presbyterian Church in New York. There it will be safe for a while.'

'How am I supposed to do that? The people of this country would burn me alive.'

The three men laughed and they said, 'No harm will come to a single hair on your head, but you need to leave Ethiopia today, or first thing tomorrow morning, with the Ark, though you will be back.'

Aaron watched the subject of their discussion intently and shuddered at the responsibility.

He had come to Ethiopia to find answers, and it looked like he had found the purpose of coming to Africa. But the Ethiopians would never forgive him; they would hate him forever, especially the Zionists, his own people.

He gritted his teeth and his eyes flashed with fear, Aaron summoned up enough courage and said stiffly, 'Who are you guys? And why was I chosen?'

'We're elders,' the third man said simply, 'we worship the Father, God Almighty. Our names are irrelevant, just call us elders,' he paused to let that sink in then continued softly, his white beard moving, 'you were chosen because it was your birth right.'

'What about Abraham and Caleb?'

'They are going with you.'

'Really?' And he burst into laughter: he was delighted. He felt light headed and happy; Abraham was not dead after all. But the laughter disappeared from his lips when he saw Abraham's body on the ground.

'Have faith,' one of the elders said and handed a bottle of olive oil to him, he took it waiting for further instructions.

'The power of life is in this bottle - it's not ordinary. Open his mouth and pour half of the contents into it. Wait about ten minutes and he will come back to life.'

Aaron took the bottle from the elder's hand and did as he the elder had instructed. He waited, but nothing happened. When he lifted his eyes, the three elders were gone.

He ground his teeth in frustration. *How am I going to take the Ark from these people?* Aaron thought sadly, they have clung onto it for generations, blood has been shed because of it, and it represents their hope against tyranny and a cruel world.

He covered his eyes with his hands and waited. A few minutes later, he was about to leave the room when he realised that the body of Abraham had disappeared.

'Abraham!' he yelled, and he heard shuffling behind him. He turned round and saw him; he was standing with arms akimbo, a huge grin on his dark face.

Aaron rushed towards him and lifted him up in the air, he swung him round the room, and Abraham protested mildly. Setting him back on his feet Aaron could not take his eyes off him.

'You scared me man, you really scared me,' he exclaimed, his eyes dancing with delight.

Abraham touched the part of his chest where the killer stabbed him, but there was no wound. His healing was complete. Aaron touched his face, a pleasant grin lighted up his features, 'I thought I would never see your dear old face again.'

Abraham chuckled and said, beaming with smiles, 'You can't get rid of me that easily, son.'

Abraham sat down on the bare floor.

He looked at Aaron and his heat filled with love, 'the archbishop sent killers to me,' and his voice broke, 'they stabbed me straight in the heart, and do you know what?'

'What?' Aaron asked gently.

'I cursed them. I wondered why they were able to attack me in the first place,' and he smiled, 'it was because you were not around, the power in the Ark has been transferred to you.'

Aaron stared at him puzzled; why would the Archbishop of Ethiopia send killers to the fragile old man who had dedicated his entire life to the spiritual service of his country?

'So if I had been around, I would have snuffed the life out of your attackers?'

'Definitely,' Abraham agreed and rolled his eyes upwards, 'you don't believe me do you?'

'I do, but not entirely,' Aaron hated what he was doing, although he had to be objective: he was afraid of contradicting him but he had to make him see reason, 'I don't think the archbishop would send people to kill you, but somebody else might. Do you think the Order of Lalibela could be behind this? Remember what Caleb told us about a mole already?'

That made Abraham very unhappy. If a member of the Order were against them, they would have to think of a strategy to thwart their plans and shame the mole.

'Do you have anyone in mind?' Abraham asked his brow furrowed.

'I don't know, and it doesn't matter anymore.'

'Why do you say that?' Abraham asked with a frown

'Something new has come up, 'Aaron looked straight at the man who had been like family to him, there was a wistful expression on his face as he said fondly, 'Papa, you asked me to call you that, remember?'

Abraham nodded and Aaron said earnestly, his eyes searching his face, imploring him to believe what he was about to say, 'I saw some primitive old men, they seem so ancient. They had these long white whiskers almost reaching the floor,' he gesticulated with his hands and sounded excited, 'they called themselves the elders, judging from their looks I don't think they're from this part of the world. They gave me the olive oil that brought you back to life.' He pointed to the bottle of oil on the floor, 'Forget about the archbishop or whoever sent killers after you, they told me to take the Ark to New York for a while.'

The look on Abraham's face was one of disbelief, how would posterity judge him for that? Aloud he said quietly, his eyes darting everywhere except Aaron's face, 'I'm going to tell you a story, my son,' he cleared his throat and said quietly, the lines on his face compressed together, he suddenly looked old and frail, 'I have dedicated my entire life to protecting the Ark, and nothing can make me waver from my true calling. That is my mission on earth. When I was a young boy, about eight years old, one rainy night I had an unusual dream about a planet very different from earth. The soil of that odd planet was red as blood, and in my dream, I saw a young boy of my age. He told me that his name was Cydonia, the same as the planet I found myself on.

This boy took me to a very big house made of glass, and I remember looking at my reflection before entering. When we entered the house, we saw a reptile with a human head and the head was weeping. When I asked the boy what the matter was, he told me that the reptile's judgement was coming nearer.'

'You think the reptile was Tyrus?'Aaron asked he didn't think the old man was making any sense at all.

'No,' he said gesturing with his hands, 'the reptile was nothing, but the boy in my dream was you.'

As he said that Aaron turned away from him and said with difficulty.

'You're old enough to be my great grandfather, how could you have seen me before I was born?' He turned to face him again, briefly hating the sight of his grinning face.

'It means that I have absolute faith in you,' he stretched his hands towards him, 'pull me up my son, we have a lot of packing to do.'

But Aaron did not move. 'How are we going to leave the country with the Ark? People would lynch us if they knew!''Pull me up, son,' Abraham repeated, ignoring his questions and Aaron complied, regretting his faithlessness.

'You don't have to worry about a thing; God wanted us to take the Ark out of here for a purpose, I'm sure He will make sure we leave the building undetected, we will carry the Ark with us, it will be invisible.'

'Are we going to carry it on our heads? I don't want to be struck down for touching it like Uzza did in the scripture, he was killed for it.'

Abraham laughed heartily, he was happy the elders gave a second chance and could not wait to see the look on his enemy's face when they met, but it seemed like it might not happen after all.

'You are not Uzza and the Lord will not smite you, so relax. Let's go and do as we have been commanded.'

They walked out of the room and Aaron heard a sound.

He turned back to look and saw that the Ark was already in a wooden box, just like in biblical times. He tapped Abraham on the shoulder and whispered, 'Look.'

Abraham laughed with gusto and walked out with easy strides. Aaron was amazed at how agile he was; it appeared his arthritis was history.

'You're walking like a young man,' he commented.

'All thanks to you my son.'

'Say, did the elders say anything about the years I have left?' he asked after a brief pause.

'No, Abraham.'

'Call me Abraha. That's my real name, and is the name on my passport.'

'Abraha,' Aaron mouthed the name smiling, and then he remembered that Peter could still be waiting outside.

'I saw Peter as I was admiring the obelisks. He invited me over to Addis Ababa.'

'That's not possible. Peter has gone to Rome with the emissaries the Pope sent to take you to the Vatican,' he said with a frown and then shrugged his shoulders, 'could have been Tyrus, but who cares now. The old fool is a loser anyway.'

'When I held you in my arms and thought that you were dying, you told me Peter was looking for me, I thought he was the mole that stabbed you...' he paused with a hurt expression on his face, 'and you knew all along that this same Peter had gone to Rome, and you said nothing.' Aaron was upset and it showed on his face.

'I thought it was Peter, but it could have been Tyrus...' he stared at Aaron, 'I was dying son, and when you're dying you see things. I didn't want you in Rome now my son; it's not safe. Besides, the Holy Father is missing,' he said simply.

Aaron stopped in his tracks, 'How do you know? He's surrounded by his guards, he can't be missing.'

Abraham's face was blank and unreadable.

'Is there something I should know, Abraham?' Aaron persisted.

'Abraha,' he corrected him and patted him on the shoulder playfully, 'and I think you need to splash cold water on your eyes to keep the foreign bodies out.' When they entered the room, Abraham's eyes went straight to the pool of blood on the floor.

'Right,' Aaron said and his hand went up to his eyes again, but Abraham pushed his hands away and pulled him into the room.

He swung around and said, 'although I have friends in the papal household who could give me inside information about the Holy Father, while I was busy being dead, I saw things too woeful to describe. The Holy Father is in terrible danger,' and he grimaced, 'I saw things that have alarmed me greatly and...' he paused and looked at him with clear eyes, 'I don't think Tyrus is who we think he is. In actual fact, I don't think he's working alone.'

'What do you mean?' Aaron asked his heart beating fast.

He wondered what Abraham was going to say next.

'Tyrus may be the son of Satan through a human mother.'

'What? How can that be?' Aaron was petrified - the story was turning wacky. Tyrus and Lucifer would be formidable foes.

'It's just a theory, but I would bet my few remaining days on it. The grand master seems to have made his appearance obvious in Rome and I'm sure that Tyrus has taken on a human form. Maybe he took the image of Peter for a while... and yes, I have more bad news for you.'

Aaron braced for the bad news: Abraham's face was shrouded in secrecy as he added solemnly, 'Cardinal Bacilio and Salvarado are dead.'

'What?'

Aaron staggered back as if hit by a hundred foot wave.

'Cardinal Bacilio was mauled to death in the Pope's library by a beast, while Cardinal Salvarado committed suicide the same day. There were roughly six hours between the two deaths.' His voice was soft; it was more of a whisper, a form of respect to the dead men of God.

Aaron couldn't think straight.

Cardinal Salvarado had been part of his family for as long as he could remember, and even though the man wanted him dead, it was still sad thinking about how died; probably miserable till the end. But Cardinal Bacilio saved him, at least Caleb had told him that much.

'I have to pay my last respects to both of them,' Aaron declared with a determined look on his face.

'Fine, when we have finished whatever we are sent to do in New York,' Abraham murmured. He went into his inner chambers and began packing.

Aaron was still reeling from the news he'd just heard, he walked round in circles confused and dazed. He scratched his head in frustration. Anyone connected to him always died. Fear gripped his heart like a ferocious beast; what would become of Caleb, Kate, and Abraham? He hadn't even been able to save the old man's life until the mysterious elders had intervened. Doubts forced him to his knees, his thoughts chaotic. Suddenly there was loud banging on the door, Aaron swore softly under his breath as he went to the door and yanked it open.

Caleb staggered into the room covered in bruises, his shirt torn in several places, his eyes swollen, and he could barely move his bloated lips.

Someone, or a group of people, had roughed him up a bit.

'There's a riot outside and the people are demanding for your head. Aaron, they've heard the news of Abraham's death.' And he bent down trying to catch his breath. Aaron said nothing but the expression on his face was grave.

Abraham came back into the room and Caleb took a few steps back staring at him. Then he fainted, hitting the ground with a thud.

He came round ten minutes later and saw Abraham's wrinkled face close to his. He screamed and tried to free himself from Aaron's strong hands.

'Hold still, Caleb,' Aaron said, finally releasing him.

He looked at Abraham and then Aaron and back to Abraham again.

'Can someone please tell me what's going on?' he pleaded brokenly his hands shaking.

'I saw three elders in the holy room and they asked me to sprinkle olive oil on Abraham and he came back to life.' Aaron explained with a smile playing round his lips; he was really enjoying Caleb's display of fear, he had thought Caleb was immune to seeing atypical happenings. At least it gave him a bit of a respite from his own misgivings about his competency as a carrier of the immense power in the Ark. Aaron controlled his riotous thoughts with effort. No one must notice his fear: a lot was resting on him.

Caleb pulled himself together and stood up with a startled look on his face.

'Oh ye of little faith,' Abraham said laughing and added, 'by the way, we have to leave the country today.'

He gaped at them as if they had gone mad, 'Are you two out of your minds,' he yelled, stomping his foot on the ground. His eyes turned red - Aaron had never seen him like that before. By now, he was becoming uncomfortable; he moved to barricade the door that led to the room where they kept the Ark. Maybe it wasn't the real Caleb.

Caleb never lost his temper; he was always cool and calm. Nothing fazed him and Aaron was suspicious about what he was seeing. He closed his eyes and started praying in Aramaic.

Abraham narrowed his eyes when he saw Caleb pulling out something from under his shirt and shouted a warning, but it was too late. The bullet rang out shrilly, startling Aaron into opening his eyes. He almost managed to dodge the bullet, but it scratched him lightly on the shoulder. He lunged at Caleb.

They collided in a battle of fists as the door swung open and another Caleb rushed in, exactly the same way his impersonator had. His eyes widened in horror when he saw his clone in the powerful grip of Aaron, and he fainted. At the same instant, Aaron's arms fell limply to his sides; the impersonator had vanished.

Abraham had been watching the whole scenario unperturbed. He'd realised that it wasn't the real Caleb the moment he'd arrived because he'd been acting strange but Aaron hadn't noticed and there was no time to explain.

'Is he the real Caleb?' Aaron asked peering down at the fallen man.

Abraham nodded.

'What do we do now?'

'He'll be all right, in the meantime I think we should pack; we have a plane to catch,' Abraham said going back to his private chambers. Aaron followed him leaving Caleb on the floor. When he entered Abraham's room, he was shocked.

The room could have come from a James Bond movie; there were about seven computers in the room, and a mini library filled to the brim with books portioned off to the side of the main room.

A big wide screen television was perched on a table, and on top of it was a DVD player but the amazing thing that baffled Aaron was in a far corner of the room. He saw three men who were apparently studying what looked like a map, but they seemed to be deaf because they communicated with sign language. On a conference table were eight landline telephones and three other men in white overalls sat at the table.

They acknowledged Aaron with a nod of their heads but he couldn't do anything. He gawked at the incredible sight with his mouth hanging open.

'When were you going to tell me that you had all this in here?' he demanded angrily.

'Africa is not the jungle usually portrayed by the west; we're enlightened you know,' he fired back and Aaron staggered under the weight of his fiery reply.

'I'm sorry; I didn't mean it like that.'

'That's all right,' Abraham said averting his gaze, ashamed of his unnecessary outburst, 'you don't really want to explore the church, you'd prefer to hole up in the small lounge outside, and nothing I do will make you do otherwise,' he explained in a calmer tone.

'Yeah,' Aaron agreed thrusting his hands into his jeans pocket, 'I'm not the adventurous type, I always stay in my corner. My brother would have been more fun if you had met him.'

'I did,' he said simply looking him straight in the eye, 'he sent me back.'

'Oh,' was all Aaron said as he turned back to leave the room, then he thought better of it and turned back, 'what are these men doing here?'

Abraham sighed and said simply, 'They're angels,'

Aaron shook his head and walked out of the room; he didn't believe Abraham. If they were angels, why hadn't they saved him, or even fought off his attackers? But he knew Abraham was full of mystery and there were certain things he would rather steer clear of.

After Aaron left, Abraham walked to a built in cupboard and pulled out a black suitcase. He opened it and took out his passport, which was lying on top of his few belongings; he opened it, looking intently at the visa he got two weeks earlier.

He had mixed feelings about the trip: by going, he had sentenced himself to death. He would be stoned to death if he should step out of the country; none of his ancestors had done what he was about to do. Even Menelik, King Solomon's son who brought the Ark from Jerusalem, would be irked at the prospect of the Ark going to the new world, but this was his duty. He now knew the reason why the elders had brought him back to give the Ark back to God. He was no longer the guardian of the Ark, Aaron was the new custodian, and in due course, the mantle would pass to him.

He heard pounding on the roof and knew their transport had arrived. He dropped his passport into the suitcase before clapping it shut, but when he stepped back into the lounge, he saw the room full of tall, lanky men armed to the teeth. By their angry faces, he knew they must be Somalis.

'Trouble,' he muttered.

32

Downtown Manhattan, New York, Aug 14

On the thirtieth floor of the battery city apartment, Joshua Cohen shifted his tired, aching back, staring at the gleaming Hudson River. His bed had been positioned in such a way that he would be able to suck in the splendid views of the river.

Joshua was skeptical about his speedy recovery, but the doctors were pleasantly surprised; they had hailed his healing as a momentous and ground-breaking miracle, and his vital organs appeared to be functioning well a mere week after his operation. He could swallow and and could hear perfectly well, he had no impaired vision and the muscles in his face were working perfectly.

But he knew things were not as they seemed; Joshua harboured a terrible secret, and no matter what happened to him, he would live for a while longer. His body may be destroyed, but no angel or demon could claim his soul just yet.

The door of the room opened and a hefty police officer entered. His face looked hard, expressionless, and lifeless. He had the features of a prison officer: well-shaped jaw, mouth set in a straight line, cold brown eyes, and slick dark hair. Joshua shuddered at the thought of countless criminals who must have crumbled under the ruthless, chilly glare.

'How're you doing, Mr Cohen?' the officer, Donald McBride, also known as 'Stealth', asked in a friendly voice, but Joshua was not convinced. They had a history. Stealth wanted to bring Joshua down, and Joshua had tried to kill him once. He watched Stealth's approach with disdain.

'I'm all right, just a little tired,' Joshua answered, looking at the man towering above him.

'Joseph is dead.' Stealth announced, looking at Joshua shrewdly, studying his every move and reaction, but Joshua gave nothing away despite the news hitting him like a sledgehammer.

He had suspected something was wrong when he'd come round and seen his secretary looking bored and definitely in need of a drink. When he asked her about Joseph, she had told him that Joseph had flu, and that had set the alarms off. Joseph would never desert him, even if he were at the point of death. Joshua was certain that Joseph would have dragged himself to his bedside.

'Damn!' he said finally, with all the strength he could muster, 'I knew something wasn't right, but definitely not death. He couldn't just die like that, Stealth.'

'I'm sorry, Mr. Cohen,' Stealth said and almost looked human while Joshua groaned like a woman in labour.

'I have some questions to ask you, but...'

'Get out, Stealth. Go, and find the killer of my son.' Joshua interrupted him harshly, hissing under his breath.

Stealth leaned forward and held his gaze for a couple of seconds. 'I'm going to find his killer because Joseph was a great guy, but I have to say this to you Mr Cohen,' and his eyes turned to slits, 'Joseph was not your son. He could never have had a corrupted soul like you for a father; I know about your sordid pact. However, there is no warrant for a man who sold his soul to the devil for fame, is there?' And he walked out of the room with a swagger, banging the door behind him.

'Arrogant son of a bitch!' Joshua swore softly under his breath, 'God! I hate cops.'

Then the enormity of Stealth's words hit him, how does that fool know about my pact? He sighed and frowned; Stealth must be a member of the Croles, or know an ex-Croles, to know his secrets.

The Croles were a clandestine and powerful cult. Members must be strictly Polish Jews; even his wife had known nothing about his involvement. The word 'Croles' struck fear into the hearts of people. They had a reputation for being ruthless and cruel, but also extremely influential. Money and fame was their motto. But Joshua was not keen to go down memory lane and think about how his best friend, Archer, and cousin, Jonathan, drafted him into the sordid world of cultism.

'Huh,' he mumbled painfully as his head seemed to explode. His nurse came into the room and was worried when she saw the expression on his face

'Are you all right, Mr Cohen?'

'I just heard the terrible news...' and he paused, looking at her fresh young face, 'McBride told me that Joseph is dead,' Joshua's scrawny hand shook with emotion, 'he's gone hasn't he?'

She averted her gaze before answering, 'That was a cruel thing for him to do. He wasn't supposed to say anything yet,' her huge brown eyes were misty as she said with a nod, 'It's true, Mr Cohen... Joseph is dead.'

'It's all right, I'll survive,' he said, but the hollowness in his voice betrayed him and, as usual, he bottled everything up and watched as the nurse changed his drip.

Joshua was grateful for the twenty-four hour care and the fact that he was able to have his own way. Rebecca Kolinsky, the hospital's director, had warned that it would be dangerous to discharge him, but Joshua was adamant.

Few days later - they released him, and the hospital management went to a lot of trouble trying to find the perfect apartment and the best care available for a person of his calibre.

'Mr Cohen, you are perfectly safe here; you'll be back to top before you know it,' the nurse reassured him in a sweet, soothing voice.

Joshua smiled. He was grateful for her kindness and thought she was more of an exotic dancer in her blue gown than a nurse, but his womanising days were over. He would use the remaining days of his life to pursue worthwhile causes.

His erratic mind soon turned to Joseph and another wave of grief washed over him like a hurricane. How would he organise the details of his life? Joseph had been efficient and competent. Joshua knew he would not last much longer without him.

'AND FOR Aaron's sons, thou shalt make coats, and thou shalt make for them girdles, and bonnets shalt thou make for them for glory and for beauty. And

thou shalt put them upon Aaron thy brother and his sons with him; and shalt anoint them, and consecrate them that they may minister unto me in the priest's office. And thou shalt make them linen breeches to cover their nakedness from the loins even unto the altar to minister in the holy place; that they bear not the iniquity and die: it shall be a stature for EVER unto him and his seed after him.'

'That's the book of Exodus, Chapter 28, verse 40 to the end.' Abraham said and closed the Bible with a glint in his eyes.

There was silence in the church office as the pastor and the church board of seven men and three women watched the journey-weary men.

Their incredible and almost unbelievable tale of how they had boarded the plane with the Ark of the Covenant, and how some ancient elders had directed them to bring the Ark for to their church for safekeeping defied all known logic.

The pastor, a small grey haired man with heavy-rimmed glasses, which had made an indelible mark on his face, was a man with incredible insight into the Bible. He was shaking with uncontrollable excitement, although he knew he would have a hard time convincing the church board to allow them to keep the relic for a while before they decided whether to keep it on a permanent basis or not. Besides, he could find out if it was the real thing or a fake. He had no idea how to achieve that, but he would.

'And you claim to be the real descendant of the biblical Aaron?' one of the board members asked with a little smile playing around the corners of his lips, which aptly suggested that he didn't buy their story.

'Yes, I can prove it with the stories of my father. Not by any genealogical research, but by the visions I've seen. I don't really expect you guys to believe me, but the things I've seen are as real as you sitting there.' Aaron answered, standing up and thrusting his hands inside his trouser pockets, 'Extraordinary, unexplainable things have been happening to me since the beginning of this month,' he paused to gather his thoughts then continued in a strong, firm voice, 'which in the Jewish calendar is the month Elul; the month of repentance leading up to Selichot, Rosh Hashanah and Yom Kippur.' He stopped abruptly, staring at everyone in the room. He had finally captured their attention.

'Some people would probably dismiss me as a mental wreck, but the things I have seen really are out of this world. The devil is out there on our streets, ready to pounce. He has very limited time now, a few days maybe, and I'm certain that a lot of people are surely going down with him, but we can prevent him from doing any harm.' Aaron stopped speaking and the silence in the room was so complete that if a pin were to drop the sound would resonate like a bomb. He swallowed hard and felt every cell in his body crying out for help, he was so exhausted.

'I'm a Jewish Christian and I believe in the blood of Christ. I believe that Christ came to the world to save me from my sins and reconcile me to God. Jesus died so that I might live and worship God as my father. I don't practice Judaism, but neither do I deny my ancestral roots.'

He kept quiet briefly, his eyes boring holes into everyone in the room, and when his gaze rested on one of them, they hastily tore their eyes away. At last, his eyes locked with the pastor's, and the pastor sensed the sincerity in Aaron's voice.

'On the first day of this month of repentance, I began an unexpected journey on a peculiar path which has taken me from London to Rome and from Ethiopia to New York in the company of these great men of exploits.' And he nodded in the direction of Caleb and Abraham and the delight on their faces showed they were absolutely behind him. He continued and this time, his voice was huskier than when he first began, 'Strange as it may sound, I've experienced untold tragedies. My parents and sister died on the same day some years back,' there were gasps and murmurs from his small audience, 'and my only brother, the only family I had left, was killed in Somalia. To this day, I have never found his body. Shortly after that, I joined a Catholic seminary and trained to be a priest, but I was plagued with series of visions. I could accurately call them nightmares; they were mostly unpleasant experiences.' Beads of perspiration appeared on his forehead, and Aaron knew it was only a matter of time; the world would simply implode if the men and women in the room did nothing. His voice was more like a hoarse whisper, 'I met a man in one of those horrific visions who tried to rip my heart out with his bare hands. He gloated and told me with a sneer on his evil face that he was responsible for the death of my family. Relentlessly - he tortured me in my dreams, until a few days ago, I saw him for real. He was still tormenting and taunting me, then he asked a strange question - he wanted the stones of fire.'

'The stones of fire? Did you just mention the stones of fire?' asked one of the board members, his eyes almost popping out of their sockets.

'Yes, he did,' Caleb answered, speaking for the first time since they had been ushered into the church office.

The man leaned forward and whispered to the man sitting next to him, who in turn did the same to the man next to him.

Eventually everyone looked at the men were subtly interrogating.

The pastor nodded his head, a sign for Aaron to continue his bizarre but interesting tale.

'I continued having these accursed nightmares until the day I was kidnapped in broad daylight from a bar in London. To my utmost fascination, my captors were the boys of Tyrus, the tormentor of my life. He couldn't get anything out of me because, as far as I was concerned, he was speaking in parables. Afterwards, those bastards kept at it, and at one point - I knew that I needed answers and that my life was in serious danger, so I decided to go to Rome and seek the answers from a family friend who was a cardinal in the Vatican. But my so called family friend ordered my execution due to reasons best known to him. But thanks to God and my friend, Caleb here, I was rescued and I went to Ethiopia where my mission was revealed.'

'And what was the mission, if I may ask?' the pastor asked, his eyes bright and fingers tapping on the table rhythmically.

Aaron looked at him and said clearly, his voice full of confidence, 'to keep the stones of fire close to my soul and prevent unscrupulous people from laying their hands on the Ark, because it contains indescribable powers. I'm the only living soul who can harness the power inside the Ark to its potential level of destructiveness. It's worse than any weapon ever conceived or made by man. Nuclear weapons are child's play compared to the incredible but destructive power of the Ark.'

'So what exactly do you want us to do?' one of the men asked and glanced at his colleagues. Aaron sensed fear permeating the atmosphere; they wanted to believe his story, yet they were afraid.

'We had express instructions to bring the Ark here, and anyone who repeats this conversation outside these walls, well...' and he left the sentence hanging.

'Could you please excuse us, gentlemen?' the pastor asked politely.

Aaron nodded and they walked out of the church office.

Once outside, Aaron asked his friends if he had convinced them.

'Yes, it was a good pitch,' Caleb said, yawning. He had bags under his eyes; they haven't had time to rest since flying to New York, and were understandably tired.

'I would give anything for a change of clothes, some real Ethiopian food, and a wide, clean bed,' Caleb said yawning again, his eyes blood shot.

'You sure need to get some rest,' Aaron said and patted his back, then walked towards the church auditorium.

He strolled towards the choir loft and his gaze rested briefly on the pews, which fanned out from the pulpit. Abraham and Caleb came up behind him, admiring the church's interior décor.

'I don't like the Gothic design, it's way too dark,' Abraham said quietly, almost whispering reverently, 'but I do love the stained glass and the way everything just flows centrally from the pulpit with no right angles.'

'I think it was designed that way to give worshippers clear views, and so they could listen to the preaching and music without straining their necks,' Caleb explained.

'Oh,' Abraham grunted and trotted to the pulpit, his gnarled hands caressed the seat as he passed by.

'The devil is afraid, you know,' Abraham said thoughtfully, though it appeared that he was speaking to himself. The others watched him, wondering what he meant by that. Caleb moved closer to him, sitting down on one of the pews very close to where the old man was standing awkwardly, leaning heavily on one of the pews.

'He thought he could trick God by laying hands on the stones of fire, the bedrock of his former glory. God gave him the stones on his creation and the reacquisition of the extremely powerful stones, coupled with the powers of the Ark could restore him to his former stateliness. I think he might be able to perform another coup d'état.'

'He had always been a trickster,' Aaron commented absentmindedly, still fascinated by the church's interior décor.

'Yes, my son,' Abraham said quietly, his eyes misty, 'but this time around, you are crucial to his plans.'

Aaron didn't like the tone of Abraham's voice; it was accusatory, as if he'd deliberately put himself in that position.

'I never asked for the stones, and I wasn't even bothered about an ancient Ark; as far as I was concerned, it didn't exist.'

Aaron growled in anger, but once the words came out of his mouth he regretted them, but refused to apologise.

Afterward, there was a frosty silence.

Half an hour later, the silence was broken when the church's board members came out of their impromptu meeting and went to the auditorium. Aaron heard their approaching footsteps and waited in anticipation for their decision.

'The Ark can stay here for a week,' the pastor announced with murmurings of approval from the three women. He cleared his throat and added, 'we would have to inform the government, of course; we wouldn't want to find ourselves in erm... in an awkward position.'

Aaron stepped forward and clasped the hand of the pastor, 'A week is not enough! Give us at least a month,' and he tightened his hold, 'the government would probably take the Ark away if they knew about it!

'We have to let the government know about this,' one of the women said coldly, pressing her lips together.

'Then it's your funeral,' Aaron said curtly.

'Calm down, son,' Abraham muttered, and apologised on his behalf, 'we're sorry, ma'am...'

'Deaconess Bernstein,' the woman said stiffly, flashing Aaron an acidic gaze before walking out with her head held high. The other women quickly followed her out of the church.

'You shouldn't have said that, young man.' the pastor reprimanded him, but everyone could see that he already had a soft spot for him, 'let's get you to your quarters, shall we?'

They filed out of the church with the pastor leading the way.

'You were pretty convincing, considering you never believed the Ark existed in the first place,' Abraham whispered, his eyes shooting daggers at Aaron as they walked outside.

'I didn't mean that. You know I didn't,' Aaron said softly, his eyes sad.

'I understand it son, and I understand you,' Abraham said quietly, patting him on the back.

Aaron nodded but said nothing.

A few yards outside the church, Lucifer, inhabiting the body of Keith Morgan stood across the street watching from a safe distance. For the time being, he dared not get too close. He turned his face upward, sniffing the air. It smelt fresh, very soon all this will be mine, he thought with a wicked grin on his face.

A pedestrian accidentally brushed past him and Lucifer lashed out in fury, severing the woman's head. Someone screamed, a woman fainted and he fled the scene on foot; he couldn't afford to tap into his powers at such an early stage of the mission. It was a busy Tuesday afternoon and there were few people around as he ran. Lucifer felt the vibration under his feet; it was coming closer than expected. It could only mean one thing: he had little time left. He would need all the resources at his disposal to get the stones but, he had to kill the old fool who called himself 'The Smiley Pope' to make things easier.

Mukta stared in horror as the woman's head rolled towards him.

He tried to run but didn't get far before strong hands pinned him down, wrestling him to the ground. He tried to wriggle free but four officers overpowered him.

The police officers holding him lifted him off the ground, handcuffed him, and led him towards a waiting police car. Mukta cursed the day he had set eyes on Fatima, the woman that had ravaged his system like a virus. He turned to look at the church; the men who had conned him into going to New York were in the church, and he swore silently to kill them. When he went to Ethiopia to ask for Aaron's help in locating Fatima, Aaron had told him to go to New York, that Fatima would be there, but he'd combed the length and breadth of the city - his Fatima was nowhere to be found. Mukta almost regretted his decision to seek out the elusive Jew, two skinny boys in Somalia had alleged that Aaron was powerful, and could see into the future. And for all his trouble, he was arrested. Despite his predicament, the only thing he could see was the beautiful face of Fatima.

Lucifer watched the police car speed off and wondered why he couldn't get any signal from the man who had been arrested for what he had done. He made up his mind to seek him out; the man could come in handy in the next couple of days.

33

Fatima banged on the door angrily, all her pent up emotions and frustration bubbling out. She stared in disgust at the cocky embassy officer.

She had braved all odds and had finally succeeded in crossing the notorious and highly volatile Somali-Ethiopian border with Abdul. The mortar shells that hit their truck killed Abdul's parents instantly. Abdul and Fatima were extremely lucky because they fell into the hands of Ethiopian soldiers who helped them across the border and booked them into a hotel.

The next day, Fatima explained her dilemma to the Ambassador of the American Embassy in Addis Ababa and he was very sympathetic and cooperative.

The embassy issued her another passport, and arranged her flight to New York, but Fatima was in a quandary; she'd given her word to Abdul that she would take him with her, but it was not as easy and straightforward as she had thought. There was loads of paperwork to contend with and apart from that, it would have to involve the Somali transitional government, and even for Abdul, Fatima was not prepared to go down that route again.

She ground her teeth and bit her nails, highly agitated. Abdul sat beside her wide-eyed and sad; he had become an orphan in a day, and for a boy of eight, that was a monumental tragedy.

At first, he couldn't really comprehend it and kept asking for his parents, but after a while he stopped, staring sullenly into space, a forlorn expression on his face.

He held onto Fatima's hand and refused to let go. She took him everywhere and when she called Andre and told him about Abdul, he had brushed him aside. After five minutes of trying to explain how urgent it was for her to travel with the boy, Andre still did not understand the urgency. She had banged the phone down on him and stalked off with Abdul on tow.

She calmed down and thought hard about what to do, and at that moment an embassy official walked up to her.

'Can I have a word, ma'am'

She looked at him suspiciously, 'I have to have him with me, he's so scared,' Fatima said.

The official agreed and they followed him.

CYDONIA

TYRUS STOOD on the beautiful outdoor terrace of the Castelvecchio, admiring the panoramic views with a cocktail in his hand, his gaze on Lake Albano. He was already thinking about his next course of action. He glanced at his Rolex briefly; it was six in the evening and the weather was already turning. He felt a little bit cold.

He put the glass on the table and wrapped his arms around his midsection as an evil grin lit up his face. He loved the carnage he and his men had been able to unleash on the sleepy town of Castel Gandolfo. He had enjoyed it very much, and when he told his father about the escapades, Tyrus had expected him to be pleased. But he was not.

Lucifer had screamed obscenities, reminded him of the little time they had left and moaned about the elders of the Grace Council.

The council would decide their fate, but Tyrus wasn't bothered. After his father's defeat in Cydonia by Archangel Barachiel, the massive angel had banished his father from the beautiful angelic civilisation, destroyed the planet and hundreds of thousands of his father's angels. Now after waiting patiently for a thousand years in the pit of darkness, otherwise known as Hades, his father, Lucifer had one more chance to prove himself worthy as a world ruler by producing the twelve stones of fire and the Ark of the Covenant. His father had not tormented humans directly for a thousand years, his demons had that privilege and Tyrus knew he hated that. Now that the grace council had released his father to appeal the decision of their decision, his father had to meet the demands of the council, or else, Barachiel and the likes of angel Uriel would hurl them back to hell.

Tyrus grimaced: not their fate, but his fate. He hated his father but also knew that he had to play the game well. It would be difficult for demons to understand his plight, but Tyrus was not looking forward to spending eternity in hell - he wanted his freedom, to live like a mortal and die like one. Tyrus had no sympathy for his father; the only thing he could think of was more power.

As foolish as he may look or sound, Tyrus knew pinning his hopes on his father was like building castles in the air.

The dictator in heaven would neither release nor pardon his father, and the sooner the old fool allowed that to sink into his diseased brain, the sooner things would work out on his end.

Then he thought of Cydonia, the beautiful rich planet that was his father's pride and glory, but Barachiel had mercilessly stripped him of that honour.

Cydonia, the red planet with the stones of fire, was the only obstacle to their redemption, and, annoyingly, Aaron had it all: the stones, and the Ark. If only the stupid stiff-necked Jew would just hand over the stones and the Ark, then things would work seamlessly. Then they would harness the full potential of the Ark and reign freely without the draconian rule of the Almighty.

Tyrus smiled with a faraway look on his features. Even thinking about it put him on the same pedestal as his father... but all he truly craved was freedom.

He sighed, clenching and unclenching his fists; there was no harm in daydreaming. Their journey and quest would simply end in disaster, but he couldn't tell his poor daddy the truth.

Archangel Michael had sentenced Tyrus to the nether region because of his parentage. He was half-human and half demon and the massive angel had problems with that.

That was the main reason he had been keen to visit Rome: to teach the Pope a lesson. In the course of their chitchat, he would gladly inform the hapless man that he was family. A wicked grin appeared on his face at the thought of the forthcoming encounter.

He was certain the frail Pope would die of a heart attack right there and then. He drank his remaining cocktail in one go and threw the glass towards the lake.

Tyrus couldn't wait to have an audience with the Holy Father, now that he had acquired the body of Father Giovanni, whenever he went he was accorded the greatest respect.

Italians were famed for that: they loved their Pope and cardinals to death. Even if they were murderers, they loved them still.

Tyrus went back inside the hotel and paid the bills, while his men escorted the Pope to their car. But as they were about to leave the lobby, a porter recognised him, and the Pope stared at the porter, his lips moving. The Pope was praying for a miracle, if the Porter had truly recognised him, help could be at hand.

The porter raised the alarm and Tyrus's demons silenced him in a hail of bullets. There was pandemonium as people ran out of the hotel lobby.

Tyrus sauntered to the car park as the Italian police drove to the hotel. He watched with disdain as officers piled out of their cars, pointing their weapons at him.

'Father Giovanni, we want you to let His Eminence go,' their commander barked the order and Tyrus's men prepared to attack, but he told them to back down, which they did.

Tyrus marched towards the officers, his eyes blazing with hatred. The commanding officer ordered him to get back. When he defied him the second time, they opened fire. More officers arrived, their sirens blaring full blast.

Tyrus fell under heavy gunfire and his men looked on with bored expressions on their faces. When the shooting stopped, Tyrus slowly got back to his feet and turned his head around. His head fell to the ground, and he began to play with it. His headless body was a bizarre spectacle, his head bounced back to his neck and he opened his mouth. All the officers, including those outside the hotel gate, melted under the intense heat that gushed out of his mouth.

Then there was an uneasy silence.

He turned back, faced the hotel and was about to open his mouth again when the Pope shouted in a very loud voice, 'No!'

Tyrus walked briskly to the Pope and struck him on the cheek. Blood trickled down his chin, but Pope Nathaniel III stood his ground, staring defiantly at the being inside the body of his trusted preacher and friend. He knew the real Father Giovanni was long gone.

The Pope gritted his teeth and spat out angrily, 'you foul little demon, how did you get to my friend?'

Tyrus raised his hand to strike him again but came to his senses. The man standing in front of him would gladly lay down his life, and his father would never forgive him if the old man died.

He lowered his raised hand and said simply, a blank expression on his face, 'I waylaid him on his short trip to the Vatican. He was going to take a vital document from the Vatican archives, so we went and collected the documents from him. Then I ate his heart. His rotten bones are in one of the stacks of files in the archives,' he stared straight into the Pope's eyes and added, 'he died quickly, he knew no pain.'

'Can I get into the car, please?' the Pope pleaded and the men helped him into the bullet proof Mercedes 4x4. They needed the old man alive and in good spirits if their mission was to be a success. His life might even be spared, or maybe not.

And he chuckled.

They got into the Mercedes 4x4 and drove away from the hotel while terrified tourists and staff watched from the safety of their rooms, afraid to venture outside. None of the tourists were able to tear their gaze away from the grotesque carnage the evil men had left behind.

Twenty minutes later, the sound of sirens filled the air as more cars pulled up outside the hotel.

Everyone had heard the news; the Pope had not perished in the great fire of Castel Gandolfo, but strange men had kidnapped him.

The kidnap of the Holy Father threw Rome into mourning.

There was no way the Vatican would choose a new Pope, and when the news filtered to the world's media that the Pope, the head of the Church, was missing, it rocked Christianity to its very foundation.

In London, Kate and Evelyn stared in amazement at the male newscaster,

'And at the moment, the whereabouts of the Holy Father is still unknown. There was condemnation all around the world today as people of all nations rallied together to pray for the safe return of the father of the Christian Church.'

'We're in real trouble,' Evelyn said, her eyes glistening with unshed tears. She missed her husband terribly, and just as he had requested in his will, she had cremated his body and taken the ashes back to London to his aged mother. The thought of the old woman filled her with dread.

Michael said he wanted his ashes to be scattered on Lake Tana in Ethiopia. Evelyn had booked her flight, and should leave London before the end of the week.

Caroline walked into the conservatory and touched her mother's neck, whispering in her ear.

A look of utter dread passed over Evelyn's face and Kate asked, 'What's the matter?'

Evelyn didn't answer.

Lola looked at her friend and a chill ran down her spine.

'I think we have some visitors,' Evelyn said and hurried to the kitchen, closely followed by Lola and Kate, but Caroline lingered behind.

They got to the living room and saw the tired face of Pope Nathaniel III, along with Tyrus. Lucifer, still in the body of Keith Morgan was admiring Caroline's portrait on the wall.

Lucifer turned to them and his face lit up when he saw Lola.

'Hey, babe, how could you leave home without telling me? The twins have been asking for you.'

'The twins are dead, you bastard,' Lola yelled as she fought back tears.

'They're alive, Lola,' Lucifer said with a shake of his head, his arms akimbo. 'I have no interest in your children, I had enough from your husband, after all, his body is fortunate to house my spirit.' and he shrugged his wide shoulders, 'they're useless to me, just as you are useless to me, Lola, I have no need for you. If you go back home, you'll find out the truth; they're with your mom.'

But Lola did not answer, watching the stranger in her husband's body. She searched his face for any signs of her husband but it was futile, Keith, her husband was long gone

Lola sighed and Evelyn pushed her out of Lucifer's reach and said coldly, 'what do you want?'

Lucifer burst out laughing, but the laughter did not reach his eyes.

'I want to eat your heart. That's exactly what I want to do to you, little witch,' he said quietly and moved closer, but she stood her ground.

They faced each other and then they heard a thumping sound; the Pope had fallen to the floor. Everyone rushed to his aid except Lucifer who had a silly look on his face.

Claps of thunder ripped through the sky and it began to rain. Evelyn touched his pulse, but there was none. She realised what Lucifer was planning to do.

They were all in deep trouble. Her ashen face tightened in rage: they had brought the Pope to die in her house. She sank into the nearest chair to her, and held her head in her hands, when *will the nightmare end?* Evelyn thought.

Then she stood to her feet and faced Lucifer; she would not go silently into the night without a fight.

Meanwhile, Tyrus was studying Evelyn, and he liked what he saw. He loved women with spirit, not whiny helpless ones. Evelyn had captured his attention; the stern faced woman defying his father intrigued him and his bones trembled.

34

Rechavia, Jerusalem, Aug 14

Seated close to the window, Shalem Armani lazily flipped through the papers on his lap, a Cuban cigar dangling from his lips. His eyes narrowed as he caught sight of what he had been searching for, he marked it down with a pencil as sweat gathered on his forehead.

Then he heard approaching footsteps.

He shut the book but an outside wind blew through the tall window and some of the papers scattered to the tiled floor.

'Let me,' a tall woman bent down gracefully and gathered the papers with her long, elegantly manicured fingers. She straightened up, a fixed smile on her full lips.

Her eyes seemed to dance with amusement; Shalem blushed at the mere sight of her. Her oval face, flawless skin, and dimpled cheeks were such a delight. Shalem's reaction pleased Rachel tremendously.

She simply adored him.

'Thank you, Rachel,' Shalem said collecting the papers from her outstretched hands.

Their fingers brushed slightly, and he nearly jumped from his seat as his face turned bright red.

'Excuse me, please,' he said and left the lounge for the bedroom, closing the door gently behind him. Shalem sighed and leaned on the door wondering why he had agreed to have Rachel with him.

Because? After all she planned the whole trip, remember? How could he forget? Still, it was difficult staying in close proximity to such a beauty, even if she was his fiancée.

Shalem swallowed hard and knew the battle was far from over; he'd refrained from heavy petting with Rachel and was not too keen on making love to her. He didn't have the nerve to confess to her that he was still a virgin.

The ordeal he had to go through at the hands of his friends was outrageous enough; they teased him constantly about his saintly status, but he had stuck to his guns, and at the ripe age of twenty-eight, he had never been intimate with a woman.

Incredibly, his good looks always made women flock around him, but once they sniffed out his naivety and innocence, they would steer clear as though he had leprosy.

Shalem grew up in a strict Catholic home. His Jewish mother was a delight, but his strict no-nonsense Catholic father made sure he turned out right. His father was the alpha and omega of his life and that of his brother. Then, one day, he rebelled and got his way. His father had wanted him to study medicine and become a doctor, but Shalem followed his heart and chose archaeology and history. He was an exceptionally brilliant student at the University of Hull and graduated with first class honours. Though his dad was immensely proud of his son's success, he was already scheming how to enforce the second phase of the plan for his guileless son.

He had made plans for Shalem to start work at the family shoe business, but he had flatly refused. He had his own plans and shoe selling was not on his list of career choices.

He'd already applied for the master's programme in archaeology at Hebrew University Jerusalem and had been successful. Repudiating his father's offers, he went ahead with the programme, finished his master's, and had further plans to go for his PhD, but his father put his foot down.

'Shalem, you're my first son. The family business is worth millions of pounds. You have had your way, you've done your master's programme, and now you want to go for a PhD? No!'

The fire in his eyes had gone but he was still as persuasive and determined as ever. His son had to join the family business as soon as possible, and he would not take 'no' for an answer.

Shalem knew he would eventually work in the family business, but he was not ready yet. He knew nothing about shoes and didn't want to; he had tried over the years to subtly drop the hint. He would have preferred going on field trips, digging, and studying the history of the world, but his father would have none of it. When Shalem realised that the standoff was breaking his mother's heart, he backed down.

'Okay, Papa,' he had said to his dad and felt his stomach rumbling in protest, 'I would like to learn the ropes now. What do you want me to do?'

The transformation was swift.

His face beaming with joy, his father had clasped Shalem in a bear hug. 'That's my boy! I knew you'll not disappoint me, Rodrigo will take you through the necessary tricks involved in the business.' He studied his son for a while then added with a twinkle in his eyes, 'Before you start, I want you to get married.'

Alarm bells rang shrilly in his head and he felt faint; another perfect plan from his dad.

'By the way, do you know the Costello family?'

'Yes, Papa. Gabriel Costello is your only friend,' Shalem had drawled, gradually despising his father for running his life for him.

'He has this beautiful daughter called Rachel; she would make a perfect wife for you. Did you know that she's a doctor?' and Shalem could see where his father was going: if he, his son, had failed to be a doctor, he might as well shop for a girl who fit the criteria.

Shalem shook his head and stood up.

'Aren't you happy, son'? his father asked with a hurt expression on his face.

'No, Dad, I'm not,' Shalem had replied angrily, 'why are you trying to ruin my life?! Let me find my own wife, for Christ's sake! This is the twenty-first century! Wake up old man.' Shalem had stormed out of the room and almost collided with his mother, but he pushed her aside and made for the door.

He had jumped into his Aston Martin and zoomed off to his friend's house.

That had been seven months ago.

He finally calmed down and when he met Rachel, his preconceptions went out the window. She simply took his breath away. They planned to get married in a lavish ceremony in Tuscany in September and he was actually looking forward to it.

Shalem's father was over the moon when he started work at the head office of his family's shoe business. It was an easy, uncomplicated life, but he desperately wanted more. Although he adored Rachel and worshiped the ground she walked on, he wanted more out of life.

His life was smooth sailing and he didn't like it one bit. Shalem wanted to court danger, go on perilous adventures and do great and daring things, not be stuck in a flashy town house in Tuscany surrounded by adoring servants and jealous extended family.

He wanted more fun, not a daily routine filled with mundane chores and endless meetings. Visualising himself in fifty years' time he saw a bored, lazy rich man. Shalem knew he would entertain the idea of committing suicide if he ended up with such a monotonous and dreary life.

When he told his friends, they thought he was crazy and had labelled him an adrenalin junkie. Maybe it was his mental state, he reasoned, but he loved adventure and would not apologise to anyone for trying to spice up his life.

Shalem opened up to Rachel, and was glad that he had. She was a keen traveller, had visited several countries, and was interested in exploring more. She suggested a holiday and chose Jerusalem. They decided to spend a week exploring the ancient city and looking up his old school mates. In a way, Rachel just wanted them to get to know each other better and have fun.

Shalem agreed and now they were in Jerusalem, holed up in a small rented apartment in Rechavia. He had also invited Yitzhak, his old friend, to come over for a cup of tea and catch up on old times.

He sat on the bed reading the life history of the Finnish scholar and poet Valter Henrik Juvelius. His mind kept dwelling on the Ark of the Covenant. He wondered where the ancient relic was, it would be fun to see such an enduring relic, Shalem thought.

He closed the book, lost in thought. He had watched Raiders of the Lost Ark and many people had laid claim to the Ark, but the thought that the greatest biblical treasure could be in Jerusalem was overwhelming.

Shalem had always been good with codes and had read the account of the prophet Ezekiel in Hebrew Old Testament. Shalem had written many articles on the Ark and even mentioned it briefly in his thesis.

He heard footsteps and quickly lay on the bed pretending to be asleep. The door opened, soft footsteps inched closer, and then he felt Rachel's weight on the bed as she slowly shifted close to him. The bed creaked and he almost choked with fear.

Leaning on one elbow, Rachel turned his head towards her and his eyes opened, locking with hers. She parted her lips in a sensual smile, and that was all. Shalem knew he couldn't hold on till their wedding day. What a shame, he thought as his hands touched her soft, smooth skin, all thoughts of the Ark completely pushed aside.

Three hours later, Shalem woke up and saw the naked body of Rachel next to him. It felt perfectly normal; he didn't feel as if he had broken any law, but he felt soiled and used. And there was a nagging question on his mind: was he normal?

He had a vague memory of what had happened. It was all a blur, but deep down he knew that was what he had wanted all along. He just didn't have the guts to ask women out. He knew he would not be able to look Rachel in the eye ever again.

It must have been awful, Shalem thought dejectedly. He was sure it had been, and, what was more, he had corrupted his body and mind. He ran his hands through his hair, regretting his brief moment of passion. If it resembled that, he thought with a frown.

He went to the bathroom, turned the shower on, and stayed under it for almost ten minutes. As the water slid down his taut muscles, he hoped all his inhibitions would dissolve. He turned off the tap and wrapped a thick white towel around his body before strolling to back to the bedroom.

Rachel was still asleep, snoring softly, her thick dark hair covering her face and the duvet barely covering her smooth thighs. Shalem walked towards the bed and covered her properly, trying to avert his gaze, but he found his eyes seeking her out. He drooled over her nakedness and felt himself desiring her all over again. He allowed himself the luxury of a smile at the irony; he believed his behaviour was ghastly and yet could not wait to experience it all over again.

'Behave, man,' he whispered hoarsely and turned away.

The devil must have possessed him, he concluded as he hurriedly dressed and walked out of the room.

He came back again and picked up the book he had been reading; he needed to go out and get some fresh air.

He closed the bedroom door quietly and sauntered to the living room. Opening the door, which led to the corridor, Yitzhak's grinning face came into view. His hand was poised ready to knock on the door as Shalem opened it.

Shalem shouted in surprise, extremely delighted to see him. They hugged each other, grinning like excited schoolchildren.

'Come in,' he invited Yitzhak inside, his face beaming with pleasure. They went into the cosy living room and Yitzhak closed the door gently behind him, his eyes taking in everything in the room.

'You're looking good, Shalem,' Yitzhak commented in a booming voice that resonated throughout the apartment, 'and you know how to live well,' and he gave a short, deep throaty laugh.

Yitzhak was a short, powerfully built man with wide shoulders and bulging biceps. His brown eyes danced with merriment and he had a pleasant looking face.

'Thanks, man,' Shalem said smiling broadly, 'are you still addicted to your excessive workouts?'

'Yeah, brother, I am,' and he grinned revealing snow white teeth.

'Are you here alone? Where's Rachel?' Yitzhak asked, sitting comfortably on the sofa. He noticed the fine worry lines on Shalem's forehead.

'She's having a nap. She's adorable, Yitzhak. I'm happy we met, even though it was arranged by my father,' Shalem said with a forced smile but Yitzhak was not fooled; he detected sadness creeping into his voice.

'Would you care for anything? Wine? Or tea?' Shalem asked with a smile, moving towards the small kitchen.

'Nah,' Yitzhak answered with a shake of his head, 'I'm good.'

Then they lapsed into companionable silence. Shalem watched his friend and realised that something was troubling him, and he did not have to wait long to find out what it was. Yitzhak stared at Shalem for a while then blurted out, 'We need your help, Shalem.'

'We? What do you mean, Yitzhak?' Shalem asked in a soft voice, his eyes wide. Yitzhak tried to explain and at that instant the door opened and three men walked quietly into the room. They stood motionless behind Yitzhak, their faces blank and expressionless.

Shalem stared at the men and excitement coursed through his veins; had his friend become a spy, or an agent?

'What's up, Yitzhak?' he asked easily.

'The Ark of the Covenant was found in Ethiopia, but then it went missing. We need to recover it, and fast: it's urgent. We don't want it to fall into the wrong hands,' and Yitzhak stood to his feet, 'we want you to help us find it. 'Yitzhak smiled, 'I knew you would be interested: I believe this is something you can do.'

Shalem was surprised.

This was not the same friend he had studied with during his master's programme, the guy that used to tease him endlessly about his gullibility and innocence. Yitzhak was now brisk, short with his words and seemingly incredibly efficient and straight to the point.

'You're not working for the museum in Jerusalem, are you?' Shalem asked, jealousy hitting him in the pit of his stomach. That was the kind of life he desperately wanted to live; a life that had meaning, a life of impact, not the boring, dreary life he would soon be condemned to in Tuscany.

Yitzhak chuckled and shook his head. Clearing his throat, he said slowly, 'Rachel is one of us.'

The revelation hit Shalem with a bang.

'I don't understand,' he stuttered, his head swimming.

'Rachel is not a doctor, Shalem. She is a Katsas, a case officer in our organisation.'

What sort of organisation is that, I wonder? Shalem thought, trembling inside. He racked his brain, and then he knew; his fiancée was working for the Israeli Secret Service.

Yitzhak was somewhat apologetic but it was too much for Shalem who staggered to his feet, stunned by the news that his father's perfect bride was not who she made out to be.

'But her dad was my father's best friend,' Shalem said with a frown. Yitzhak had trouble looking him straight in the eye.

'Yes,' Yitzhak agreed with a nod of his head, 'that's truly her real dad; he was also an agent before his retirement. I'm sorry, but I can't say more than that.' His voice was grim and reluctant. It was as if he was suddenly not too keen on the idea of Shalem working with Mossad.

Looking at it in a new light, it was not as bad as Shalem had earlier thought. Having a spy for a wife was more interesting than if she were a doctor. Their family life would be filled with adventure upon adventure, and spies' stories would be the normal talk around their breakfast table each morning. Then the image of his father's face crossed his mind and he swiftly brushed it aside.

'You don't have much time to think about this,' Yitzhak said, and there was a hint of pressure in his voice, 'we certainly don't have that much time left. You have to make a decision now, old friend.'

Shalem's cloudy eyes sought his friend out, but Yitzhak still refused to hold his gaze, 'Would Rachel still go ahead with the wedding?' he asked, suddenly afraid of losing her.

It was surprising how the tables had turned against him.

He was revolted at their earlier intimacy but now he couldn't bear the thought of living without her. Or is that because of the information I've just heard? Inwardly he disagreed; it was a simple case of the veil covering his eyes disappearing.

'Yes, my love,' Rachel answered from the doorway, fully dressed, her dark hair pulled back in a ponytail and her full red lips open in a smile. She looked ravishing. Shalem's throat felt dry suddenly and he walked towards her with deliberate steps.

'You wouldn't have given away your secrets, would you?' Shalem asked, cupping her face in his hands, his heart pounding. He felt different, light headed, but he was no fool; he knew the catch, things could get ugly.

'No darling, I wouldn't,' was her simple answer and she slipped into his arms, speaking against his chest, 'but it's dangerous, our lives are sold out to defend Israel...'Rachel paused briefly, staring into his soulful eyes. Her eyes were misty, and tears threatened to fall at any moment.

'I didn't know I would fall in love so fast, but you were so gentle and kind...' and she chuckled, 'though a little naïve, but who can find that kind of man nowadays? I wouldn't give you up for the whole world,' and she shuddered, but Shalem didn't know whether it was with delight or dread. Her voice was laden with emotion, 'I wouldn't.'

They held each other tightly.

There was a single cough and they turned to Yitzhak. His other pals were gone.

'Yes?' Shalem said quietly, his jaw twitching and heart pounding against his ribcage.

'Thank you, brother,' Yitzhak said and clasped Shalem's hand for a shake, 'I'll be in touch soon, and please stay indoors; there's a little riot going on outside, it's to do with the Pope or something like that.'

'Okay,' Shalem said and Yitzhak left the room, closing the door gently. 'What riot is he talking about?' he asked Rachel, his eyes devouring her every move.

'The Pope has been missing for some days, didn't you know?' Rachel asked, looking at him strangely. She slipped out of his warm embrace and walked to the kitchen she flung over her shoulder, 'The Pope was abducted by aliens, I think,' and she gave a short laugh before continuing, 'but my boss wouldn't believe me. I believe in UFOs, do you?'

'No,' Shalem answered, shaking his head slightly and marvelling at the swift transformation in her. Rachel seemed to have peeled off her cloth of pretence. She talked freely, her eyes lit up, her voice was rich with emotion, and she found in him an attentive listener.

Thinking back to the explosive passion they had experienced earlier, he wondered why he had always shied away from sex, but now it seemed so right waiting for the right girl. Even though he wished, they had waited until their wedding night.

'Do you think we should be doing this together, as a couple?' she asked, coming back into the room with two glasses of red wine and she set them down on the centre table.

'We have a lot to talk about, Rachel,' Shalem said seriously and pulled her into his arms again. But before his lips claimed hers, she wriggled free, grabbed the two glasses of wine, and ran into the bedroom, giggling.

Shalem was hot on her heels when he heard a single shot. By the time he got to the room, Rachel was on the bed, flat on her back, a single gunshot wound to her forehead.

The wine glasses littered the tiled floor, fragments poking fun at his dreams of a happy ever after, their contents spilled all over the floor.

Shalem froze in his tracks and let out a blood-chilling scream. Yitzhak and his gang burst into the room. The only thing Shalem saw was the shocked expression on the face of the woman who would have been his wife.

35

Aaron stood motionless in the doorway, the empty space in the middle of the room screamed mystery and he gritted his teeth in anger.

The Ark had vanished.

Abraham almost crumpled to the floor in shock; he was shaking so badly that Aaron quickly grabbed him by the elbow and led him to a chair.

When Abraham sat down, Aaron's eyes strayed to the window and he saw three men loading a wrapped box into the back of a van.

He almost bolted after them but common sense prevailed; they couldn't possibly have stolen the Ark. Or could they?

Caleb stood silently behind Aaron. His face went a shade darker as he debated the best course of action. They all kept quiet, staring forlornly at the empty space. A few agonising minutes later, Caleb left the room determined to speak to the pastor.

He walked with brisk strides towards the lift.

The seventh floor of the pastor's quarters had the markings of a safe, secluded building, but they had been wrong. The pastor had promised them safety, yet someone had stolen the Ark.

Who would steal from weary old monks?

Caleb grimaced with a shake of his head, and walked on.

Still in the room, Aaron held Abraham's frail hands and their eyes locked briefly.

He stood up without a word and headed for the door before he remembered the words of the three elders about the rod.

They specifically told him to have it with him at all times, but he had forgotten to take it with him when they had gone out that morning.

He returned to the room and walked briskly to the built in wardrobe. Opening it, he crouched and rummaged inside his bag. His face lit up when he saw the rod. Aaron grasped it tightly and a tremor went through him as it disappeared into the palm of his hand.

'Be careful, my son,' Abraham said, stifling a cough, 'the Ark can't go far with that rod in your hand.' Aaron looked up sharply with a smile on his face, is there anything the old man doesn't know about? He doubted it.

'Don't tell me you have seen the three elders too?' Aaron asked fondly, loving every inch of his wrinkled face. He had come to accept him as a father figure; more like a grandfather, he thought and suppressed a smile.

Aaron walked towards Abraham, squatted in front of him and felt the familiar tightening of his chest. He managed a grin to hide his pain.

'My son,' Abraham said, lifting an emaciated hand to stroke Aaron's face, 'you've grown into a fine young man. When I first saw you, you were frightened, but you hid it well. Now, you're strong and fearless. Demons and vile spirits are now shaking with dread; they don't know what you're up to.'

They stared at each other for a long time as Aaron fought back tears.

He swallowed hard and a feeling of sadness engulfed his entire being. He was not as fearless as he looked. Sometimes he was fearless, but at other times, he was simply as a two-year-old boy afraid of thunder. He tried to shake off the feeling of sadness, but could not.

Aaron stared at Abraham's face, his feeling of dread mounting with each agonising second. Abraham's eyes welled up.

'My time has come, my son,' he said and coughed hard. Aaron couldn't stop the tears; they spilled onto his cheeks, travelling like two hikers on to his crisp white shirt.

'Don't forget this, my boy,' he continued tonelessly, 'please take my body back home. I want my body buried with my ancestors. I knew those ancient elders were up to something,' and he gave a short laugh, 'they simply wanted me to tag along. Now I think my mission is complete, and like Christ, I would say... it is finished. I have run the race and I have kept the faith.'

Aaron nodded, unable to speak. There was a strong bond between them, and they both knew it.

'There is one more thing,' and Abraham's eyes grew brighter, his countenance had undergone a swift transformation 'Peter is the mole in the Order of Lalibela, but you can't tell Caleb just yet: the news would destroy him.'

'But why would he do that?'

Aaron was angry, 'You loved him like your own son!'

'He doesn't believe in you; he thought you would steal the Ark and everything that connected it to Ethiopia would be erased. He could not let that happen. Ethiopia has survived for centuries on her own, free from outside rule and the Ark symbolises that. I also think he has lost faith in Caleb's leadership.'

Abraham took a deep breath and held Aaron's hands tightly, 'Take me to bed, please.'

Aaron carried him in his strong arms; he hardly felt his weight, he was as light as a feather, but his face was still shining and radiating with such intensity that Aaron knew the old monk had seen God's glory.

Caleb came back into the room in a rush. He watched the tenderness between the two men and gently slipped out of the room again.

Standing outside the door, his breathing coming in quick, short gasps, he ground his teeth in regret. Everything had gone horribly wrong; Abraham looked like a soul inching close to death's door. Caleb now doubted the rationale behind bringing the Ark to the United States, but it was too late for regrets he reasoned. His frustration mounted like a tornado.

Inside the room, Aaron propped Abraham's head comfortably on the pillows and held his bony hand in his, praying for God to give him more days to live.

Abraham opened his eyes sharply and admonished him, 'Stop praying, my son; it's my time!'

'How did you know I was praying?' Aaron asked, shocked at his sudden outburst.

'I just knew, Aaron the priest,' and he chuckled. 'I wish I could stay with you a little bit longer and tell you lots of things; there are many things to say, but sadly I have to go now, my angels are around.'

There was silence and Abraham whispered inaudible words as his eyes fluttered to a close.

'You're now the official caretaker of the Ark of the Covenant,' Abraham said weakly as his smile faded like a receding shadow.

Aaron knelt by the bed, watching the shallow breathing of the man he had come to love and respect. Seconds later, Abraham grunted and lay still.

Caleb entered the room gingerly, like a man walking on eggshells. He stopped in his tracks when he saw Abraham's face; it looked darker than usual, and a cold alien feeling crawled up his spine.

His worst fear was confirmed when he saw the stiffness of Aaron's back and head; he was like a statue. Caleb realised that the revered monk and caretaker of the Ark had died.

'Goodbye, Abraham,' Aaron whispered and stole a quick glance at Caleb. He stood still like a sculpture, his eyes not leaving the body of Abraham, and Aaron didn't want to think about what was going through his mind.

Caleb probably regretted their ill-fated trip. Aaron did as well, but that would not change anything. He touched Abraham's cold body, expecting him to wake up and speak to him in his funny accent.

Knowing that was a fantasy, he stood to his feet, still watching the dead man. They should probably call the police, but Aaron was not up to it. He hated the finality of death; it was always excruciatingly final.

But he must complete the mission.

There was no Ark or three elders to give him instructions on what to do, only a distraught and confused Caleb.

'We have to tell Pastor Geoffrey about this tragedy,' Caleb said as though he had read Aaron's thoughts.

Both men were devastated. Caleb tried consoling the younger man by moving closer to him, but Aaron flinched and stepped back. His bloodshot eyes looked strange.

'I really need to be alone, Caleb,' he said quietly and his voice broke. Caleb hesitated briefly but when he saw the desperation in his eyes, he decided to leave him for a while.

Caleb left the room quietly.

He rubbed his hands together and walked to the lift. He had to see Pastor Geoffrey. He had met an empty office when he checked earlier. *Hopefully he should be back now,* Caleb thought.

Abraham's death left a sour taste in his mouth. He suddenly felt tired and defeated. For a brief moment while he was in the room, Caleb wished he had not set eyes on Aaron, but, in a way, the young Jewish man had become his cross.

He entered the lift and pressed the button for the ground floor. When the lift got to the third floor, it stopped abruptly. Caleb's temper continued to mount. Waiting for a minute seemed like an hour.

'Oh God, I can't be stuck!' he exclaimed angrily and pressed the alarm, but nothing worked. He took out his mobile and dialled the number written on the wall in case of emergency. Pressing the mobile to his ear, there was nothing, just a crackle, then silence.

'Hello, can someone hear me? I'm stuck in the lift!' he barked into his phone but there was no response. He dialled Aaron's number, but he had switched off his phone.

Caleb was now frightened.

He tried not to panic but it kept gnawing at him, biting his insides like a disease, and eating away at his mind like a cancer.

Something was wrong.

He dialled the emergency number again, but the same eerie, distorted sound filtered out from the phone.

'Calm down, old boy,' he said and managed a shaky laugh.

When he looked up and saw the vent, he knew if he could pull it off and climb out he might be able to get to safety. Or get crushed if the lift should start up, a warning voice said shrilly in his mind.

Caleb sat on the lift floor and wondered if Tyrus had anything to do with the lift not working. If he did, he was not in the right frame of mind to fight him.

Suddenly, there was a jolt, and the lift started moving again. But instead of going down, it went up, very fast. Then he knew. A shadow loomed over him, and when Caleb looked up, he was staring into the face of the abyss.

The last thought on his mind was Peter.

Pastor Geoffrey checked his wristwatch more than once. He had told his guests the board's final decision to inform Washington about the relic in their custody. But that had been two hours ago, and they were supposed to give him their final answer. Deaconess Bernstein was not making things any easier, but he understood her concerns.

The pastor left his office and walked out of the chapel; he might as well check on his guests in their rooms.

He strolled briskly across the church courtyard towards the house, and then he saw him. Writhing in pain on the paved floor, close to the lift, was Caleb. Pastor Geoffrey rushed towards him.

'Oh my God!' he kept muttering as sweat broke out on his forehead. He bent down, touched Caleb's neck, and felt a faint pulse. There was no visible wound but Caleb seemed to be slipping away fast.

'Don't die on me, mister,' Pastor Godfrey said gently, taking out his phone and calling for an ambulance.

A low growl sent the pastor's pulse racing. He looked around wildly, but there was no one around. He stood and moved away from Caleb, whose fractured breathing was coming in short bursts. Pastor Geoffrey hurried to the office; he hoped the ambulance would get to the church as soon as possible.

Tyrus watched the pastor's retreat with a snigger. He was finally having fun, all thanks to his father. He stepped closer to Caleb and turned him over with his bare feet. He was tired of carrying the slightly overweight body of Father Giovanni, and, strangely, his skin had begun to peel off, so he needed a change of body anyway. His dark eyes scrutinised Caleb from head to toe, and Tyrus liked what he saw: a strong, healthy man.

Tyrus suppressed a giggle because he knew that he had found the perfect match - the perfect body.

'You are a hunk of a man, you know that, don't you?' he asked with a belch, fanning the rotten odour with his upturned hand. He opened his mouth revealing fangs and the ground shook, but when he bent his grotesque head to tuck into his prey something else caught his attention.

Stillness. Time practically stood still, and Tyrus realised his mistake. With furrowed brow, he took a second look at his victim. Caleb was no longer moving. He was dead, and that was not good. His victim was supposed to be breathing; his blood must be warm to complete the transformation.

Tyrus growled and flung Caleb away, breathing like a wounded lion. His eyes glowed like embers; he was already concocting a lie to tell his father when he heard the grating sound of the doors to the lift sliding open. Aaron's fiery gaze rested on Tyrus's rotting head. The venom in his voice was enough to melt a mountain.

'Are you looking for me? You filthy, hell bound monster!'

Silence.

Tyrus didn't know what to do.

He had merely breezed in to possess Caleb's virile body, not engage in a fistfight with the hotheaded priest.

'No!' Tyrus screamed and sank into the ground.

Aaron's hands fell limply to his sides, his breathing uneven. He moved slowly towards Caleb's body and his legs felt like ancient mountains; he could hardly lift them.

Staring at his friend, Aaron knelt beside him and buried his head in Caleb's smooth neck, but the tears refused to flow. Breathing like a woman in labour, he closed his eyes and lay beside Caleb, listening to the sound of his own breathing. He had no tears left to shed. He was numb with grief.

The drama of the day had been horrendous. How could I lose two great men within minutes of each other? Why would those stupid elders send me on an impossible errand? Aaron was angry but there was no outlet for his anger.

So he just lay there, looking forlornly at the sky which seemed to mock his despondency. He noticed a dark cloud forming and his aimless thoughts picked up on the heavily built angel. Uriel, the mysterious being he saw in the Vatican: big, fanciful, and useless. Why didn't he swoop down in his angelic splendour and save him from the terrible evil dogging his steps?

Aaron believed he was a companion of tragedy. It was like a plague; he always lost the people he loved. If he could, he would have gladly taken his own life, but he knew the consequence of that, the hottest part of hell.

Suicide was a sin and demons would torment him with relish.

Again, his sad eyes sought the bright morning sky, and the vastness of the clear, unassuming sky did something to him. It heralded banished memories; they flooded his entire being like a tidal wave, and his despair ended as the welcoming sound of a siren tore into the air.

Abraham, Caleb, and even the Ark are gone. *There is nothing left but death,* Aaron thought, desperately seeking respite from within, but finding fear lurking in every corner.

Abraham and Caleb could have gotten it wrong; maybe he wasn't really the right candidate for this 'saving the world from total annihilation' thing. It was more or less a mirage.

Aaron turned his attention back to Caleb; he studied his strong jaw, well-set mouth and black wavy hair. A sad smile danced around his lips; he had never really looked at him at such close range. *Caleb was a good-looking chap,* Aaron thought with a sigh.

And he waited.

Waiting patiently for the men who would turn his life into another mystery, but as far he was concerned he would now prefer hell.

The rhythmic sound of pounding shoes on the paved floor grated on his nerves as the officers inched closer.

Aaron clenched his teeth.

They towered above him, flashings their badges. A visibly upset Pastor Geoffrey peered down, staring at him. Aaron glared at the officers, a bored expression on his face.

One of the officers bent down and began to speak but Aaron was temporarily deaf. He looked lost.

The officer straightened up and beckoned his partner over. They spoke in hushed tones for a couple of minutes.

Crime scene investigators, men in white overalls, arrived with their paraphernalia. One of the officers helped Aaron to his feet and led him away. Pastor Geoffrey couldn't look at Aaron or the body of Caleb. There was nothing to say.

Aaron knew without an iota of a doubt that the pastor had defected from his faith; he could be wrong, but he felt sure of it. It was ironic that even Tyrus had fled when he'd seen him, but a mere mortal had scuppered all his lofty plans. He shook his head sadly; he thought it would be Tyrus and his demons, but it was a man.

Outside the church, a crowd had begun to gather.

Police officers stood sentry, trying to fend off the crowd. Police vans had blocked the road, cutting off traffic. Passers-by strained their necks to watch the unfolding drama. Many gaped at Aaron when he emerged, sandwiched between two officers, hands cuffed together.

A woman held out her mobile phone, took some pictures, and strode off, a grin plastered on her face. Before noon, the picture would appear on her Twitter feed.

Logan, Darren, and Jonas stood in a corner chatting, oblivious to the unfolding drama.

Logan was the first person to see him.

His eyes almost popped out of their sockets. Aaron in New York and in handcuffs? In his wildest imagination, he never thought he would just stumble upon Aaron, and what's more, in New York. *What a long shot,* he thought. Quickly working out how the new development would work in his favour.

He glared at Aaron as they led him away like a common criminal. Logan stood still for a while, contemplating what to do.

'Hey, guys, that's Aaron Cohen,' Logan said, pointing at the police car pulling into the traffic on the ever busy Fifty-fifth Street.

'Really? Are you sure?' Jonas asked.

'Positive,' Logan answered with a frown. It would be bad if Aaron disappeared again.

'What do you want to do?' Jonas asked carefully, searching Logan's face for clues.

'Why not find out from Pastor Geoffrey?' suggested Darren, 'at least Aaron was taken away from here. You might be able to find out more. We can't go to Ethiopia now that he's here, can we?'

'No,' Logan answered with a thoughtful frown, 'something's not right: I can feel it in my bones.'

'Please don't drag us into more of your riddles,' Jonas said with a grin, 'I think you're all right now that Keith Morgan, aka Lucifer's gone.'

'Don't you think that he'll be back?' Logan asked in a trembling voice.

'No,' Jonas answered, going back into the church, 'I haven't seen him in my dreams, I would like to see Lola, Evelyn, and Kate though; we shouldn't have allowed them to go.'

'They decided to go back to London. Don't forget that they're adults,' Darren said following Jonas into the church, 'I think we should just wait and see what happens. Aaron is here now, and that's all that matters.'

'I'll go check on Joshua Cohen then. I'm sure he would like to see Aaron,' Logan said.

'You do that. We'll be here when you need us,' Jonas said smiling.

'Thanks guys,' Logan said and walked away from them.

Jonas and Darren turned their attention to the man looking at them from across the road.

'We need to protect Aaron now. Lucifer must not get to him in this vulnerable state.'

'Do what you have to do,' Uriel said from behind them and their faces brightened when they saw him.

'What took you so long?' they asked in unison.

'I was held up in traffic. The session will begin soon and time is running out for him,' and Uriel beckoned to the man still staring at them.

‘Who is he?’ Jonas asked, ‘I haven’t seen him before.’

‘He's the prince of Persia. He's here to help Tyrus and his father.'

‘That means the hordes have arrived?’

‘Yes, I'm afraid they have. But Aaron is powerful - they can’t get to him,’ Uriel said, his eyes glistering.

‘But they can get to those dear to him.'

'Yeah, like Caleb. But Abraham had to go, he was tired.'

'Poor boy, he must be mad.'

Uriel agreed with a nod and said, ‘Brothers, you have to go to London. I’ll see to it that Aaron is safe; he will be with you tomorrow.’

‘Okay,’ and they moved away.

Jonas turned back and asked, ‘Where's the Ark?’

‘The Ark is invisible but it's with Aaron. Wherever he is, the Ark will be there, as long as he has the rod with him,’ Uriel said, and before they left he added, ‘I hope Logan doesn’t know who you really are?’

‘Nope,’ they answered in unison and disappeared inside the church.

'If Logan realised we're angels, he would probably ask us to make him rich.' Darren said with a grin and Jonas laughed.

They were fond of Logan, even though all he thought about was money.

'Good boys,' Uriel murmured and flew away, his fiery gaze reprimanding Persia who followed his every movement. Uriel disappeared into the air, moving faster than the speed of sound, his golden sword gleaming in the sun. Persia turned sharply when he heard a whizzing sound and saw Lucifer by his side.

They were eternal allies but Lucifer was still suspicious. He loved and trusted no one. In spite of that, they had to pool their resources, even though Lucifer and Persia hated each other's guts.

'How was the boy?' Persia asked with a stiff upper lip, obviously displeased at being summoned from the abyss. He had made up his mind to stop fighting Lucifer's battles; the only reward he'd got for his trouble was banishment for eternity. His dark, lined face creased up in a scowl as the events, which preceded their fall, assailed his mind.

All the strategy and planning had started on a certain day; it was a bright morning in Cydonia, a beautiful, red planet inhabited by angelic choristers. Their job was simple, they sing all day long, worshiping God every minute. Lucifer was the head of the choir, a powerful favoured angel whom God loved.

But Lucifer wanted more. The angels had finished the morning worship and were trooping back to the sanctuary to relax and prepare for the midday worship. He saw Lucifer looking rather pensive and a little subdued. After a little prodding, Lucifer hinted about a 'no show,' when he asked him to explain, he said mysteriously, 'I need to have a word with Big G.'

And that was all.

He tried to get more out of him, but Lucifer maintained sealed lips. Persia was the coordinator of the choir; Lucifer was the head of the worship team, and the closest to the throne of grace. So if there was anything brewing he should have known about it. Persia ignored the surreptitious glances from other angels and went about his duties. By midday, he had heard all the gory details.

Lucifer was tired of being second fiddle to God, tired of the dominion given to man, angry about the unending worship and irked by the incessant adoration heaped on man daily. The love and attention was like a dagger to his soul; it was like spikes through his dark heart.

Lucifer believed he had God where he wanted him. Big G trusted him, loved his voice, and would be shocked when he spat in his face.

Soon, he thought, he would ascend above the thrones of eternity and extinguish the seven spirits of God!

How wrong he had been!

Persia stopped his reminiscing and cast a furtive glance at Lucifer, who looked smashing for a disgraced entity. He wondered who the poor man was - another poor soul.

Persia regretted his decision to join the rebellion. Archangel Michael wanted to give him a leeway, a brief moment of clarity to think things through, but he didn't. Promises of power from Lucifer sealed the deal, and sin found its way into his treacherous heart.

His knitted brow was the only indication that his mind had travelled to distant lands. Lucifer was a smooth operator; he had promised lower cadre angels promotions and free reign if his insurgency succeeded. Persia would have been a spoilsport to decline such mouth-watering offers. Greed also played a major part. The thought of being in charge and ruling alongside Lucifer was too good an offer to throw away.

Their daily routine had been to spend every single minute that ticked by singing and worshiping the Almighty. Sometimes it did get stale, but they had to do it. Lucifer immersed himself in the stones of fire, supernatural stones carved with God's breath and available only to the purest of souls. The stones of fire increased Lucifer's strength while Persia grunted at the mess Lucifer had created.

Even if he had wanted redemption, it was far from his reach and he knew he would never attain it.

They had gone too far to be welcomed back into the fold of grace. He reeked of filthiness and knew that

God had blocked his loving grace from him and his kind forever.

He let out a sigh and stared at Lucifer, wondering if the latest attempt would work.

Within days of his hearing at the mount of mercy in the city of grace, Lucifer seemed to have better plans and Persia was keen to discover what he had up his sleeve.

Lucifer did fulfill some part of the bargain, but it was a mere fraction. Their foolproof plans failed, and soon, Archangel Michael sent them hurtling down to Earth. Persia made the abyss his home and every thousand years he popped to the surface world.

Persia let out a deep sigh when he recalled the look of disappointment and horror on the face of Archangel Michael when his treachery had been exposed. There was no way he could have extricated himself from it all, and he loved Angel Michael. But that was light-years ago; they hardly spoke anymore when their paths crossed.

He glanced at Lucifer, and wondered why his empty-headed son believed they could win. Even if they managed to lay their hands on the stones of fire and the Ark of the Covenant, God would not reverse their punishment. Persia knew about the stones of fire that Uriel had imbedded it in the fabric of a man's soul, the descendant of Aaron the high priest. If Lucifer had asked his opinion, he would have told him to accept the judgements meted out to them. The truth was they'd been disobedient, and had to pay the price.

'You need a body,' Lucifer said smoothly, glaring at Persia's strange appearance. He had a human head, the torso of lion and the legs of a horse.

'I'm all right as I am,' Persia said nonchalantly, still angry.

'Sorry for dragging you in,' Lucifer said slowly, his lips heavy. Persia was the prince of the power of air, and he needed his help more than ever. He was an expert in controlling humans, and with all the legions of controlling spirits at his disposal, Persia couldn't be more useful.

'This time around, your operation will not be clandestine in nature. We're going to use everything we've got.'

'Okay. But for a change, I think I'd like to be a woman,' Persia conceded, a rueful look on his bearded face.

'Talk about the power of a woman,' Lucifer remarked.

36

CIA HQ, Langley, Virginia, Aug 15

As the head of covert operations, Brian McDaniel didn't really exist. At least, he hoped he didn't. He tried not to draw unnecessary attention to himself and had done so for his twenty-nine years in clandestine service.

Brian dealt with the bureau's dirty work.

He had never been married, and his parents gave him up for adoption shortly after his birth. At fourteen, Brian tried tracing his birth mother, but only ended up with one of her cousins. Aunt Greta loved him but died two years later.

Brian had been pleasantly surprised to find out his dead aunt had left him two hundred and fifty thousand dollars. His aunt's gruff looking lawyer informed him that he would have complete access to the money when he turned twenty-one, but on one condition; he must serve his country. Aunt Greta wanted him to be a great man, and that was what young Brian McDaniel did. He joined the bureau in 1978 after graduating from Harvard, where he'd studied law.

Brian was sharp, intelligent, and a workaholic.

He began his career as a core collector operations officer and gradually rose through the ranks. In the course of his career, he had experienced extreme failure and untold emotional upheaval, but he kept a tight rein on his emotions; he neither flipped nor faltered. He was what the bureau needed as their clandestine chief operations officer.

Brian lived and breathed patriotism. He had killed and would kill again to obtain vital information that could be of importance to the security of the country. Brian's superiors loved his attention to detail, but there had been failures and compromises. Terrorists feared him; he always seemed to know their next move. Word was out in Washington that he could progress in his career if he wanted to, but Brian loved clandestine service; nothing else mattered as far as he was concerned.

He scrutinized and analysed the files in front of him but was not reaching any conclusions. The phone on his desk rang sharply, but he ignored it.

Brian stood to his feet, heading for the office of the director. The contents of the files in his hands disturbed him, and his intuition was always right.

He knocked once and entered the big but moderately furnished office of the director.

Brian was average height, slim with bushy eyebrows; his whining voice was his Achilles heel, so he had devised a cunning way of speaking. He spoke slowly and clearly; he was never in a hurry and always made sure that he got his points across.

He stood silently in the middle of the room, waiting patiently for Director Roberto Costello to turn round and acknowledge his presence.

Roberto was glued to the window, deep in thought. He knew Brian was in his office, and he knew he had come to compound his headache rather than alleviate his pain.

'What have you got, Brian?' Roberto asked softly, his thoughts far away.

The disappearance of the Holy Father had been giving him great concern, despite trying to push it out of his mind. He couldn't remember the last time he attended Mass; his job made it almost impossible to have a life.

'I have a letter from one of the church elders of Fifth Avenue Presbyterian Church in downtown Manhattan.'

'What significance is that to national security?' the CIA chief fired at his director of operations. 'A lot, if you'd just glance at the contents of the letter,' Brian persisted indignantly, slightly piqued by the director's lack of interest.

At last, he turned away from the window. Brian glanced at the CIA chief briefly and noticed the worry lines. Roberto Costello was very handsome; even though he was fast approaching his sixties, he still looked good. Roberto attended his local gym regularly, and it showed.

He had toned muscles and a full head of dark curly hair, which he had repeatedly tried to straighten whenever he popped into his local salon, while his bushy eyebrows and clean-shaven face gave him the appearance of a Sicilian godfather. He was a Washington veteran, had served in Congress, and was once the chief of staff in the White House.

He adored Pope Nathaniel III and couldn't bear the thought of any harm coming to him.

Absentminded, he stretched his hand out and took the letter from Brian. He read through quickly, and mid-way, walked to his chair and sat down.

When he finished reading, he glanced up, waving the letter in his hands. 'Who else has seen this?'

'Just you and I,' Brian answered, unmoved by the reaction of his boss.

'Get me the White House and the director of national intelligence.'

'Yes, sir,' Brian said and left the room.

How could the Ark of the Covenant be in New York? It sounded preposterous. Did he even believe in it? It was necessary to see the Ark before they could make any decisions, and they must handle it with diplomacy. Different nations would lay claim to the holy relic if it did exist.

Roberto bit his nails, a habit his mother had tried to stop, but had failed miserably. It was ironic that as a Catholic he didn't believe the Ark existed. *What a joke,* he thought grimly.

He felt strange and light headed.

The Ark was reputed to contain radioactive material and, rumour had it, that it could level mountains and destroy millions of armies with a whiff of its holy fire. Apart from biblical times, could it be true?

Roberto closed his eyes, swivelling round in his executive chair deep in thought.

If the Ark had half the power it was rumoured to, then they had to find it, and anyone even remotely connected to the holy relic must face serious questioning.

Things don't add up, he thought with a shake of his head.

The Pope had disappeared into thin air, the Ark resurfaced in New York, and everyone appeared unperturbed. At least the Vatican had grudgingly issued a statement saying everything was under control, but the

Italian prime minister had not made any comment, and the White House had conveniently kept its lips sealed.

Roberto rubbed his hands over his face and stood up; he had to see the president. It might not directly have any link to the US yet, but he knew anything could happen and the sooner they found the Pope, the better for all concerned.

He left his office and closed the door quietly.

A whizzing sound heralded Tyrus's arrival in Roberto's the office. He sat on the chair the CIA director had just vacated. Waiting patiently, he tapped his gnarled claws on the mahogany table; he knew that Roberto would soon be back.

Exactly five minutes later, Roberto Costello opened the door of his office and saw something like an apparition in his seat. Tyrus flicked his hand and the door slammed shut with such brutal force that all the papers on the table flew about like kites. The letter Brian gave Roberto glided towards him, landing at his feet.

Roberto bent down on one knee and picked up the letter, trying in vain to control his shaky legs. He crumpled the letter in his hands and Tyrus laughed heartily, baring his fangs. Roberto controlled himself with an effort as beads of sweat gathered on his forehead like ants on a mission.

'Who are you, sir?' Roberto asked coolly, wiping his face with the back of his hand. If only he could pray, he gritted his teeth and swore under his breath. He regretted neglecting his faith; a few psalms would have done the trick.

His mother would be furious if she were alive and saw her beloved son shaking like a leaf before an apparition.

'I want you, Roberto,' Tyrus screeched, clasping his hands together, 'I'm a demon, the nearest to the throne, and I need a body now.'

Keep your cool, don't show any fear. Roberto thought, but his hands were already clammy with sweat.

Tyrus's head was expanding. He desperately needed a new body, but it was becoming a tough job. He watched Roberto shrewdly, and liked what he saw.

'Your body will suit me till the hearing,' Tyrus said conversationally, picking a clog of wood from a hole in his face, and spat it on Roberto desk.

This is not happening, Roberto thought desperately. He wanted to reach for his holster and draw his gun but knew it was futile. If he could reason with him, maybe he could buy some time. Then he remembered Anna, his two-year-old granddaughter. She would be expecting him; he had promised to take her to see the president at Camp David. Would the evil monster sitting in front of him allow that?

He doubted it very much.

Roberto gathered some courage and with slow, measured steps walked towards Tyrus. He stood in the exact spot Brian McDaniel had stood a few minutes earlier.

'Sir, I think I could be of more help to you than just providing you with a body.'

Tyrus gave him a quizzical gaze, a slow grin spreading to his rapidly deteriorating face, or at least, something that vaguely resembled a face.

'Fire away,' he conceded, pushing the chair backwards, swivelling back and forth.

Roberto racked his brain but nothing came out. And when he opened his mouth, the first words he said seemed to intrigue Tyrus as he clapped his hands together and motioned him to speak louder.

'I'm a Christian.'

'Hmm... I'm impressed, but that's not good enough.'

Roberto! Think hard! He thought desperately, and something refreshing occurred to him.

'I have a brain tumour.'

'I only need you for seven days, though I know you're lying,'

Tyrus said and gave a short laugh; he was fast losing his patience.

'Why did you choose me?' Roberto asked, glaring at his tormentor in disdain.

'I chose you because of your close link to the Vatican. Roberto, you adore Nathaniel III, or whatever that stupid title you gave him was.' Tyrus replied standing up and inching towards him without his feet touching the floor.

Roberto's hands unconsciously reached for his nose, the stench emanating from his unwanted guest was sickening. His stomach rumbled, he doubled over and vomited on the rug-covered floor.

Tyrus pulled him up, tore his shirt with a flick of his hand, and opened his mouth wide. Suddenly, a brilliant light shot out of Roberto's body. Tyrus staggered back, stunned.

He couldn't believe it.

The only force that could have inflicted such a wound on him was one of the stones of fire. Had he bitten off more than he could chew?

With a deep growl, a force pulled him away from the fear stricken Roberto. Tyrus crashed through the window and disappeared when he hit the ground.

Roberto clutched the chain and cross around his neck, shocked at his close encounter with death. His hands shook as he removed the tiny gold chain around his neck and examined it.

It had been a gift from his grandmother, and the chain seemed ordinary enough except for the inscription on the back of the cross. On closer inspection,

Roberto found a whitish coloured stone imbedded in the cross and his grandmother's words, spoken on her deathbed, echoed in his mind.

'This was a gift from a dear old friend, Betto,' and she'd smiled when she called him Betto; she was the only one allowed to call him that.

'Wear it always, son; it's a gift from God.'

With shaky hands, his grandmother put the chain around his neck. He had been nine years old and the chain had stayed around his neck until he'd joined the Marines.

He had not worn the chain for years, but before he'd left home that morning, his wife had seen the gold chain among her jewellery, and she had asked him to wear it. He did, and it eventually saved his life.

He ambled to his desk, his breathing heavy. He slumped into his chair. No one should find out about what had just happened. But how would he explain the pungent odour and the broken window?

Later he lifted his head and put the chain back around his neck. He pulled out his mobile phone from his trouser pocket and called his wife. Fortunately, for him, Vivian was an ardent believer; she was the only one who would actually understand.

37

Joshua stared at Logan as if he had seen a ghost.

'What do you want, you son of bit-...?'

'I'm so sorry I haven't had a chance to see you...'

Logan cut him off nicely, 'but the constant police presence outside your door at the hospital was discouraging. I really tried.'

Joshua didn't believe him for a second.

'I'm sorry about Joseph, I really am,' Logan said easily, his eyes on Joshua's flushed face.

'Where have you been all this time?' he asked weakly.

'I've been around,' Logan replied evasively, the image of the beautiful woman he'd met at the hospital came to his mind, 'I saw the hospital administrator, one Ms Rebecca...' Logan noticed Joshua's tired eyes and his heart went out to him.

'She told me,' Joshua said allowing a hint of smile around his dry lips, 'I just wanted to be sure you hadn't spent all my money on women and booze.'

Logan scrutinised the tastefully furnished room, impressed with Joshua's taste. *I'd better get down to business,* he thought. He saw a chair beside the bed and lowered his frame into it.

'I've found Aaron,' Logan said in a clear, rich voice, and he waited.

The transformation was swift; it was as if a light from heaven shone on Joshua. But for the drips attached to his frail arms, he would have jumped out of bed.

'Where is he? Please tell me, I need to see him now.' Joshua cried out, tears of joy in his eyes. Logan began to feel uneasy. He fumbled for the right words.

'He's alive and well, but he can't come to see you now; he is helping the FBI solve a case.'

Alarm bells began to ring.

That was how everyone had lied to him about Joseph's death. Joshua glowered at Logan, his lips trembling, and said as calmly and firmly as he could manage, 'Tell me the truth, now!'

'Whoa, whoa, hold it big guy. He's cool, I swear!'

Joshua's expression was totally unexpected. He had a deranged glint in his eyes and surprisingly for a hardened man like Logan, he pitied him. Joshua's hands shook when he spoke and his voice was faint, like the voice of a ghost in a Friday night horror film.

'He's under police protection. Some strange things have been happening to him. I think he's a troubled man,' Logan said quietly, biting his lip for the last statement.

'We live in a troubled world, Aaron is no different,' Joshua snapped angrily, jumping to Aaron's defence, 'I'm sure he's a fine young man.'

'He is,' Logan agreed, staring at his palms; it was the best way to avert the deep, penetrating gaze of the renowned criminal lawyer, 'but I repeat that he's really troubled...' then he tried to hold Joshua's gaze, ' I don't mean that in an offensive way, I swear.' Logan added gently.

'Tell me what you know,' he commanded in a stronger voice.

'Aaron is experiencing strange things that are beyond any rational human explanation. Nightmares, visions in the dead of night, ghostly assailants; the list is endless.

And there is always this lost look in his eyes...' Logan paused briefly, trying to collect his thoughts, 'his nightmares are mainly associated with death. He went to Ethiopia briefly, and then came back to New York with two Ethiopian monks who died in suspicious circumstances.'

'How do you know all these facts? And where is Aaron now?' Joshua asked softly, his excitement plummeting.

'The police took him,' Logan said simply, ignoring his first question.

Joshua's eyes narrowed into slits at that revelation, his mouth set in a thin line. In spite of Aaron's misadventures, the most pleasant thing was that Logan had seen his brother's son. It was the first bit of good news he'd heard since Joseph's death.

He could finally atone for his sins.

Joshua let out a deep sigh and Logan felt sorry for him; he cut the picture of the embodiment of sadness. Joshua stared at him and said forcefully, his eyes sad, 'You've got to help me find him, Logan. You need to find out where they've taken him. Investigate what really happened. I have a hunch someone set him up.'

'Set up by whom? Or do you think he was set up by the Church of England?' Logan sneered, all his pity flying out of the window. He needed cash, but he was getting tired of chasing shadows.

'I'll give you a million dollars if you can bring my brother's son to this house,' Joshua paused as if gathering his thoughts, 'No; I want you to take him to England. I'll give you an address of a friend who will take care of you, and I'll meet you there.'

Logan was dumfounded.

A million dollars would certainly change the story of his life completely. His mum would finally be proud of him and he could go back to Jackson Mississippi and show the local folks that he had finally made it.

He scratched his stubbly jaw; he hadn't shaved for two days, and his skin itched like hell. He knew he had a mountain to climb and valleys to cross; Aaron's case was mysterious, and the Ark's ominous. He remembered his new friends: Jonas, Darren, and Zach. He was sure that they would be happy to help him.

'I'll do anything for you, boss,' Logan said with a wide grin.

'There is a catch though,' Joshua said slowly, 'you don't get paid until you take him back to England.'

'Do you expect me to eat sand while I'm chasing your psycho nephew?' Logan almost bit his tongue when he saw the look of utter despair crossed Joshua's face.

'I didn't mean it, I'm sorry,' Logan apologised profusely, standing up and making a show of leaving.

'That's all right,' Joshua grunted and added, 'you seem very bright and eager, but a foolish and unwise man. Take my advice and you'll live a longer, happier and more fulfilled life. Don't serve money, let money serve you.'

'That's if you have it, Mr Cohen,' Logan chipped in warmly, feeling a bit relaxed and at ease.

Logan loved money; if you had been poor, you would too.

'Please bring that black suitcase over here,' and Logan turned round and saw the suitcase. He picked it up from the couch and handed it over to Joshua.

He opened it and took out a chequebook, scribbled on it with a flourish and handed the cheque to Logan. He took it and gaped at the amount written on it.

Joshua smiled and said, 'I knew you needed the money, but no booze or women until this is over. It's also important for you to keep a low profile, you know what I mean?'

'I do, Mr Cohen,' Logan replied still, shocked at the amount of money.

He walked with quick strides towards Joshua who lay on his back.

Joshua seemed to be enjoying the look of surprise on the handsome features of his visitor.

'This is a cheque for two million pounds, not in dollars man,' Logan exclaimed and his voice was shaking, 'I haven't done anything yet.'

And he put the cheque in his breast pocket.

Joshua chuckled and said with a beaming face, 'I have millions tied up in properties scattered across the globe. I have millions in stock and hundreds of millions of dollars in accounts all over the world. I can afford to be very generous.'

'You have that much money? How come...? Did you inherit it?' Logan sat on the chair, staring at Joshua in fascination.

'I've been around for a while and I've dabbled in a lot of lucrative deals, but as God would have it, and in His infinite wisdom, He gave me no heir. So tell me, who should inherit my vast fortunes?'

'You can always spend it on good causes. In Africa, or Asia, even here in the states,' Logan said, hardly recognising his own voice.

He looked at Joshua in a new light. Logan had known the man was rich but not to that extent. A lonely, dying rich man; how he wished he were in Aaron's shoes.

'I've made my fair share of donations to charity,' Joshua said with a glint in his brown eyes, 'and now go and pay that cheque into your account and get my Aaron to England... hurry up, please.'

'Consider it done, sir,' Logan said standing up, and then strode briskly towards the door.

Joshua said to him, 'I wish you Godspeed, my son.'

Logan turned back briefly and bowed before opening the door. Three hefty men faced him, and they looked angry. Logan retraced his steps and heard Joshua's startled gasp.

The men barged into the room and punched Logan's face; he couldn't even scream. The only thing he remembered was the cheque and his legs wobbling for a brief second before he crumpled to the tiled floor with a dull thud.

AARON RESTED his head on the table while the interrogation officer paced up and down the bare room.

He stopped in front of him, tapping his index finger on the table. Aaron lifted his head, staring straight ahead, a vacant look on his face. Brian McDaniel pulled up a chair and sat directly in front of him.

Brian had got a call from an agent in the New York Police Department who alerted him to a suspected double homicide in Fifth Avenue Presbyterian Church. The case was important because the pastor of the church had confirmed that the Ark existed.

On the spur of the moment, Brian had decided to go down and handle the interrogation himself, but the suspect hardly spoke a word and it was hard for Brian piece all the facts together.

He had concluded that NYPD could not charge the suspect for the murders of the two Ethiopian men until they gathered more evidence.

However, the post mortem results he received indicated that the men died of natural causes, so there was no case. He had simply wasted his time.

Brian turned his attention back to the distraught man; Brian needed to know the location of the Ark of the Covenant.

'The Ark is gone, sir. I don't know where it is,' Aaron said suddenly, breaking into Brian McDaniel's thoughts.

'Excuse me? Could you repeat what you just said?' Brian asked, taken off guard.

'I don't know where the Ark is. Three men took it from the church house where we were staying. I think you should be speaking to Pastor Geoffrey; he might be able to help you more. I want to mourn my friends in peace.'

Brian sighed and knew his hunch had been right. The officers should have brought the pastor in for questioning. Then a thought struck him and he asked, 'Mr Cohen, are you in any way related to the renowned criminal defence lawyer Joshua Cohen?'

Aaron put up a blank expression.

'Nope,' he answered, hoping Brian would leave it at that, but he pressed on nonetheless.

'I've been digging into your family's history and I'm absolutely sorry for everything you've gone through.'

Aaron said nothing. All he could see was Caleb's body on the floor and Abraham's cold body in the church house.

'Sir,' Aaron stared straight into Brian's eyes and said quietly, his voice breaking, 'I don't know anything about what you guys want. I don't know where the Ark is, I don't know who killed my friends and I don't even know why you think I should know a man that bears the same name as me. Just let me go. I want to go home. I have to get to England,' he paused for a minute and his head dropped, but when he lifted it again, his voice was stronger and more convincing.

'I have enemies your nukes and intelligence can't destroy. If you or your little troopers here want to live, you had better let me go; anyone remotely connected to me dies. At least you've read that in your sordid little file, I'm sure that things can't get better than this.'

Brian stood up and walked out of the room without a single word.

When he got outside, he met the officer in charge of the case and said to him, 'I'm going back to Virginia. Let him go, but if you suspect anything please don't hesitate to contact me.'

Brian had just made the biggest mistake of his career by dismissing Aaron. On his flight back to Virginia, he sat next to one of the most beautiful woman he had ever seen in his life. The life he had led for almost twenty years was one of celibacy. Right beside him was a woman he would love to take home. Dim the lights and have a little romantic dinner, followed by small talk beside the fire. Afterwards, everything should sail smoothly.

He cleared his throat and said with a broad grin on his face, 'Hi.'

The woman looked sideways and returned his grin with a wide smile. Encouraged by the woman's easy smile, they got talking, and when the plane landed in Virginia, Brian didn't go back to the office.

No one saw him again.

The woman's name was Rebecca Kolinsky.

38

Shalem Armani held Rachel by the waist and then hugged her tightly. He pulled away, trying to engrave her face into the fabric of his soul. His voice broke when he spoke, 'Don't ever pull that kind of stunt, ever again,' and he pulled her into his arms again while she chuckled and lifted her face off his shoulder.

'They wanted to know if we'd be good together. In fact, I suggested it,' and she laughed.

Shalem loved the richness of her voice.

'And now?' he asked uneasily, 'how did I measure up?'

She moved away from him and the thought of her skin on his made his blood hot; just a few more weeks and they would be married. He doubted he could hold on for the big ceremony in Tuscany; they just had to get married as soon as possible.

'I don't know, Shalem,' she said fondly with a sweet smile.

His heart almost broke in two at her breath-taking beauty; her full red lips and her bright eyes, although what finally captured his heart was her easy smile. Her lips usually tilted to one side whenever she was smiling and her eyes were ever so bright. He desperately wanted her to be the mother of his children.

They held each other for a while and Shalem wondered how his father had been able to ensnare Rachel. It was unbelievable that she was in the secret service - she didn't look it.

Shalem had always thought that agents were manly looking, or at least the female ones.

'I want to start a family as soon as possible, Shalem,' and she looked up at him with her huge brown eyes, 'I don't want to be an agent anymore.'

Shalem was shocked but didn't show it. In a way, her decision pleased him. After the nasty experience he'd had, he was not too keen on having adrenalin-pumping thrills anymore, especially with his soon to be bride.

'Why do you want to quit, darling?' Shalem wanted to know.

'Yesterday was not all an act.'

She cleared her throat and swallowed hard, 'Somebody tried to kill me; must have been one of our agents.

I don't why, but I suspected Yosef, one of Yitzhak's men.

'Is he the big bloated guy with the wicked looking eyebrows?' Shalem asked trying to take it lightly, but inside he was shivering like a bird with flu.

'Yeah,' she answered.

Yitzhak had moved them from their rented apartment in Rechavia to a safe house in Tel Aviv. He had also visited that morning and they'd even spoken to their parents who seemed confused by their sudden decision to get hitched quietly, but Shalem assured them that a bigger ceremony was still in the offing.

Shalem stared at her. Everything was becoming too confusing, 'Is that why Yitzhak moved us from Jerusalem?'

'I think so, but I could be wrong,' and she slid into his arms again, looking up at him.

The only thought in Shalem's head was kissing her passionately, but he controlled the urge and listened with rapt attention.

She placed her hands on his wide chest and said with a cute little grin playing around her lips, 'I want to be a mother, Shalem. I want to watch our children grow. I love family life. It's funny when you continually moan about how boring your life is,' she paused and placed her index finger on his lips, 'you are the luckiest man alive, Shalem Armani, and I love you to bits.'

'I love you too, Rachel,' he said huskily and bent down to kiss her, but she moved away giggling like a schoolgirl.

'I've got a wedding to plan,' she said, and her voice echoed in the great villa.

'It's just a small ceremony, darling,' Shalem said with a smile.

It was suddenly quiet and he chuckled at the thought of the impeding wedding. Things seemed to be moving fast, but he liked it. The thought of getting married now appealed to him. The boring life he used to despise had become a paradise on Earth. The thought of their children running around in their villa in Tuscany was clearer now.

Love surely makes things better, Shalem thought. He removed his coat, then loosened his tie and threw it carelessly on the sofa.

Yitzhak had told him that they needed to lie low and remain incognito. It finally occurred to him that their lives might actually be in danger, and he wondered why.

They were staying in a large, luxurious villa, and they had access to the internet, which was a huge relief for him. Men with blank faces waited on them hand and foot. Shalem suspected that everyone in the villa was an agent, but he didn't care; as long as he was with Rachel, he could dine with the devil.

He sat on the sofa and wondered why people were keen to find the Ark of the Covenant.

Not that he wouldn't be thrilled to see it, but if there was so much mystery and power associated with it, he might as well steer clear of it.

He heard a door opening and looked up. It was Yitzhak with a tall man dressed like a priest.

They all shook hands, and Yitzhak introduced the man.

'This is Father Hezekiah. He will be performing your wedding this evening,' he said smoothly, avoiding eye contact with him.

Shalem was stunned.

'This evening? Why?' he asked incredulously. Things were certainly spinning out of his control.

'We have to leave for New York tomorrow night, and since Rachel has decided to step down from field trips, I thought it best that things move up a notch.'

'You didn't even have the courtesy to consult me before you decided to just spring this on me? What, or who, exactly do you take me for, agent Yitzhak?'

By now, Shalem was angry. He tried to control it but failed woefully. It was absurd that Yitzhak think he would flow with this ridiculous idea.

Rachel must have heard his raised voice because she rushed to the lounge and saw Shalem's flushed face.

'Honey, what's the matter?' she asked, placing a protective hand on his shoulder.

'We're getting married tonight, so says Emperor Yitzhak,' he sneered, shaking with rage.

Rachel was shocked; she had never seen him so angry.

'Maybe there was good reason for it, darling,' she said softly, pulling him gently into the large bedroom they shared.

'We have to trust him, dear,' Rachel said placing both of her hands on his flushed cheeks. Eventually he calmed down, pulling her into his arms, 'what have I gotten us into, my love?' he murmured into her hair.

'Everything will be all right, Shalem. We have to play along,' she said reassuringly, her big eyes imploring him to believe her.

'Okay,' he said and sighed, 'but he said I have to go to New York tomorrow night.'

The news caught her off guard. A scowl appeared on her face and she asked, 'Why? Did he tell you why you had to go tomorrow?'

He shook his head studying her face.

She looked scared, and he had a sudden urge to protect and shield her from harm.

'Honey, I'll be all right. I'll make it clear that the only condition that would make me go is the promise of your safe arrival back home.'

'But you need to be briefed about the nature of the assignment, you can't just go...' and he silenced her protests with a passionate kiss.

When he lifted his face, she had her eyes closed, and her breathing was uneven. She looked ravishingly beautiful as Shalem stared at her with pride.

'Honey, I can't wait to be your husband and I promise to love you for all of eternity,' he said, and meant every word.

She opened her eyes.

'I can't believe that I can love a man the way I love you,' she whispered, 'and I don't mind being Mrs Armani right now.'

They stared at each other. Love seemed to pour from every available pore on their bodies. They went back to the lounge and met a horrific scene.

Someone had slit Yitzhak's throat and the priest was lying on the floor, a six-inch knife protruding from his stomach.

Icy coldness glided through them as they stared at the carnage unleashed. Gradually, the priest opened his eyes and lifted his hands with great difficulty. Shalem and Rachel rushed to his side at once.

The priest held their gaze and with the last strength in his body said, 'I now pronounce you man and wife,' and he gave a gold chain to Rachel.

She took it with shaking hands.

'Father, who did this to you? Can you please talk? Tell us Father.'

He wanted to speak but blood gushed out of his mouth and he coughed painfully as he held Shalem's hand, 'Hosts of de-...' and his breathing became shallow. He had stopped breathing.

'C'mon, let's get out of here,' Shalem said.

'Wear the chain, Child,' the father said strongly, opening his eyes for a fraction of a second before gasping for breath like drowning man. His hands fell limply to the floor.

Shalem closed his eyes and took the gold chain from Rachel's hand. She pushed her hair up with one hand and Shalem fastened the gold chain around her neck.

'How could this happen?'

'This is the work of highly trained assassins,' Rachel replied, and they went back to their room. She opened the bedroom wardrobes and took out two Berretta 93R automatic pistols. She worked swiftly, her demeanour that of a woman going to war.

Shalem stared at her with something akin to wonder; Rachel was in her element, her eyes were cold and hard. She threw one of the pistols towards him and he caught it in mid-air, he turned it in his hands holding it firmly.

'Can you shoot?' Rachel asked in a whisper as she armed herself with rounds of ammunitions.

'No, but I'll learn,' he answered and she tip-toed to him and gave him an ammunition belt, which he also strapped to his body.

'What now, Wife?' Shalem asked as beads of perspiration popped on his forehead.

'We wait, Husband,' she replied, glancing at him, and the look on her face was murderous.

Shalem waited anxiously. He'd wanted adventure, and it was apparent that he had gotten more than he'd bargained for. Someone, or a group of killers, had murdered his friend and the priest in cold blood. The killers could still be prowling around the villa.

They waited.

Then they heard a crashing sound.

39

Camp David, Maryland, Aug 16

It was a beautiful sunny afternoon. The president of the United States stretched to his six foot seven inches on the sofa reading a newspaper, while his wife of thirteen years clutched a novel.

Their three children were playing somewhere in the presidential Aspen lodge; their robust laughter filtered to them occasionally.

Joseph Levin leafed through the pages, but his mind wasn't really there. He had decided to go to Camp David on the spur of the moment, Chief of Staff John Dock tried to make him see reason and stay put in Washington at least for that weekend, but Joseph Levin had had enough of the bickering and politics.

He wanted to clear his head and relax with his family at the cool, secluded Maryland Catoctin mountain retreat.

He stood abruptly and dropped the paper he was reading on the centre table.

'I'm going for a walk, darling. Care to come along?' President Levin asked, closing the gap between him and his wife. He gently pulled her to her feet before holding her head in his hands. She did not resist, but rather she gave him her brightest smile.

'Mr President, you know I'm reading,' she said sweetly but with a determined look on her smooth black face.

He pulled her into his arms and kissed her soundly on the lips.

'I love the mountain air. Walking will do you good, honey.' He persisted with a boyish grin that always melted her heart into submission, but this time she refused to budge.

'No, Joseph; run along now. I'll be here when you get back.'

'Okay, Dorothy,' he gave up and walked to the door while she went back to the sofa.

'It might get chilly, honey; why not take a coat?' she called after him.

When he didn't answer, she stood up again and approached him cautiously, smacking him on the butt.

'Ouch,' he feigned pain and pulled her hair.

She gave a mock scream as their three boys came into the room laughing.

'Mom, can we all take a walk with Dad?' Richard, their eldest son, asked.

'Sure,' Dorothy agreed, going back to the sofa. She sat down, watching her family as they trooped outside the lodge, followed by two secret service agents.

Her sister walked into the lounge, an inscrutable expression on her face. She sat on the sofa the president had vacated, watching her.

'What?' Dorothy asked with a knowing smile. Everyone knew how addicted she was to novels, and nothing relaxed her more than reading.

'I wonder why you didn't go out for a walk,' Natasha said, touching her hair and crossing her long legs.

Natasha was twenty-six and a law graduate of Harvard. She wanted her sister to be glamorous like her predecessors, but Dorothy was the most conservative First Lady Natasha had ever seen. Although her simplicity had endeared her to millions of American women, Natasha was not buying it.

Dorothy was the epitome of womanhood; strong, hardworking, and faithful to her family and country. As recent poll results showed, she seemed to be winning the popularity contest - not that she cared about such trivial things.

Dorothy had been born into a wealthy African-American family. Her dad had been a civil rights activist, one of the closest friends of Martin Luther King.

Until his death a couple of years earlier, Dorothy's dad believed that one of his six daughters would a become governor, but Dorothy had other plans. She hated the business world and politics left a sour taste in her mouth. She had always dreamed of becoming a cardio-vascular surgeon, and a couple of years later, with lots of hard work, she'd achieved her dream.

She eventually won her dad over; until she brought Joseph Levin home. Joseph was Jewish. Initially, the relationship didn't go down well with him, but he eventually overcame his reservations and gave his blessing. Joseph had a warm personality and it didn't take him long to win Dorothy's family over. When Joseph decided to run for senate, she supported him all the way.

Two years into her husband's presidency, Dorothy had been juggling her commitments to St. Luke's Episcopal Hospital, being the First Lady, and a mother to three energetic boys. It wasn't easy, but she was coping well, at least in the eyes of the world.

She was ecstatic about their weekend retreat to Camp David, a laidback place tucked away in Maryland's Catoctin Mountains. She thought perhaps, the refreshing cool air would cleanse her crowded spirit.

However, her ever-cheerful face hid a painful and distressing problem. She was a sleepwalker. At times, she had pleaded with her husband to chain her to their bed.

One incident left an indelible scar on her mind. She had woken up one night and found herself naked on the lawns of the White House. She often wondered how the papers never got hold of the story, because her husband had been the one who carried her back to their room. If the media did know about it, they had never leaked the story to the public. Despite how hard it was to keep secrets in Washington, hers had been well kept.

Her strange condition began shortly after the swearing-in ceremony, and to make matters worse, she had started hurting herself in her sleep.

Joseph wanted her to see a psychiatrist but she refused. Dorothy had argued that it was stress, and she had promised to scale her commitments down, but he was not convinced.

Dorothy's gaze flickered to the heavily made-up face of her sister and she changed her mind. She knew Joseph would be furious over her indecision, but she wanted to feel the mountain air on her face; Jeffrey Archer could wait.

Dorothy and Natasha left the Aspen lodge followed by an agent. They strolled in silence. Natasha glanced down the road and saw a blonde woman approaching their lodge. The woman wore a bright red skirt suit, her lips parted in what closely resembled a mocking grin.

'You have to go back inside, ma'am,' the agent said crisply, his eyes on the strange woman. He spoke rapidly to the earpiece attached to his neck. In a matter of seconds, a dozen marines materialised from the surrounding trees.

Natasha hurried inside the lodge while Dorothy stood her ground. There was something magnetic and strange about the woman. She couldn't place her finger on it, but she would bet her life that she had seen her before. Maybe she'd met her in one of the numerous dinners organised by the White House, or some charity event? Dorothy knew the face so well. She watched the woman's approach, and her suspicion mounted with each step the woman took.

Dozens of guns trained on the woman did not deter her, and she never flinched.

As she inched closer, Dorothy felt the cold hands of fear. From the corner of her eye, she watched the agents in surprise; they were not following normal protocol. By now, the agents should have done something; either issued words of warning or ordered the woman to stop her approach.

The agent standing close to Dorothy was shaking uncontrollably and Dorothy almost laughed.

She watched with a feeling of utter helplessness as the specially trained men dedicated to protecting her and her family stood like statues.

The woman stood close to her and seemed to sniff her. When Dorothy looked straight into those green eyes, her blood turned cold, and every thought flew out of her head.

The icy red lips parted in a smile and she extended her hand for a shake. Dorothy complied and the woman clasped her hand in a vice-like grip; she cringed. When she finally released Dorothy's hand, she was feeling dizzy.

The weather changed dramatically. The wind hissed in rage and the trees seemed to clap their hands in fury. Thunder ripped through the clear sky and Dorothy screamed at the men standing like zombies watching her and the woman, 'Find my family!'

They were galvanised into action.

'My name is Rebecca Kolinsky. I'm here to have a word with the president,' the woman said in a sleek, smooth voice.

Dorothy forced a polite smile to her face and invited Rebecca inside the lounge. She took her straight to a mini conference room. About five agents tagged behind them and she heard the familiar drone of a helicopter, but the unusual raging weather continued.

Rebecca Kolinsky sat on one of the chairs and Dorothy sat close to her. She didn't know how the woman came to be in the camp, but it was a serious security breach.

Dorothy cleared her throat and asked quietly, 'How did you get so close to the camp?'

'I flew,' Rebecca answered.

After a few awkward minutes of silence, President Joseph Levin entered the conference room, flanked by security agents.

Another rumble of thunder struck and Rebecca stood to her feet, ambling towards the president.

'We need to be alone, Mr President,' she said in a matter of fact tone, and Joseph Levin knew he was talking to no ordinary woman.

There was something sinister and evil about her.

Joseph was curious as to how she could have slipped into the camp without anyone spotting her.

Camp David was supposedly the most secure place on Earth for him due to the high altitude.

The camp was one thousand eight hundred feet above sea level, which made it a very cool, relaxing place to be after the stress and humidity of Washington.

The retreat camp was always on high alert, but he was slightly irritated at having to cut his walk short over a woman and dodgy weather conditions.

As far he was concerned, there was no human born of a woman who could frighten him.

He dismissed the entire security web around him, but Dorothy stayed.

'She must leave, Joseph,' Rebecca Kolinsky demanded in a cold, flat voice. Dorothy looked at her sharply.

'Who the hell is this woman, Joseph?' Dorothy asked her voice dangerously low; Joseph knew she was very angry.

The door was yanked open and another set of naval officers entered carrying submachine guns but again, the president dismissed them.

'I'm the prince of Persia,' Rebecca said and flicked her hand. Dorothy was flung into a wall and she landed on the floor with a thud.

Joseph slapped her hard around the face and her head jerked backwards. Joseph staggered towards Dorothy fearing the worst. When he found that she'd merely fainted, he breathed a sigh of relief.

'What do you want?' he asked looking up at her. For the first time in a very long time, Joseph felt the cold hands of fear eating away at him and he shuddered.

Rebecca was a new kind of threat; the one he had no real answer to. He was feeling helpless and Joseph hated that. He tried to take charge of the situation by cradling the head of his wife and whispering into her ear, but her arms had gone limp.

Rebecca walked to where he was and said quietly, looking down at him with disdain, 'I want the Ark of the Covenant and a young Jewish boy named Aaron Cohen within three days. I'm not a very patient woman, so I would really appreciate it if you used every power at your disposal.'

President Joseph Levin nodded.

He believed in the supernatural, but in his wildest imagination, he never thought he would come to see a demon in human flesh.

'But if you could sneak up on me here amidst tight security, why can't you find this guy yourself?'

'That's none of your business,' Rebecca retorted and turned to go. Then, on second thoughts, she glared at him and said, 'I know all your secrets, and I won't hesitate to expose you.'

There was glee on her face, and her voice was hoarse.

'Your romance with the American people would be over; imagine the kind of horror that would create. Besides, Brian McDaniel is dead. I killed him to celebrate my return to Earth.'

And with that she stalked out of the room, slamming the door so hard that Dorothy opened her eyes.

'What does she want?' she asked weakly.

'Nothing I can't give her, my love,' he said holding her tenderly, his mind far away.

He'd gone to the camp to have a bit of 'me' time, but instead the devil had stolen his peace. All his enemies in Washington were nothing compared to this. How would he deal with the situation?

He carried his wife out of the conference room and met dozens of agents and marines staring at him anxiously.

'It's all under control,' he murmured with a nervous smile, but the words had scarcely left his mouth when deafening clap of thunder ripped through the sky with such intensity that it sounded like a bomb. Electricity surged through the sky as torrents of rain fell hard.

President Joseph Levin walked to their room and lay his wife down on the bed, as gingerly as he would a day old baby. Their children gathered around the bed, watching their mother. They looked scared.

'She just slipped,' he explained slowly, trying to diffuse the tension in the room. They didn't seem to believe him. Natasha walked into the room with a dazed expression on her face.

'What happened?' she directed the question at Richard.

'Dad said she fell,' Richard answered, peering down at his mom. His eyes spoke volumes, but his mouth stayed shut.

'Oh my God,' Natasha whispered tearfully.

'She'll be fine,' the president muttered as the doctor came in. They all left the room and the doctor quickly examined Dorothy while President Joseph stood silently in a corner, a look of gloom creeping onto his features.

The doctor turned to him and said, 'she doesn't seem to have any broken bones, just the swollen forehead. I strongly suggest we take her back to Washington as soon as possible, so we can run further tests. Just some precautionary measures; I don't think it's anything to worry about.'

'Thank you, Doctor,' he said, shaking the doctor's hand.

The doctor left the room, closing the door firmly.

Finally, alone, the president walked to the bed, sitting at the edge, his eyes sad.

Should I tell her the truth and risk incurring her wrath? How would she react if she knew I had a daughter? President Joseph thought.

He didn't know how much the woman, or the prince of Persia as she called herself, knew.

'My God, why do you want to expose me now? And who the hell is Aaron Cohen anyway?' he grumbled and ran his hands through his brown hair.

Should I confess to the affair? It was ages ago. She was only an intern, and now she's dead anyway! Joseph was torn between telling the truth and keeping a tight lid on things. Another bolt of lightning flashed through the window and heart-wrenching thunder struck again. This time around, it sounded more like a nuclear bomb.

An agent rushed into the room without bothering to knock.

'Mr President, we have to evacuate you now, sir; there is a little skirmish outside.'

Several agents crowded into the room forming a tight column, and the president heard the voice of his son screaming out his name.

'Leave me alone,' he uttered and he pushed past the wall of specially trained marines. He ran out of the room and into the corridor. The first thing he saw was the sprawling body of Natasha. He stumbled along and saw his personal aides on the floor. It seemed they had been electrocuted; their faces were frozen.

President Joseph felt hands pulling him but he pressed on towards the living area, screaming out the names of his boys, 'Richard! Daniel! Eleazer!'

But there was no answer.

Years of training to control his emotions crumpled. He convulsed into sobs as he searched furiously for his children. They seemed to have gone.

He staggered outside the Aspen lodge and saw the body of the naval commander right on the lawn.

He froze.

Whoever attacked Camp David had reduced it to rubble. Fire raged in all directions, and then he saw them. They were like helicopters; there were hundreds of them, hurling thunder like arrows. President Joseph Levin had never witnessed such a terrifying or gripping sight.

They were like aliens - powerfully built aliens with mammoth wings and mouths that spat fire. It was like something out of a Steven Spielberg film, yet very real.

He stood rooted to the spot and saw smoke billowing to the sky. A marine made a futile attempt to engage in combat.

He was vaporised instantly.

Then, like a sweet melody in the rain, Joseph heard his son's voice, 'Dad, Dad, wake up! Stop screaming!' Richard was shaking him vigorously and he jumped up, a wild look on his face.

The president stared back at almost twenty pairs of eyes.

'How long have I slept?' he asked his croaky voice hardly above a whisper.

'Just a couple of minutes, I think,' Dorothy answered in her southern drawl, a smile playing at the corner of her lips.

'Thank God,' he murmured and headed for his room, 'c'mon everyone, we're going back to Washington, now!

'No, you can't do that, Dad; we just got here!' Richard protested hotly.

'Well young man, that was a presidential order,' Dorothy said ruffling his hair playfully as she stood up and followed her husband.

'What's that all about, dear?' she asked, placing a delicate hand on his shoulder, 'you said you wanted to have a walk with the boys, and the next thing you went back to the sofa and nodded off. I told Richard to let you sleep for a while, and then you were hollering at the top of your voice.'

He turned to her and said, 'I had a very frighteningly dream, honey; it looked so real. I believe from the bottom of my heart that we should leave now.'

Dorothy sensed his fear and it was quite surprising; he didn't believe in dreams. Her Joseph was a carefree soul.

She tried another tactic, 'Do you want to talk about it?'

He was trying to suppress his anger and frustration.

'No,' and it was emphatic.

'Okay, if that's the way you want it, I'll get the boys ready.' She planted a brief kiss on his cheek.

Twenty minutes later, they were all set to go, but as they walked to the helicopter, the president saw Roberto Costello and the woman he had just seen in his dream.

Rebecca Kolinsky. They approached cautiously. The president stared at the CIA chief wondering if his dream was happening so soon. He glanced briefly at the sky and noticed the gathering clouds. He stole a quick look at the woman walking elegantly beside the CIA director.

She was wearing a blue dress, which clung to her shapely body. He swallowed hard as they came up to him.

Dorothy hated her immediately.

40

Aaron opened the door to his London flat and looked round. Everything was just the way he'd left it. He was about to go to the toilet when he noticed a familiar handbag. It was Kate's.

The sight of her bag gladdened his heart.

He went to the toilet and came back, then collapsed on the sofa. He glared at the piles of letters neatly arranged on the kitchen table, but ignored them.

Every bone in his body screamed out in protest. The past few weeks had been a living hell.

He would have gladly died with his friends, but he had not. He might as well continue with his mundane existence.

He would be ready for Tyrus and his gang anytime; at least the Ark was history. He left the living room and went to his bedroom. The first thing he saw was the freshly made bed, and he groaned.

'You're so untidy. Didn't your ma' spank your behind for being so messy?' Uriel smiled when he saw the look on Aaron's face.

'You can't get rid of the Ark; it's come home,' he said warmly and his wings began to open.

Aaron noticed the wrapped box beside his bed.

'How did that happen? Who stole it in the first place?' Aaron fired the fusillades of questions at his friend.

'I did!' Uriel answered with a chuckle, 'Tyrus and his gang were closing in, so I went on to plan B, got a few pals and sent them to the house, they took the Ark and I used the flowery stick the elders gave you in Ethiopia to tie it to your person. It's a lot of spiritual jargons and you may not understand it.'

Uriel seemed to be enjoying himself but Aaron didn't find it funny. He was spent and the sight of the Ark set his blood on fire.

'I think you'd better take that back with you to wherever you've come from; I'm sick and tired of it. All my friends are dead and my family has been totally erased from the surface of the planet, what more do I have to lose? Nothing, do you understand me?'

Uriel watched his every move while Aaron glared at him before continuing in the same angry tone, 'God is seated in His pompous throne playing my life like a game of chess. What have I done to Him to deserve this kind of treatment? I think He just enjoys inflicting untold hardship on me; he was there when my parents died, and I will keep repeating that until the day I die!'

Uriel still said nothing; he waited patiently for him to vent his anger, which Aaron did. 'He killed Abraham and Caleb while Tyrus and his gang were having a field day. Right now, they're probably having a laugh about their massacres. I even heard from the pastor in New York that some sick psychos razed the Pope's summer residence to the ground. And the Pope? He's simply disappeared into thin air. I can see Tyrus's signature all over this, but what has your God done? He's done nothing! He's ignored his children while His rival is having a field day!'

Aaron gritted his teeth in despair.

'I'm through with you, your God, and that stupid Ark. So, you better take it with you and leave me well alone. I need some peace before your God slays me.'

His hands fell to his sides.

Miraculously, he felt relieved; happy, even.

He jumped on the bed, plumped the pillows, lay down and raised his knees, waiting for Uriel's response.

Uriel sat on the bed facing him with a silly grin on his face.

He understood where Aaron was coming from, and it was not his place to tell him, but he would. After all, things were not as they should be.

'You have to work on that anger of yours. It could get you into trouble. It's raw, volcanic, spontaneous, and unnecessary. I hope you remember these words, Aaron; anger rests in the bosom of a fool. Don't allow the enemy of your soul to use that against you. God did not kill your parents, or the rest of your family for that matter. The devil was responsible for that. Abraham died because it was his time to go, and Caleb was fearful. He could have fought Tyrus but he didn't, and he paid the ultimate price: his life. Do you think the Almighty enjoyed seeing his children suffer? On the contrary, the only thing you need to do is reach out to the Holy Spirit and He will help you fight. He will give you the grace to withstand the onslaught of the enemy. He will even fight on your behalf, if you allow Him. But with the volcanic eruption that is your anger, he will be far away from you. He is life in its entirety, the spirit of the father on Earth, the embodiment of the trinity.'

Uriel stopped speaking abruptly, fastening his eyes on Aaron. Aaron flinched under the scrutiny and turned his face away.

'I think it is time for you to have a woman. You need to get married.'

'Says who?'

'You need her, Aaron.'

'I don't want to draw her into this. Besides, am I not supposed to stay celibate as the caretaker of the Ark?'

Uriel ignored his argument and pressed on.

'Kate is already into this deeper than you think. When she comes in soon, she'll tell you the most incredible story you've ever heard...' and Uriel added with a twinkle in his eye, 'she's bringing someone to see you. I hope you'll be able to keep your mouth shut for a few minutes and hear her out,.'

'How on earth do you know about Kate?'

'I'm an angel, remember?'

For an angel he was incredibly handsome. He had deep brown eyes, which seemed to see through one's soul. He was very tall, over seven foot and well built. Apart from his wings, he looked ordinary enough, with thick dark wavy hair, a bronzed complexion, and dimples on each cheek.

Aaron couldn't help but admire him. He would have broken many hearts if he had been human.

He continued his appraisal of the angel, wondering what Uriel did when he was not snooping around.

Uriel heard Aaron's train of thought and said simply, with a sparkle in his eye, 'By the way, I'm the keeper of the Tartarus, otherwise known as Hades. It's the eternal pit where the devil has been, and will continue to be, incarcerated. I keep the key to the gate of the pit. I'm also the prince of the presence, the fire of God. I also have the privilege of staying in the throne room,' and he gave Aaron a boyish grin, 'I'm a great traveller and see to the affairs of the Almighty. I have many other roles that I won't bore you with. One day we'll probably have more time to chat, okay?'

Uriel's face began to glow with such brilliance that Aaron had to shield his eyes.

'Are you leaving me now, Uriel?' he asked timidly and squint his eyes, all traces of anger gone.

Uriel nodded as he stood up.

'When am I going to see you again?'

'Soon, Aaron. In the meantime, don't forget about the spirit of the father. He's right here with you; remove bitterness from your heart and you'll ascend to a higher level than you ever thought possible. No matter what happened here today, the spirit of the father will never leave you.'

'That's very comforting,' Aaron said quietly, 'but I can't see him like I am seeing you, can I?'

'No, you can't. Just ask Him to come and He will breeze into your life and give you more power. He will increase your faith, and believe me; you might not even need me anymore. I'll say to you Aaron, son of Cohen; you'll meet at least two members of the council apart from me.'

'What are you talking about?'

Uriel changed the topic and his wings fanned out in glorious splendour.

His white linen robe began to sparkle.

Suddenly, a ring of glossy laurel leaves entwined with moss encircled Uriel's thick, wavy hair.

'All earthily forces will be used to find you, and they will, but it's your wit that will ensure you succeed. Your courage, your perseverance, your faith: it's all you!'

Uriel's eyes shone like the sun.

'Aaron, you're the only one who can win against this onslaught from Tyrus and Lucifer.'

And he was gone.

A breeze whistled through the window, and Aaron's heart seemed to expand, feeling as though it might burst out of his chest. He re-adjusted the pillows, mulling over Uriel's words. Ten minutes later, he fell asleep.

KATE HAD been lucky to flee Evelyn's house undetected. She hoped her friend and her daughter would be able to escape as well.

Naturally, the only place she could think of was Aaron's flat; her mom would never welcome a stranger into her home.

Aaron's return was a delightful miracle and she could not wait to tell him about her escapades.

Kate strolled towards Aaron's room; her feet barely making any sound. The door was ajar, so she peeped through and smiled, watching him sleep.

Aaron stirred in his sleep, muttering inaudible words, punching the air furiously. She was confused. Going into the room did not seem like a great idea, so she waited, watching the bizarre scene. Then he lay still. Kate was immobile for at least two minutes. When she was satisfied that he had slipped back into dreamland, she moved away from the door.

She turned back again to catch a last glimpse. Aaron was snoring softly; he looked relaxed, like a newborn baby.

How she loved him so!

Her heart fluttered with excitement and she held her hands to her breast, a wistful expression on her face. She was completely smitten, head over heels in love. She had broken every known law of her mother's; she had fought with demons and won.

Kate was a very different woman now- she knew what she wanted, and that Aaron needed her more than ever. She was tempted to fling her arms around his neck and smother him with kisses, but that could wait. A contented smile lit up her face and she went to the living room.

Aaron was extremely clean. His small living room looked neat and well organised. Kate sunk her aching feet into the soft cream rug and went through the plans all over again. If she succeeded in bringing the dying Pope to Aaron's apartment, it would give Evelyn and her daughter the chance to make a run for it, and she would be able to explain everything to Aaron.

But it was Evelyn who worried her; although Kate was against her impending trip to Ethiopia, she had no say in it. It was too damn soon.

She had heard about the chaos engulfing Ethiopia after the Ark and its caretaker disappeared. Most countries had closed their embassies in the East African nation due to the escalating violence. Kate wanted Evelyn to wait at least a month before travelling to Lake Tana to scatter Michael's ashes. Telling Evelyn her concerns was simply out of the question; she didn't have the guts to do so.

The sound of a car broke into her thoughts like a bolt of lightning, and she was on her feet in a flash. She parted the curtains and peered outside. Evelyn was alighting from a Ford Escort. Kate didn't bother to check who was sitting in the back of the car before she left the apartment, darting down the stairs.

Kate was grinning from ear to ear. How Evelyn had managed to sneak out without those hoodlums finding her was beyond her. But she had escaped, and that was all that mattered. Kate was sure the Pope must also be in the car.

Her face spread into an open smile, but the smile froze on her lips when she saw her bullet-riddled friend. Evelyn had collapsed a few feet away from the car, gripping the urn that contained her husband's ashes tightly.

Kate looked round wildly, but the street was quiet; there was no one. She raced towards Evelyn and bent down, taking the urn from her hands and putting it beside her.

'It was a trap, Katie,' Evelyn whispered weakly, her pale face contorted with pain. Blood was dripping from the side of her mouth.

'Oh my God, who did this to you?' Kate asked, her lips trembling.

'The Pope is still with them... Lola escaped but I couldn't help the Pope...' and Evelyn's voice faded away, her lifeless eyes boring into Kate's tearful eyes.

You've got to call 999, Kate, she thought.

Luckily, she had her phone in her jeans pocket; she pulled it out and dialled the number for the emergency services. Kate spoke rapidly into the phone while beads of perspiration trickled down her face. She described what she'd witnessed and with a sigh of relief, snapped her phone shut. The woman at the other end had promised to dispatch an ambulance crew.

Then her eyes strayed to the back of the car. She noticed some movement and stepped back, wondering if the killer was still lurking around. Then she heard the unmistakable sound of someone whimpering. Who could that be? she thought feverishly.

She stared at Evelyn's ashen expression and suddenly felt cold.

What's happening to us? What should I do?

Kate felt her head spinning. She tried to think of what Evelyn would do - call the police? No, she'd only called the ambulance. I should have called the police first, and then the ambulance, she thought with a sinking feeling at the pit of her stomach.

Then maybe go upstairs and wake Aaron; he could help. Surely Evelyn would have acted in that order.

She heard the whimpering again, but Kate could not think straight.

She crouched beside Evelyn and wondered if she should check the car. Uncertainty and fear assailed her already frayed nerves. She wanted to go back to the house but couldn't bear the thought of leaving Evelyn alone.

Kate checked her wristwatch wondering why it was taking the ambulance so long, and she made up her mind. Lifting the urn containing Michael's ashes with her shaky hands she stood to her feet and approached the car.

Every step she took resounded in her mind. She wondered if she had made a wise choice.

Inching her way slowly, Kate stared at the pitiful picture of the frightened child. It was Caroline, Evelyn's daughter. She was huddled on the back seat, shivering and obviously distressed. Kate bent over and stretched her right hand towards her, beckoning her to come out.

Then she saw the gun and everything became a blur. A booming sound was all she heard, and the urn containing Michael's ashes dropped from her hands, falling to the ground.

Kate fell backwards and landed on the ground, hitting her head on the pavement. She was stunned and, strangely, her eyes sought the clouds. She stared at the mocking sky, her head hurting like hell.

She was not afraid to die, but the pain in her shoulder was excruciating and she had difficulty breathing. Kate's mind went straight to Aaron, sleeping soundly in his room, oblivious to the unfolding tragedy outside his apartment.

What a cruel joke, she thought and felt herself slipping away into a doze, but she willed herself to remain focused.

Then Kate heard Caroline stepping out of the car, walking over to her. Her dainty steps were like the hordes of hell.

Kate wondered if it was the end. Then she heard a dog barking in the distance, and she felt her shirt was soaking with blood.

Kate even remembered Evelyn, then Michael's ashes. She wanted to live and she fought to stay awake. A lone tear forced its way out from behind her right eyelid, seeping through and sliding down her cheek.

Water, she wanted a glass of water badly. A face appeared, then a familiar voice. Slurred voices, jumbled like a web. She couldn't hold on anymore as she embraced the welcoming power of darkness.

41

East Ham, London, Aug 17

The early morning sun emerged as a lone figure cut across the road. The man struggled with his breathing and had difficulty walking, but he trudged on nonetheless. He turned into a quiet street and dogs started barking furiously. He managed a rueful grin as he pulled his weight along.

To a percipient onlooker, he would appear drunk. But he wasn't; he was just tired.

He got to the last house on the street, entered through the door, and grunted in pain as he barged into a room.

He was the embodiment of rottenness; the remaining flesh on his face had fallen off and his tongue was hanging out.

Lucifer stared at him with disdain and spat on the floor.

'You look the worse for wear, son. I presume you couldn't get that CIA guy?'

Tyrus shook his head sadly, upset at his failure. His claws had begun to fall off. He crumpled to the floor, cutting a sorry picture. He was badly injured and was still shaken from his ordeal in Roberto's office. He couldn't even fly; the destructive effect of the radiation had also damaged his wings - it sliced them off of his flagging frame.

He was not expecting any sympathy from his father; rather, he expected a tongue-lashing. However, he desperately needed a body. He didn't want to go to the nether region without first acquiring a fully formed body.

Lucifer walked towards him, heaved him up, and slammed his disintegrating torso against the wall. Tyrus growled and fought back, hitting his father on the cheek. Enraged, Lucifer opened his mouth and fire consumed Tyrus. He dissolved into sulphur, disappearing in a haze of smoke. But less than thirty seconds later, he was back, a crazed look on his rotten, bony face.

Tyrus faced his father, glaring at him in disdain, frustrated with his weakness.

Lucifer took a cigarette from his suit jacket and lit it. He put the cigarette between his lips and puffed away.

'The prince of Persia will be here shortly, son. He has a body for you. The guy is also a weakling; I reckon you'll be a perfect match.'

And he walked out of the room. Ten minutes later, his head appeared in the doorway, 'Evelyn is dead, and Kate is dying. Evelyn's daughter shot them both,' the revelation was followed by maniac laughter and he continued, 'I did it all - I healed Caroline and the doctors had no choice than to release her from the Psychiatric hospital - Then I possessed her body and shot Evelyn, she was such a talkative. Michael was stupid and I finished him off too. Besides, he was hampering my plans.'

Another bout of laughter followed.

'Can you imagine their foolishness? Evelyn actually thought they could actually escape!'

When there was no reaction from Tyrus, Lucifer sauntered back into the room staring at him.

'What's wrong with you, son? You lost your balls?' Why are so quiet?'

Still, Tyrus said nothing. His nostrils flared in frustration as he struggled to breathe through his disintegrating nose.

Suddenly, for no obvious reason, Lucifer shouted, his eyes bloodshot, 'I don't want the hordes of hell fighting my wars again. Never again! I now have the chance to take back what belongs to me! Those stones of fire rightfully belong to me. And the bastard with those potently powerful stones is that stupid Jewish boy and you know something, son?'

Tyrus's dead, sunken eyes stared straight at his father.

'What?'

'Though I don't want the hordes of hell on this, I can't do it alone. I still need your help, and Persia's. Angel Uriel will see to it that I don't get the stones, but when there's a chance this could work, I won't give up. Throughout the centuries, throughout the ages, I've never given up. I've never lost my nerve or effectiveness. I'm still a force to be reckoned with, and if this kangaroo appeal court organised by God is anything to go by, I'll give it my best shot. I might not be a genius but I'm an achiever, and I swear on my name that I'll get those stones and Aaron will herald the powers in the Ark on our behalf.'

Tyrus's voice was passionate and pained at the same time.

'Believe me, Father, it's time to go home and call it a day. Release the Pope and let's go home.'

Tyrus was wise enough to know that he had a very short time left, and his father's glowing speech only added to his discomfort. He couldn't understand his father's obsession with the forces of heaven. Going by the experiences of the last few days, humans were tougher nuts to crack than he'd thought.

'No!' Lucifer shrieked and kicked the walls in frustration. If his only son was ready to give in, what chance did he have?

'Damn it!' Lucifer swore under his breath.

God's only son did such a fine job by sealing his fate and taking the power, the seals, and the keys of life and death from him. Now that he has been given a chance to redeem his time, a chance to beat the big guy in the cloudy and densely perfumed room at his own game - the seed from his loins wanted to tuck his tail between his legs and run. Lucifer would not allow it. He was determined to make his son fight and conquer as he had done, time and time again.

'I'll give you my bloodline son. It's the remnant of my purity, the last of my powers before Archangels Barachiel and Michael chased me out. You'll have a new body and you'll fight for what rightly belongs to you. This is home, you idiot!' And Lucifer' eyes glowed with the passion of his words, ' I want that to sink into your mouldy head.'

'What's that, Dad? You call this place home?' Tyrus asked weakly, every ounce of strength in his body ebbing away.

'Your dad wanted you to have a chance at greatness, a chance to ascend above the throne and stars of God,' Persia said appearing in the room in the body of Rebecca Kolinsky. A man was in her arms.

'This is so not happening,' Tyrus declared, sick and tired of their games. If only he could become a mortal, but the chances were slim. Perhaps there might be some leeway for him. His face lightened as a thought occurred to him.

Lucifer smiled broadly, rubbing his jaw with pleasure.

Things were going as planned.

'The American president has promised his full support for our cause. He knew I would kill his precious son Richard and...' an evil gleam appeared in her eyes.

Tyrus watched with a mounting feeling of dread; he was scared of Persia, who seemed to be enjoying his new role as a woman.

'I told him in no uncertain terms that his love child and sordid little secrets would be exposed if he didn't do what we wanted.'

'Good job, Persia,' Lucifer said grinning from ear to ear. His eyes travelled to the man trapped in her powerful arms, 'and is this is who I suppose it is?'

'Affirmative.' Persia said, putting the man on the bare floor, 'I forgot to mention this, but I also killed a man in the hospital's car park. He smelt of fear, and I needed fresh human blood.'

'When?' Lucifer asked curiously.

There was a gleam in his eyes before he answered,

'A couple of days ago, I was just roaming about and I saw him fidgeting. He was just an easy target, and I also followed his wife and killed her too..'

'Good for you. I don't even want to know the details. ' Lucifer said gratefully. He felt great. They might still be able to pull this off.

Lucifer turned his attention back to Tyrus and beckoned to him. He obeyed and stood up with difficulty. His bloodline was fading fast. He would play along, and then strike out on his own when the time was right. He would not spend eternity in the nether region; he had to negotiate his way out.

Father and son stood facing each other and Rebecca left the room, giving them some much-needed privacy.

'Your bloodline will fuse with this man,' and Lucifer directed his gaze to the unconscious man, then turned to Tyrus again.

'I'll give you more of my bloodline and this man lying at your feet will live, but I have to tell you this,' Lucifer's eyes turned red, his thick eyebrows raised for emphasis 'You might not be permitted to see the confrontation for a thousand years, you may even be banned from seeing me for a season. Do you understand?'

Tyrus considered what his father had said and shook his head, 'No, I don't.'

Lucifer tried to control his temper but failed miserably. He snapped angrily, alarmed at Tyrus's naivety, 'What's wrong with you, crack head? I'm sure it's your human side that's messing you up. I'm beginning to doubt your importance.'

Tyrus fell at his father's feet and worshiped him.

'Forgive me dad, I was so tired today. I promise I'll not fail you.'

Lucifer squatted, glaring at him coldly,

'You can't fail me, son, because if you do, your case will be worse than mine. I'll personally ask my demons to lock you away in the hottest part of Hades and throw away the key. You know what I mean by that?'

'Yes, Dad.'

Lucifer stood up and pulled his son to his feet. He walked to the next room with quick strides, and then came back with an ancient looking knife. He handed it over to Tyrus who took it with a questioning look.

'You have to stab me through the heart. I'll plunge into the abyss but I'll be back tomorrow morning - still with the same body. You must drink every single drop of blood in my body, son. By doing that, my bloodline will flow through your veins, making you one million times more refined, strong, and powerful. You will finally have the body of this man here, permanently. Even when we visit the grace room to see God, you can't change your body. You'll fight all your battles in this fellow's body, until we've won. Then you can do as you please.'

Tyrus swallowed hard and nodded.

'Now, let's go to the other room. Persia has erected a small altar for us. I want to get this over with,' Lucifer stopped for a brief second and turned to his son, 'I also invited Azazel.'

He brushed aside Tyrus's protest with a wave of his hands, 'Angel Raphael was taken care of, if we are to have a free trial, the hosts of heaven will agree to any terms. God must be seen to be impartial; you know He's the all-knowing and wonderful father who allowed me and my friends to plague the human race. Now he wants to end it all and we are going to give him a battle he'll remember with a shiver on his gleaming throne.'

Tyrus left the room in suppressed rage. Azazel was a demon he hated with a passion.

In the demonic hierarchy, Lucifer, Tyrus's father, currently inhabiting the body of Keith, revered Azazel. He had orchestrated part of Lucifer's rebellion during the fall of Cydonia. In retrospect, Lucifer wished he had listened to some of his suggestions; perhaps he would have won the great battle of Cydonia.

They despised Azazel in heaven. In Hades, some respected him, and on Earth, witches worshiped him in their droves. Some even considered him the father of whoredom, prostitution, and bestiality. Tyrus wondered why his father had involved Azazel in their set-up.

Lucifer threw Tyrus a sideways glance and shook his head as he thought of the craftiness of Azazel. He had been and still is incredibly gifted. Lucifer had secret admiration for him, though no demon knew that.

Azazel had fathered a child before anyone could blink, while he, Lucifer, the king of the power of the earth, waited two thousand years to father a child through a human. Azazel's daughter, Amelia, lived in a newly refurbished ancient house in the south of France.

Lucifer bent down to shift the man. The man opened his eyes and began to scream.

42

Joshua glanced at Logan briefly before moving closer to the full-length mirror, studying his own reflection. He looked different; no one would have believed that a few days earlier he'd been at death's door.

Logan was not impressed; neither was he keen on staring at himself in the mirror. He was still nursing a sore jaw and bruised arms. Thankfully, all his bones seemed intact.

However, he was beginning to question the impulsion behind pursuing his career as a private investigator. It could land him in big trouble.

The day he finally wrapped up his deal with Joshua Cohen would be the happiest day of his life. His only consolation was the cheque; he kept checking it every second. At least if he were to be crippled, he would do it in style.

The three bullies who had paid them an impromptu visit had a contract with Joshua. Logan was not bothered about the practical details of it all, but it was obvious that something was not right. The men roughed them up a little and bundled them into a black limousine parked in the underground garage. They'd spent the night in the cold, damp basement of a rundown building. By first light the next day, the men shoved them into the street. Joshua was gracious enough to call for one of his bulletproof Jeeps; one was already waiting for them when they got out.

They were presently inside Joshua's grand bedroom at his Washington home. After a couple of phone calls, Joshua told him that they would be leaving for London in a few hours. Logan couldn't wait for the whole charade to end.

Out of curiosity he asked, 'What did you give in exchange for our freedom? Who were those men?'

'I gave something that was not mine,' Joshua replied smoothly, dabbing cologne on his jaw. Logan allowed himself the luxury of a smile. The old man sure looked good, and the way things were going, if he behaved responsibly, Joshua could be more generous and add a few million to the cheque he had already written.

'Those guys used to be good friends, but I did a deal and it went sour. Naturally, they wanted their pound of flesh. I would have given it to them but spilling my blood was not part of the agreement. Shakespeare sure knew what he was talking about.' Joshua smiled.

Logan, however, was uneasy.

He knew that beneath the gay mood of Joshua Cohen, the man was living on borrowed time and was, and always would be, the target of many people. Joshua had legions of enemies waiting to feed on his flesh, and Logan sure didn't want to be an accidental target; he still had so much to live for.

Joshua finished dressing and stole another quick look at his reflection in the mirror. Satisfied, he picked up his suitcase, handed it over to Logan and said in a crisp authoritative voice, 'I believe we have a plane to catch, son.'

They strolled out of his palatial bedroom and into the hallway. Logan's eagle eyes admired the splendour boldly displayed.

Forcefully, he dragged his eyes away and focused on the task before him. Joshua had enough dough to splash on things that he thought were mundane and unnecessary. He shrugged his shoulders, but his roving eyes sought a second look and he felt a pang in his stomach.

Logan was jealous.

It's so unfair, he thought sadly. Some people had billions of dollars in their accounts while people like him had to struggle to make ends meet on a daily basis. Then he remembered the cheque he had.

'Well, that's something,' he murmured and Joshua gave him a quizzical look.

Logan chuckled, a smug look on his face and he walked with a slight swagger. Having that kind of money was somewhat cool. The most important thing would have been for him to take the cheque to his bank, but that was out of the question with the way things were going.

They walked briskly to the front door and a neatly dressed man in a black striped suit opened the door for them. Joshua acknowledged him with a quick nod of his head and handed over a white envelope. The man's face creased up in a smile.

They strolled towards a Mercedes 4x4 while Joshua stood still for a while, his eyes glued to the house.

He swallowed hard and his eyes filled with tears. Joshua remembered the great times he'd spent with his wife in the home, and he felt a pang of pain.

Life is such an illusion, Joshua thought. One day you believe you have it made, have all the answers, and the next thing you know, you're grasping at threads, trying to live out your days in makeshift glory.

Life is so transient, he thought again and his legs felt heavy. They were like stones. Joshua believed in the law of atonement; whatever it took, he would make restitution and atone for his sins.

With a determined look on his weary face, he turned away and wondered briefly if it was all worth it; the quest for success, dominion, and wealth.

He kept winning case upon case, thereby inflicting on humankind men that were best left with the devil. He had sold his soul to greed, money, and power. He never lost a single case. Most people held him in high esteem, but was it worth it? What had he really achieved?

He sighed.

He dragged his feet, his legs moving him towards an unknown destiny. His heart was heavy. It was as if someone had placed a slab of concrete on his soul.

In the words of King Solomon, 'Vanity upon vanity, all is vanity.'

He had lived his life in vain. However, if he made it safely to London, redemption could be within his grasp.

That gave Joshua hope; he could still sing again.

Logan walked ahead of his pensive boss with long strides, his lithe physique the picture of youth and virility. Joshua gazed at him with a little envy. He longed to be in his shoes; if he could turn back the hands of time, he would do things differently. If only he were twenty-five again. Would he have taken that oath of destruction that fateful night?

He climbed into the back seat of the car while Logan sat with the driver in the front. The driver moved away from the driveway as Joshua took one last look at his home. He turned away, tears of regret threatened to drag him down into the quagmire of his sordid past. Joshua travelled down memory lane.

Archer, his childhood friend, had invited him out; he'd called it 'a boys' day out'. Joshua was still reeling from the shock of his brother Benjamin eloping with a girl, and Archer was always there to offer words of comfort and friendship. His parents trusted and encouraged their friendship; they were reassured by the fact that Archer was always in the synagogue with his parents. They considered him a proper example of a perfect young man. How wrong they were.

Archer was like the devil incarnate. He knew how to put up a good front, knew the perfect words to say, and the places to be at the right time to ensure people would go home and tell his parents how well behaved he was.

However, at a very young age, he began to dabble in the occult and astral travel; the first and seventh planes were nothing to him. Archer knew a whole lot about angels and demons, and different kinds of devilish talismans were not beyond him. By the time Joshua realised how deeply involved Archer was in Satanism, Luciferianism, the 'Left Hand Path', dark Paganism and all sorts, it was too late to extricate himself from the tangled web of demonic influence.

It was almost impossible to get out from the perverse network of lies and evil, but he should have done something about it.

Joshua was afraid of the repercussions of defection.

Archer got more angry and violent. Joshua began to toe the line, believing that soon enough he would get out, before he got in too deep. But he never summoned enough courage.

Then the rituals and murders started. First, it was just casual meetings with a couple of members at coffee shops, and then, as the number of members grew, their egos and confidence doubled.

Initially they met in alleyways, dreaming and exchanging ideas. Then Archer killed his first victim, and his ruthless thirst for blood had begun. Archer grew bolder and richer. Brooklyn was under siege by Satanists; people disappeared only to resurface later, mutilated beyond recognition. It was gory. Joshua winced as he remembered all the details, and he closed his eyes in agony as the brutal memories overwhelmed him. He almost choked.

They'd had men in Washington who had been sympathetic to their beliefs. One thing led to another and before he knew it, Joshua was actually enjoying it. By the fall of 1969, he had reached his peak. His parents were dead so he could do as he wished. He married his college sweetheart, who knew nothing about her husband, except that he was an up-and-coming lawyer.

Joshua remembered his first and last kill with horror.

The girl was four; his neighbours' only child. The details were vague, but he knew he had abused and strangled the poor girl. Shortly after that, he shot to fame.

Yet the more his influence grew, the more he became depressed, until that fateful night when Archer came to his house with bright eyes.

He seemed high on drugs.

They went into his study and Archer had told him that they were going into the big league; a meeting with the grandmaster, Lucifer.

'I can't come,' he had whispered, 'my wife is getting more suspicious.'

Archer would have none of it and, as usual, Joshua succumbed and they went to the meeting.

It was like a big gala event in Denver, Colorado. Of course, he lied to his wife about a conference he had to attend.

It was a three-day affair and it was very tiring. Goat meat was on the menu; how he hated goat meat!

When he got to Denver, he had called Archer who had been in Denver three days before the event and told him he had some last minutes preparation to make.

'How long are you going to stay in London?' Logan asked suddenly, breaking into Joshua's reminiscing.

Logan was tired of the silence; it made the short trip to the airport long and boring.

Joshua sighed and answered with a faraway look in his eyes, 'I don't know, Logan. I want to see Aaron before I make any other plans.'

'Right,' Logan agreed, rubbing his hands together. Then he wondered why Darren and the rest of his friends had not bothered to call him; that was very unusual. They hadn't seen him for two days, yet nobody had bothered to call.

He made a mental note to call Darren when he landed at Heathrow.

There was no way he could explain anything to him now. Besides, Joshua's erratic mood was beginning to worry him.

Logan noticed the goat demon tattoo on Joshua's chest. He seemed to be flaunting it, as though he actually wanted him to see it.

Logan had heard about the Croles - they had the exact same tattoo. He wondered what his mother would think if she knew.

The only thing Logan wanted was the money; when he'd had enough, he would stop.

When will you realise that it's enough, blood money! A voice whispered in Logan's mind, but he banished the thought to the far recesses of his mind.

He was a businessman, and that was the end of it.

Logan tumbled away into a doze; *a quick nap would be good,* he thought and was soon nodding off.

Joshua glared at the back of Logan's head and his old desires came back, though he suppressed them. All he wanted was to see his brother's son, but he was struggling with the image of Logan's strong neck. His lean, hard face gave him the shivers.

'I'm not a cannibal,' Joshua said under his breath and Logan's eyes opened in a flash, he turned to look at him.

'Did you say something?' Logan asked with a worried frown.

Joshua nodded, unable to speak. His eyes were bloodshot; the poor kid had probably heard him and he couldn't control his urges any longer.

'Stop the car, now!' Joshua barked suddenly.

The driver jumped in fright, his foot slammed on the brake, and he lost control. Tyres screeched on the empty road and the powerful 4x4 swerved dangerously. The car somersaulted thrice before landing on its roof on the sidewalk.

Logan was conscious throughout the minute of mayhem. His legs felt like jelly, and he hoped that they were not broken. He tried to push the mangled door open but it was hopeless. Then he heard an eerie sound coming from the back of the car. Logan turned and he froze

Joshua's face had gone through a bizarre transformation. He seemed surreal, as if he were wearing a grotesque mask. Joshua reached for him. Logan did the only thing he knew how to do well; he found himself crawling out of the car and as far away as his wobbly legs would allow.

Logan had never fought for anything in his life; he had always run away. He stood far off, watching the wreckage of the car in disbelief. He pinched himself to be sure that he was not dreaming. When he looked at Joshua his face had changed back to normal, but there was still a deranged look on his face.

The driver appeared dead. His head was on the steering wheel with his hands hanging limply at his sides. Logan stared in horror as Joshua turned his attention to his driver. Logan began to scream.

When he heard the welcome sound of an ambulance, he tried to move away from the accident. A small crowd had gathered and Logan spotted Darren among them. He hurried towards him.

Logan grunted, opening his eyes.

It was all a dream, Logan thought with relief, thankful that it was not real, and he came to a simple decision. Casting surreptitious glances at the driver whose attention was strictly on the road, he devised a means of escape. He stole a quick look back and saw Joshua sleeping, snoring loudly. His face looked pale.

Logan saw the deep longing in Joshua's mind and was not comfortable with it. It was all so confusing.

'You'd better keep your eyes open, you fool,' Logan murmured under his breath and the tight-lipped driver glared at him, muttering inaudible words.

Money is not everything, Logan thought and made up his mind to get away from Joshua as soon as he saw the opportunity. Then he saw his chance.

The driver was travelling at forty miles an hour, which was slow for Logan but perfect for what he was about to do. He opened the door and jumped out. He screamed when he landed on the road; the driver swerved dangerously but later regained control. Logan stood to his feet and dashed away from oncoming traffic.

'Freedom!' he shrieked.

'IT WAS one of the best days of my life,' Shalem croaked out in a husky voice and his eyes filled with tears, 'I asked for a friend and I got a brother,' his voice broke and he choked back tears. It was hopeless, and he stepped down from the pulpit.

Friends of Yitzhak had gathered to talk about him. The actual burial had been done in the morning, and when Shalem stared at the body of his friend covered in a white shroud with no coffin, pain racked through his body. The rabbi prayed in Hebrew, but Shalem did not hear a word of what the preacher was saying. His mind was miles away, and in a matter of minutes, it was all over.

Shalem went back to his seat and sat down. Rachel held his hand, squeezing it gently. Other friends and family spoke glowingly of the dead man whom they unanimously called a patriot.

Three hours later, they were at the airport on their way to Italy, but Rachel was expecting trouble. Yitzhak's death was still a mystery; it made no sense at all. As she had suspected, Yosef had appeared unannounced the day Yitzhak died with six men in tow and ordered them out of the villa. Rachel was suspicious, but Yosef took control of everything and insisted they leave the city for their own safety. Shalem had stood his ground; he wanted to pay his last respects to his friend. And he did.

Rachel turned to her husband with a strange look on her face, 'Honey, do we need to go back to Italy in a hurry?'

Shalem's brow creased in a frown; what was she playing at? Then he understood perfectly.

'Well,' he drawled in his best southern accent, 'we can get to Italy tonight and check right out again.'

'Excellent,' she beamed, giving him her sexiest smile. She linked her arm through his and they moved towards the immigration officer who had been watching them with interest.

'Newly-weds?' she asked with a broad smile.

'Yes,' Rachel nodded, breathless.

'Hope that smile stays twenty years on,' the woman added pleasantly, her eyes twinkling.

'It will,' Shalem asserted, grinning, and he dropped their hand luggage. He noticed something peculiar about the woman; she kept moving her head sideways. Rachel and Shalem exchanged glances.

Afterward, they went through the metal detector, picked up their hand luggage, and strolled to the departure lounge. Yosef was watching them with some secret agents who were obviously bored. When he saw them disappear through the departure gate and go through the security checks, he took out his phone and dialled a number. He spoke rapidly and clicked the phone shut: mission accomplished.

Yosef beckoned to his colleagues, and they marched out of Ben Gurion International Airport, satisfied that Rachel and Shalem were out of their hair.

Shalem stopped for a moment and held Rachel by the shoulder.

'I don't think we should board this plane; that immigration woman was trying to tell us something.'

Rachel stared at him impatiently, and then she shrugged. What did they have to lose? There was really no reason to hurry when they intended to come back.

'Darling, it's just a gut feeling,' he said, gesticulating with his hands, 'I might be wrong, but I could be right.'

'So, what do you want us to do?' she asked quietly, studying his face. His eyes were glowing with suppressed excitement.

'We should find a place to sleep tonight, and tomorrow morning we can just tell the airline a fib about how terrified we were of travelling by air. We could say we get paranoid at times and just panicked. Let's just wait and see what happens.'

Suddenly Rachel's face went through a series of emotions, 'Do you think... are you thinking what I'm thinking?'

He nodded and she was livid with rage,

'That wicked son of the devil killed Yitzhak.'

'Maybe Yitzhak wanted to be killed to save your life,' a familiar voice said behind them.

The same immigration officer checked them was smiling, extending her hand for a shake. They took turns in shaking her hand and Rachel turned to her husband, and he was grinning like a Cheshire cat.

'Just a gut feeling,' he whispered easily.

'Could you two please come with me? I have a lot to tell you guys.'

They followed her into an empty office and she closed the door gently, walking to the centre of the room.

'I'm an angel.'

Rachel and Shalem nodded; words were unnecessary. Long shadows came over the room and a small glow from the woman's forehead mingled with the shadows. Shalem covered Rachel's eyes with his hands, but she pushed them away.

'We need you, Shalem. There is a silent war of wills going on presently, and if Lucifer wins, it would be devastating for us.'

Rachel and Shalem looked at each other, stunned. They rubbed their faces to be sure they were not dreaming.

'What are you talking about?' Rachel asked, watching the unfolding scene with something akin to terror. The woman's feet were now off the ground. Her golden hair cascaded down her back and her wings opened up, flapping vigorously.

She began to tell the story of Cydonia, which was an angelic civilisation and the cherub who once ruled the red planet, which was Lucifer. How Archangel Barachiel reduced it to rubble, at the battle of Cydonia. The angel spoke of Lucifer as one of the beloved of God, how God later found pride and deceit in him, how God released him for a season to allow him appeal his sentence. As her voice droned on, Rachel and Shalem slid to the floor in a trance.

43

NASA HQ, Washington, Aug 18

David Maser held the picture of his daughter in his hand, staring at it intently. She had grown into such a beauty. He held his breath for a second, remembering when she was born. He was afraid of the sight of blood and had cowardly left the delivery room to wait outside. His daughter came screaming into the world fifteen minutes later.

Chloe brought joy and laughter to his life; his two sons were great boys, but Chloe had been, and still was, the apple of his eye - until she'd met her current boyfriend. The young man had a repulsive aura about him. He was extremely good looking with a clean cut family, but David was uneasy. Jude was too smooth, too neat, and it was as if he had fallen from another planet.

Everything fitted into place with Jude. He'd got his science degree in mechanical engineering from Yale

University and was planning to go for his master's at the prestigious Princeton. His parents were top-notch politicians; his mother, a beautiful Russian, was connected to a former president, and they had billions in their account.

Maser was worried. Chloe had fallen in love. He could only hope it was with the right man.

He sighed.

David, a very large man, loved his family; he had never cheated on his wife, and many of his friends considered him too 'ordinary', but he liked his own personality. He was a man given to few pleasures. The only thing that drove him was his family and his job.

However, it seemed his picture-perfect world was veering off course.

The unexpected news at breakfast had exacerbated his uneasiness. As the scene played out in his mind, he shut his eyes; perhaps he would be able to expunge it from his memory.

A spoonful of cornflakes had been in his mouth when the bombshell dropped like the one on Hiroshima.

'I'm pregnant, Dad. Jude and I are moving in together.'

'Are you nuts?' he had blurted out and almost choked, 'we're church folks! My only daughter will marry before moving out of my house.'

'Dad, have you forgotten that I'm twenty-four and already living on my own?' she had fired back, her face inflamed with anger, 'what difference does a wedding certificate make?'

'It means togetherness, trust, enduring love, and complete commitment to one another. That was the way God intended marriage to be,' her mother quipped, her eyes sad.

Ellie Maser's petite frame shook with shock; her only daughter living in sin.

It was beyond comprehension.

Chloe had pushed her chair back angrily and as she did so, hot tea spilled onto David's white shirt.

She fled the room and they heard her stomping about.

Five minutes later, she came back to the kitchen, her face drenched with tears.

'You'll be informed when your grandchild arrives,' and with that, she stormed out of the house, banging the door so hard the building shook.

A sharp knock on his office door brought him back to reality; his secretary poked her head through and said, 'David, everyone is waiting for you; the meeting is about to start.'

'Yeah, sorry, I'll be with you in a minute. Thanks, Jessica.'

She nodded and closed the door.

David stood up, flicking imaginary dirt off his crisp white shirt. He remembered the brown tea stain, and his daughter storming out of the house.

When Chloe had left, he hurried up the stairs to his room and closed the door. He leaned on it and saw his wife sobbing profusely on the bed.

He'd tried to console her, but to no avail.

Reluctantly, he left her and walked to the second room, which they used as a walk in wardrobe. He changed his shirt and went back to the bedroom, but his wife, Ellie, had left.

He hurried downstairs and saw her at the dining table looking intently at something in her hand. David moved towards her, pulling her to him. He sniffed her hair, and then nibbled her ear gently. She laughed; her huge brown eyes were puffy and red with tears, yet she was laughing.

She moved out of his embrace, and there was a glint in her eyes. David knew she was up to something.

'Take this, darling.'

David stared at her outstretched hand; there was a tiny gold chain in it. He took it with a frown on his face, examining it.

'Where did you get this?' he asked quietly.

'It was a gift from my grandmother,' she answered sadly.

'Why the starry eyes, baby?'

Ellie tried to smile but failed, 'she gave me the chain before she died,' there was a faraway look in her eyes, 'the chain holds some of the powers of the ancient Ark of the Jews, and it will protect us.'

David had the urge to laugh but made his face as expressionless as possible.

'Okay, but why are you crying and laughing at the same time? Was it because of Chloe?'

She nodded.

David studied the chain, and handed it over to her.

'I'm laughing because I'll soon become a grand-mother, and crying because I don't know what will happen to our Chloe.'

'You heard her; she's all grown up,' he could hardly keep the sarcasm from his voice.

'Chloe is a good girl...'

Ellie's voice trailed off.

'Yeah, I know,' he agreed, but that didn't stop his anxiety.

'Sit down,' she commanded with a hint of laughter in her voice. He obeyed, glad at the change in her mood.

Gently, she loosened his tie and put the chain around his neck.

'How do you feel?' she asked.

'I feel great,' he said, standing up and holding her hands, 'don't worry about Chloe; she'll be all right.'

'I'm not worrying about her,' she said, moving a strand of auburn hair away from her eyes, 'I'm worried about her boyfriend. There's something sneaky and atypical about him. He doesn't look right... I don't mean physically. Do you understand me?'

David let out a deep sigh and nodded.

He understood perfectly. Ellie was a Sunday school teacher and a deaconess at their local Baptist church. She was the epitome of the perfect American wife and her only daughter having a child out of wedlock was too much for her to bear.

'I promise you, honey, she'll be all right,' he had reassured her, pulling her into his arms again, but he had a sickening feeling in the pit of his stomach.

They had been married for thirty years and had three children. Their eldest son was currently in Iraq, their second son was in the US Navy, and Chloe, the apple of her mother's eye, had grown wings and flown out of the safety of the nest.

David was a senior scientist at NASA mission directorate in Washington; but one with a difference. He believed in God and had absolute faith and trust in humanity.

He believed human beings have the capacity to invent and create a better world. Ironically, he didn't have a clue on how to handle his daughter; it was as if she were possessed by a demon.

Chloe had totally shut him out of her life, but she hadn't been like that before. He remembered how pretty she looked on her prom night; so innocent and beautiful, more like an angel. Then things changed rapidly. She rarely answered his calls and had started attending strange religious meetings with Jude; it was now affecting his work.

His colleagues noticed the vacant expressions, the disjointed speech and the irritable behaviour, and they were concerned.

David always shrugged it off.

'I'm working too hard,' he'd say, or, 'I'm having trouble sleeping.'

David grunted. He couldn't even remember Jude's surname and his daughter was living with him.

What a tragedy.

David inhaled and then expelled an exaggerated breath. He made up his mind to focus on his job and push thoughts of his daughter and her boyfriend aside.

He stepped out of his office into the long corridor. David was a man with a heavy heart trying to hide behind his job.

NASA was preparing another launch into space and as the chief scientist; he needed to be on top of his game.

David tried to shake off an odd feeling creeping up on him; the feeling of somebody watching him.

It was preposterous, he knew that, but the feeling persisted.

Then a great idea occurred to him. A holiday would ease his pain a little. He decided to take his wife to London, her favourite city. Maybe a week away from their normal surroundings would cheer them up, but the thought did not raise his spirits, rather, it seemed to dampen them.

David shrugged his shoulders, walking through the long corridor to the conference room with his chaotic thoughts.

AARON RACED to the front entrance of King George Hospital in East London, his heart in his mouth. He went straight to the accident and emergency department where a nurse told him to wait for visiting hours. The good news was that Kate had survived the attack. The bad news was that he had no idea how serious the damage was.

He glanced at his watch; could he wait for two hours? He gritted his teeth, pacing up and down the waiting room. Later, a petite nurse walked up to him.

'She's in Erica ward but heavily sedated at the moment. If you come in the evening, you might be able to see her.'

'Thanks for your help, I appreciate it.'

The nurse nodded and disappeared inside the ward. Aaron was happy at the news that Kate would be fine. He folded his arms over his chest and felt someone beside him. It was Uriel.

'You have an uncanny way of sneaking up on people, you know?'

'She'll be all right, buddy. Kate should be the least of your worries now; you've got bigger fish to fry.'

'She almost died, how do you think that made me feel?'

'You didn't pull the trigger. Look, Aaron,' Uriel's tone was now patronising, 'the die is cast. We need to go.'

'You'd better speak plain English; Shakespeare is long gone.'

'I'm serious, dude; we have to go now!'

'First I'm 'buddy', now I'm 'dude',' and he chuckled, 'London is changing your language. You ought to be speaking like this – thou art the son of man, what sayest thou Aaron of East Ham?'

'What meanest thou?' Uriel said, enjoying the banter, but his eyes were deadly serious, 'we need to go!'

'Go where, Uriel?' Aaron asked, irritated.

'There is a church on Fleet Street here in London; The Temple Church, have you heard of it?'

Aaron turned away, but Uriel pulled him by the hand and forced him to look at him.

‘The hour has come, Aaron; we have to go now.’

There was something authoritative about Uriel; he seemed on edge, even afraid.

'I want to tell Kate that I love her.'

'You haven't?' Uriel was surprised, ' I thought you guys were in love.'

'We are,' he lowered his eyes, 'I haven't expressed my true feelings.'

Uriel didn't know what to say. The kid had gone through a lot, but they were running out of time.

An ambulance pulled to a stop at the entrance of the hospital. They watched paramedics struggling with a stretcher.

The stiflingly humid heat was almost unbearable. The men worked quickly as sweat dripped from their bodies like blood. Aaron watched the men with something akin to wonder. The merciless sun beat down on them, but it had no effect; they were racing against time trying to save a life.

Aaron swallowed hard, and it occurred to him that soon he would have to confront his fears head on. He moaned in annoyance, rubbing his tired eyes. He knew it was no use arguing with Uriel. However, if there was something he was looking forward to, it was an end to his exhausted existence.

Since the beginning of the month he had been running from pillar to post, completely unsettled. Anytime he remembered Caleb and Abraham, his heart broke into a million fragments.

'Let's go,' Uriel said after a prolonged silence and they moved away from the entrance of the accident and emergency department towards the car park. A beautifully dressed woman emerged from the hospital; she wore a bright red skirt suit with patent black shoes and a black clutch bag to match. She looked straight at Aaron, and he suddenly felt uneasy.

'C'mon, let's hurry up. We don't have all day!' Uriel snapped, almost pushing Aaron away from the woman's line of vision. They approached Aaron's battered Audi, and opened the door.

'We'll go to your flat first, erect a perimeter to ward off evil spirits, then to the church.'

Aaron nodded, and then asked as he drove furiously through Goodmayes Street, he asked, 'Who was that?'

'Believe me Aaron, you don't want to know. I promise to tell you when we get home.'

A fearful angel; that was new, and Aaron could not help sniggering.

'Contrary to your opinion,' Uriel said with a glint in his eye, 'I'm not afraid; I'm only protecting you.'

'I'm only protecting you,' Aaron scoffed, mimicking Uriel and stole a quick glance before turning his attention back to the road, his hands firmly on the steering wheel, 'was that lady in red one of your winged friends up there?'

'That was no lady. She's a very powerful demon in the hierarchy of darkness,' Uriel replied with a furrowed brow.

'And she's presumably out to get me before D-day, huh?'

Uriel ignored him, and after driving in silence for a while, Aaron asked curiously, 'Whose body do you inhabit?'

'Russell Katz is a German Jew married to a lovely Ethiopian scientist by the name Angela. He's a surgeon and he lives in Maryland. That's all I can say for now,' he answered brusquely.

'Now who's giving the attitude?' Aaron laughed.

Uriel wanted to keep a straight face but failed, and he joined in, tapping his hands on his powerful thighs while watching Aaron's skilful driving.

'You are a funny human being,' Uriel commented quietly. After that, neither of them said a word until they arrived at Aaron's apartment.

Aaron parked his car in the street. When Uriel got out of the car, he noticed a queer looking bat flying dangerously low. He scanned the vicinity and saw nothing amiss, but when he smelt the air, he realised they could be walking into a trap. Aaron was already moving towards his apartment.

Aaron slotted his apartment card in, the door opened, and he disappeared inside the building, taking the stairs two at a time to his second floor flat. He opened the door, jogged through his hallway and was about to step inside his living room when he stopped for a moment, sensing a presence. There was an eerie silence and his apartment was darker than usual. A light from his desk lamp flicked on, illuminating the leather surface on which it stood. He hesitated briefly, wondering what to do. When Uriel realised the danger Aaron was in, he yelled out a warning, 'Look out!'

It was too late.

An explosion rocked the building and seemed to tear his flat apart. Debris was strewn everywhere. Swiftly Uriel unfurled his wings. They were strong and shimmering and he flew emerging inside the building. He pulled Aaron away from the monstrous inferno, and they vanished.

The explosions continued to rip through the apartment block. People ran out of their homes scared stiff. Smoke and dust mingled with the afternoon heat making the atmosphere a mini hell.

Less than fifteen minutes later, the sound of a fire engine was a welcome relief to the residents, but as the truck loomed into view, Tyrus was furious. Aaron had disappeared; he had failed again, and this time he had failed himself.

He turned away from the mayhem, scratching his head. When he passed a car, he saw his reflection. He was now a barrel-chested man with short brown hair and muscles that would melt the heart of any woman. He had possessed the body Reverend Mathew Peters, a war veteran wanted by the American government for countless murders. Though the poor bloke had been recuperating in hospital from burns when Persia, a.k.a Rebecca Kolinsky, had kidnapped him, his father had repaired Reverend Mathew's body. Tyrus couldn't complain; his father had done a great job. He felt new, except for the rottenness of his soul.

'Maybe I need a woman,' he thought aloud and roared with laughter. Then his mood plummeted as his mind dwelled on his present predicament. His great plans had gone up in smoke, again. If he had succeeded and Aaron had died, surely his father's dreams would have died with him. With his brand new body, Tyrus would have been able to live like a human.

He had no hope of redemption. Besides, whose side would he be on? God had already rejected him and if Lucifer were to reject him as well then life would be hard indeed.

Tyrus vehemently loathed Hades.

His skin crawled at the thought of the disgusting and horrible evil in that pit of hopelessness. Tyrus gritted his teeth; he would not go back, he was resolved on that point. He hurried towards Evelyn's house, which had been their hideout since they'd arrived back in London.

He had to come up with a good plan, and fast.

Tyrus knew he would incur the wrath of his father when he found out about his little escapade. *I could always tell a fib*, he thought with a grin. After all, his father was the king of liars.

44

Darkness loomed ominously, swelling like a pregnant woman as an eight-year-old boy picked his way through the ruins. He was extremely thirsty, though he knew no one could assuage his thirst. He stopped for a moment, examining something under his feet. The boy bent down and picked it up. It was a stone - a very small, shining stone. His face creased up like a wrinkled orange as his intense gaze rested on the stone. Then with a satisfied grunt, he dropped it into his pocket.

The boy yawned and felt a hollow sensation spreading to his stomach. He was sad because of the utter desolation of the red planet, and his mouth watered at the thought of his mother's homemade cake with ice cream; what a futile dream, he thought gloomily. He trudged along, his feet making a tapping sound as he walked along the vast red planet.

But the boy was not alone. Three hundred thousand monsters watched him from a distance of about five hundred yards, and it was obvious by the look on their anxious faces that they were apprehensive, which was a very strange sight indeed. How could a skinny boy scare a host of demons?

Their human faces were mere facades. They had horns on their heads and paws instead of feet; their hairy bodies were home to steel armour, and one could easily trace along their bulging arms to powerful, gleaming swords in their large stubby hands. Smoke emerged from holes where there should have been noses and they hummed incomprehensible words.

A giant man with the hind part of a dinosaur, a wide hairy chest, and thick black lips bellowed in what must have been a terrifying voice indeed, but the boy was oblivious to it. He didn't hear a sound. A goat like figure trotted behind the massive dinosaur man.

'What haileth thee Lucifer, son of the morning?'

'That worm, there!' Lucifer roared contemptuously, his eyes shooting daggers at the innocent boy who was engrossed in searching for more stones in the red sand.

'How did a humanoid get in here? What kind of power brought him to my world?'

'He's your enemy,' Azazel revealed flippantly, 'he'll be responsible for your eternal damnation.'

'How did you know that, huh? You filthy, smelly goat!' Lucifer boomed, moving menacingly towards him.

'Patience, master. I have friends in high places. I roam the earth and eat the sacrifices of the sins of men. I've heard that your little rebellion will attract a hefty punishment, and I'm not really bothered, why should I?' he scoffed, then lowered his head, muttering,

'You relegated me to the background and surrounded yourself with idiots with no brains but brawn. And me? I've got it all; brains, brawn, and a way around Metatron. This place will go up in flames and everything will be destroyed. You'll have nothing again, brother,' and he dissolved into uncontrollable laughter as he jumped through the divider of time and space, a tiny opening beside the stones of fire, a means by which Azazel commuted.

'He's not to be taken seriously,' one of the monsters said, and then the sudden blasting of a thousand trumpets almost damaged their hearing.

A force lifted Lucifer above the bright red planetary body into a cloud-like vehicle. The boy saw the cloud and cried with joy, waving his hands frantically. The cloud stopped and the same force gently lifted the boy onto the luxurious cushions inside the cloud. The boy sank into it and his weary face broke into an infectious grin, but Lucifer glared at him, imagining the boy's skinny neck in his vice like grip. The cloud driver appeared; he was a short, stoutly built angel with a chubby face and long black beard. He patted the boy on the head, ruffling his hair and then moved the cloud swiftly along the pathway to heaven.

They delved into space and the boy stared in fascination as they passed stars and meteorites.

'Spectacular!' the boy murmured.

'Hold still, guys,' the cloud driver bellowed as they approached the black hole. The boy's face began to stretch in fear while Lucifer was relatively calm, even placid. There was a loud hissing sound and the boy lost consciousness.

He came to and was surprised to see the cloud driver bending over him, 'Are you all right, son?'

'Yes, sir,' the boy answered.

The cloud glided smoothly into the vastness of heaven, moving at the speed of light. The cloud driver moved closer to the boy, tapped him on the shoulder, and his eyelids fluttered to a close. Gently, the cloud driver pushed him out, and he plummeted head first into freedom and disappeared from view.

Lucifer glowered contemptuously at the cloud driver who merely smiled and dropped him at the mercy gate, and then drifted away. He glared at the huge pearly gate; its brilliance almost blinded him. Uriel opened the gate and Lucifer stepped in with a suspicious look on his face. Immediately, a thick fog with tendrils like arms enveloped Lucifer, encircling him like an anaconda and rendering him immobile. The only thing he could move was his mouth so he could speak.

Uriel, Raphael, and Michael left him beside the mercy gate while Metatron came out of the grace cathedral. Lucifer watched Metatron's approach with envy as his eyes lingered briefly on the radiance of heaven. The towering city of gold radiated and sparkled with light, which streamed unhindered through the walls adorned with countless precious stones.

Metatron walked with easy strides. His flesh was like flame and as he inched closer, his eyes shot bolts of lightning, melting the fog. Lucifer was free. Metatron's hands shook with power, his veins were on fire, and when he laughed, the sound was akin to that of a thousand trumpets.

Whimpering like a child, Lucifer lowered his massive head. His body suddenly broke out in sores as he writhed in agony.

Metatron stood silently before him, and his close proximity made Lucifer groan as unbearable pain shot through him.

He began to address Lucifer, 'your days have been measured, oh Lucifer, son of the morning, prepare to defend thyself. Father has heard your threats; therefore, you can no longer set foot in the throne room. The stones that were your covering are no longer yours. The only way you can approach the throne of mercy is through a child from your loins. This is your only chance, oh Lucifer, son of the morning.'

With a guttural shout, Metatron flung Lucifer out of the mercy gates, never to set foot beyond it again.

'I'll get you, Metatron. I promise; if it's the last thing I do, I'll get you.'

Lucifer's voice echoed through space and he crashed onto Cydonia with such brutal force that fifty thousand of his army perished. They dissolved into sulphur, hurled straight into hell fire.

Lucifer, still inhabiting Keith Morgan's body woke up with a start.

Why was I dreaming like a mere mortal? he thought angrily. Only men dream, he should not; after all, he was a supernatural being - the head of them all. His stony gaze swept across the room and he saw Pope Nathaniel III staring at him.

The Pope gave the impression of being tired, gaunt, and frail, but incredibly, he felt more alive than ever. It was surreal that the words of scriptures should come to pass in his lifetime.

The devil, the accuser of men, was nothing and no one; a powerless, rebellious spirit who terrified the sons of men with lies and illusion. The Pope gave him credit for that. Lucifer was a cunning spirit who had no power except the ones that God had bestowed on upon him. Lucifer prospered on the fears of men, which was what propelled the monster in him to rule and reign with such viciousness.

'What the hell are you staring at?' Lucifer yelled angrily and his voice rose a notch, 'I would have killed you but for my son, who pleaded with me to spare your stinking regal butt.'

'Go ahead, Lucifer, son of the morning,' Pope Nathaniel taunted him quietly, coiling up on the bed, 'kill me if you dare.'

Lucifer chuckled and moved towards him, his eyes gleaming 'Don't tempt me.'

'Where is that son of yours? And the hordes of hell that normally accompany you? Have they deserted you?' the Pope asked scornfully, his emotions reaching a fever pitch.

The Pope had been subjected to humiliation, kidnapped, beaten, starved, and several of his cardinals had been brutally murdered; it was time to put a stop to it.

But how? he wondered.

He served God and his fellow men with a true heart and would love to die in peace, not held captive by that Lucifer, who turned out to be a circus clown desperately clinging to stardom and relevance.

Lucifer eyes turned bright yellow and spikes erupted from his forehead, but then he changed his mind. An evil smile made a slow ascent across his face.

'Nathaniel, I've been around for a very long time. I'm the god of this world, make no mistake about that. Don't think I'm vulnerable or alone at all. The only reason I'm still keeping you is because I need your blood for the final sacrifice,' his eyes turned to slits, 'after all, the mother of my son came from your family tree. Have fun with my pets.'

He strode out of the room. As his footsteps receded into the distance, the Pope let out a deep sigh.

Then he heard a deep, eerie wailing sound; it came from the four corners of the room and was accompanied by a nasty smell that permeated the atmosphere.

Four beasts emerged from the floor of the room, their yellow eyes glowing, and their uneven breathing forceful as they moved towards the Pope with stealth. He was certain that death was imminent.

The beasts were bull terriers crossbred with hyenas. Their tongues hung out, dripping blood; they were different from the bloodhound the Pope saw in Italy.

Two surrounded his bed while the other two guarded the door; the Pope wanted to speak, but one of the dogs lashed out, biting him on the cheek.

'No prayers for you, son,' said a voice from by the window.

Pope Nathaniel turned in the direction of the voice and was stunned to see his mother watching him with her usual smile, her lips parted slightly.

The Pope was shocked but quickly recovered; the devil was an illusionist, he could use the form of anyone.

She wore a flowing red gown with a crown of gold on her head. He rubbed his eyes before looking at her again; it was his mother all right. That must be one great illusion and even he was impressed. His mother had died thirty years before and had been a woman of grace and charity. It was not impossible that his beloved mother had saddled herself with evil spirits.

Or had she?

He stared at the woman; she greatly resembled his mother, and maybe that was where it ended.

Pope Nathaniel watched and waited.

'I'm your beloved mother, son,' the woman alleged as she came closer. He dug his hands into the bed and his eyes never strayed from her face. Her eyes turned bright red, and when she smiled, her teeth were those of a shark.

Pope Nathaniel belted out a sudden scream. A sharp piercing scream that halted everything in its tracks; even the animals took notice, and they moved a few inches away from the bed.

Time practically stood still.

When he stopped, colour rushed to his cheeks and he looked dazed. The Pope fell back on the bed, exposing a tiny gold chain around his neck.

'Devour his flesh!' the woman ordered in a loud voice and the beasts moved in for the kill. A sudden glimmer of light from beneath the Pope's white gown flashed, incinerating the beasts instantly. The bright light emanated from the tiny gold chain around his neck, which had a shining stone as a pendant.

Echoes of their screams hung heavily in the room. The woman backed away from the slumped body of the Pope, fighting an imaginary foe. She thrashed about wildly, stumbling and tripping over the furniture. She screamed in anger, enraged - her face contorted like a woman in labour. Her continuous screams reverberated throughout the semi-detached house and she dissolved into sulphur, her once beautiful face eaten away by unknown forces. A few seconds later, the bright red gown twisted, coiling around her burning carcass. Then an eerie sound reigned.

The Pope's breathing was coming in short gasps, but he was out cold, oblivious to the on-going melee.

45

Temple Church, London, twelve noon, Aug 18

Peter walked briskly through the busy street, his eyes darting everywhere. He stole a quick glance at his companions - three tall men in dark shades who followed closely behind. The men looked like tourists with their flip-flops, brown baggy shorts, and rucksacks strapped to their backs.

Several people gave the men cursory glances. A woman coming from the other direction breezed past and took out her mobile phone.

Peter did a U-turn and hurried after the woman, who stopped in her tracks when she felt a light tap on her shoulder. She looked up at the tall, lean man standing in front of her, her blue eyes wide; she appeared flustered.

He smiled, revealing a strong and clean set of teeth. The woman relaxed a little and when he began to speak in flawless English, every form of suspicion disappeared from her mind.

They were engrossed in conversation for almost five minutes and the woman pointed towards the Temple Church, which was about two hundred yards from where they were.

The men watched Peter, their anger building steadily. At last the woman walked away and Peter went back to meet his companions, with a ready explanation for his behaviour.

'What was that all about?' one of the men asked. His wide chest and bulging biceps belied the impression he was trying to make of being a tourist. He bore a close resemblance to a scowling nightclub bouncer; his clean-shaven head and gangster's ring on his index finger sealed the deal. He looked deadly and ruthless.

'Sorry, Cedric,' Peter said, trying to diffuse the tension, but his eyes was gleaming insanely. 'I was trying to find the right direction for the church. I have a hunch that Aaron will be there. He has many questions to answer, like how he killed our brothers. It's judgement day for him.'

Andre was not sure he had heard right. He stared at Peter and felt like shaking him until he saw reason.

'Hey, guys,' he said, waving the Bresser safari binoculars in his hands for emphasis, 'we're not here to exact any judgement; this is not the jungle. If anything should happen, we'll all be cooling our heels in jail. I just want to know how my uncle died, that's all.'

Andre's cheery face went through many different emotions, from uncertainty to bewilderment until finally it settled on apprehension.

The men nodded in agreement but Peter brushed aside their fears.

'Far from it, I just wanted to know what really happened - nothing criminal in that. Besides, he has questions to answer about our national treasure, the Ark of the Covenant. The Ark disappeared when Aaron left Ethiopia.'

'But we're not sure yet that he was involved in the Ark's disappearance,' Andre commented dryly.

Andre had noticed an animalistic brutality in Peter and he was getting more uncomfortable by the day.

He had agreed to go to London to discover the truth about what happened to Caleb and Abraham, but it was obvious now that he had made a mistake. Maybe he should go back to Ethiopia and partake in the national burial of the two great men.

Peter controlled himself with an effort.

'We shouldn't be discussing this here... now,' he said earnestly, 'let's just pop into the Temple Church and see if Aaron is there; my sources told me he would come to the temple today.' Peter had hardly finished speaking when an elegant woman captured his attention and, strangely, the woman was walking towards them.

Andre turned in the direction of Peter's gaze and his face creased into a smile as the woman walked up to him and planted a kiss on his cheeks.

'Hey, babe, meet my friends. We went to university together here in the UK before everyone parted ways,' Andre said with a satisfied look on his face. 'My wife,' he added, still smiling as he introduced the woman to his friends. She shook their hands.

'Buddy, you didn't tell us your woman would be here,' Peter said, reluctantly removing his gaze from her beautiful face.

'Fatima was very persuasive. I agreed at the last minute.'

She felt Peter's lingering gaze on her and disliked him instantly.

Andre and Fatima held hands as they walked in the direction of the church, oblivious to a man who had been tailing her. The man stopped briefly and stared at her long and hard before he followed stealthily, taking tentative steps.

The man clenched and unclenched his fists as his blood began to boil and perspiration appeared on his forehead. He remembered Fatima's hot body beneath his as he'd claimed her several times. The picture was entrenched in his mind; it was like a virus in his blood, and all he could think of was having her in his arms again. She belonged to him and no one else.

In retrospect, Fatima had unwittingly turned him into her slave; she had captured him with her beauty and innocence and turned his life into a living hell. His eyes had a murderous gleam. He would rather kill Fatima than allow her taunt him with another man. Then he would take his own life, that way, they would be together forever.

'Mukta!' someone called from the throng of people moving up and down the high street. He turned round swiftly, astonished by the familiar, high-pitched voice. Then he spotted him. Mukta had thought he would never hear from Rahal again, and he watched his approach with delight.

Rahal was like a brother to him and he was glad to see his gangly frame. Although, he was the last person Mukta had expected to see.

'What a pleasant surprise, Rahal! What on earth are you doing here?' Mukta gave him a bear hug, the pleasure evident on his voice.

'I came with some friends for a day out. What are you doing here, boss?' Rahal asked still smiling.

Mukta stared at him and liked what he saw.

Rahal looked different; he had more flesh on his body, his wild shifty eyes looked more focused, and he was more handsome. It had been a few days, or weeks,

Mukta could not remember. He scratched his head, laughing nervously; he had totally lost track of time.

'Fatima is going to that church,' Mukta answered, pointing, and then lowered his gaze, almost afraid to look up knowing that he had not heeded Rahal's advice.

Rahal said nothing for a while. When he did, his voice was very low.

'She's poison to your soul, boss. Let her go.'

'I can't, brother,' Mukta disagreed with a vigorous shake of his head, a crazed look on his face, 'I love her.'

'That's obsession, not love,' Rahal said quietly and quickly changed the topic, 'how's the homeland?'

'Not the same without us, brother,' Mukta said with a sad grin, 'I have to go.'

Rahal hugged him and Mukta moved back, suddenly emotional. He was reluctant to leave Rahal but he had to go. He noticed Rahal's teary eyes. Mukta wanted to say something but could not; it was as if something was blocking his throat.

Rahal left his former boss and merged with the teeming crowd. Mukta watched him until his form became a distant blur and Lucifer's dark looks replaced him, his mouth set in a thin line - he was still inhabiting the body of Keith Morgan.

Lucifer nodded and Mukta frowned, wondering if he had met him before. He acknowledged Lucifer with a tilt of his head, but Rahal's words stayed on his mind, and for the first time since he left Somalia, he questioned his motives and feelings.

His feet felt like two heavy stones as he trudged on towards the Temple Church. The spring to his step had gone. The weight of all the murders and atrocities he had committed in the past rested heavily on his soul, pressing him into repentance. He wondered why his boy, Rahal, could whip up such strong emotions in him. He suddenly lost the desire to pursue Fatima. He wanted to start afresh, to be a better man, but he wondered whether he had gone beyond redemption.

As if in a slow motion, he turned back and saw Lucifer still watching him. His daughter's face appeared, and Mukta stifled a sob.

Somalia! he thought and a shudder went through him.

Mukta had trouble breathing. If I could turn back the hands of time and undo all the atrocities I have committed in my quest for revenge, I would gladly do so.

'But in life, there are no second chances, are there?' a voice whispered in his mind. Mukta moaned aloud as guilt racked his body like a tidal wave and he staggered on his feet, faces muddled together as events flashed through his morbid mind. How could he forget? His breathing became uneven as he stumbled on his way. People were staring at him but he didn't care. The weight of sorrow clung tightly to his soul. He had helped maul his country to pieces; if only he could help salvage and build Somalia up again.

His face contorted in pain when he realised how he had thrown his life away. He remembered when had waved goodbye to Britain, never to return. Now he was back, a rapist on the trail of an innocent woman, a woman he had kidnapped and molested. Shame rested upon him heavily like a thick cloak.

He had killed thousands of innocent people, destroyed his homeland, dipped his hands in blood, and was responsible for the damage to his soul. The brutality of his guns had abruptly shortened several destinies. his swords had swum in the blood of the rich, the poor, the righteous, and the guilty. He had presided over countless massacres and he had actually thought he could get away with it, but with Rahal's words, the weight of his sins crushed him, and he felt naked and exposed.

Mukta had wanted to avenge the death of his family, yet he had turned into the very monster he was trying to fight. Could he still find salvation in a world he helped destroyed?

Mukta's mind drifted back to the well-dressed man he had seen earlier. He turned and, just as he had expected, Lucifer waited, watching him with arms akimbo, a silly expression on his face.

'Who is this guy?' Mukta questioned aloud.

Lucifer had walked into the police station in New York and secured Mukta's bail; the police hadn't been able to find any evidence that he had killed a bystander by chopping her head off.

So they released him, simple as.

Mukta was on the tail of Aaron, the man everyone claimed had the power of the gods to help him find Fatima, the woman who had enslaved him since he'd set eyes on her, and inadvertently, he'd stumbled upon the object of his quest.

Aaron and his pals had disappeared into a church and Mukta found himself in a cold damp cell. When Lucifer arranged his bail, he'd attached a clause to it. Mukta must help him find Aaron, and Lucifer had promised to help Mukta get Fatima but he had other agendas.

Lucifer wanted to use Mukta to start a fight, and in the ensuing melee, he would swoop down on Aaron and capture him, he had no intention in helping Mukta, for all he cared, the poor man deserved to die for all the murders he'd committed.

The problem was, Mukta seemed to have forgotten him already, and Lucifer was definitely going to do something to rectify that.

Mukta stopped at the south gate of the Temple Church, staring at Fatima whose upturned face glowed with love and contentment. Her partner's mouth came down on hers. Mukta's blood began to boil, and he did the sensible thing by turning his eyes away.

She still had a very strong hold on him.

'Somali warlord turned to jelly by a woman,' Lucifer whispered in his ear, and Mukta jumped in fright.

Lucifer laughed, mocking him incessantly, 'You can't go through with it, can you?'

Mukta had the urge to punch the smirk off his face, but he controlled his growing anger. Instead, he asked, 'Who are you?'

'Who are you?' Lucifer spat back at him, his face twitching. 'I'll tell you who you are,' and Lucifer's eyes turned bright yellow, 'you're just a number, a soul to be harvested to my kingdom. You have killed for me and the blood of your victims decorated my altars, their cries of torment filled me with joy; I swam in their despair and laughed with derision at their pain. Their sorrow gives me strength and I bask in the glory of their tragedies. I promised to give you your heart's desire, and you want to scorn me with your refusal? You men of the earth have no honour.'

And he was gone.

Mukta looked around wildly, his hands shaking; he had spoken to Beelzebub, the devil. Mukta's restless eyes noticed what looked like two Knights Templar on horseback outside the church; it was an eerie sight. He heard the neighing of horses, but when he looked closely, they were mere statures.

With quick, deliberate steps, Mukta entered the church's courtyard and sank to his knees. At the same time, Fatima laughed in response to something Andre had said to her, and she glanced briefly to admire the stature of the two Knights Templar on horseback.

Fatima froze when she saw Mukta on his knees.

'Forgive me, oh God,' Mukta prayed in agony. The weight of his sins pressed him down and he turned his eyes to the sky, 'God Almighty, forgive my sins. Have mercy upon me, a sinner. Jesus, son of God, save my soul.'

Mukta's mood changed, and a great peace settled on his soul as joy filled his heart. It was so cheap, he thought with a smile. The gift of salvation was cheap. He knew without an iota of a doubt that his life had taken a good turn. And then he saw Fatima again.

His body began to tremble. Their eyes locked for few seconds and Fatima's heart seemed to stop as memories of her ordeal in Somalia flooded her mind. It was as if someone had taken a cleaver and hacked her heart from her chest. Her legs turned to jelly and she slumped to the ground and fainted.

Mukta saw her fall and, without thinking, he stood up and ran towards her. Two gunshots rang out in quick succession and everyone ducked their heads.

Rahal appeared from nowhere, tears streaming down his face with a gun in his right hand.

He had killed Mukta. He had warned him to leave Fatima alone, but he would not listen. *Serves him right*, he thought.

Lucifer collided with Rahal like a whirlwind.

'Sorry,' Lucifer mouthed the words and walked away. He had stabbed Rahal.

Rahal fell down and his friends rushed to his aid. He tried to keep his eyes open but they were so heavy, then the pulling started.

Someone kept tugging at his shirt, pulling him. He tried to fend them off, and when he succeeded, he struggled to his feet, panting and short of breath.

He felt light, like a leaf blown by the wind. Staring at his feet, he noticed a shadow, and when he scanned the object, he realised that it was his body. The truth finally dawned on him; he was stone dead.

Rahal watched in incredulity as an ambulance came to an abrupt stop. Paramedics rushed out and placed him on a stretcher, and then the ambulance's door slammed shut.

Rahal cringed inside. His body floated out of the ambulance. There was no wind, just an uncomfortable silence.

He tried searching for Mukta. Rahal was certain that he had killed Mukta, yet he could not locate him.

Then he saw it, and his heart sank.

It was a gigantic fireball; it reminded him of a hurricane. The fireball came forcefully towards him and swallowed him up. Inside, it was over one thousand degrees, and he flesh began to burn.

Rahal saw Mukta in the company of beautiful winged creatures, and his eyes seemed to dance with pleasure. Rahal was stunned. When? How? But there was no one to answer him.

The tumultuous fireball began to choke him and he started screaming. Incredibly, he could still see the ambulance, which slowly found its way through the surge of people that had gathered. He stretched out his hands, crying for help, but he merely grasped hot, empty air.

He watched his friends huddling together, crying, but he was helpless. Pain consumed him and became his bride; it clung to him, biting, choking, and eating him alive. It felt like millions of needles were incessantly poking his body and his hands had started to peel off. It was like a rain of acid, wind, and fire.

After what seemed like eternity, a mighty rushing wind blew him out of the fireball and gave him a brief spell of respite. Relief washed over him - maybe there was hope for him. But his reprieve was short lived. A force flung him violently to the ground, and when tried scrutinising his surroundings everything was hazy.

The only thing he could make out was that he was in a queue, a very long queue. He saw Mukta in front talking earnestly to a very young looking man at a massive gate. Mukta's eyes streamed with tears, drenching him.

The man at the gate exclaimed in a loud voice, 'Enter into the joy of your Lord,'

Angels enveloped Mukta into their midst and they whisked him away. Rahal heard his name and a massive angel swooped down and led him towards an enormous gate. He found himself standing in front of a man sitting on a colossal throne. The man had a large book in front of him, and he flicked through it in an instant.

When the man looked at him Rahal lowered his head, staring at nothing in particular. Moments later, he summoned enough courage to face the man. Rahal saw compassion and love in his eyes. He also noticed the man's hands; they were long and beautiful, like a woman's hands.

They locked eyes for what seemed like eternity and he asked, with the gentlest, yet most powerful voice Rahal had ever heard, 'Why did you kill your own flesh and blood? Why did you murder your brothers and sisters?'

Rahal knew he could not lie. He had to speak the truth, which was a rarity. 'I chose to, My Lord,'

The man was very cross.

'I'm not your Lord. Depart from me, you worker of evil.'

Rahal swallowed hard, he was not about to be tossed into hell without a fight, 'I rid the world of an evil man. I preserved a lot of lives, My Lord,' he cried out.

The man frowned and said quietly, 'You are not the judge of his soul. His life was not in your hands. He repented of his evil deeds, he regrets all that he has done, and our father pardoned him. His judgment was not in your hands.'

'Please, give me a second chance!'

But the man turned his face away and Lucifer appeared as a whirlwind.

Rahal disappeared into it, screeching, and fighting empty air. Fire danced on his skin, eating his flesh and soul; his blood-curling scream reverberated throughout the crowded Hades.

'Give him the VIP suite,' Lucifer ordered and hordes of evil spirits flew to do his bidding.

Lucifer's spirit went back to the Temple Church in London.

He appeared unruffled, watching the church intently, waiting for Aaron to make an appearance.

The prince of Persia appeared, still in the body of Rebecca Kolinsky.

'Yes?' Lucifer grunted.

'Trouble on the home front,' Persia said, looking at him disdainfully.

'Fire away,' he said curtly. Persia had a way of getting under his skin. He had begun to regret bringing him on-board.

'Your son has taken the Pope to an unknown destination. We've combed everywhere, but we can't find them.'

'I own the world; find me that bastard, who calls himself my son,' he shouted, kicking his legs on the fence of the church and tugging at his hair.

'You're causing a scene,' Persia said stiffly, 'and you seem to have forgotten the word "Please".'

'Please, maggot, find them,' he snarled and hurled Persia against the fence. Passers-by stared in shock at the brutal display of violence. By the time Lucifer realised that he was in his human body, two police cars had screeched to a stop a few meters away. Two police officers sprung out of the cars and Lucifer sensed his control slipping away. He decided to throw all caution to the wind.

He opened his mouth wide and balls of fire consumed the two officers and their cars. People scampered away and Lucifer heard the drone of a police helicopter overhead. By now, he was raging mad.

'I'm the king of the world. The world is mine and all the inhabitants therein,' he bellowed in fury, growling as the ground began to heat up, melting like rubber. Soon, cracks appeared as fire erupted out of the ground.

Scenes of massacre, chaos, and blood followed. The ground beneath the south gate of the church split in two and a blast of hot air spurted out.

The Temple Church was under attack from the king of darkness. Lucifer had discarded his human form in the middle of the church's courtyard and had transformed into a hideous creature. The gruesome beast opened its ferocious mouth and, with a deafening shriek, the eight hundred year old church began to burn, pillars, and all.

Peter and his friends, as well as other tourists in the church, were terrified. Trapped inside, they hurriedly made their way towards the round, which was the oldest part of the church. But the fire was relentless, consuming everything in its path.

Amazingly, the effigies of the knights were not burning, but the slender Purbeck marble column was already absorbing heat.

The master of the temple tried to calm the petrified visitors but it was useless; they watched in horror as the fire raged towards them. The master of the temple looked up at the nave, he stared at the pillars and his eyes travelled to the altar, praying for succour, but none was forthcoming. This was a different kind of threat, different from the attack on the church during the Second World War. This fresh threat had the full backing of hell, and he was very afraid.

He tried in vain to maintain a dignified approach. Bizarrely there was no smoke, just a mad, raging inferno. Everyone jumped with fright when they heard a strange sound; it was a heavy thumping, like a giant walking with quick strides and they held their breath as they waited for the worst.

'Don't panic, let's move quietly outside,' the master said, but nobody moved; it was as if they were all under some form of spell. They strained their ears. Someone coughed, and that seemed to galvanise some of them into action.

They rushed towards the side entrance of the temple, and suddenly, they heard a baby chuckling. Instinctively, the master of the temple knew that it was no ordinary child and told everyone to save themselves, but Peter stood transfixed.

A baby boy was crawling towards him, his eyes glowing and Peter couldn't move. Cedric tried pulling him back, but he didn't budge. Cedric left him and followed the others out through the side entrance.

Then there was silence.

46

Kate sat on the bed wondering why her mother was late. A nurse walked past her room and smiled. She returned her smile, pondering where they had met. There was something vaguely familiar about her.

She glanced at her wristwatch and was dismayed to see that it was quarter to six in the evening. By seven visiting time would be over. She lay back on her bed, watching people coming in and going out. She must have dozed off because she felt a gentle tap and was relieved to see her mother, and to add to her joy, her father also stood sheepishly at the foot of her bed, looking down at her with tears in his eyes.

He moved closer and held her in a tight grip, afraid to let go.

'Daddy,' she sobbed quietly, 'I've missed you terribly.'

Her father took out a white handkerchief and lovingly wiped tears off her face. When she calmed down, her mother watched them fondly. She wiped a tear from the corner of her eye, blinking rapidly and smiling with relief at the same time.

'I'm home, Katie girl. I promise never to leave you or your mother again; I'm home for good, baby.'

They stayed with her for an hour and left when visiting time was over. Kate was in high spirits. Seeing her father had changed her preconceived notions about her parents' marriage; things might work out after all.

According to her mother, she was like a cat with nine lives, having cheated death twice. Yet Evelyn and Michael had not made it. Her mood changed at the thought of her friends, and deep sorrow engulfed her, preventing her from sleeping.

Social services had taken Caroline away. Police were still investigating whether the little girl truly had killed her mother, and they told Kate that they were not looking for anyone else.

The events of that night had been terrible. She had tried her very best to banish the images from her mind, but it was futile. How she'd managed to escape with a bullet lodged in her shoulder blade remained a mystery.

Doctors had performed minor surgery on her shoulder and had successfully removed the bullet. The problem she had now was working out how Caroline had got hold of a gun. And why had she shot her own mother?

Kate was sure that Caroline had not shot her. It could have been an illusion or a mirage. Lucifer was probably trying to score a point, but if Caroline was innocent, who'd killed Evelyn? The mystery deepened further; Michael's ashes had vanished from the scene of the shooting.

Who killed Evelyn?

The questions kept ringing in her mind. It was the last thing on her mind when she went to sleep and the first thing when she woke up. Kate sat on the bed, unable to sleep or concentrate on anything. The next thing she heard was footsteps. It sounded like a great crowd trapped in a building and trying to escape. Will there ever be an end to my torture? she thought in despair.

She gritted her teeth and waited, and the noise subsided to murmurings. Still Kate waited and her eyes strayed to her wristwatch, it was eight on the dot. She pressed the button close to her bed for attention, but no one came.

As if jolted by electricity, she yanked the drips from her left hand and hurriedly changed from the hospital gown into her own clothes. She didn't know where she was going, but she could not stay on the ward; something was not right. Outside, she saw nurses on the floor looking pale and lifeless. Kate sprinted out of the ward, her heart beating wildly. She took the lift to the outpatient ward and was dismayed to find that it was the same everywhere.

She ran outside the accident and emergency department and saw cars rammed together, their horns blaring. Just outside the entrance to the hospital was a bus stop. She hurried towards it and prayed for a bus.

Everywhere she looked, people were lying on the floor. It was a terrifying sight, and then she heard the sound of approaching footsteps. They were quick, purposeful steps. Kate braced herself for whatever was coming. She turned round and saw a man standing in the shadows, very close to the entrance of A&E. Kate controlled herself with an effort.

'Calm down, Kate, that's not Tyrus,' she said to herself, and the unexpected blasting of a bus horn brought a smile to her face.

She waved at the bus frantically; it was the number 387 heading for Barking Reach in East London. The bus screeched to a stop and the door swung open. Kate jumped on, looking back, but the shadowy figure was gone. That was when she turned her attention to the driver. He looked massive, extremely good looking and his clear blue eyes seemed to gleam. He smiled, exposing perfectly even teeth.

'Hello, Katie baby,' and she froze when she heard the voice. Only one person was allowed to call her that.

Aaron held the handrail for support as Uriel sped through the deserted road. He stared at her as if imprinting her face on his mind. They collapsed into each other's arms, and Kate let go of her bottled up emotions, weeping softly. Aaron wiped her tears with his free hand, kissing her soundly on the lips.

'I love you, Kate,' he said solemnly, laughing with joy and relief.

She raised her hand to touch his face, her eyes questioning him.

'I met with a minor accident at home,' he explained and studied her bandaged shoulder. 'I'm so sorry about Evelyn,' he whispered, his eyes dark with sorrow.

'You knew?' she asked, and the surprise was evident in her voice. She studied him. Aaron had changed; not physically, but there was something stronger, more resilient about him. Her eyes danced with affection as she said, 'You left me alone at that hotel in Kent.'

He smiled, apologising profusely, 'I'm sorry, my love...I have so much to tell you, darling, but first I want you to sit down,' and he led her to a nearby seat. That was when Kate was able to survey her surroundings; the bus was full of grey haired old men.

She stared at Aaron, expecting an explanation.

'Friends,' he murmured with a grin as Kate snuggled close to him.

'I've been to hell and back,' she whispered, remembering the man outside the hospital and the extraordinary incident she had just witnessed. She told him everything, and Aaron swallowed hard. Kate noticed that his hands were shaking.

'That man used to be a good friend, but he's dead now...gone,' he said slowly with an air of mystery about him.

'Dead? How can that be...' and then she understood what he meant by that; someone must have taken possession of the man's body.

'Was that Tyrus?' she asked tentatively.

'Nope,' Aaron shook his head looking at her sharply, 'how do you know about him?'

'We have a lot of catching up to do, honey,' Kate said with a great sense of safety as she snuggled close to him.

'The man you saw is Lucifer, and he must be raving mad about his son. It's like the son had bailed out at the last minute,' he added quietly.

'Tyrus was not the boss?'

Aaron shook his head but said nothing. He held her tightly as the bus travelled at top speed, *and for an angel that's some driving,* Aaron thought with a faraway look on his face.

CYDONIA

The bus sped on with brute force; they were almost flying.

47

Washington DC, Aug 19

Joshua Cohen struggled with the ropes around his hands, cursing continuously and glancing at the window nervously. The early morning sun streamed through the sole window in the room and his only thought was his nephew.

A man towered over him and sneered,

'You freaky perverted old man, where the hell is Richard? What have you and your cultist friends done to him? I'll keep you here for a month if I have to; just tell me where Richard is!'

Joshua stared at his accuser, wondering out to convince him of his innocence.

'Believe me, Stealth, I don't know what you're talking about,' Joshua pleaded with him, 'by now I should be in London. You have kept me unlawfully for forty-eight hours. I don't know who Richard is, and I don't know where he is; what gives you the impression that a frail old man like me could kidnap anyone? All I can think about is my brother's son in London.'

Stealth kicked the chair in front of him in frustration.

He walked up and down the bare room and, for once, he hated his job. He took a fleeting look at Joshua and saw a spent old man desperate for some kind of redemption.

He grunted and thought long and hard. This time around, he might have gone too far, but he knew the sordid secrets behind the façade of the man sitting before him.

Stealth frowned, looking at Joshua shrewdly; he appeared to be telling the truth, and seemed lost and truly ignorant about what he had been asked. Maybe it was time to stop Joshua Cohen's investigation, Stealth decided.

Stealth was a man driven by an insatiable desire to solve every case brought to his attention. He absolutely hated failure, but with the way things were, President Joseph Levin would have to come clean and tell the nation about his missing son.

He stared at Joshua and spat out, 'How did you heal so fast? We all believed you were going to die.'

'God works in mysterious ways,' was Joshua's apt reply.

Stealth removed the ropes and Joshua massaged his bruised wrists, but something kept bothering him. His eyes followed Stealth keenly.

'What are you looking at?' Stealth barked.

'Why did you take so many officers to arrest me at the airport?' Joshua asked, but already knew the answer. He shrugged his shoulders as pain racked his body, his wrists seemed to be on fire, 'and how did you know that I was travelling outside the country?'

'The name Logan sound familiar to you?' Stealth asked, looking at him without pity. He still hated Joshua, but he had decided to give him a break; unless he broke the law, Joshua was a free man.

'Logan Stone told us where you were. Thank God your plane was delayed...' then he added as an afterthought, 'he kept babbling about you being a vampire and stuff like that.'

Joshua went rigid.

How could Logan have known about his past? He stood up and asked weakly, 'Can I go now?'

'Yeah,' Stealth answered, sobering up a little, 'I'm sorry about the shabby treatment; the president's son went missing three nights ago at the White House. We were combing everywhere and...' he avoided eye contact, but Joshua was impressed.

Stealth may be harsh and hard but he was definitely a good man.

Joshua nodded and walked away, but he came back, popping his head through the doorway, 'Does the president believe in God?'

'Yes, I should think so,' Stealth answered and frowned, 'why do you ask?'

'Tell him to ask the whole country to pray for his son. The young man's life is in danger.'

Joshua left the decrepit building, and his driver was already waiting for him. He turned back and saw Stealth in the doorway with his officers looking at him. Slowly, Stealth lifted his right hand in a wave, and Joshua waved back.

Before he got to his car, he stared bleakly at the sky and noticed the clouds gathering. In the occult, that was an ominous sign; he was not supposed to proceed. Should he go back and tell Stealth that he was afraid? A man who had hated him for years? No, he shook his head and walked the few remaining steps to his car.

He got in and his driver gave him his mobile phone.

'Logan has been calling, sir,' his driver said. He looked exhausted, but Joshua was not keen on asking him what was wrong.

'Thanks,' he took the phone and listened for a few seconds then clicked it shut.

'That idiot left me high and dry and now wants to know my plans. Drive me to the airport, please.'

'Not so fast, Joshua,' a familiar voice said coldly.

Joshua's eyes opened wide in shock and the hairs at the nape of his neck stood on end. He noticed that his driver had vanished, and he knew his time was running out.

Had his sin found him out at last?

'Archer?' Joshua stammered, 'you're dead!'

'Well, I'm here now, so that makes me very much alive.'

Stealth was watching Joshua, wondering why his car was not moving. Out of curiosity, he decided to check and strolled towards the car. Joshua wanted to warn him to stay away, but he could not. He felt a sharp pain in his chest and he groaned, scratching the back of the driver's seat in desperation. Archer began to laugh; it was sinister and bone chilling laughter.

'Please, let me see Aaron. Please, Archer, I would gladly give my soul back,' Joshua begged.

'I can't do that, brother,' Archer said and plunged a six-inch knife into Joshua's chest. At that instant, Stealth got to the car.

He peered inside and saw a knife protruding from Joshua's chest, but there was no else in the car.

'God, another case!' Stealth said. As he stepped away from the car, the ground began to shift. He tried to escape but the gulf began to widen and he slipped, wedged between the car and the opening. Stealth called out for help, but nobody came. Everybody had vanished.

He realised with dismay that he had come to the end of his life, and he remembered what Joshua had said earlier. He said a quick prayer as the ground swallowed both him and the car.

The ground closed, and there was a ghostly silence.

SHALEM AND Rachel passed through immigration and walked outside Terminal Five of Heathrow Airport in London. Rachel sniffed the air and laughed heartily.

'I love London.'

'You should have told me that, darling. We could have ditched Italy for London,' Shalem said and planted a kiss on both her cheeks. They were like two teenagers in love.

Outside, they hailed a black cab and got in.

'Where are you going, sir, madam?'

'Please take us to the Hilton Hotel in Park Lane,' Shalem said looking at his wife, 'aren't we forgetting something?'

'Our luggage,' they shouted in unison, giggling like schoolchildren, 'excuse us, please,' and they climbed down from the cab. The cab driver stepped out to help them with their luggage.

After loading everything into the cab, they settled in the back, whispering sweet words to each other and grinning from ear to ear.

The driver, a jolly looking man with a thick moustache and around orange face, the result of a fake tan and sun bed, asked curiously, 'Are you guys just dating?'

'Nah,' Rachel answered with a big smile as she ran her hands through her hair, 'we're newly married.'

'Ha,' was all he said.

A few minutes later he said, 'There's been some trouble in London, don't be surprised if you see cops everywhere. A bloke told me a guy blew himself up in a church on Fleet Street, killing scores of people.'

Shalem and Rachel exchanged glances; they were supposed to meet their London contact at the church.

'What really happened?' Rachel asked her expression grave.

'I live in Hackney,' the cab driver said with a pleasant look on his face. It was obvious to Shalem and Rachel that he was chatty, but that could be helpful. 'My neighbour is Ghanaian and she had wanted me to go to her church for ages...' he stopped abruptly, waiting for their reaction, and then he cleared his throat and continued, 'She told me the devil has come to London to vent his anger on the residents...' He tightened his hold on the steering wheel, 'she told me the apocalypse is here,' and he laughed heartily, 'she said the US president is coming to London, and there is this rumour that the president's son is missing. Probably kidnapped by Al-Qaeda or the Taliban, but I didn't believe a word of what she was saying.'

'So why are you telling us?' Shalem asked coldly.

'Don't be offended,' the cabman quickly apologised, 'I was just trying to make small talk. Just be careful though, strange things are happening. The other night my daughter couldn't sleep; she told me she saw an alien on London Bridge, can you believe that? Possibly UFOs I think,' and he roared with laughter.

When neither of his passengers said a word, he kept quiet, finally getting the signal. Rachel looked at her husband and touched the tiny gold chain around her neck. Neither of them knew the extent of danger they were walking into.

Shalem changed his mind, 'Mate, can you please drive us to the Sheraton Hotel close to the airport instead?'

'My pleasure,' the driver said with a smile, checking his rear view mirror for vehicles.

Rachel looked at Shalem with a frown and whispered, 'Why don't you want the Hilton Hotel again? We've already booked, and for your information that was one of my favourite hotels.'

Rachel was obviously annoyed.

'And we can cancel,' he said softly, trying to pacify his wife. There was something vaguely familiar about the driver. He couldn't put his finger on it, but he was definitely sure that they'd met before.

'I don't want to be far from the airport. Yitzhak was murdered by his own people; I don't want to risk our lives, love.'

'But we have to go to the Temple Church on Fleet Street first thing tomorrow morning.'

Rachel was not happy. All she wanted was to plan her big wedding in Tuscany. She wanted to live a normal life, but her new husband fit the perfect description of an adrenalin junkie.

However, the words of the angel they'd met in Tel Aviv were still fresh in her mind. Until they succeeded in their present assignment, Tuscany would have to wait.

48

The street was deserted and ominously quiet as Tyrus drove the powerful Mercedes through the small village of Harmondsworth near Heathrow. His face was like an ancient mask as he pondered on his rebellion. His father was probably in consultation with that stupid Azazel and the prince of Persia, but he needed to do this. If he had any chance of redemption only the Pope could help him buy some time and, maybe, he could wriggle his way out of the league of demons.

The car surged with power and they sped through the village. They passed nice looking pubs and headed straight for St Mary the Virgin Church. With his brow furrowed in concentration

Tyrus's powerful arms expertly manoeuvred the steering wheel of the Mercedes. The Pope said nothing and wondered what they were going to do in the twelfth century church. Maybe the church would soon reek of blood.

It was a grim thought, but it was better for him to face reality.

It was Sunday evening, yet everywhere was extremely quiet.

'Better for everyone to stay in their homes, I guess,' the Pope murmured under his breath. Tyrus gave him a cursory glance and parked outside the south aisle of the church.

The warmth and serenity radiating from the church astounded the Pope. Tyrus on the other hand seemed to have a problem with his breathing. However, after a while, he regained his composure and got out of the car. The Pope followed suit, his eyes not leaving his captor for a second.

For a few minutes, Pope Nathaniel III studied the exterior of the church, which was predominantly made of flint rubble with stone dressings. His sharp eyes noticed that the upper part of the ancient church was made of red brick, and he did not miss the domed cupola and the embattled parapet with angled pinnacles.

Tyrus strolled towards the twelfth century doorway as though he owned the place, and the door opened of its own accord. They marched in with easy strides, Tyrus leading the way. Pope Nathaniel expected the church to be cold, dark, and stuffy, but on the contrary, it was warm, bright, and had a homely feel to it. Tyrus stole a quick glance at the Pope and chuckled before speaking.

'Feel free to explore, Your Eminence. We could be here for a long time.'

'Thank you,' Pope Nathaniel said, his eyes riveted on the altar. He ran towards it and sank to his knees, 'Have mercy upon thy unworthy servant, Oh lord. Forgive me my sins, let your eyes blot out my transgression and make me see your glory.'

'You aren't seeing any glory yet, old man,' Tyrus said, joining him at the altar, 'I have a long story to tell you, and who knows; you might be able to help me out.'

Pope Nathaniel III made the sign of the cross and stood to his feet, facing his adversary.

'What have you got to say?'

Tyrus sighed. He dug his hand into his trouser pocket and a mysterious glint appeared in his eyes. He wore a three-piece suit and looked very dashing, like a corporate lawyer. The Pope wore the same type of suit, and though he appeared frail, it looked great on him. Tyrus had given him the suit before they left London. The Pope was glad of the short trip to the village; it was like a breath of fresh air. He'd hated the house in London. It was worse than being in the castle of Elizabeth Bathory, the Hungarian countess and worst female serial killer in human history, the Pope thought, his heart beating fast. At last, whatever was coming to him would not be too far away now.

Tyrus took out some documents sealed with a red band. Pope Nathaniel looked confused and wondered what Tyrus was playing at. Tyrus handed them to him and Pope Nathaniel took out his reading glasses, glancing through the ancient documents. After reading a few paragraphs, he glared at Tyrus and demanded furiously, 'Where did you get this? This was a fake,' but the Pope's hands were trembling.

'I got it from your pal, Father Giovanni, before I took his heart.'

Tyrus answered with delight.

Pope Nathaniel grimaced and tears came to his eyes as he tried to explain the contents of the document.

'It's true; the whole thing was a hoax. The Knights Templar were innocent of all the allegations levelled against them. King Phillip IV of France forced Pope Clement V into issuing the Pastoralis Praeeminentiae, a papal bull that came into force on 22 November 1307. It was communicated to all Christian monarchs to take hold of any Knights Templar within their domain and confiscate their properties. The king ordered the arrest of over six hundred Templar knights, including the grand master of the Order, Jacques de Molay.'

'So,' Tyrus seemed to be enjoying the Pope's discomfort. 'the curse of Jacques de Molay will find fulfilment now. You're the only man alive who can stop it, because you're a relative of Pope Clement V. There's still a curse hanging on his head and that of his generation for what he did during the medieval inquisition against the Knights Templar,' and Tyrus shrugged his shoulders walking over to a sixteenth century oak pew in the church. He sat on it, watching the Pope with a bemused expression on his face.

'The Knights Templar was becoming too powerful for so many people, especially King Phillip of France, but Pope Clement V secretly absolved them of the so called heresies they were alleged to have committed.'

Pope Nathaniel III tried to defend the Catholic Church but no words came.

'So, why hide the Chinon parchment, which pointed to the fact that Pope Clement V absolved the Knights Templar of all the trumped up charges against them, in the Vatican's secret archives?'

Tyrus asked.

'It has been published and will be publicly published again, I promise,' the Pope answered and pulled a face, 'why are you suddenly defending an Order that has been extinct for almost a thousand years? You are the son of the devil; there can't be a seed of goodness in you.'

'You're wrong again, Your Eminence. I might be the son of Satan, but I have free will. I can choose what I want to do. And anyway, you are my blood.' Tyrus dropped the bombshell.

'You must.... be j-jo-king!' The Pope stammered, staggering back towards the door.

'You're going nowhere. It ends today,' Tyrus said in a booming voice. He stood up and marched purposefully towards him.

'The curse of Jacques de Molay brought me to life. Your sister was my mother. I did not ask to be born. You can't even imagine the horror I have seen, the terrible atrocities I have committed; I killed Bacilio and many more like him. My father gave me free rein to do what I like, when I like. I have lived both in Hades and on Earth, but I want to live here, now!'

His eyes turned bright yellow, his voice bellowed and the church trembled as if an earthquake had hit it.

'You liar!' the Pope shouted. That angered Tyrus who charged towards the Pope like a bull, flinging him across the church. The Pope hit the wall and screamed out in agony, sliding to the ground

'I only ask to live; I didn't ask to be born. I hate my father and don't give a damn about God, I just want to live a normal life: to have a girlfriend, have sex, drink beer and go on holidays to Spain. Is that too much to ask? But while my father wanted to rule the world, my mother was a whiny, shameful little girl who had sex with a stranger in a seedy hotel in Paris, fifty-nine years ago. And you claimed that you had no sister! You disowned your own flesh and blood.' Tyrus's voice was low and he spoke slowly, as if soliloquising. At the same time, he moved closer to the helpless Pope.

Tyrus's eyes were glassy with emotion and Pope Nathaniel III knew without an iota of a doubt that his death was imminent.

When Tyrus got to where he lay helpless, he towered over him and exclaimed in an outburst, 'You were too consumed by your silly little faith to notice how pale Marianna was. She was pregnant with me, and your mother knew about it all along. In actual fact she arranged the whole thing; she was a witch!'

'My mother knew?' Pope Nathaniel asked in disbelief, his voice hardly above a whisper. When he sat up, all the bones in his body screamed out in protest.

'Yes, my dear uncle,' he stressed the word 'uncle' disdainfully, 'what do you think happened to your real dad?' And he gave a short dry laugh that was punctuated with coughs.

He cleared his throat and continued, 'Your real dad was the man who adopted you after your 'supposed' dad, the man your mother married, died in the First World War.'

The Pope swallowed hard.

The revelations were relentless; they hit like a flood, and it was too much for his weak heart. Nevertheless, Tyrus continued the onslaught, oblivious to the emotional pain he was inflicting on the Pope.

'Your dad's best pal, Raymond de Goth, had been having an affair with your mother before you or your sister, Marianna, was born. He also introduced your mother to the occult, of course. He had great wealth and was instrumental in having your dad drafted into war – more like the biblical King David who couldn't wait to have Uriah's wife to himself, so sent the poor man to the front where he certainly became mincemeat.'

Tyrus's eyes were now bright red as sweat poured from his face like the Nevada Fall, 'your mother's husband was Aidan Aengus, the brave one, and you went to stay with his sister when Marianna was supposedly killed.'

'What happened to my mother?' he asked quietly, shaking uncontrollably.

'She died a month after you arrived in Ireland, don't you remember?'

'I do,' Pope Nathaniel III replied, his eyes bright with unshed tears, 'I just wanted to be sure you were telling the truth.'

Tyrus suddenly closed his eyes and began shaking. Pope Nathaniel knew this might be his only opportunity to escape, and he tried standing up, but he could not. It was as if his lower body, especially his hipbones, had a life of its own.

'Oh, my God,' Pope Nathaniel murmured under his breath. He had dislocated his hipbones so badly that he prayed the pain would kill him before Tyrus did.

Tyrus stopped shaking and staggered to the altar, holding his head in his hands and groaning in pain. When he got to the altar, he sank to his knees and his groaning became louder.

Pope Nathaniel took a quick look round the church, desperately searching for a way of escape. He prayed for someone to come to his rescue.

But the church was as silent as the grave, except for the ragged breathing of his nephew. The Pope gritted his teeth and closed his eyes; that devil couldn't possibly be the son of his sister.

'Marianna,' Pope Nathaniel called her name softly and the enormity of the words Tyrus had said hit him like a sledgehammer.

The memories came flooding back.

Their villa in the Languedoc part of southern France had been filled with punctuated voices while he tried to read in his room; he could not forget that sunny day in May, 1950.

'Mom! Mom!' he'd called out, frustrated with the relentless noise. How he hated to be disturbed whilst reading, but what met his gaze when he got down stairs was his sobbing mother and three police officers.

'What happened?' he had asked no one in particular.

Their housekeeper had looked at him with sorrow-filled eyes and she said, 'Marianna is dead!'

That was the only thing he remembered.

The rest of the day passed in a blur; his dad had died exactly a year earlier, and now his only sister was gone too.

Tyrus got back to his feet while Pope Nathaniel stared at him anxiously, and all the hostility was gone. He seemed to be struggling with his breathing.

'This is a holy place, Father,' his red eyes were now bright yellow, 'I don't think I can stay here any-more.'

He scuttled to the entrance of the church, but Pope Nathaniel called out to him.

'Please wait, Tyrus.'

Tyrus did, turning back abruptly and ambling to the wounded Pope.

'What's wrong with you?' Pope Nathaniel asked gasping for breath as sudden pain shot through his thighs.

'I'm dying. I thought I could finally make my peace with God.' Tyrus said sullenly and he looked like a perplexed teenager.

'But...'

'Yeah, I know, Henri Bernard de Goth,' he interjected, calling Pope Nathaniel III by his real name. A crooked smile appeared on his face, 'I took my father's bloodline so I could help him trace Aaron Cohen, the guy that caused all these problems in the first place, but I guess my father wouldn't allow the thought of defeat to enter his head. Archangel Michael once defeated him, yet he would not listen. He alleged that God gave him until the end of this month to prepare a case of absolution, and the only way he could be pardoned was to take the stones of fire from Aaron.'

'The devil has no blood,' Pope Nathaniel III revealed quietly, looking up at Tyrus sadly, 'he's made of flesh and bone. He was a former Cherub, and they don't have blood flowing through their veins. I thought you of all people would have known that.'

'But I ate his heart, and there was blood flowing like a river,' Tyrus insisted, alarmed. What had he done? He scratched his head in frustration, 'I had to do that to be stronger, and he promised that I'll have this body for eternity...' he added in a whisper

'You should have known better, Tyrus,' Pope Nathaniel said wisely, 'your father was very close to God before the rebellion. He is powerful and can conjure up any illusion he wants you to see. He is the father of deception; he lived before the first Adam. Don't forget that he's very crafty and cunning - how do you think he compelled Eve to go against the instructions of the Almighty?'

'What should I do, Holy Father?'

Tyrus's obvious vulnerability touched the Pope, but he knew that Tyrus was still potentially deadly.

'I don't know...' and he hesitated before his next utterance, the Pope didn't want to be caught in the crossfire. It would be a precarious situation for him.

'Your birth was different from that of normal human beings; I don't know if you can be redeemed.'

'Indeed, he cannot,' a voice rang out shrilly from the doorway.

A tall shadowy figure strolled into the church majestically, but stopped just before they could see his face.

The church began to shake like a leaf dancing in the rain.

'Is that you, Dad?' Tyrus asked flatly, moving backwards, his face contorted in horror. The dire punishment awaiting him was terrifying, even more so when he remembered his father's statement before possessing the body of Reverend Mathew Peters.

'You can't change from this body until Judgement Day.'

That meant God could judge him as a human and not a supernatural being. He would have to rely on that. Tyrus made the sign of the cross and said the Lord's Prayer.

There was a horrific guttural sound and the shadowy figure was gone. Pope Nathaniel and Tyrus both heaved a sigh of relief.

'He's gone!'

'Yeah,' the Pope said in a nonchalant tone, 'but he will be back.'

Tyrus stared at the Pope and felt a little bit of compassion, but the overpowering evil in him squashed it before it manifested. Nevertheless, Tyrus struggled against the evil spirit, refusing the urge to devour the flesh of the wounded Pope. He said forcefully, his breathing irregular,

'Your sister is alive in Abruzzi, Italy. She has been living near you all her life and has dedicated her life to God. She is a hermit. I had wanted to hurt her, but I could not. I think she wanted to purge her mind and body of the memory of my father.'

They heard movement outside the church and then several voices, which were getting nearer. Tyrus and Pope Nathanial III looked at each other.

Shalem and Rachel burst into the church with flushed faces. The Reverend Canon Amos Bradwell, the clergyman in charge of the church, followed them. They stopped short when they saw the Pope on the floor and Tyrus's anxious face.

'Go to them, now,' Tyrus said through clenched teeth as his body filled with smoke. It was obvious that he had resigned himself to his fate. God would incarcerate him in the nether region, reserved exclusively for the angels who had rebelled after Lucifer fought his bitter battle and lost.

'Help me!' Pope Nathaniel shouted. Shalem rushed to his side and gently carried him in his arms.

'Get out, now!' Tyrus screamed, and the sound was dissonant and menacing.

They rushed out of the church as Tyrus exploded into fragments. The booming sound echoed throughout the village, and people trooped out wondering what was happening. The once sleepy village was now a beehive of activity as anxious villagers filled the street.

Lucifer, inhabiting the body of Peter stood at the church gate, watching the scene. His nose flared as his eyes turned dark grey, and his chest heaved up and down.

His rage built up steadily. The spirit within him growled and he lurched forward, but he restrained himself and held onto the gate for support.

He lifted his face and stared at the blazing August sun. The weather had been unstable for two days; sometimes there were scattered showers, and at other times, it was stiflingly hot. Lucifer turned his attention back to the church, watching intently as a man carried the Pope to a car. He tore his gaze away and turned on his heels, running away from the church. The situation was gradually turning nasty, but he still had a trick or two up his sleeve.

Despite the shock of Tyrus's betrayal, which came only twenty-four hours before the deadline to find Aaron, this time, nothing would be able to stop him. He had to find the stones of fire, the Ark, and an altar to perform the rite of restoration. He strode purposely out of the village, knowing that it was time for him to call in the reserves.

49

Canary Wharf, London, Aug 20

Uriel went inside the hotel room and smiled when he saw Aaron's beaming face. Three other men entered the hotel with Uriel, and Aaron stared at the men apprehensively.

'Relax, friend,' Uriel said, smiling, 'they're for us, not against us.'

'Uriel,' Kate called his name reverently, 'have you returned the bus?'

'Yes I have, Katie,' he answered with his usual easy smile, 'along with the men who came with it; I did that ages ago.'

She giggled and lay on the bed. Kate felt at ease and at home with all the men in the room. She had come to trust Uriel, even though she still refused to believe that he was not human. As far as she was concerned, Uriel looked like a movie star, with his huge biceps and baritone voice that resonated round the room.

She glanced at her phone and a brief smile crossed her face; Aaron was hers, and she was content with that.

Aaron had professed his undying love for her, which had compensated for his absence and the bizarre experiences she had gone through since the start of the month. Kate knew it was time for her to go home and see her parents but she was reluctant, even though she was confident that Aaron would not leave her again; he was free from the shadows of his tragic past.

The ring on her finger sparkled, and as she stared at it, her heart filled with love. Aaron sat on the bed and took her left hand in his, kissing it gently. He smiled broadly and said in a very husky voice, 'I'll see you tonight. I'll come to your house, I promise.'

Kate looked at him and realised that he was going away again. All the feelings she thought she had banished from the recesses of her mind resurfaced, and she began to shiver.

The unpleasant memories were inexorable. From the day when the bloodhound bit her in Central Park in New York to the day Evelyn died, the memories flooded her mind like a virus and she began to weep softly. Aaron took her in his arms whilst Uriel and the three men left the room.

'Please, don't go,' she pleaded desperately, her fear totally blinding her to reason, 'I have a feeling I won't see you again.'

She touched his face with her right hand.

It was as if she wanted to etch his face on her heart forever.

'Kate,' he called her name softly, 'it all ends today. I have to go or none of us will be safe. There is a prowler out there, and I'm the only one who can stop him. He will destroy everything in his path...' he paused to let that sink in, 'didn't you watch the news this morning?'

She nodded, bright eyed and Aaron felt like taking her into his arms again but restrained himself. There would be plenty of time for that.

'The body of the son of the American president was found mutilated in Hyde Park a few minutes ago. The president was at Downing Street talking to the prime minister about world peace at the time. No one knew his son had been missing for days. What about the explosions on the Jubilee line this morning? Or the fact that some random bloke found the Pope in a church in Harmondsworth? The Pope was missing for over a week, and you knew how he was when you met him. Michael and Evelyn are dead; rescuers found Keith Morgan's under the rubble of what was once the Temple Church on Fleet Street. The guy causing so much carnage was looking for me. I have to confront him. I can't hide or run away any more or millions of people may pay dearly for it. Shall I go on?'

Kate shook her head, unable to speak. Her trembling stopped and the door opened. Uriel poked his head through, his demeanour had changed; he seemed to be in war mode.

He said quietly, 'Are you ready to go, Katie?'

'Yes,' she answered and stood up from the bed. Her legs were shaking, but she put on a brave face for Aaron even though her knotted stomach trembled with fear.

She picked her bag up from the table and stared in shock at a familiar face on the television. It was her mother, begging her to come home. She was giving an interview at their family home concerning her disappearance from King George's Hospital.

Kate swallowed hard and walked out of the hotel room without a backward glance, her head held high. Meanwhile, Aaron lay down on the bed with a sick feeling in the pit of his stomach. He wondered what, or whom, he would soon be fighting. Humans? Fallen angels? Rebellious demons? Aliens?

He had a daunting task before him, but he would just have to summon his courage. He could not back out any more. Still, he felt ill prepared and did not have the faintest idea about what was going to happen. The strangest thing was that Tyrus and his gang had simply disappeared from his radar, though it was obvious that they might have gone underground to gather reinforcements. Aaron knew he had to preserve his strength for whatever lay ahead, and the only way he could do that was to get enough sleep.

He closed his eyes and slipped off into a dreamless slumber.

DAVID AND Ellie Maser stared at the skyline, questioning why the weather had suddenly turned dark and gloomy. Ellie went into the bathroom to have a shower while David removed his tie and jumped on the bed. The thought of his wife's soft skin next to his sent his blood racing. He waited patiently.

He had seen the relief on the faces of his colleagues when he told them about his decision to spend a week in London. Most of them had his best interests at heart. He had lost concentration, and although things would be on hold for a week, it was a much-needed holiday.

Ellie came back into the room in a white towel. Without warning, claps of thunder ripped through the sky, and Ellie jumped with fright, her eyes wide in panic. David stood up and gently led her to the bed. He rolled his sleeves up and took her body lotion from her makeup bag. He put a generous amount into his hands and rubbed it with gentle strokes all over her body.

She moaned with pleasure and, in a matter of minutes, was fast asleep.

David smiled and covered her with the duvet. He hurriedly undressed and entered the bathroom for a quick shower. The thought of his wife's naked skin on the bed filled him with desire, but when he came back out of the bathroom, his heart almost popped out of his chest. His wife was floating in mid-air with three weird birds, which resembled bald eagles, circling round her and shrieking incessantly. Thankfully, Ellie's eyes were shut; she was still sleeping.

David watched the birds with apprehension. They were small with long beaks and their colour was dark grey. David was a keen bird watcher and knew that the birds were a very strange breed.

He knew he had to do something, and then he remembered the chain around his neck; Ellie had warned him never to take it off, he charged towards the birds, yelling to distract them from his wife. He lifted his hands revealing the chain around his neck, and the stones on the golden chain sparkled. A white light shot out of the stones and the birds flew out through the window, flapping their wings vigorously.

Ellie hit the bed very hard and screamed out in pain. She sat up panting. 'I just had a terrifying nightmare. You won't believe what I saw...' she said in a small voice, her eyes darting round the room.

'I would,' David interjected quietly, a tender look on his face, 'I saw the nightmare here, live.'

'You did?' Ellie asked quietly.

Her husband nodded and held her hand in his; he looked at her and said slowly, 'Tell me the story of this golden chain I'm wearing.'

But before she could, there was a deafening explosion. On impulse, they moved towards the window, staring open mouth at the unlikely scene before them. They must have been in their millions; the same birds that attacked his wife now filled the skyline. A plane had crashed into the hotel adjacent to theirs.

'What a terrible time to visit London,' David said, wondering how they would get back home.

In a burst of spontaneity, David hastily put on his clothes and Ellie did the same. He took his wallet and suitcase from the table, and their eyes were drawn to the television. The monotonous voice of the prime minister was asking for calm, warning everyone to stay indoors. No one should venture outside, 'We are on top of the situation,' the prime minister promised, but David was not convinced. They just had to get back home.

'This is so strange; it's like something out of a horror film,' he commented dryly.

They left the television on and went out of their room. They saw other people trooping out of their rooms one after the other, everyone speaking at the tops of their voices. David clasped Ellie's hand in his, marching forward like a soldier with his head held high, but something caught his attention. When they went to enter a lift, there were four men already in it. One of the men had a very tiny golden chain, which was an exact replica of the one David was wearing. The only difference was that the stone on the other man's chain was much bigger and it illuminated the lift.

They entered and David's eyes were unwavering as he stared at the man. Ellie deliberately stepped on his shoes, but he didn't notice. When he couldn't hide his curiosity any more, he coughed twice and apologised before saying in a raspy voice, 'Sir, where do you get that gold necklace?' And he pointed to Aaron's neck. Before he could reply, Uriel asked David, 'Where did you get the one around your neck, sir?'

'It was a gift.' David answered. By that point, he was feeling very uncomfortable.

'Six of these precious stones were carved from the throne of grace in the Holy of Holies,' Uriel said looking intently at David and Ellie, 'You were chosen to be here today...' he paused before adding kind-heartedly, 'tell your wife to go back to your room. This hotel is one of the safest places you could be in London right now.'

'She was attacked by some strange birds,' David's voice quavered with emotion when he spoke, 'I thought she was going to die...' he blinked his eyes several times, 'we just came in today from Washington.'

'Great,' Uriel said with a sparkle in his eyes, 'your president is here mourning his son. Those birds you see are the hordes of hell, and they will obliterate everything in their path if nothing is done to halt their advance.'

'I can't stay alone,' Ellie cried out timidly, her eyes clouded with tears, which threatened to fall at very short notice.

David held her close as the lift stopped on the ground floor. They stepped out and saw the hotel lobby full of nervous people. David and Ellie moved away from their new friends who were talking animatedly with each other.

'How long do we have to wait?' Aaron asked Uriel with an agonised expression on his face.

He watched with dismay as daylight turned to utter darkness. The birds filled every available space in the sky.

'People are dying by the hour. The devil and his agents are wreaking havoc on the city,' Aaron complained, frustrated by Uriel's nonchalant attitude.

'We have to wait for the others to join us,' Uriel said tersely, towering above the sea of people babbling away, trying to make coherent conversation, but failing miserably.

Aaron watched with apprehension as the shrill cries of the birds grew in intensity; he knew he had to do something.

A few minutes later, he saw a guy he suspected had been tailing him when he was in Ethiopia.

The man's eyes locked with his briefly, and the next thing Aaron knew the man had merged with the teeming crowd.

Suddenly, there were gasps of amazement as two people staggered inside the hotel covered in blood. Their clothes were in tatters; they were almost naked.

Rachel and Shalem slowly made their way through the throng of frightened people. The front of house manager pushed his way through the crowd, and he took them upstairs.

'So, what do we do next?' Aaron asked slowly, tapping his right foot on the marble floor.

'We're just spectators;' Uriel told him softly and his eyes gleaming, 'the ball is now in your court. You can go and kick his stinking backside to where it belongs. I'm only the gatekeeper of Hades. I'll wait for you here while these men accompany you.'

Aaron's gaze rested on the men. They were young black men dressed in denim jeans and white shirts. Aaron hesitated for as a brief second, and then with a deep sigh, he strolled towards the main entrance of the hotel.

Opening the door, a blast of hot air hit him in the face and he turned to Uriel for support. Uriel raised his hand in a short wave, but his customary smile had vanished.

The ball is truly in my court now, Aaron thought, his heart pounding with such viciousness that he felt faint. If a pin had dropped, it would have sounded like a bomb; everywhere was deathly quiet.

All eyes were on Aaron and his companions. With a determined look on his face, he decided against the main door; he closed it and opened the side door. They walked out into certain death; at least that was the thought on David Maser's mind. But something extraordinary began to happen to him - the tiny gold necklace around his neck began to glow with such power that someone screamed.

'Hey, everyone, that guy is full of light!'

People stared at David Maser, and he tried to make a run for it but could not, something seemed to have glued his feet to the floor. Ellie watched helplessly.

The lift door opened and Shalem stepped out with Rachel. They had changed their clothes, and their wounds appeared cleaned. They headed straight for the front door, but David caught Shalem's attention who whispered into Rachel's ear. She nodded and moved near David and said to him, 'You have to protect everyone in this building; those screeching creatures you see outside will try to come in again, but you can fend them off.'

Ellie noticed the gold necklace around Rachel's neck and she asked, 'If I may ask, how did you get that gold chain?' and she pointed to Rachel's neck. A shadow passed through Rachel's eyes for a fleeting second, and then it was gone.

'It was a wedding present,' she snapped hoarsely, walking away from her.

There was a loud crash as three enormous bald eagles landed in the lobby. A woman screamed out in horror, crumbling into a heap on the floor. Rachel turned back swiftly. She was ready to confront the creatures, but Shalem held her back.

'Let him deal with it,' he said at the top of his voice for everyone to hear.

David hurried to the direction of the noise and saw one of the eagles carrying a woman in its massive beak. The woman was no longer moving. He didn't know what to do. He stood there staring at the creature and something unusual happened; the eagles were engulfed in flames, and their agonised cries filled the air. In a matter of minutes, they were reduced to burning coals.

The woman hit the marble floor with a dull sound; the crowd surrounded her, watching for signs of life. David bent down to check her pulse. The burning coals raced towards him with a ghostly sound; his gaze flickered as he braced himself for the worst. A dazzling light radiating from the gold chain began to suck the coals up. It dawned on him that the necklace could actually suck in the killer birds.

The woman opened her eyes and David knew what he had to do.

50

Fatima looked on with interest as the nurse expertly bandaged her bruised knee. With the dressing done, she lay back on the bed, her two hands cradling the back of her head. It had been strange when she woke up and found herself on a hospital bed with Andre's anxious face peering down at her.

When she remembered the events of the day she froze in panic, but Andre held her tenderly, whispering into her ear,

'Mukta is dead, darling. A chap just walked up to him and shot him. I believe he died on the scene.'

'How do you know?' she asked with her heart beating rapidly.

'Because I saw it, moreover it was all over the news.' he answered and his tone was angry. Fatima understood his reaction absolutely. He moved away from her and walked to the window, staring at nothing in particular. Fatima watched his stiff back with apprehension.

Andre had taken her kidnap calmly. He had hurriedly arranged their wedding when she got back from Somalia, even though she wanted more time to recover from her ordeal, but he would have none of it. Her mother supported him and they went ahead with the wedding.

Now her worst fear had been confirmed - she was pregnant. But whose child was it? Fatima recoiled with horror at the possibility that it could be Mukta's. How would Andre take the news if it were?

Pushing her sad thoughts aside, her mind dwelled on safer issues and she groaned out loud wondering how Abdul, the young boy whose parents saved her life in Somalia, was coping without her at home. Abdul appeared to be adapting well to his new environment, and she couldn't wait to finish the rest of the complicated paperwork and officially make him her adopted son.

She heard light footsteps moving closer to her bed and was surprised to see Peter looking a little bit dishevelled. Fatima smiled and was about to speak when she saw Andre right behind him. Andre squared up to him. Neither of them said a word, but when Peter's eyes rested on Andre's neck and saw the glimmer of light from a tiny gold necklace, he scampered towards the window and simply disappeared.

There were gasps of astonishment. People who witnessed Peter's disappearance from the ward were stunned. A man had vanished in broad daylight, right before their eyes. Andre's mouth was suddenly dry, because what he had just seen was more bizarre than Peter's disappearance.

'Where is it Peter?' Fatima asked with a worried frown on her face.

'I don't know,' Andre answered and lowered his voice, 'we have to leave London.'

He had expected Fatima to say something, but when she didn't he continued, 'I saw a bald eagle, darling, it was huge. I think we should leave; I have a weird feeling this city will descend into anarchy in a matter of hours. We can still get out now.'

Fatima stared at Andre, confused by his incoherent words.

First, Peter had vanished, and now her husband was babbling, not making any sense.

'I've been discharged, Andre and I think we should go and look for Cedric and Peter; they're your friends. Then we can all go back home together.'

Fatima's sharp eyes caught a glimmer of light from underneath Andre's shirt and she smiled, 'I see that you're wearing the gold chain your uncle gave you...'

and she looked at him fondly, 'he must have been a nice man, I wish I'd met him'

'Yeah,' he mumbled some words, and everything passed in a daze as they went through the motions of signing the discharge register. When they got to the front of the hospital, they saw military men armed to the teeth and fighter jets flying past. It would have been a fantastic view, but the soldiers seemed to be on edge; it was as if they were expecting an attack at any moment.

Andre held Fatima's hand and they walked with quick strides to the bus stop. They were torn between loyalty and survival, but Andre was prepared to do the sensible thing by getting them out of London alive while they still had the chance.

AARON DUCKED behind a wall, scrutinising his environment. The towering buildings in Canary Wharf made it difficult for him to plan his next move.

The three men who followed him out of the hotel had since left him, and he didn't have enough time left to be angry.

He glanced at his wristwatch and realised that it was three in the afternoon.

Fear gripped him as he stared at the skyline anxiously. Aaron had been amazed, but also suspicious, when he left the hotel and saw that everywhere was clear. There were no huge man-eating raptors, and the bald eagles, which had been causing havoc, had vanished. The air smelt fresh and clean, however he noticed that there was a slight increase in wind.

The sky was bright, the sun shone brilliantly in all its glory, and he wondered if he was going nuts, but he knew it was a transient peace. It would not last.

He touched his neck and felt the huge stone on the gold chain. Why had things changed so horribly for him? Why did he trust everything Uriel told him? Why hadn't he questioned him more on so many riddles, bits, and pieces that did not add up? What if he did not survive? What would be his fate? He was getting more confused as the agonising seconds ticked by.

When it happened, the noise was deafening; Aaron stared at the ground in terror, and there was tightness in his chest and throat. Then he looked up and saw something emerge like a very dark mountain. It was a comet falling from the sky; a gigantic mass of ice and rock. Aaron was not sure what it was, but he knew it was not good. He thought he would fight the devil man to man, but not like this.

He gawked in horror as the object inched closer. It was colossal. *Uriel is a cruel messenger,* Aaron thought sadly. He could have at least warned him that the earth and its people were facing death and destruction on this scale. What were the scientists doing? NASA should have discovered the evil monster, with all their technology, it was preposterous that such a massive object would be heading towards earth and they could not detect it.

But Aaron also knew that Lucifer was responsible for the incoming comet attack, and he wondered why it was so elusive. Then he remembered the instructions of the three elders in Ethiopia, they had warned him to take his bath at exactly five in the morning with a change of raiment for three days but he'd totally forgotten - could his negligence be responsible for the attack, or had allowed it?

He had no answer to his own question.

If Aaron had seen Lucifer, he would have tipped his hat off as sign of respect; the bad boy had finally pulled his last trick by releasing a comet upon London, he was not expecting that at all. Nevertheless, it was obvious that Lucifer had failed, because he couldn't get the Ark or the stones of fire but rather than concede defeat, Lucifer would rather bring innocent victims down with him. There was no one way Lucifer would be able to fight for his rights to the stones of fire.

All sorts of thoughts went through his head as he watched. Thoughts of all the things he would not be able to do filled his mind, and an overwhelming feeling of incredible sadness and sorrow came over him. Faces of people he knew flashed through his mind and he looked around in alarm. What could he do?

He knew he was on the Lord's side, so why couldn't he win? In spite of his own mistakes, how could Lucifer still rise, he was a fallen angel - he wasn't supposed to have such ruthless power. Why the woman he loved, and the city should die such a gruesome and ferocious death was beyond him.

There was no respite for him as tears streamed down his face. He watched on in agony. The events surrounding the twin towers crossed his mind fleetingly, and at the same time, he looked at his wristwatch again. It was one minute and forty-nine seconds past three.

The dark mass landed on the HSBC building and a vast area in Canary Wharf, with devastating effect levelling it. The resulting ripple tore buildings down like an angry monster. The towering buildings of Canary Wharf fell like a pack of cards, and the earth started to burn as acid rain fell in torrents.

Aaron hurriedly tore the gold necklace from his neck, staring at the beautiful chalcedony stone imbedded in the pendant. A single tear fell on his ashen face; it was the tear of a failure, and he braced himself for impact. A bright white light shot into his heart from the stone and he watched grimly as plumes of black engulfed the earth. Incredibly, amidst the rubble and destruction, he could see clearly, it was as if he was in a bubble and he understood why death hesitated, he was the carrier of the Ark. He couldn't die except he wanted to, the light from the stone overpowered him, lifting him up above the devastation.

Aaron screamed angrily, as bright light engulfed him - the last thing on his mind was Kate.

POPE NATHANIEL III sat on the papal throne on the balcony of St Peter's Basilica in the Vatican, staring forlornly into space. Although Tyrus had spared his life, there were moments when he wished he had died. If his death had alleviated the excruciating pain in his heart, he would have gladly laid down his life.

Later, he lifted his hands to pray for the throng of worshipers, but as he did so the bright sky turned to grey and debris began to fall; the sun completely blocked by a travelling blanket of gases and dust.

The Pope made the sign of the cross and the crowd hurriedly dispersed from the square. A cardinal came rushing into the Pope's private chamber, a look of terror on his face.

Pope Nathaniel III bowed his head for a very long time.

When he lifted his face, the only words he said were, 'God bless the souls of the people of London.'

The cardinal left him, and Pope Nathaniel sat still, staring into space. The words he had just heard slowly blackened his heart with unquenchable sorrow.

A giant comet of about thirty kilometres had killed almost six million people, and the energy released from the object had been worse than any nuclear weapon ever made by man.

After his miraculous escape from Tyrus and his father, the Pope had thought the worst was over. He had rejected every form of celebration on his safe return, but had instead buried his friends who died in the great fire, which engulfed his summer residence. The only task left for him was to find his sister in Abruzzo, but his staff told him that she died the same day he left London.

That revelation crushed him.

'What a futile world. What a waste of life; such vanity and endless folly,' he said aloud and allowed himself the luxury of crying again; he wept bitterly for the millions of people who lost their lives and, at the same time, marvelled at the miracle of the survivors.

About two million people had survived the nuclear-like destruction.

London had been, and would always be, a formidable city. The great fire, which devoured London about five hundred years earlier, had not crushed the city; the great city had bounced back.

'Can that great city live again?' The Pope whispered as his head slowly dropped to his chest.

51

Lake Tana, Ethiopia, Aug 29

Kate opened the urn and threw the ashes and urn into the lake. Her hands fell limply to her sides. The guard took her right hand gently and led her away from the edge. She stifled a sob and allowed herself to be led away like a child.

She rummaged through her bag while her Ethiopian guard watched with interest. She found what she was looking for, a small diary, and she held it to her chest with a deep sigh.

The erratic Ethiopian weather gave a loud warning in the form of rumbling thunder; the guard glanced at the sky with a worried frown.

'It's going to rain soon, ma'am. I think we'd better get going.' Kate nodded and trailed after her guard, inch by inch, to their papyrus reed boat.

Everything she did was like a chore; breathing, eating and living were tasks that she was grudgingly performing. However, she was so pleased that she had gone to Ethiopia.

The lake had a calming effect on her, a kind of spiritual discovery.

A sad smile crossed her face; she now understood why Aaron had fallen in love with Ethiopia. She was a proud, beautiful, untainted country with a very rich history.

She watched the lake and saw different species of birds flying without a care in the world. Kate wished she could become a bird and fly away.

Such wishful thinking, she thought as she admired her environment. Kate would have loved to explore the ancient churches and monasteries, but it appeared she would have to content herself with scattering Michael's ashes in Lake Tana, as Evelyn had wanted to do before she died.

Kate got into the boat and sat as still like a statues for the ninety-minute journey back. The sound of the Blue Nile filtered to her in the distance. She lifted her face upward as drizzles of rain began to fall and, without warning, tears slowly streamed down her cheeks.

Her sorrow was of such magnitude she often wondered how she would survive. Kate stared at the body of water and her spirit broke.

'If only Aaron were here,' she whispered softly, but deep down she knew it was futile; this time around, Aaron was not coming back, along with millions like him who had died.

Millions!

She shuddered at the thought. London had literally become a ghost town, and the whole world was still reeling from the shock.

An overwhelming feeling of emptiness engulfed her; what was she going to do with her life? How could she pick up the shattered pieces and move on?

She sighed again, staring at her black dress. It was getting soaked, but she couldn't care less.

Her Ethiopian guard was throwing casual glances in her direction occasionally, but Kate was oblivious to where she was as her mind played out the events of that fateful day. It had been exactly nine days ago when she left the Marble Hotel in Canary wharf.

Uriel had driven her outside London. What intrigued her most was her complacency; she had not bothered to argue or ask why he did not take her home.

Egerton was a quiet, idyllic village and that fateful Monday afternoon, when she was ushered into a very large reception room, she had felt the cold hand of fear tying her stomach in knots again, but she brushed it aside. Aaron trusted Uriel, and so she had no cause not to do the same.

She sat on a plush leather sofa and a cheerful woman breezed into the room with a cup of tea and biscuits.

Uriel left soon afterwards, and, strangely, after eating a biscuit, she rested her head on the soft sofa and dozed off.

After what seemed like a few minutes' nap, she felt a light touch on her shoulder and woke up with a start. She was surprised, and somewhat embarrassed, to see many people in the room staring at her awkwardly. Uriel was among them and he broke the news to her. Words failed the eloquent and confident Uriel who struggled for a few seconds.

'London is gone, Katie,' he said solemnly, as though he were reading a funeral dirge.

'How can London be gone?' she asked stupidly, standing to her feet.

'There was a comet,' Uriel began, and Kate marched towards him and slapped him hard around the face.

Uriel stepped back and continued as if he had not been interrupted,

'It could have been worse. Aaron stopped the others from colliding with your planet; as I speak, there are many more of these comets and asteroids heading directly towards Earth. The stones of fire embedded in Aaron's gold chain prevented this catastrophic event from happening the way it was meant to.'

She glanced at the strangers in the room and saw the truth in their eyes. Kate sank onto the sofa, her world collapsing before her eyes.

'This particular comet couldn't have been averted. Aaron fought hard, but he could not stop the advent of that particular comet. If humans had stopped fighting each other, wasting huge numbers of lives and amounts of money by making mountains of destructive weapons, they might have stopped it. God has given humanity wisdom which could have been used to prevent this kind of tragedy.'

'You're worse than the devil, Uriel. Why didn't you stop it? Huh?!' Kate snarled, glaring at the sad looking figure staring down at her with his clear blue eyes.

'I could not, even if I had the power to. If the devil had laid his hands on the Ark and Aaron, Earth would have ceased to exist. It would have been total annihilation,' Uriel said and added after a short pause, 'Aaron wanted you to have this,'

Uriel gave her a small book and a vase.

She took the book, putting the vase beside her feet, and she opened the first page.

Aaron's smiling face beamed out at her and she hurriedly closed the book.

'Things will pick up again, I assure you, Kate. I'll be checking up on you, I promise.'

'Don't ever come near me again,' she said through gritted teeth and turned her face away; she would not show her weakness.

'There is an evacuation bus just outside the village. It's best if you go, Kate. An arrangement has been made for people to leave the country for a while; you can come back after a few months. It's just to let the dust settle, I suppose.' Uriel said softly and held out his hands, she obliged and finally collapsed into his arms, sobbing quietly.

Uriel walked her out and when they got outside, she was shocked to see the village deserted.

'Everyone has left, we're the last ones,' Uriel explained gently and Kate began to cough.

The weather was grey and gloomy. No one would believe it was August; it was like the darker days of winter.

They got to the bus and Kate held his hands briefly, then she stepped on it.

'I'm sorry,' he whispered and the bus began to pull away. Kate turned to steal a second look at Uriel and saw a man coming up behind him.

Who is that man? She wondered.

Kate's days had begun in a blur and ended in a daze, but she was not alone. The next day, she left for France. She spent two days there and then went to Ethiopia. Everywhere she went, people wore long faces;

it was a disaster, which touched billions of people, and now humanity was scared.

Kate stared at the pelicans sitting quietly on Lake Tana as her mind returned to present day, and something dropped in her spirit. The Earth was like those pelicans; probably aware, but oblivious to the threats outside their environments.

Kate wondered what to do with her life, if comets or asteroids allowed her to live. She was not a religious person, but as she took out Aaron's diary and began to read, the hair at the nape of her neck stood on end. The words on the pages jumped out and Kate realised that life was about to be brutally distorted.

Her hands began to shake violently.

CHLOE MASER walked around the empty house. She was still in a state of shock.

Her parents had simply disappeared along with millions of Londoners.

She slumped on the sofa, picked up the remote control for the television, and saw their front door on the national news.

She jumped to her feet and yanked the door open. The flash of lights from cameras momentarily blinded her, but it was the faces peering at her from a few meters away, which almost turned her insane.

'Dad? Mum?' she screamed, running down the short steps into the arms of her parents. Her mother's tears soaked her hair and, slowly, they climbed back up the steps and stood in the doorway. David Maser turned and waved to the cameras.

Once inside, Ellie Maser held her daughter. There was no sign of her three-month pregnancy, and Chloe held her mother tightly while whispering into her ear, 'I lost the baby. And I have left Jude, Mum. He's a Satanist. You were right about him all along, Mum.'

Ellie closed her eyes in obvious relief while David gazed at them with warmth. He ran his hands through his receding hair, happy to be home. It still felt as if he was dreaming.

In faraway Jackson, Mississippi, Logan Stone watched the Masers on the news with his mother by his side.

'Mom, it was horrible,' Logan said with tears in his eyes, 'we were lucky. I think we were deliberately spared to warn the world of the impending danger currently surrounding us. Scientists were shocked; they never saw it coming. The comet hit London with a bang, but no one saw it coming, Mom,' and he wept like a child while his mother comforted him. Then he remembered something.

He stood up from his chair and went to his room. He found what he was looking for; the cheque Joshua

Cohen had given him. Without thinking twice, he tore it to shreds and went back to the living room.

Logan Stone was a changed man.

SHALEM AND Rachel huddled together on the bed, staring into space.

They had been like that since they got back from London, and Shalem's dad was becoming increasingly worried.

But Shalem always smiled whenever his dad asked him about the terrible events in London.

'How could we have survived that intense heat?' Rachel asked.

'We were not there, love,' Shalem answered, turning to look at her, 'the hotel was moving; that was why we weren't vaporised. Someone, or something, moved us out of there in the nick of time.'

'No one would believe us if we said that,' Rachel whispered, eyes bright, 'people will think we're crazy.'

'I don't care what anyone thinks,' Shalem said with a sigh, 'but I do know that I would definitely love to step into my father's shoes. I've had enough adventures to last me a lifetime.'

They snuggled on the bed while Shalem's dad paced up and down in his study, seriously disturbed by his son's behaviour.

ANDRE ENTERED the church and sat down on a mat. The burial of his uncle Caleb and Abraham, the caretaker of the Ark, had been a quiet affair. He was not too keen on knowing more about the Ark of the Covenant, or its miraculous journey back to Ethiopia after it had been stolen. Neither was he remotely interested in joining the Order of Lalibela.

He had seen enough death and destruction to last him a million years, but his dear old mother had insisted that he join the respected Order. He had gone to the church to satisfy her, but he did not intend to become a member.

Outside the church, Kate gazed at the ancient building, watching it keenly. Fatima strolled outside and saw something in Kate's expression, which drew her to the young white girl. She looked lost in her surroundings, but there was something vaguely familiar about her.

'Hi,' Fatima said with a broad smile.

'Hello,' Kate returned her smile. Fatima walked towards her and they began to talk.

Fatima had seen her at the Marble Hotel, a day before the comet hit London. She knew they were survivors, and survivors look out for each other.

52

Roberto Costello pulled up outside the Maser's home and got out of his car. He walked briskly to the front door and pressed the bell. Someone pulled the curtain aside and peered out; Roberto showed his badge, and the door opened.

About an hour later, Roberto and David left the house and got into his car. They drove for a while, and David noticed that Roberto's hands were shaking.

'Are you all right, Robert?'

'Yeah, I'm fine. I just can't believe that I'm actually doing this.' Roberto stammered, checking his rear view mirror constantly, but no one was following them. After driving through the streets of Washington for half an hour, he turned back and drove David Maser home.

They got out of the car and strolled into the house. David took Roberto to his study and poured him a glass of whisky to calm his nerves. Roberto sat down on the leather sofa, sipping his drink. David poured another drink for himself and downed it in one go.

'What exactly can I do for you?' David asked with a yawn. He had had a long day and would have preferred to crawl into bed with his wife.

'I wanted to see you, and driving through the city with you gave me a semblance of normalcy. I just need a friend.' Roberto said, his voice quavering with emotion.

David was confused but he tried to conceal it. The CIA director needs a friend? It was beyond reasoning. *There must be a reason for this strange behaviour,* he thought. David was an intensely private man, and he would not pry into Roberto's affairs or ask unnecessary questions. Although they were friends, most times, they just sit and enjoy each other's company, like their impromptu drive though the street.

'Strange bed fellows,' his wife had commented once.

'I'm really sorry for my eccentric behaviour, but do you happen to have one of these?' Roberto showed David his gold necklace; the stone sparkled in the dimly lit room.

David nodded and removed his own, holding it in his hands.

Roberto collected it from David and compared the two; they were exactly the same length, but the stones were different. He gave it back to David.

'I've been having these weird dreams about the events of August the twentieth,' Roberto began in a grief laden voice, 'is there more that I could have done? I wasn't there for the president. I should have stayed with him.'

'The British people also lost their prime minister and more than six million of their citizens,' David said in a very quiet voice, almost a whisper, 'I also felt responsible. We believed that comets and asteroids couldn't possibly collide with Earth, but we were wrong, and this could happen again.'

His eyes shone with raw emotion as he continued, 'We identified comet Catalina but we didn't think it posed any threat to Earth. I'm not sure whether it was the same comet that slammed into London, but I'm convinced that we were wrong.'

'But there is more,' Roberto said and his hands were visibly shaking, 'have you considered the spiritual aspect? The end of times, as in the book of Revelation?'

'No, not really.'

'I pray this is not the beginning of the end.'

'I hope so, too,' David said, and there was an uncomfortable silence between them. An awkward cough from David broke it and Roberto stood up, taking the cough as a cue for him to leave.

David realised the man was troubled. Putting Roberto's thoughts aside, something else was nagging at him. He reached out to touch Roberto on the hand, but he reacted so violently that David was visibly shaken.

'Sorry, I didn't mean to scare you,' David apologised profusely, taken aback by Roberto's nervous reaction. 'How did you know I had the gold necklace?'

'I saw you and your wife on television.'

The CIA director replied and recounted his encounter with Tyrus. How the director of covert operations, McBride, had vanished shortly after Tyrus paid him a visit.

'I was sleeping with my girlfriend at the Marble Hotel when the comet hit.'

'Have you told your wife?' David asked quietly, finally understanding the depth of the man's guilt.

'No, I couldn't tell her. Can you believe that she was the one who gave me this necklace, which has repeatedly saved my life, yet I couldn't keep my devious manhood in its place?'

David grimaced and patted him on the shoulder. Roberto held David's hands for a while and they hugged.

He had tears in his eyes as he watched Roberto stagger to his car.

When his car moved away, he was relieved, but it was short lived. He heard two shots ring out shrilly. Ellie and Chloe ran out of their rooms and were relieved to see David.

Forty-five minutes later, the body of the CIA director was placed in an ambulance. David dragged his aching body into his house and slammed the door.

The gold necklace around Roberto's neck was gone. The marks on his neck made it obvious that someone had forcefully taken it.

Fear began its gradual ascent to David's heart. Someone out there was interested in the gold necklace. If the CIA director were such an easy target, how long would it take before they found him?

It was not a very comfortable thought, and, as he lay down beside his wife, he remembered the two bald eagles he fought off at the Marble Hotel in London. They had not been ordinary birds. His hands slowly touched the necklace, and he knew he would not sleep a wink.

The next morning, David hurriedly gathered the astronomers in his department, and scientists from the Jet Propulsion Laboratory in Pasadena, California, for a crisis meeting. Everyone appeared to be on edge, and, unknown to David, there was more bad news.

Joe Darwin of the JPL said firmly at the onset of the meeting, 'We're technically not out of the woods yet. We've identified at least three comets and seven asteroids heading straight for us.'

There was complete silence in the room.

'What is the level of threat?' David asked in a hoarse voice. It was as though someone was strangling him.

'We, erm...' Joe cleared his throat for more emphasis, 'have awarded this new threat a score of ten of the Torino Impact Hazard Scale, bearing in mind the recent occurrence in London.'

David stared at each man in the room, mumbling under his breath, 'God help us.'

A GIGANTIC man with bulging biceps dragged someone down the dingy, narrow pathway. Suddenly, there was a blood-chilling scream, but the man continued what he was doing. An enormous gate flung open and the man pushed the being he was dragging into the pit. There was a long wrenching cry, punctuated by grunts as the prisoner fell down the twenty million foot pit.

Finally, there was an uneasy silence.

The gate swung to a close and the man turned the key, dropping it into the skin bag strapped around his waist.

He sauntered back the same way he had come and began climbing some steps. He climbed the stairs for four hours before he reached the landing, which had another gate.

The young man at the gate nodded with a grin when he saw Uriel flying away into the clouds. He winked at Aaron who winked back with a chuckle.

'I hope you rot in there, Lucifer,' Aaron whispered, watching Uriel's ascent.

Thoughts of Kate filled his mind; he couldn't wait to see her again. Uriel had promised him he would see her soon.

'You'll see her soon,' Uriel repeated aloud the words Aaron was thinking, and he was right behind him.

'I thought you'd gone.'

'I can't leave you here by yourself. Besides, it's your turn to monitor Tyrus's progress in the nether region. He won't stop wailing; I think he needs to see a familiar face.'

'Okay,' Aaron said and his wings fan out in glorious splendour, 'he should have known that he would be confined there, after all, he did killed himself and was part of Lucifer's plans to herald the end of days,' he added.

'He would never learn, but he's locked up now, never to torment people again!' Uriel said. His clear blue eyes fastened on Aaron's face and he said slowly,

'It's absurd that Lucifer thought he could win, considering the fact that he couldn't lay his hands on the stone of fire and the Ark.'

'If he had acquired the stones and Ark, what would happen?'

Uriel was silent a while, and when he answered, his voice was strangely cool,

'It would have changed the order and balance of things. Barachiel had won the battle of Cydonia when he defeated Lucifer and his hordes. If Lucifer had succeeded in acquiring the Ark and stones of fire, Earth will simply cease to exist.'

'What are the stones of fire? Aaron asked curiously.

'It's the law and it's what govern existence, what makes God, God!' Uriel answered and his eyes began to glow, 'the stones in the gold chain you had was simply symbolic, it's the law that govern universe and all there is, and would be. It's a deep mystery, and I can't explain it all to you, only God could do that.'

'But why did I have those horrible dreams?' Aaron asked quietly, his eyes searching the face of his friend, 'what's the connection between me? Cydonia, Tyrus, Barachiel, and Lucifer.'

'It's very simple, you represent the law, just as the son of God was crucified and endured incredible pain, you had to go through the same process, although a wee bit different. Jesus represents the mercy of God, you were also the carrier of his mercy, and you stopped the total annihilation of the human race. You've met Barachiel, and you witnessed the onset of the battle of

Cydonia, this was a sort of baptism into the supernatural. Lucifer and Tyrus knew God had chosen you, and they tried to frustrate that calling of God on your life. Barachiel won the battle in Cydonia, in other words, you are Barachiel in the physical. That was why I was able to take the Ark of the Covenant from that New York church to your house in London, and then transfer it back to Ethiopia. You are the embodiment of the Godhead, a representation of the spirit of God. '

Uriel's explanations further deepened the mystery and if Aaron continued questioning him, he was not sure he would be satisfied by the answers. But he trusted Uriel now, and even though he spoke in parables most times, he was a cool angel.

'I must confess, I don't understand it all, but I guess you've said it all,' Aaron said with a short laugh.

'In layman's words?'

And Uriel's eyes seemed to dance with delight, 'you saved the world. You did a great job Aaron and I'm proud of you.'

'Thanks Uriel,' Aaron said and gave him a brief hug.

A shadow crossed Aaron's face and he said quietly, 'I wished no one had died.'

'You never know, you might be able to change the past,' Uriel said.

'How?'

'It's simple, you fight it!' Uriel flapped his massive wings, his eyes twinkling with mischief, disappearing as trails of light followed his gradient into the clouds.

Aaron smiled and shook his head, if only it was that simple, how joyful it would have been - to be able to undo the past. He flew towards the divider of time and space, wind rushed past his eyes, which usually tickled him.

Then the music started in his spirit. His soul and body burst into songs of praise and he flipped over, somersaulting with bouts of laughter trailing behind him as he flew through space. He was excited. Thoughts of Kate always excited him; he never stopped loving her, and he missed her every single second. And if he were to take Uriel's words to heart, go to the past, he would do his best to stop the onslaught of Lucifer. If he had his way, no single soul would be lost.

Simeon appeared in front of him, his face shone with delight as he flew past Aaron. His beaming face broke into a full-throated laughter, he moved closer and playfully pulled Aaron's cheeks, Aaron laughed as they circled each other, their wings flapping in controlled motion.

'I'm so glad you're safe.' Simeon said his eyes bright.

'Same here brother,' Aaron said, glad that his brother had found redemption, Simeon had always been a simple soul, which was why he'd gone to Somalia, to help people in distress.

They flew away in different directions as Aaron stared at the brilliance of the city above him. It was a beauty far beyond words.

'What can I say, huh?' and he laughed heartily, the sound echoing through the vast space.

'I'm home,' he whispered, plunging to the nether region of space where they held Tyrus.

As he flew, Aaron sighed with contentment in appraisal of the beautiful city he had just left. Everything he thought he had lost, he had truly gained.

He'd lost no one. Not even Kate.

53

The End

Royal London Hospital, twelve noon August 29

It was bitterly cold outside and Kate was shivering uncontrollably. She wondered why the weather had suddenly turned and in August! She trudged along the ward, lost in thought. Aaron had been in a coma for thirty days since the accident they'd had on their way back to London from Stonehenge.

She always had been a survivor and had survived the accident without a scratch. She still could not piece the riddles of the accident together. The agonizing thing about the unfortunate incident was Aaron's coma; doctors had warned her it could take years before he regained consciousness, and even after that, the road to complete recovery was hazy. They had warned her without sugarcoating their words.

But Kate believed in luck. Somehow, she had faith that Aaron would come out of his coma. She had rented an apartment very close to the Royal London Hospital to be close to him. Her parents had been amazing; they had supported her all the way, and she was delighted when Aaron's uncle, Joshua Cohen, called her from Washington to say that he would be coming to see Aaron. He was due to arrive at the hospital very soon.

She glanced at her wristwatch: it was twelve noon. She smiled at a nurse who breezed past her with a cheerful smile.

Kate closed her eyes briefly and suddenly felt dizzy. The stress was finally getting to her, but an amazing thing happened.

She saw someone walking towards her with arms outstretched.

It was Aaron, and she fainted.

She came to and found herself on a bed surrounded by doctors, 'Are you all right, Miss Summers?' they asked quietly.

'I'm fine,' she answered and attempted to get up, but they held her down gently.

'I saw Aaron,' she whispered.

They exchanged knowing glances and one of the nurses said, 'I'll come back in half an hour, and then you can come see him.'

'Thanks.'

They left; Kate had never been that embarrassed in her life. They probably thought she had faked it.

Half an hour later, they allowed her to visit Aaron's room.

He lay on the bed looking calm and relaxed. Kate moved closer and held his hand while she blinked back the tears that were threatening to fall. She sat down on the only chair in the room.

'Aaron, please come back to me. I want you to come home.'

She kissed his fingers, saying in a grief-ridden voice, 'don't keep me waiting forever, honey. I want to be your wife...'

A short pause and she added, 'I believe in your God now,' she swallowed hard and continued, 'I saw you outside, and you know what? I just fainted. The doctors thought I was trying to get their attention, but now I believe you. All those things you told me and the dreams you've been having, I believe it.'

Kate stopped speaking, her hands covering her face.

'It's okay Katie, I'm back.'

She stared at Aaron and a tingling sensation began to move slowly from her toes up to her head. She felt weak; was this hallucination, or had she heard correctly? Had Aaron just spoken to her? She shook her head in a bid to clear it and Aaron opened his eyes slowly, staring straight at her. His eyes looked sad and bloodshot.

'Don't alert the doctors yet, Katie,' Aaron's voice was hoarse, he coughed and grimaced.

'The doctors thought you'd be in a vegetative state for years.' Kate said, her eyes filling with tears.

'They thought wrong.'

'Is this the real Aaron? Or am I dreaming?' she gasped, trying in vain to control her erratic breathing and the tremor in her voice.

'I could ask you the same question,' and his eyes slowly filled with tears, 'I thought I'd lost you.'

'You can't, darling; we're stuck together for the long haul.'

And she felt like screaming at the top of her voice, but she reined her emotions in; it was still too early, the doctors needed to examine him and give him the all clear.

'I have amazing stories to tell you, Katie. I've seen mysterious things, and they looked so real. I saw heaven and I was even in hell. I saw things beyond description.'

'The doctors won't believe this.'

'We have to get out of London, Katie. Something bad is going to happen.' There was a sense of urgency in his voice.

Kate was drawn to the gold necklace around his neck; she had not seen it before. She closed her eyes, and when she opened them, her gaze was still glued to the chain. She wanted to speak, but thought better of it.

So many coincidences, so many weird things that couldn't be explained. Kate knew without a doubt that Aaron's mental state was okay, but when she had read through his journal a creepy feeling began dogging her steps, and ever since she hadn't been able to think straight.

What if the end is truly near? Everything that had a beginning must surely have an end, she reasoned, is the earth going to pass away? What hope is there for humanity if everything should go up in smoke? What hope do I have? Her mind raced through a million things while Aaron watched her with concern. She cast her mind back and was sure she had not noticed the necklace before.

Kate had done her own research while Aaron had been in a coma; most of the things she thought he was rambling on about were true. Like the face of Cydonia region of mars. Scientists had been coming up with all kinds of theories, but what if humanity were about to disappear in a puff of smoke? She shifted her weight to one leg as her mind raced through the pages of scripture, especially the book of Revelation. She had devoured the Bible voraciously and other prophesies by notable scholars, especially Nostradamus, and what she had found made her uneasy.

There was certainly life after death, and as much as people tried to avoid the topic, humans were still mortal, and there were higher spiritual forces outside the little world called Earth that were truly in control of the affairs of men. However, a part of her still clung to her realistic view, even if that part was slowly drowning in despair.

She wrung her hands in confusion; she should alert the doctors, a person couldn't just come out of a coma bright eyed like Aaron had. There could still be some underlying problems.

'Is there anyone important visiting London today, Katie?' Aaron asked softly.

'I don't know, why do you ask?'

'Canary Wharf will be razed to the ground...a comet is going to hit London in a few hours; we don't have much time. We have to go now.'

She swallowed hard and looked around wildly, 'If what you're saying is true, Aaron, I have to think of my parents too, and a whole lot of other people. Let's find a way of telling the police,' she conceded quietly, trying to calm him down. She was sure it was his usual nightmare.

Are you sure? a quiet voice whispered in her mind. She shrugged her shoulders defiantly, looking for excuses and loopholes as to why she should not believe Aaron, but her defences were slowly crumbling.

'Nobody can stop this thing, except me...' and a shadow crossed his face, then he added, 'and we're certainly running out of time.' He attempted to sit up, but Kate gently pushed him back.

'Katie,' Aaron said softly and held out his hand, she took it, staring at her, and then he began to speak,

'I witnessed things beyond words, Evelyn and Michael died in the visions, everyone I knew perished. I even went to Ethiopia...'

'You had always loved Ethiopia, ' Kate said with a smile.

Aaron nodded and continued his bizarre tale, 'I met three wonderful men in Ethiopia but one after the other they all died. It was a horrible vision, but the good news is, I could stop the impending carnage. I would love to do everything within my power to prevent Lucifer's rage and save as many people as I can. Lucifer had a son called Tyrus who wanted to kill me...' and his voice trailed away.

Tears gathered in her eyes again, but she knew she must be strong. Aaron had certainly been seeing things, and he had been immobile for a month; she should take his words with a pinch of salt.

Wiping the tears from her eyes with the back of her hand she said, 'that's not possible, Aaron.'

'I'm saying the truth my love,' he said earnestly, his eyes imploring her to believe him, 'I saw people's secrets, I witnessed Michael's passing and his subsequent judgement.'

His face softened with a faraway look in his eyes. His last statement caught Kate's attention.

'What happened to Michael?'

'He sailed through,' and Aaron smiled, 'Michael went to heaven.'

'That would be comforting,' Kate said quietly, sarcasm creeping into her voice, 'I could just call him up and say, 'Michael, you know what? My boyfriend said when you die, you'll go to heaven!'I bet's he'll be delighted to hear that!'

Aaron sighed, then said softly, 'Kate what you believe or don't would not change what's going to happen. All I know is, we have to leave now, and I want you safe.'

'I believe you honey,' she unconvincingly, 'but it's going to take a while for me to process all that information. '

'Then you have sealed our fate.' He said a strange look on his face.

Her heart sank as she strolled outside looking for doctors.

She didn't want to make Aaron suspicious by pressing the button beside his bed, but what she saw outside the ward sent a chill down her spine. People were running in different directions. She ran back to Aaron's room and found his bed empty. She began to panic and then saw him limping towards her.

'Let's go, Katie,' he said quietly.

'Where can we go?' she asked. Her knees were knocking together and could barely support her weight, 'your uncle will soon be here.'

A deranged glint appeared in Aaron's eyes. He reached out for Kate, and slowly they walked out of his hospital room.

'While I was in a coma, I fought with the devil. I was in Ethiopia and stole the Ark of the Covenant; I saw how my uncle died, I saw angels, and I saw demons. I even saw Evelyn and her husband...' he paused before continuing in a shaky voice, 'if by night fall we're still alive, I'll tell you everything, but I know these things will come to pass. Around my neck is a gold necklace with a strange combination of stones as its pendant, and in my pocket is the red silk robe I tore from Barachiel, the angel who destroyed Cydonia. The devil has been defeated again, but I don't really have an answer as to why this is happening. He failed to get what he wanted, and so millions of us will have to pay. Maybe the world is paying for her sins, or we have simply used up all the resources at our disposal. Either way, I know the apocalypse has begun.'

As he uttered those last words, claps of thunder ripped through the sky. Kate was grateful that she had brought her father's Jeep, but what about her parents? What about the millions of people doomed to die?

She felt so powerless.

'I saw too many things, and I know if we don't leave now, we'll be amongst the dead. We'll all die today.' Aaron predicted sadly.

But he remembered the words of Uriel, his angelic friend who stayed by his side throughout the visions. He could change the past and save the future, but reality was a little bit different. The most important person to him was Kate, once she was safe, he could then plan his next move.

As they moved through the ward, they heard explosions and Kate saw a little girl in a hospital gown. She wanted to reach out for her, but the girl ran blindly towards the wall, her ear-splitting scream exploding in Kate's brain.

When they got outside the hospital, she saw stones of fire falling from the sky.

She began to shiver and a sickening feeling started to develop in the pit of her stomach.

Aaron had been right all along.

A sense of urgency quickened their pace, and they hurried across the road.

Cars were crammed together on the narrow road, their horns blaring and Kate knew there was no escape; everyone wanted to leave the city.

'We can't drive through this massive holdup. We have to walk towards the underground; even if the trains aren't still running, we might be safe there. That's what people did during the blitz when the Germans were bombing London.'

Barely had the words left Kate's lips when a thunderous sound almost damaged their ears. They looked up and all the blood in their bodies seemed to dry up. The cloud was darkening and the ground began to quake. Aaron didn't wait to see what would happen; he grabbed Kate by the hand and they ran blindly into Whitechapel underground station, bumping into terrified commuters.

They jumped through the barriers and ran down the escalators. They kept going down, and Aaron knew that they might be going to their burial ground. They got to the underground platform and still felt the tremors. They moved to a corner, holding each other tightly.

'Close your eyes, Kate. No matter what happens, don't open your eyes.'

'I'm scared, Aaron,' she whispered, shivering.

'Don't be Katie, either way our faith will see us through.' he answered, pulling her closer.

Strange sounds permeated the atmosphere and the temperature in the underground increased to over sixty degrees. The heat was terrible; their bodies were soaked with sweat as they held each other for dear life. Carnage and death reigned supreme outside the station and all around London.

Then there was an eerie silence.

Aaron gently pushed Kate away as his body transformed into that of a glorious being. The temperature in the underground gradually stabilised.

Aaron's feet were off the ground, and an unknown force held him aloft, suspended in mid-air. His eyes began to glow brilliantly and the hospital gown he wore disappeared from his body, a blue and white tunic replaced it and a small crown was on his head. A sword was in his right hand, while a staff was in his left.

'I have to go, my love,' he said in a husky voice, 'but I promise to come back for you. We all make our own destinies; let me go and make mine.'

Kate was unable to speak.

He flew close to her, cupping her face in his strong hands.

'I have the power to stop this, darling,' he said earnestly, his eyes shining brightly 'let me know that you're with me on this.'

'I am, Aaron, and I wish you God's speed.'

His lips came down on hers briefly, and they clung together for a long time. Kate wrenched herself away from him crying, 'Go, Aaron. Go,' and she sniffed back tears, 'whatever it is, this earth is the only home we have. Please hurry.'

Rapturous clapping erupted unexpectedly and Kate watched in awe as white clad, winged creatures appeared, flapping their wings. Angels filled the underground with their overwhelming presence and exuded supernatural strength.

It was an awesome sight.

Aaron had not been hallucinating after all; all the things he saw were real. Kate mumbled a prayer in a whisper, her heart filled with love, pride, and uncertainty. She watched as the company of angels flew up the escalator. Aaron followed them, but glanced back and gave her a smile.

It was full of promise.

'I love you,' he mouthed the words and she nodded, torrents of tears clouding her visions.

'I love you too, Aaron,' she replied, and they disappeared from view.

The fate of London and the world was now in their hands, and she began to pray.

HOW IT MUST END...

'And the seventh angel poured out his vial into the air;

and there came a great voice out of the temple of heaven

saying it is done.

And there fell upon men a great hail out of heaven...'

Revelations 16: 17, 21a

THE AUTHOR

Seyi David loves to write and she has done that for several years. She has worked as a reporter, teacher and accountant. She had a brief stint as an actor while at the university before she finally decided to write novels full time. She is a committed blogger and a columnist for Black Heritage Today, a London based Magazine, and Rev Up Media.

Her first novel, 'The Impossible President' sold out of its first print run in 2004. She wrote a short story, 'Tales of Five Lies,' which gripped readers worldwide. 'The Feet of Darkness,' her second novel is still on sale worldwide.

Seyi lives in London with her husband, Kay and three children, Samuel, Elizabeth, and Emmanuel.

Acknowledgements

I am immensely grateful to a number of people who gave generously of their time and helped make this book a reality. In particular, I would like to appreciate Erika Sanger and Chloe Pilsbury, my editors at Arrow Gate for their insightful comments. It really helped. I am also grateful to the staff at Arrow Gate for their patience through every stage of the writing. Any mistakes inherent in the book are entirely my own, and I apologise for them. I also appreciate Andrew Brown and his wonderful design team, thank you for a beautiful cover.

I am also grateful to Deola Jide for reading the manuscript several years ago and giving it the thumps up, and to my very good friend, Stella Alhassan thanks for your kindness.

Thank you to all my blogger friends worldwide, thanks for your friendship. Above all, to my wonderful husband, Kayode David, for his constant encouragements.

SD

www.ingramcontent.com/pod-product-compliance
Lightning Source LLC
Chambersburg PA
CBHW060209030726
47499CB00004B/967

* 9 7 8 0 9 5 7 5 9 3 0 3 9 *